G.

Pantheon Books
New York

John Berger

A Novel

Library of Congress Cataloging in Publication Data

Berger, John.
  G.

  Reprint of the ed. published by Viking Press, New York.
  I. Title.
[PZ4.B4965Gab 1980] [PR6052.E564]   823'.914   80-8031
ISBN 0-394-73967-1

Manufactured in the United States of America

98765432

For Anya

and for her sisters in Women's Liberation

ACKNOWLEDGEMENTS

In this book there are a few unacknowledged quotations in the text:

Page 15: 'One minute in the life of the world is going by. Paint it as it is.' is a quotation from Cézanne. Source unknown.

Page 21: paragraph which begins 'He was poorly equipped...' from 'Personal Reminiscence of Garibaldi and the Garibaldini' by the Rev. H.R. Haweis. Quoted by G.M. Trevelyan in *Garibaldi and the Making of Italy*.

Page 28: paragraph which begins 'Animals do not admire each other...' Pascal, *Pensées*, No. 685.

Page 43: paragraph which begins 'Honey may be either healthy or toxic...' Lévi-Strauss, *Mythologiques III, L'Origine des Manières de Table*.

Page 54: paragraph which begins 'All history is contemporary history...' R.G. Collingwood, *The Idea of History*.

Page 66: paragraph which begins 'An assault on the town hall ...' From a contemporary account. Source untraceable.

Page 95: paragraph which begins 'The land surface ...' *Encyclopaedia Britannica*, Edition 1911. Entry: British Empire.

Page 228: paragraph which begins 'I despise this dust of which I am compounded', Saint Just, *Discours sur les Institutions Républicaines*.

Page 253 and following pages: in the account of the battle of Auvers Ridge, I have drawn heavily on the research done by Alan Clark and published in his book called *The Donkeys*. I have also quoted sentences by him.

For the writing of this book the author acknowledges assistance from the Arts Council of Great Britain.

Other acknowledgements to friends are too deep and intensive to tabulate.

J.B.

I.

I.

The father of the principal protagonist of this book was called Umberto. He was a merchant from the city of Livorno and he dealt in candied fruit. He was a short fat man who looked shorter because of the largeness of his head. To women not unduly frightened of gossip and public opinion, the unusual size of Umberto's head may have been attractive. It suggested obstinacy, weight and passion. Most of the women of the merchant class in Livorno or Pisa were timid. Consequently he had gained among them the reputation of being monstrous. He was called 'La Bestia': a word nominally justified by his rudeness, his leering and his arrogance, but nevertheless retaining in their usage just sufficient of its rawer meaning to both feed and suppress the feelings of attraction they unconsciously felt. It was significant in this respect that they never called him 'La Bestia' in front of their husbands. The nickname was reserved for purely feminine conversations during the afternoon.

Umberto's wife, Esther, was the daughter of a Jewish Livornese journalist, who had been a liberal. She married Umberto when she was twenty. Her father disapproved of the marriage because he considered Umberto coarse and uncultured but he refused to act against his liberal principles by forbidding it. When she was twenty-one her father died suddenly. The mystery of her own poor health began with his death and gradually established the foundations of a lifelong right: the right to be less than present, the right to withdraw. It seemed to Umberto that he had married a ghost. (All ghosts for him were connected with women and their supernatural tendencies.) It seemed to her that she had married a

3

beast—although at that time she did not know how her women friends referred to her husband.

Esther led a full social life in the provincial city. Scarcely an afternoon passed without her visiting or being visited. Nobody refused an invitation to her dinner parties. Her secret—and it was partly the secret of her husband's power in Livorno—lay in her appearance. She had a very pale skin, dark brown hair which she wore tightly drawn back from her face and slow-moving eyes with heavy shadows beneath them. Both her face and her body were exceedingly thin. Yet she did not look sickly. The sickly emphasize the unpredictability of the flesh: there is a kind of pathetic and grating sensuality about them. Esther looked delicate, fragile, as though she were made of some material other than flesh: a material which had been wrought and intricately finished so that there seemed to be no danger of it ever changing.

To her circle of friends and acquaintances in Livorno Esther's physical character was a sign of unusual spirituality. It was she who understood what they aspired to. It was she who appreciated better than any of them Faith, Beauty, the Longings of the Soul, Forgiveness, Innocence, Filial Piety, Love. If a guest, when talking, wished to evoke the spirituality of his experience, he turned towards her for confirmation; one nod from her, even the slow lowering of her eyelids, was sufficient to make him feel that he had been understood and that therefore he was telling the truth.

When women were alone with her, they talked of themselves. In talking they tended to present themselves in as bad a light as possible, for the worse they made themselves out to be, the more licence they would have afterwards when she had approved of them. It was her approval they sought. They gained it as soon as they had finished talking. It then became clear to them (and each time it was a surprise) that since she had listened with interest and made no critical comment (which she never did), she must approve of what they had done or intended to do. She was like a father confessor who belonged to their own sex.

None of this would have been possible however without her husband. Had it not been for Umberto, she might have been suspected of being a saint, instead of just looking like one. And this

4

would have been fatal for her social position. She might represent certain spiritual values, but she must first and foremost represent them, the bourgeoisie of Livorno. The fact that she was the wife of a successful candied-fruit manufacturer preserved her for them. More than that, she was the wife of a man notorious for hard bargaining, coarse manners and heavy appetites. Consequently they believed it was impossible that living with him had not to some degree corrupted her. And this corruption, which could never be entirely refuted, prevented her spirituality from ever appearing excessive or embarrassing.

Similarly, the fact that Esther was Umberto's wife saved him from appearing too extreme. Without her, he might have been reckoned a profligate. With her, it was possible to believe that he had been tamed.

○

The mother of the principal protagonist was a woman of twenty-six, whose first name was Laura. Her mother was an American, her father, now dead, a general in the British army.

I see Laura and Esther, who never met, side by side as they must have appeared sometimes in Umberto's mind. Laura is short with fairish hair and a slightly snub nose. Beside Esther she looks like a dumpy child. Yet her bearing is not altogether childish. She wears expensive clothes with skill—though not with Esther's dignity. She talks a great deal in an insistent voice; Esther listens. Esther's hands are tapered and sensitive; Laura's are podgy and squat. Laura's eyes are hazel-coloured and when she wants to give warning of her disagreement she opens them very wide. When Esther disagrees, she closes her eyes. If Esther were surprised whilst taking her bath, she would 'freeze' like certain wild animals and remain absolutely motionless; if Laura were so surprised, she would clap her hands over her breasts, huddle up her body and shout.

Each was jealous of the other: Laura because she believed, on the evidence of a photograph which she had persuaded Umberto to show her, that Esther had all the natural feminine qualities she lacked; Esther because she suspected that Umberto spent vast amounts of money on his American mistress.

Laura had been married in New York at the age of seventeen to a copper millionaire; after two years she left him and she came to Europe to join her mother in Paris. She had met Umberto, three years ago, on a passenger ship going to Genoa. Umberto courted her with a concentration and persistence such as she had never dreamt was possible. He made her feel, she wrote to her mother, like Cleopatra. (The ship had come from Egypt.) They immediately spent a month together in Venice.

He arranged for singers, she reported to her mother, to accompany us at night, either side of us, in gondolas. I will remember it always. He made funny jokes about his hands being like crabs. You would love him! Which is why I shan't bring him to Paris yet! He has friends everywhere and there is a ball we should have gone to here. He wanted to order me a dress. But, believe it or not, I told him that I would prefer not to go. And so instead we went to the island of Murano.

During the next three years he met her in Milan, Nice, Geneva, Lugano, Como and other resorts, but he never allowed her to come near Livorno. When she was not with him, she returned to her mother's rich American circle in Paris, where she never admitted that her Italian lover was a merchant in candied fruit. She took singing lessons (until she decided, despite her teacher's protestations, that she had no talent) and she interested herself in the theories of Nietzsche.

Whenever Umberto arrived to meet her after a period of separation and she first saw him approaching, she was struck by the improbability of their relationship. His lack of subtlety and his provincial ostentation in matters of money offended her. In New York, she said to herself, he would have been a waiter in a restaurant whom she and her friends would not have deigned to notice. But after an hour or so of his company she could no longer see him critically. It was like entering a tower which she could not leave until he departed. Inside the tower she was both mistress and child. She played there, either gravely or frivolously, with whatever he gave her. She could look out from the tower but she could never see the tower from the outside. The tower was their love affair. During the months when she did not see him, she thought of him and his passion for her and her own feelings about him as though they were a place. She could visit and revisit it; she visited it, too, in her dreams; but nevertheless it was a place in which she never stayed for long.

○

Umberto, who as a young man had worked in New York for a firm that imported olive oil and Italian vermouth, speaks English fluently but with a strong Italian accent.

Ah! Laura, the grandeur of the mountains! And the lake so calm and peaceful. It is a beautiful thing the peace at the end of a day, but you are more beautiful, *mia piccola*. And it is only with you that I can share such peace ... To think that I came under those mountains, the tunnel is fifteen kilometres long, fifteen. It is a marvel of science to make that—fifteen kilometres through a mountain. And on this side of the mountain, *passeretta mia,* you are waiting for me.

(The St Gothard tunnel was opened in 1882. Eight hundred men lost their lives in its construction.)

Umberto and his mistress are driving in a carriage from the station at Montreux to their hotel. Umberto has just arrived. Laura finds him more improbable than she has ever done. He puts his arms around her and tries to lick her ear. She pushes him away.
What do you think I am? she says.
My Laura, my Laura, he says, I think you are my Laura.
From the inside of his overcoat he pulls out a packet, tied with pale blue ribbon. He inclines his head and offers the packet to her on the palms of his hands, as though offering something on a tray. She accepts it. He lets his hands fall down on to her hips. She makes a point of looking at them there to discourage him from continually making such demonstrations in public. (They have argued about this before. He says the inside of a cab is like a private room in a restaurant. She has replied that you don't make a public place private just by paying a little more!) The backs of his hands, covered with

wiry black hair, are very familiar to her. His hands have authority; they arrange things the way he wishes. At the dinner table with his business colleagues in Livorno his hands construct in front of their eyes large invisible models of schemes with which they consider themselves fortunate to be associated. At the wholesale market his hands guarantee the quality of the fruit they touch approvingly and spoil the fruit which they reject. He leans back to watch her open the present.

Inside is black tissue paper and inside that a green velvet Juliet cap decorated with pearls. Laura gasps. Umberto takes this to be a sign of delighted surprise.

The pearls are the real ones, *passeretta mia*.

On this of all days, she thinks, a cap like this is for a girl of sixteen or seventeen, a kind of toy, a bauble. Her lover's lack of judgement suddenly infuriates her. She equates it with his trying to bite her ear within two minutes of their meeting. Why is it, she asks, that he has always refused to notice her likes and dislikes, why has he never learned?

I couldn't wear it, she says, I would look ridiculous in it, it's for a young girl just out of convent school!

In the half-light of the cab it is difficult to make out the shape of the cap, but the three lines of pearls look like a necklace lying on her lap.

There's no point in my pretending is there? You would only be disappointed because I couldn't wear it.

We'll buy you a necklace, he says.

It is her independence that he loves. She travels anywhere to meet him. She reads the history of the place before they arrive. She shows him chateaux and fountains and she always knows what she wants to do. Yet he has only to put his arms round her and she becomes as docile as a sparrow. That is why he calls her *passeretta mia*.

We will eat, he says, a banquet in our room with the Swiss white wine you told me was like a fish with a knife—do you remember?— and afterwards we will go to bed, *passeretta mia*, and tomorrow we will look for the necklace, and if we do not find one here which pleases you, we will go to Milano in a few days.

In bed Umberto has always found his mistress surprising. His impatience now is partly the result of his not being able to fully believe that he will once more be surprised. Upright, she is brisk, strong-willed, independent; lying beside him she has always been delicate and pliant and the touch of her hands has always been lighter than he could remember later.

She had sparse, unusually fine pubic hair as soft as silk thread; her nipples were small and pink and when he kissed them they became red; when her head was thrown back and she smiled, baring her teeth, her upper and lower teeth did not quite touch— between them the space for perhaps a grain of sand to pass. The delicacy and susceptibility of her body had never failed to surprise Umberto and to rouse him to violent passion.

I will keep the velvet cap, she says, and one day perhaps I will give it to my daughter!
She lays her hand on his arm.
Delighted, he says: Ah my little one, you are mad, quite quite *matta.*
Matta (mad) was the term of endearment he applied most often to her.

For Umberto madness is native to Livorno: he sees madness in the massive monolithic warehouses, eyeless and mute like deserted forts, in the four Moors chained cursing to the monument of Ferdinand I of Florence, in the conglomeration of stuffs with which the capacity of the city is overfilled, in the rectangular spaces of sky cut out by the massive regular buildings above the dark canals, in its shifting population, in the blankness of its walls, in the indeterminacy of its spaces, in its smell of poverty and superfluity, in its furtive opening to the sea.

Madness is native to the town, he believes, but it breaks out only spasmodically. Each time reminds him of the first time, in 1848 when he was ten.
The bridges, the indeterminate spaces, the quays, the Piazza San Michele by the four cursing Moors, the decks of the ships and the rigging of the masts which lined the furtive opening to the sea, all were filled with a crowd, a crowd vertically dwarfed by the massive geometric buildings, but horizontally extending without cease, despite ever tighter and tighter concentration: *i teppisti!*

Such a crowd is a solemn test of a man. It assembles as a witness to its common fate—within which personal differentiations have become unimportant. This fate has consisted, so far as its own memory is concerned, of continual deprivation and humiliation. Yet its appetites have not atrophied. A single pair of eyes, met in that crowd, are enough to reveal the extent of its possible demands. And most of these demands will be impossible to meet. Inevitably, the discrepancy will lead to violence: as inevitably as the crowd is inexorably there. It has assembled to demand the impossible. It has assembled to avenge the discrepancy. Its need is to overthrow the order which has defined and distinguished between the possible and the impossible at its expense, for generation after generation. In face of such a crowd there are only two ways in which a man, who is not already of it, can react. Either he sees in it the promise of mankind or else he fears it absolutely. The promise of mankind is not easy to see there. You are not of them. Only if you have previously prepared yourself, will you see the promise.

Umberto feared the crowd. He justified his fear by believing that they were mad.

Men ran with the crowd and harangued it. The summer heat of 1848 made the boy Umberto sweat even at night in bed. The faces of these men were swollen to apoplectic proportions and the sweat ran down their faces like tears.

Umberto considers that a sane man should always try to see himself as an exemption from the rest of the world: then he will be able to see what he can or cannot take from the world. According to him the madman demands all or nothing! *Roma o Morte!*

Umberto cannot leave his wife. Neither by way of his children (for he has none) nor by way of society can he find any sense of succession or continuity; he is alone, abandoned in time. To continue his business and gain concessions he is forced to be amiable, not once but a thousand times, to people whom he dislikes or even hates. He can never speak to anybody of more than one tenth of what is on his mind.

Ah my little one, you are mad, quite, quite mad.

What Umberto calls madness is what threatens him. Not what threatens him personally—another merchant, a thief, the man who will cuckold him—but what threatens the social structure in which he lives as a privileged being.

His privilege is more important to him than his life, not because he could not survive without his American mistress, four servants at home, a fountain in his garden, hand-made silk shirts, or his wife's dinner parties, but because implicit in his privilege are the values and judgements by which he must make sense of his lived life. All values stem from his belief—that his privileges are deserved.

Yet the sense he makes of his life does not satisfy him. Why must liberty, he asks himself, always be retrospective, a quality already won and controlled? Why is there no liberty to pursue now?

Umberto terms madness that which threatens the social structure guaranteeing his privileges. *I teppisti* are the final embodiment of madness. Yet madness also represents freedom from the social structure which hems him in. And so he arrives at the conclusion that limited madness may grant him greater liberty within the structure.

He calls Laura mad in the hope that she will bring into his life a modicum of liberty.

Umberto, I am going to have a child, and perhaps it will be a girl. If it is a girl (Laura has seized upon the subject of the cap in the hope that it will make her announcement less stark. She is happy at the thought of being pregnant, she thinks continually of what her child will be like, but she finds the announcement humiliating). If it is a girl, I will give her your Juliet cap on her fifteenth birthday and she will look beautiful in it.

The cab has arrived at the hotel. A porter is holding the door open. Please shut the door, says Umberto. Then he instructs the driver to drive them slowly along the lake-side. The driver shrugs his shoulders. It is raining and it is getting dark and there is nothing to see of the lake.
Are you quite sure you are right? asks Umberto.
Quite sure.
Have you been to a doctor?

Yes.
How was he called, this doctor?
He was a doctor in Paris.
What did he say?
He said it was true.
He said it was true?
True.
The doctor said so?
Yes.

The word *true* echoes at last with the authority of the doctor and this authority offers Umberto the means of coming to terms with the news. He must demystify it, he must make it manageable and negotiable, he must give it a colour so that it can be handled, so that it loses its initial infinite, entirely abstract whiteness.

I am the father, says Umberto.
It is a statement, not a question; but Laura nods her head. She can see no advantage to either of them in his being the father.
Why didn't you tell me when you wrote to me?
I thought I could explain better when I saw you.
Umberto's head is teeming with calculations of what can and cannot be done in Livorno to accommodate his illegitimate son.
How long—he makes a counting gesture with his hand.
Three months.
We'll call him Giovanni.
Why Giovanni? she asks.
Giovanni was the name of my father, his grandfather.
And supposing she is a girl?
Laura! he says. But it is not altogether clear whether he is suggesting this as a name or expressing surprise at his mistress's suggestion that a child of his might be a girl.
How do you feel, my little one? he asks.
In the mornings I don't feel so fine, but it passes, and in the afternoon I feel quite hungry, and I don't know why we are driving up and down the lake-side like this, it is so dismal, and I would like to eat some cakes. They make a special sort of cake here which my mother is always talking about, of almond paste.
You know, I have never had a child, he says, and I was—how do you say it?—*rassegnato*.

He tries to put his arms round her. She struggles.

You are the mother of my child, he protests. It is not far from being a wife. If I could, I would make you my wife.

It might seem that in such a situation this was an honourable response. Yet far from satisfying Laura, it infuriated her. He is turning her, transforming her at this moment, she feels, into his wife in Livorno—into his wife to whom he has always wanted to say 'You are the mother of my child', but has never had the opportunity. She, Laura, is now the mother of the child of the paterfamilias. And just as she has been transformed, so too, she fears, has his wife in Livorno: Esther will now represent all that is seductive and free and not inexorable. For two months she has been peaceful and happy at the thought of her child. But to bear a child for a man, and to be condemned to bearing it for him irrespective of her will—she starts to sob.

She allows herself to be comforted. Umberto is the cause of her distress, but he can alleviate it. Not by removing the cause—which is the fact of his being the father elect—but by temporarily surrounding her with his own physical presence so that her awareness of herself and her bitter destiny starts to dissolve, as the outlines of a gate dissolve in the dusk or the words of a letter become illegible in the gathering darkness of a room. In his arms she feels her interests receding, and her name, with the intonation it once had when she was a child, emerges from some remote repository inside her and surfaces everywhere through her childish, so easily irritated, skin.

When she touches the straying, grey, mane-like hair brushed back above the ears of his massive head, it is with the amazed inquisitive touch of a child.

When Laura was a small child she realized, through her own observation and by way of remarks made by her mother, that there were certain secret aspects of a woman's body which might be prized above all others and which could equally well be more shameful than anything else in the world. As she grew up, she became convinced that in everything which related to these aspects she was peculiarly sensitive. She had only to be frightened (or so she believed) for her fear to bring on menstruation. If a man touched her in a certain way on her shoulder, she would feel a convulsion in her womb. Ordinary brassieres would chafe her nipples. She used to be ashamed of this sensitivity because it made her awkward and irritable. But she also used to be glad of it because she believed that one day she would be able to share her secret with a man who would become as infinitely curious about it as she was herself.

O

At the hotel they have dinner served in their own suite. Laura is still tearful and Umberto tries to distract and entertain her with outlandish stories about the intrigues of Livorno. When the meal is over, he takes off his jacket, undoes his collar and tie and says:
Come my little one with eyes green.
She appears reluctant.
If it is dangerous, my sweet, we will lie side by side and hold hands —no more—like children.

She has never for one moment doubted that she wanted to have the child. The child will be hers like nothing else in her life has been. She has no dread of the scandal it may provoke because she has her own fortune and can live wherever she likes, and also because she believes that the individual will should never bow to- the demands of conventional morality. Indeed she will enjoy demonstrating her defiance as she did when she married against her family's wishes at the age of seventeen, and as she did when, two years later, she told her husband in public to leave and never come back.

She lies in Umberto's arms, content to be held but indifferent to his passion. If he lies still, she is pleased. She finds it acceptable for him to cherish her; she finds it absurd for him to desire her. She has never before been able to ignore Umberto's advances because they have offered her an opportunity to show him the intricate sexuality of her body which has always seemed to her to be as unpredictable, as delicate and as pure as an almond hidden in its two shells. Her immunity now surprises her. Her child has already offered her the gift of self-sufficiency.

To the physical well-being of the mother of his son Umberto is prepared to make every concession. He lies quiet. Confusedly his mind returns again and again to the mechanics of the forthcoming event. Within them, he feels, is the solution to all problems.

He lies with his hand between her legs, a finger between the lips of her vagina. Warm mucus encloses his finger as closely as if it were a ninth skin. A little earlier he felt with his hand on her stomach, a little below the navel, a small lump.

Instead of his entering her, his son will come out of her. It occurs to him that the very form of the vagina, which he had always assumed was as it was in virtue of his function, has in fact evolved to meet the exigencies of the outward journey of a third person. He is reluctant to withdraw his finger. There is no change to be felt. He moves his finger to confirm this. Not since he first heard about it as a child has the phenomenon of birth seemed more surprising to him.
One minute in the life of the world is going by. Paint it as it is.
What has been conceived are the essentials of the character about whom I wish to write.
Umberto pulls her violently towards him, holding her far shoulder and rubbing his face against her hair. He realizes how violently they are now exposed to the world, bereft of every exception. He is ignorant of all the details of childbirth, but his premonition of the rough, violent outward journey of the small lump grown large and human forces him to recognize how similar they are to other couples.

In the last gesture of tenderness she will make towards him, she holds his head in her hands.
Lie still, she says, think of the child.

He remembers a morning when he visited a friend who deals in flowers and has a number of large greenhouses on the road to Pisa. The glass of these houses is painted over with a green wash (the turquoise colour of the sea) to diminish a little the power of the sunlight for the flowers inside. This wash is painted on the out-side and any passer-by can draw with his finger on the glass because the wash when dry rubs off at the slightest touch. As Umberto walks past the greenhouses, away from the road, he notices the drawings. At first they depict lovers' hearts with arrows through them and initials, then came crudely drawn naked figures standing upright, then a woman lying on her back, legs apart, slit visible. Finally, drawn larger and bolder than all the preceding ones, a cunt with hair above it and below it a cock with hanging balls. It is inconceivable that he himself would ever draw like that. But he recognizes that the two of them have become the subject for such a drawing.

Previously every part of her—like their liaison—has seemed to him to be secret and exclusively for the two of them: the secret has now been divulged: there is a third person involved, his son.

Donna mia! Donna mia! he cries into her hair.

O

I did not sleep well. What you told me, our news—you can say that? like what we read in the newspapers—this was beating in my heart all night. Laura, I want to make change in my life, I want to make space in my life for you and for our son.
Are you so sure the child will be a boy?
I have the feeling I have a son.
I have no feeling about it being a boy or a girl, but then for me it's unimportant. I will be glad of either. I would not like to have a plain girl, for her sake not for mine. It is simpler for a boy. His looks don't matter.
I am proud of you. I am proud of my son. I want to hide nothing.
You couldn't hide us if you tried!
I wish to give you all you need.
We are not asking for anything.
Laura, I will tell you something. Perhaps something you have not understood. In all my life, always, I have been rich enough to do what I wish. When I was younger, my wishes were more modest. But now I am ambitious. Ambitious for you and for our son.
Why are you talking about money? Money has nothing to do with it, absolutely nothing. I never think about money.
I was speaking of the feelings in my heart and my plans. I want to tell you how proud I am.

What are your plans?

You, the two of you, must come and live in Italy where I can see you.

Come to Livorno, you mean?

Livorno is an unhappy mad city.

And your wife is there! That is why you call it mad.

She is not from Livorno.

She lives there. Waiting.

Waiting?

Waiting for you to come back.

Passeretta mia, you know I am married. You have known since three years.

So we mustn't come to Livorno. So we must become your illegitimate wife and your illegitimate child. Do you know what we call that? Bastard. It's your bastard. But it's my child. And that's why we can't come to Livorno.

Do not be excited.

Why have you never let me come to Livorno? Because you were frightened we would be recognized.

I wanted all possible things to please you. I wanted the days we spent together to have no shadow on them. I feel that still. I want it. But now we have more than days together to share. I can hardly believe what has happened to us, to you and me, to me, Umberto, and to you, Laura. Everything is changed.

What will your wife say when you tell her that you have installed your mistress and your bastard child in the town?

She will say nothing.

You propose to tell her?

No.

And you imagine she will not know?

Naturally she will know, but she will say nothing.

And you say you are proud of us! You are not a father. You are a man with a weakness for a little American tart.

I beg you not to shout and say words like that. *Passeretta mia,* what has changed you?

This is what has changed me. (She thumps her stomach.)

Yes, he has changed everything. I want you to live in Pisa. I have seen a villa there, a beautiful villa with a magnificent English garden and tall rooms with painted ceilings. Once it belonged to a *Conte.* I want to buy it for you, Laura.

And we are to wait there for you to visit us. How many times a week? Every Tuesday and Friday?

Or you could live in Florence, in Fiesole above the Arno which is a corner of paradise.

When you have installed us, what do you propose we do? How can you be so stupid? Can you not see that we would be prisoners in a jail?

Jail! You would be free to go wherever you wished.

Who would we meet? Who would we talk to?

I would arrange Italian lessons for you.

That is why you want to call him Giovanni!

I would like him to speak several languages. Then he will be able to travel. I have not travelled enough in my life.

Umberto, I cannot believe you are being serious. You should know better than I what kind of country Italy is. Nobody would know us. We would be outcasts. A woman who is not married with an illegitimate child.

My dear, you are married.

Not to you I'm not.

One day I may be in a position to marry you.

You mean you will get a divorce?

In my country to make a divorce is almost impossible.

So you cannot marry me.

My wife is a sick woman.

I see. We shall wait in our jail until she dies. And then you will be gracious enough to make us respectable. How do you dare to make such a proposal?

I love you.

Love! What is it? It's a word you use to get what you want. Like all men.

It is a word you have used too, Laura.

Yes, I was in love with you when we went to Venice three years ago. You were like no man I had ever heard of. You could have made whatever you liked of me. But you did nothing. A woman isn't like money that you put in a bank and it will bring you interest without your doing anything about it. A woman is a person. How do you expect me to live ten months of the year, kicking my heels until you somehow contrive to make a little trip to see me? That is not a proper life.

All this I intend to change. You will live in Pisa or Florence and we will be together often and without interruption. The boy will see more of me than many boys see of their fathers. And I will make him my heir. Let us try to make a life together for all three of us.

Four!

Four?

You have forgotten you are married.

I have explained to you already.

You say you are proud. Me? I am ashamed. You make me ashamed for all of us. How could I look into the eyes of my child whilst waiting, day after day, year after year, for news of her death?

Sit now, *passeretta mia*, and I will talk to you. I am older than you. I am nearer to the earth. If I compare us to most, we are fortunate. You do not know what their lives are filled with. Life is never as we want it. It is of no use to ask for everything. In the end you get nothing. Our life will not be a perfect one—that is for those who believe in the good God after they are dead. But it will be better, and I will make it better, than you believe possible. We have both been mistaken. I am older than you and I have been mistaken more. But not you either can begin life again like an innocent *fidanzata* of seventeen. With you I have the last chance of happiness. I know it. No chance will come again. You have come to me like an angel to deliver me. Angels come once only. I will spare nothing to make you happy.

Would you come and live here?

I can try. But how can I? It is too far.

Too far from your home?

From my business.

Your business comes before us?

My business is for my son. He will inherit it. He will not be poor.

You intend to disinherit your wife?

I have told you what will happen.

You are shameless.

No, I am not shameless. I see things for how they are. I want you and my son. Without both of you my life is over. All my life depends on this one chance. I love you as nobody else will love you. Not even a younger man. He will not be as faithful to you as me. I know what you are worth, believe me. Come to Pisa. Give me the opportunity to show you—

—Where I shall be in jail.

I will be a father to our son. If you knew what paternal feelings are filling me, if you knew how patient, how adoring, how proud I will be as a father! In him I will see you. He will have your impatience and your love of dreams.

And what will he have of you?

You know what they call me in Livorno behind my back, I have told you already, they call me *La Bestia*. That is because I am cunning and close to the earth. Perhaps he will have my realism.

You, realistic!

Yes. You will see. We have one chance now. There will be no more opportunity.

What do you mean?

For you to be the mother of your son. For me to be the father. For all three of us to be happy.

I intend to bring up my child as I choose, not as you choose. I will teach him myself. If he is a boy, he will begin life with the advantage of never having been told lies. If she is a girl, she will be loving and sincere and realistic. No child of mine is going to be satisfied with your half-measures. And to make sure of this, I will devote the next ten years of my life to my child.

You deny me the right to my own son?

You have none.

Laura!

It's too late to call me now.

The sheets on the unmade bed, the carpets, the furniture, the wrought-iron balcony outside the window, the lake which is the colour of steel and lavender, the Alps—everything within their sight—is unaffected by the rapid beating of each heart.

O

The principal protagonist was conceived four years after Garibaldi's death.

Garibaldi was hero.

Garibaldi defeated his country's enemies. He inspired the nation to become itself: to anticipate its own identity.

Garibaldi was what every Italian wished to be. It is in this sense that one can call him the national genius. There was not an Italian in Italy—not even among the loyal Bourbon troops of the Kingdom of Naples—who did not wish to be Garibaldi. A few hoped to become him by fighting him: some, like La Farina in Sicily, by betraying him. Cavour in Turin became him by using him. What stood between a man and his becoming Garibaldi was not his own identity but the wretched state of Italy: a wretchedness which each interpreted or suffered according to his own theories or position. For the peasant it was the impossibility of leaving his land: for the constitutionalist it was the inefficiency of conspiracy.

When men set eyes upon Garibaldi they amazed themselves: until that moment they had not known who they were. They met him as from within themselves.

He was poorly equipped and almost in rags; he had nothing but a sword and a pistol. 'What induced you,' I said, 'to give up ease and luxury for this life of a dog, in a camp without commissariat, pay, or rations?' 'You may well ask,' he said, 'I tell you a fortnight ago I was in despair myself, and thought of giving up the whole thing. I was sitting on a hillock, as might be here. Garibaldi came by. He stopped, I don't know why. I had never spoken to him. I am sure he did not know me, but he stopped. Perhaps I looked very dejected, and indeed I was. Well, he laid his hand on my shoulder and simply said, with that low, strange, smothered voice that seemed almost like a spirit speaking inside me, "Courage; courage! We are going to fight for our country." Do you think I could ever turn back after that? The next day we fought the battle of the Volturno.'

On 7 September 1860 Garibaldi entered Naples.

Venù è Galubardo!
Venù è lu piu bel!

The Bourbon garrison of several thousand occupied the four castles which dominated the city. The king had fled. The castle cannons were trained upon the city. There was a rumour that Garibaldi would arrive—not with his troops and redshirts on horseback—but alone and by train. The streets were empty under the white glare of the sunlight and the muzzles of the cannons. Nobody knew whether to believe the rumour. Timidly everybody hid indoors. At 1.30 in the afternoon Garibaldi arrived at the station. Half a million people surged into the streets, on to the quays, climbing, pushing, running, shouting—regardless of the cannons and the consequences—to welcome him, to commemorate the moment at which they were living.

Garibaldi was not a military genius of the first order. Politically he was easily deceived. Yet he inspired a whole people. He inspired them, neither by authority nor by divine right, but by representing the simple and pure aspirations of their youth, and by persuading them, through his own example, that these aspirations could be realized in the national struggle for unity and independence. What the nation found sacred in him was its own innocence.

All his characteristics fitted him for such a role. His physical strength and courage. His virility. His long hair down to his shoulders, carefully combed after battle. The simplicity of his tastes and appetites. 'When a patriot,' he said, 'has eaten his bowl of soup and when the affairs of the country are going well, what more can anyone want?' The island to which he retired whenever there was no task for him to perform and on which he lived as a farmer with his sheep. His patriotism which confounded his theoretical principles. (A republican, he recognized the authority of Victor Emmanuel.) His amour propre. His sense of humour. The fact that he was eloquent by gesture rather than word. 'I believe if he were not Garibaldi, he would be the greatest tragic actor known.' (Because he did not talk, men of different or opposing opinions supported him and believed that he supported them.) His ignorance of motives in the world as it was. His impatience.

In what other kind of man could the nation of Italy find its better half in order to become united?

By way of what other kind of man—with his absolute personal integrity—could the majority of the nation be so successfully deceived?

The way in which Garibaldi inspired the nation led to moments of danger for the emergent ruling class. If Garibaldi was what every Italian wished to be, his wishes, so encouraged, might go further than the expulsion of the Austrians and the Bourbons. Garibaldi was a threat to order, not only because his methods were conspiratorial, but because he inspired.

The massing of the crowds in Naples under the mouths of the cannon became a saturnalia which lasted for three days.

Calabrian peasants believed that Garibaldi, like Christ, could perform miracles. When his redshirts were desperately short of water, he fired a cannon into a rock and water gushed from it.

Garibaldi honoured the memory of Carlo Pisacane, martyr of the Risorgimento, whose writings influenced the thinking of a generation of Italian socialist revolutionaries.

'The propaganda of the idea is a chimera. Ideas result from deeds, not the latter from the former, and the people will not be free when they are educated, but will be educated when they are free. The only work a citizen can do for the good of the country is that of co-operating with the material revolution: therefore conspiracies, plots, assassinations, etc., are that series of deeds by which Italy proceeds towards her goal.'

Yet Garibaldi was effectively constrained by his alliance with the existing ruling classes. His gestures defied them: the political consequences of his victories confirmed them. The national genius was used to create the pre-conditions for a bourgeois state.

After Garibaldi's death, there was scarcely an Italian city or town which did not have a street or piazza named after him. Throughout Italy his name was spoken or written thousands of times daily. Yet this name was as irrelevant to what now occurred in those streets and piazzas as the blue sky above.

O

In Paris Laura feeds the new-born child at her breast. It is as though the milk which flows from her is the quicksilver of an extraordinary mirror. In this mirror the child is part of her body, the number

23

of all her parts is doubled: but equally, in this mirror she is part of the child, completing him as he desires. She can be object or image on either side of the mirror. She can do unto him or she can be done unto by herself. The two of them, so long as the nipple remains in the mouth, revert to being parts of an indispersible whole whose energy will lead to their being separate and distinct as soon as the child ceases to suck.

She asks: What need have I of anything more? The boy will grow, but by looking at him, I can again inhabit him.

Her nerves and sensibilities answer her own needs perfunctorily; they continuously strain across space and through his flesh to anticipate and answer his. Her feelings are distributed in his body like veins. When she touches him, she has the sensation of touching herself made innocent.

She wants to worship him because with her he seems to transcend the world as it is. She desires to be totally committed to him, so that this commitment amounts to a rejection of all other claims. She wants with her baby to start an alternative world, to propose from his new-born life a new way of living.

2.

2.

Laura did not achieve the new way of living with her baby which she had wished. She had not reckoned with the sheer force of routine in a rich nineteenth-century household. Had she decided to live by herself with her illegitimate child—and this would have meant becoming a bohemian—she might have succeeded. As it was, in her mother's house in Paris, her plans were defeated by nursemaids, chambermaids, the housekeeper, her mother's doctor. It was not possible for her to be with the child for more than a couple of hours a day. It was not possible for her to occupy herself with all the daily chores connected with looking after him—washing linen, ironing, cleaning the nursery, preparing his food, etc.; there were servants to do such jobs. The most that she could achieve was bathing him in the late afternoon under the eyes of the nurse and the maid who brought up the hot water.

Nor could Laura explain what she wanted. If she had said that she wanted to be always within sight and touching distance of her son and that for the next few years in her life everything else should take second place, that she wanted to live with him as an equal, crawling when he crawled, walking when he walked, speaking his own language, never being more than a few steps ahead of him, if she had said this she would have been treated as hysterical. An infant, like everything else in the nineteenth century, had its own place—which was unshareable.

Umberto implored her to let him see his son. Laura refused to answer his letters and told her mother that the boy's father had gone out of his mind. Two years passed. Laura's mother remarried and returned to the United States. Laura went to London and there, through some acquaintances who quickly became close friends, was converted to the cause of Fabian Socialism. It was arranged that until she had found a house, the boy should stay for a few months with Laura's first cousins on a farm. Laura was to come down by train to visit him every other week. The cousins were in debt. Laura was able to raise money on their behalf through her mother. In London she became more and more involved in her political interests. The secret of life, she considered, was no longer hidden in her own body but in the evolutionary process. Her visits to the country to see her son became rarer and rarer. The boy appeared to thrive in the country. The French nurse was sent back to Paris and an English governess installed. The cousins (a brother and sister called Jocelyn and Beatrice) agreed that the boy should continue to stay with them. On that farm the boy spent his childhood.

Animals do not admire each other. A horse does not admire its companions. It is not that they will not race against each other, but this is of no consequence, for, back in the stable, the one who is heavier and clumsier does not on that account give up his oats to the other, as men want others to do to them. With animals virtue is its own reward.

At that place the minimum of flesh covers the bone of the skull, but even on this thin, thin soil the fur grows. The bone casing is almost concave. On either side of the space is an eye, large with its depths uncovered. It is the frontal centre of the head. In man there is no equivalent place. The sense organs are too concentrated, the eyes too close together, the face too sharp. By contrast the face of a man is like a blade with the cutting edge facing whoever approaches.

On this almost concave field of fur with its thin soil, you rub your hand and the animal nods in accord. But the palm of the hand is too soft: its pads muffle the contact. You clench your fist and rub again: this time with your knuckles grazing against the animal's skull. His eyes remain open, placid and undisturbed because for him there can be no danger which is that close.

It begins like this in childhood. But grown men, overcome by grief or remorse, thrust their foreheads, skullbone to skullbone, between a cow's eyes.

The term 'dumb animal' sinks deep into Beatrice's mind. It implies neither condescension nor pity. But the animal's inability to speak is somehow related by her to the almost concave field between the eyes.

Until puberty the horns mystify her: or rather, not so much the grown horns but their growing: the stumps which she feels with her fingers like rock beneath the fur. During adolescence they supply her with a model for what is happening to herself. The growth of the horn, she begins to understand, does not represent the animal's mere submission to time passing: it has nothing to do with patience: it represents time acquired. Cattle carry their horns as men their years of experience.

Without the presence of animals (such as she has felt all her life) the farm would be intolerable to her. She does not coddle the lamb that has to be brought indoors. She has no regrets about a cow which has gone dry being sold. But without the animals the farm would oppose her as uninhabited and inert: time passing would claim it as it claims a hollow tree. It is the animals who stand and eat and (at night) sigh and graze and wait and breed between her and the lifelessness of the stars.

During her childhood the animals are owned by her father. His power is manifest in them. Like her, they do his bidding. And to them as to her he speaks softly. To everyone else he speaks roughly and is ill-tempered.

She is twenty-four. Her face tends to be laterally over-stretched— as though her ears are constantly pulling her mouth into a smile. In consequence her full lips are always slightly parted, her white teeth just visible.

At a garden party she may look to a stranger from London like a still eligible daughter of a country gentleman. (Though her father is dead and she keeps house for her brother.) Yet when she moves, she may surprise and slightly disturb him. All her movements and gestures are, despite her small size, curiously emphatic.

The neighbouring gentry describe her amongst themselves as hoydenish and so explain why she has not married.

Her actions, whatever they may be — walking across a lawn, cutting a rose, opening the oven when supervising the cook, folding linen, stepping into her skirt and petticoat when dressing — all suggest this disproportionate force which is the result of her unusual sureness of decision. Once she has decided upon a course of action, any consideration which might modify it she instantly dismisses as a detail. There are no details within her life; they are all exterior to it.

Beatrice is a woman without morality or ambition because she is incapable of surprising herself. She can propose nothing unfamiliar to herself. This self-knowledge is not the result of prolonged introspection but, rather, of having always been familiar, like an animal, with the patterns of action and reaction necessary to satisfy her own unquestioned needs.

It is possible that I make her sound like an idiot. If so, I do her an injustice.

The farm is at the bottom of a valley with hills rising steeply up from it on three sides. The house, built about a hundred years earlier, is large with many chimneys. At one side is a walled fruit garden: and behind the house a steeply rising lawn. The stables and dairy and outhouses are laid out along the valley. Perhaps once when the condition of the farm was different, its situation suggested a well-chosen and protected site. Now the hills seem to overshadow it a little.

Since her father's death both house and land have deteriorated. The brother's interest is in his horses and little else. They have had to sell land. In the father's time there were five tenant farmers on the estate: now it has been reduced to their own 500-acre farm.

The house still maintains standards. A pantry maid still spends two whole days a week cleaning the silver. Every winter afternoon a fire is still lit in the master's bedroom. When the master is out hunting, a groom still acts as second horseman. Every June there is a well-attended garden party on the sloping lawn beneath the two magnificent copper beeches. But the house is becoming too big for the household. On the land jobs are deferred or postponed. Thus, because it is slightly under-inhabited and underworked, there has begun the slow process of depersonalization which will end, in twenty-five years' time, with the place being turned into an Officers' Convalescent Home.

Beatrice's brother, Jocelyn, is five years older than she.

Large and handsome with very pale blue eyes. One's first impression is of a man likely to be master of any situation. But this impression is quickly succeeded by another. Very little seems to impinge upon him. He has acquired a certain manner of reacting but behind this is an extensive passivity. One wonders why one's first impression was so wrong. And then suddenly something occurs to him, his eyes sparkle and with the conviction of his whole large body he says: And that was a damned fine thing to have done! The authority of his judgement (even to a boy who knows no history) appears to be based on all that has been worth preserving from the past. And then—as if relapsing into that past itself—he becomes profoundly and secretly passive again. What is it that makes him so elusive?

To understand him closely we must consider him from afar. Towards the end of the last century the English upper class faced an unusual crisis. Their power was in no way threatened: but their own chosen image of themselves was threatened. They had long since accommodated themselves to industrial capitalism and trade, but they had chosen to continue the way of life of an hereditary, landed élite. This way of life, with its underlying assumptions, was becoming more and more incompatible with the modern world. On one hand the scale of modern finance, industry and imperialist investment required a new image of leadership; and on the other hand the masses were demanding democracy. The solution which the upper class found was true to their own character: it was both spirited and frivolous. If their way of life had to disappear, they would first apotheosize it by openly and shamelessly transforming it into a spectacle: if it was no longer viable, they would turn it into theatre. They no longer claimed (except purely verbally) justification by reference to a natural order: instead they performed a play upon a stage with its own laws and conventions. From the 1880s onwards this was the underlying meaning of Social Life—the Hunts, the Shoots, the Race Meetings, the Court Balls, the Regattas, the Great House Parties.

The general public welcomed the apotheosis. Like most audiences they felt that, to some degree, they owned the performing players. Their one-time rulers appeared to have become their romancers. Meanwhile during the diversion the upper class—at its class centre —habituated itself to its new and necessarily more disguised exercise of power. Like a phoenix it was to rise again from its own ashes, for the ashes were only those of its regalia, finally used as theatrical costume.

Jocelyn is an impoverished and peripheral member of this class. The Hunts and the Point-to-Point Races he goes to are comparatively undistinguished ones. But this increases his need to believe that the play is life and that the rest of life is a suspended empty interval. This is why he is elusive and why, when he is off-stage with no lines to speak or actions to perform, he becomes unusually passive. But let us be clear: it is not because he wants limelight or applause (on the contrary, he would consider them vulgarities), but because he believes that the play is reality.

His costume for the part: top boots with mahogany-coloured tops, spurs, cord breeches, a faded swallow-tailed pink coat, a white stock, a low-crowned top hat, a short leather crop with a long lash.

From November to April he hunts four days a week.

I must emphasize that I have used the word 'play' as a metaphor so that we can appreciate the essentially artificial, symbolic, exemplary and spectacular nature of the occasion. But the scene and the props are real. The winter weather, the hounds, the coverts to be drawn, the fences to be jumped, the country that is there to be ridden over, the drag of the fox, the fatigue of the man who has thrust all day— these are real: and the physical experience of these is all the intenser because of their symbolism which every hard-bitten hunting man feels.

To be mounted is already to be a master, a knight. To represent the noble (in the ethical as well as the social sense). To vanquish. To feature, however modestly, in the annals of battle. Honour begins with a man and a horse.

To get well away with the hounds is to be intrepid. To be ingenious. To be the respecter of nothing but the pace.

To hunt is the opposite of to own. It is to ride over. To dart in the open. To be as men as free as the straight-necked dog-fox is as fox.

To meet is to ride with others, who whatever their character know something of these values and help to preserve them. All that is opposed to these values appears to be represented by the invention of barbed wire. (The wire that, later, millions of infantrymen will die against on the orders of their mounted generals.)

Jocelyn is riding home early one December evening. The horse is caked with mud. He slips from the saddle and, although at first he is so stiff that he cannot stand upright but is bent like a man with a stick, he walks beside the horse's head. Its ears are cocked well forward. Just two more miles old fellow, he says. The two proceed side by side. The man runs over in his mind the main incidents of the day. What happened to him and what his friends had recounted of their day. In the marrow of his tiredness is a sense of well-being, even of modest virtue. He is convinced that just as the consequences of a crime—an act of treachery, for example, or a theft—often spread outwards to involve more people and further actions, so, too, within a medium of cause and effect which he cannot name or quite visualize, the consequences of an act of honourable horsemanship must emanate outwards with tiny but endless effect. He looks up at the sky. A few stars. And in that vast space he feels the absence of gigantic horses that once darted through it.

The boy listens on the stairs to their talking in the bedroom. Later he will realize that the cadence of their two voices is like that of a couple talking in bed: not amorously but calmly, reflectively, with pauses and ease. (Some evenings his uncle goes to bed early, and on these evenings his aunt takes a hot drink up to his rooms. She calls it—with a laugh—a nightcap.) Their words are not decipherable to the boy on the stairs. But the manner in which the male voice and the feminine voice overlap, provoke and receive each other, the two complementary substances of their voices, as distinct from one another as metal and stone, or as wood and leather, yet combining by rubbing together or chipping or scraping to make the noise of their dialogue—this is more eloquent than precise overheard words could ever be, eloquent of the power of the decisions being taken. Against these decisions no third person, no listener, can appeal.

In the summer of 1893 there was a drought for three months. When at last it rains in a great storm, he runs out and the earth smells of meat.

On his hands is the smell of horse and harness. Its components derive from leather, saddle soap, sweat, hooves, horsehair, horse breath, grass, oats, mud, blankets, saliva, dung and the smell of various metals when moisture has condensed upon them.

He brings one of his hands to his face to savour the smell. He has noticed that sometimes a trace of it lingers until the evening—even when he hasn't ridden since early morning.

The horse and harness smell is the antithesis of the cowshed smell. Each can only be properly defined by reference to the other. The shed smell means milk, cloth, figures of women squatting hunched up and small against the cow flank, liquid shit, mulch, warmth, pink hands and udders almost the same colour, the absolute absence of secrecy and the names of the cows: Fancy, Pretty, Lofty, Cloud, Pie, Little-eyes.

The horse and harness smell is associated for him with the eminent nature of his own body (like suddenly being aware of his own warmth), with pride — for he rides well and his uncle praises him, with the hair of his pony's mane and with his anticipation of a man's world.

He knows some of the terms of this world but he believes that all of them refer to something which nobody ever mentions. He assumes that the men around him have, for their own reasons, a need for secrecy comparable to his own. When he enters their world — and follows Captain Elwes' hounds — he will learn their secrets.

MISS HELEN

Between the ages of two and five the boy has three governesses. The last one is called Miss Helen.

In the schoolroom in the wing of the farm furthest from the kitchen and the yard, there are no men; there is only the boy. He is sitting at the high desk, his feet dangling in the air, reading out loud. She is in an armchair which she has turned round so that she can gaze out of the window.

When it seems that her attention is entirely taken up by what she can see through the window, he deliberately makes a mistake so as to re-attract her attention. Sometimes his mistakes are unintentional.
. . . all thrush summer the birds were singing.
Thrush?
Yes, the speckly bird.
Thrush summer?
She gets up from the chair, smooths the front of her dress where it

is pleated round her tiny waist and comes behind him to look at the book.

All through summer. Thrush indeed! OUGH not RUSH.

She laughs. He laughs and in laughing throws his head back against her dress.

It was a good mistake, a thrush is a sort of bird.

But not a sort of preposition.

Falling in love at five or six, although rare, is the same as falling in love at fifty. One may interpret one's feelings differently, the outcome may be different, but the state of feeling and of being is the same.

A pre-condition is necessary for a five-year-old boy to fall in love. He must have lost his parents or, at least, lost any close contact with them, and no foster-parents should have taken their place. Similarly, he must have no close friends or brothers or sisters. Then he is eligible.

Being in love is an elaborate state of anticipation for the continual exchanging of certain kinds of gifts. The gifts can range from a glance to the offering of the entire self. But the gifts must be gifts: they cannot be claimed. One has no rights as a lover—except the right to anticipate what the other wishes to give. Most children are surrounded by their rights (their right to indulgence, to consolation, etc.): and so they do not and cannot fall in love. But if a child—as a result of circumstances—comes to realize that such rights as he does enjoy are not fundamental, if he has recognized, however inarticulately, that happiness is not something that can be assured and promised but is something that each has to try to find for himself, if he is aware of being essentially alone, then he may find himself anticipating pure, gratuitous and continual gifts offered by another and the state of that anticipation is the state of being in love. You may ask: but what does he have to offer in exchange? The boy, like a man, offers himself—not altogether impossibly. What is impossible, or at least very improbable, is that his beloved will ever recognize either his offer or his anticipation for what they are.

What—he asks—is a preposition?

A preposition is part of grammar. It's always in front of a noun and it tells you what the noun is doing.

But—you protest (as she too would protest, with vaguer words)—
a boy of five is not sexually developed and the basis of falling in
love is sexual.

Every morning he hears her washing in her bedroom. Every morning he considers entering her room and surprising her. He could
enter on the excuse of being frightened or of some fabricated need,
but to do so would be to appeal, to claim as a child: and because
he is in love with her, his lover's pride prevents this.

At night in bed, alone, he examines his body part by part to
discover the source of the mystery which inflames him. (Her
presence, as now when she is standing behind him and he still
has his head against her dress, makes his heart beat faster and
his limbs feel weak, as after a bath that is too hot.) He examines
his nose, his ears, his armpits, his nipples, his navel, his anus, his
toes. Finally he arrives at his erect penis, which, he already knows,
will afford him a half-answer. He caresses it to bring on the waves
of familiar sweet pleasure. The frequency of the waves increases
until suddenly they turn to pain. He categorizes the pleasure as a
good pain because the only other sensations he knows which
approach the intensity of this one are indeed pains.

Can we do some singing, he asks.

Unlike his previous governess, Miss Helen, who is unusually lazy,
appears to have no strict programme for the lessons she gives to
the boy. They do whatever suggests itself. Instead of having three
distinct and formal lessons, they pass the morning together. For the
boy this establishes a kind of equality between them. It allows her
to moon.

She goes to the piano and sits down on the round stool that can
twirl round like a roundabout.

Let me turn you, he says, let me turn you.

From behind her he puts a hand on either hip and pushes. She lifts
her feet off the ground so that her shoes disappear beneath her
skirts. Slowly she revolves.

He has a face like a monkey, darling, but with deep dark eyes. He's a funny little fellow, he really is. He keeps on looking at you and in the end you have to turn away. I've no idea what goes on in his head. In two days' time she is going to London for a week.

He has noticed (and considers it unique to her) that her clothes always feel warm.

She puts her feet down.

What would your uncle say if he could see us now?

He never comes to this end of the house. And if he did, he would come on his horse and look through the window.

Involuntarily she glances towards the window.

Let me turn you again.

No.

The no is almost petulant.

Then sing your song, he says, the one I always like.

Which one do you mean?

The one about Helen, your song.

She laughs and touches the side of his head.

Anybody might think that was the only one I could sing.

Her voice is thin, not dissimilar from a child's. When she is singing, it seems to him that they are the same size and a well-matched couple. He no longer listens to the words of the song ('I would I were where Helen lies . . .') partly because he knows them too well and partly because he does not believe in them. The words thus discounted, he hears her singing her song, in the same sense as a bird sings its song. Whilst she sings, he might be asking her: Helen, will you marry me? And whilst she sings, she might be answering: Yes. But he would not believe it, because he is fully aware that in consideration of everything in the world, except themselves, it is impossible.

Her eyes are slightly lowered, as though she were reading music instead of playing by heart. Her rather heavy eyelids, half covering her eyes, are smooth, rounded and without a fold. Once he came upon her asleep in the hammock at the top of the lawn, and there was a fly on her face.

She imagines herself singing lightly and sweetly 'her' song to the boy she has been employed to look after, being overseen by Mr John Lennox, prospective Liberal candidate for Ross-on-Wye, and then his coming up to her and saying: I had not dreamt that amongst all your other gifts and accomplishments you had such a sweet voice.

The mystery which inflames him and at night in bed stiffens his penis leads the boy to ask a number of questions. But the questions are asked in a mixed language of half-words, images, movements of the hands and gestural diagrams which he makes with his own body. Thus, the following are the crudest translations.

Why do I stop at my skin?

How do I get nearer to the pleasure I am feeling?

What is in me that I know so well and nobody else yet knows?

How do I let somebody else know it?

In what am I—what is this thing in the middle of which I have found myself and which I can't get out of?

He is convinced that by means of the same mixed language in which he asks these questions, she can answer them. All the formal questions he asks her in the schoolroom and which she answers (What makes rain? What does a wolf really eat? etc.) are a mere preparation for this.

Her hands on the keyboard. Pale hands with thin fingers, and very short nails. On Sundays she wears white gloves: when they walk back from church he takes her hand. He is fascinated by an old fascination: her fingers touch the keys in two very different ways. Either they touch them so lightly that no sooner have they touched them than they desist and fly on; or else they descend heavily upon them, pressing the keys down and keeping them down, so that he can see the unpolished sides of the adjacent keys. It is then as though she forces her fingers through the piano. The last note dies away.

Now you play and I will sing for you.

What do you want to sing?

I'll sing your song back to you.

Beyond the age of six or seven it is very unlikely for a boy to fall in love—at least until adolescence. He knows too many people. The world-that-is-not-himself begins to become multiple, to separate out into many different people, any one of whom may confront him as somebody different from himself. When he is five this may not yet have happened.

Lacking parents, he is still searching for one single person to represent all that he is not, to confront him as his other half and his opposite. If the person he finds is entirely distinct from him—in experience, in role, in background, in personal interests, in age, in sex, if the person is, in the most extensive sense of the word, a stranger to him and yet is continually and intimately with him, and if, in addition to all this, she is pretty and nubile, then he is liable to fall in love.

You may still insist that effective sexual passion is missing. You may present his naked five-year-old body to prove your argument. (Twice a week in his bath he offers the proof himself to his beloved.) But what little he lacks physically, he makes up for metaphysically. He senses or feels that she—by being all that is opposite and therefore complementary to him—can make the world complete for him. In adults sexual passion reconstitutes this sense. In a five-year-old it does not have to be reconstituted: it is still part of his inheritance.

He begins to sing, regardless of the words, intently watching her fingers on the keys. He takes the opportunity of stepping closer and resting his cheek on her shoulder.

Miss Helen is soon replaced by a tutor.

The boy seeks no explanation and is offered none. He is used to accepting decisions as indisputable facts. He has no sense of any ultimate authority residing in any one person: and consequently the idea of appealing against decisions does not arise.

With his ear to the bark, he listens to the tree. He has never yet dared to listen to a dead tree. There are quite distinct categories in his own mind into which he fits trees. Ones he likes and ones he does not like (without reason). Ones that are too easy to climb. Ones that frighten him a little to climb. Ones with a view at the top and ones without. There are also more complicated categories. Trees are alive but not alive as animals are. What is the difference? First, the tree is more accessible. Second, the tree is more mysterious. Third, the tree is immovable. Fourth, the tree can hide him. If he carves on the bark of a tree, he does not believe that the tree feels pain. If a large branch is lopped off there is neither the sound nor the smell of pain. Nevertheless when he is pressed against the bark of a tree, it feels alive to his own skin to a degree that is more comprehensive than his categorical reasoning. When he touches an animal, the animal's will intervenes. There is a tree which, when he is as high as he dare climb, he kisses. Always in the same place.

O

The day, when once it is established, is barely noticed in itself; continuous interests claim us; only if there is a dramatic thunderstorm, a blizzard or a partial eclipse of the sun may we momentarily forget the pursuit of our own life. But at the beginning or end of the day, at dawn or at sunset, when our relationship with all that we can see is in process of rapid transformation, we are inclined to be as aware of the moment as of what we fill it with—and, often, more aware. In face of the dawn, even the supreme egotist is tempted to forget himself. Thus I assume that the experience of day breaking or of night falling is somewhat less subject to historical change than the experience of days themselves.

On certain days he is allowed to breakfast in the kitchen with the farm-hands. He has worked at the limits of this special licence, and slowly, week by week, he has extended them so that Breakfast in the Kitchen now signifies getting up as early as he wishes, going out, wandering where he likes, and making his appearance in the kitchen with the head cowman at 7.30.

On several winter mornings, a few months after Miss Helen's departure, the boy has left the house when it is still dark and climbed the steep lawn to the copper beeches.

What he feels when he looks down at the lit windows of the house and dairy is the icy complement to the burning mystery of his own body in bed. Every lit window suggests to him the room within. Through each window he pulls out the drawer of the room. In it is warmth, safety and his own familiarity with the life he is living. But he himself is not in it. He is in the darkness by the beech trees. The range of his senses in this darkness and in the cold is so restricted that he has the sensation of standing in a little hut, scarcely larger than his own body, with one side open where he looks out. A question which this time he cannot even formulate in a mixed language resides somewhere between the house and his hut. In the field, higher up the hill, are sheep, slightly lighter than the dark, like breath on a windowpane giving on to total blackness. He is aware that the sheep will always remain exterior to the question he cannot formulate. As soon as there is enough light for him to see his own feet the hut disintegrates and with it the presence of the question he cannot ask.

He goes down to the yard and stands in the doorway of the cow-shed where the head cowman and two dairymaids are milking. The boy pats the rump of each cow and calls it by its name.

The tea for Breakfast in the Kitchen is different from tea in the schoolroom. The cups too are different: thick-lipped and almost as large as basins.

The taste of the tea which he drinks as hot as he can bear to is a strong but thin taste. It lines the mouth with its thin covering: the surface of the covering non-absorbent and shiny like that of mica which they use for lantern slides. Within the mouth, so lined with the taste of tea, there is also the extra-strong exaggerated taste of sugar. This is a taste whose effects are not confined to the mouth. Sweetness is like Eurydice's thread: it leads from the tongue down the throat and then, mysteriously, through the stomach to the sexual centre, to the tiny region (distinct in a male from the sexual organs themselves) where sexual pleasure accumulates before extending outwards in waves. It is sugar that first induces us to love life.

Honey may be either healthy or toxic, just as a woman in her normal condition is 'a honey' but secretes a poison when she is indisposed . . . in native thought, the search for honey represents a sort of return to Nature, in the guise of erotic attraction transposed from the sexual register to that of the sense of taste, which undermines the very foundations of culture if it is indulged in for too long.

The kitchen smells of bacon and labourers' boots.

The cook, standing by the range, watches the seven men and three maids eating with an expression of apparent surprise on her face. If she is not harried, it is the expression she habitually wears when watching people eat the food she has prepared. The surprise cannot be at the fact that they eat it with such appetite—for this can surely no longer surprise her. Perhaps it is less personal: the elemental surprise provoked by watching anything being devoured and then apparently ceasing to exist.

His aunt strides into the room, ruffles the boy's hair and then turns abruptly to walk to the low window by the dresser. The maids at the table glance at her timidly. She has gone to the window to see whether she can see her brother. When she is not occupied with the house or some aspect of farm management which her brother has neglected, as soon as she is unoccupied, she becomes anxious and impatient to see him. Like a newly-wed wife she becomes attendant upon him. She has observed that his growing up has disabled him, making him ineffective. What she admires in him is the unwounded boy of twenty years ago. It is to that boy that she has remained faithful.

The other boy, who is drinking his tea, watches her. Her face is close to the window-pane, almost touching it. He knows that she is waiting for his uncle. He has often seen her waiting like this. He slips away from the table and out of the door through the pantry and into the courtyard. Keeping close to the wall of the house, so as not to be seen from inside the kitchen, he creeps round until he is underneath the window at which his aunt is standing. He pauses a moment, a little excited and on the brink of laughter at the thought of the trick he is about to play.

She is waiting for my uncle and bo! it's me!

He climbs on to a water trough, slowly straightens up and presses his nose against the window-pane. His head comes level with her midriff. For an instant she does not notice him: her eyes are still fixed on the middle distance where she expects her brother to turn into the yard. The boy has time to glimpse from below her face with its fixed gaze. Then he sees her lower her eyes, perceiving him. In changing focus her eyes brighten. As they do so, she smiles and he laughs. Bo!

NUMBERS

A blackboard has been installed in the schoolroom. It is no longer a woman's sitting room or a nursery. There are schoolbooks on the bookcase. A map of the world, a large area of it pink the colour of a hunting coat to denote the Empire. A clock has been fixed to the wall. An era passed with Miss Helen and the boy recognizes that it is irrevocable. As irrevocable as the fact that he has no father. But the latter fact he has been told, the former he has told himself.

If I see you looking at the clock again, we shall continue our arithmetic this afternoon.
This afternoon I'm going to go riding with my uncle.
If necessary I shall speak to your uncle.
It will make no difference whatever you say.
I beg your pardon?
I'm going to go riding with my uncle.
Stand up!
The tutor also rises, and walks slowly across to the piano. It is a ritual walk, quite unnatural in its slowness, so that the boy may recognize it and foresee its meaning. From the wall above the piano he unhooks a cane.
What is the punishment for impertinence?
One stroke across both hands, sir.
He holds out his hands, palms up.
He has learnt how to come to terms with this punishment. After a

44

stroke the tutor always stares intently into the boy's face—as though searching for a proof. The boy's determination to control his face must exactly balance the smarting of his hands. If he over-clenches his face, he becomes self-conscious of his expression and position, and, continuing from this, he may become self-pitying and so cry. If he under-clenches it, the sting in his hands may rise for expression to his eyes and throat quicker than he can control them. Thus he must estimate exactly on each occasion how hard the tutor is going to hit him. He gauges this by the tutor's breathing and by how, beneath his waistcoat, he draws in his stomach. If his estimate proves correct so that he reveals nothing, so that the tutor searches his face in vain, the boy scarcely suffers at all.

The boy receives one stroke on his left hand if he persists in repeating the same mistake as the tutor was forced to correct on the previous day (e.g. until has one 'l' not two): for a mistake repeated more than three times on the same day, he receives a stroke across the right hand: for insubordination (as now) a stroke across both hands: for rank disobedience three strokes. At first this systematized tariff of punishment surprised the boy: by now it seems no more arbitrary than the time announced by the hands of the large clock on the wall. One hour can seem interminable: two hours out of doors can pass unnoticed.

Which is the larger, two thirds or three sevenths?

The boy stares out of the window at Basset's Wood and senses that there is a trick in the question.

The tutor tells himself that he likes his new charge but that the boy's wilfulness must be checked lest it be his undoing.

In the cook's sitting room there is a grandfather clock. The ticking of this clock has a hypnotic effect upon the boy, alone in the room. Its promise of a seemingly endless time lulls him; but the way the ticking fills the time, whose passing it records, oppresses him. He has thought of smashing the round window in the clock through which he can see the brass bob of the pendulum, always continuing to swing slowly from side to side after he has abandoned the attempt to count two or three hundred swings.

The cook's cat settles on his legs and increases the hypnotic effect. It purrs as he rubs its ears. His trance-like state is hung like a hammock between two branches of awareness: the endlessness of time within the house which he can never successfully imagine destroyed (he is seven and a half and he has lived in the house for over five years): and the unconcerned, categorically separate life of the animal on his lap. The warmth of the animal, permeating his breeches, paints the wall of his stomach and the tops of his legs hot.

TWO MEN

Descending to the house at dusk through the wood above the beech trees. An autumn evening. Puddles. A red sky. Smoke rising straight from the chimneys. The wooden noise of a pigeon flying from one copse to another. Cold rising from the ground: now at waist level. Having a dog with him changes his sense of distance. Objects and events impinge less persistently. There is more space around him. The dog, circling him, charges and worries the frontier of the unknown back: the opposite to what a dog does when it herds sheep together. The unknown is persistent. What is it that cannot happen? And the child answers himself: Nothing. What is it that can happen? And the adult answers himself: Nothing. He is a child and he walks through the wood like a child.

Twenty yards ahead of him the dog starts to bark. Poachers poaching? As with much else at this stage of his learning, the idea of poachers has led to a mystery. His uncle speaks of them as of murderous criminals: beings with whom and for whom there is no mercy because they stop at nothing. (Poachers are the equivalent in his uncle's code of public danger to the city mob in Umberto's.) Yet listening to the farm-hands talk and being quick to interpret their winks and sign-language laughter, he has learnt that some of their friends are poachers. A man said: If the magistrates had ever gone hungry ... The boy asks himself, are all poachers hungry?

But the notion of being hungry, of being so hungry that you poach, is the most mysterious of all. Dogs jerk their heads eating when they are hungry. In the dusk he sees the possibility of men jerking their heads when they eat to satisfy their extreme hunger. He refuses either to run or to slow down. He knows the fear is inside him. He is carrying it like a full jug. Above all it must not be spilt, for then it will be uncontained and will flow over everything.

The dog stops barking and stands quite still, ears pricked, one front paw raised. There is the unmistakable wood-noise of a booted, two-legged walk: twigs, wet leaves, roots record the sound in their own manner. Two men appear. They have sacks draped over their heads and tied round their waists. In places the sackcloth is damp and dark. They are men he has never seen before. One of them has a bottle in his hands. Sonny! one of them shouts, and the other tells the boy there is no need to be frightened.

He stands absolutely still lest the jug spills. They have square heavy faces like the ones carved on the two top front corners of the wardrobe in the room where the dairymaids sleep. They ask him to come with them. We shan't hurt you, the one with the bottle says. They speak to him as to a child. In this there is a certain kind of security. What is your name? they ask him. He tells them. They walk on. Nothing that has so far happened to him has prepared him for this walk through the wood beside the men in sackcloth: yet he is uncertain about how exceptional it really is. Will it turn out to be an incident that his uncle or his tutor will explain to him? Or is it already beyond their power to explain? Where are we going? he asks. The man with the bottle says: We have something to show you. We want you to see something. It is too dark to distinguish the faces of the two men.

Stop. Wait. One of the men goes off and comes back with an unlit lamp, like a carriage lamp. The man with the bottle pours from it into the lamp. The boy can smell the paraffin. When the lamp is lit and turned up they continue walking. The dog disappears whimpering into the darkness further along the track. Nobody says a word. The light from the moving lamp appears to cast shadows upwards into the sky.

The man in front stops and holds his lamp up above his head. What can you see? Peering into the darkness, the boy makes out three branches lopped from a tree, laid across the track; but the shape of these branches is entirely familiar and it is this which frightens him. He has already recognized them. They are horses' legs. The man's arm moves a little and one edge of a horse-shoe catches the light, like a nail in the branch. The legs are entirely still. What do you see? A horse on the ground. Only one? asks the man with the bottle whose voice is always gentler than his companion's. I don't know.

Come on, says the other man, what are you stopping for? He climbs up on to a bank and holds the lamp still higher. There are two horses, both on their sides. Massive dray horses. Their positions contorted, as though they had fallen on to their knees, broken their legs and then rolled over. The only sound now is the dog sniffing at one of their mouths. Are they dead? asks the boy? The man with the bottle, the man with the gentler voice says: Wait. What do you mean? demands the one with the lamp. You were always a fool, says the other and turns to the boy. Look, sonny, I'm going to kill them now. You can see they can't get up can't you. So I'm going to kill them.

The man on the bank lowers the lamp. You'd better watch him if he says so, he says to the boy. The man goes to the head of the first horse, bends over and strikes it. The boy can't see what he strikes with. Perhaps it is the bottle. He does the same to the second head. Not one inch of the horses' flesh such as the boy can see in the lamplight so much as quivers from either blow. The man stands upright, nothing in his hand. So I killed them, you saw I killed them, didn't you? The boy knows he must lie: Yes I saw you. The man approaches him, evidently pleased, and pats him on the shoulder. There is blood on his hand which reeks of paraffin. So you saw, he says. Yes I saw, says the boy, you killed two horses. He is aware that it is he who is now talking to the man as to a child. You killed them very well, he hears himself saying again.

We will take you back now, says the man, and if anybody asks you, you tell them what you saw me do. We'll light you back with the lamp.
Can I go? says the boy.
We'll take you back, sonny.

I know my way, says the boy, even at night.

No terror on the way can match the disgust he feels for the man in front of him: it is a disgust to the point of nausea. In a moment the smell of paraffin will force him to vomit.

Can I go?
Don't ever forget what you saw me do.

Away. The lamp invisible. The smell of paraffin present but now imaginary. He feels his way between the trees.

His fear is overcome, both his fear for himself and (for it is different) his fear of the unknown: not overcome by an appeal to will-power or the summoning up of courage—how often can such direct appeals of a purely formal morality ever work?—but overcome by another, stronger, revulsion. It is beyond me to create a name for this revulsion: the ones I can think up all simplify. It has nothing to do with the slaughtering of horses or with the sight of blood. It is a revulsion not uncommonly felt by children and men, but one that quickly disappears never to recur if systematically ignored. With him it was always to remain stronger than his fears, for he never ignored it.

He emerges from the wood at the top of an incline above the farmhouse. The slope, far too steep to plough, has been left uncultivated and is overgrown with bracken. As he comes down it in the dark his foot catches in a skein of bracken and he falls forward. Unhurt, he begins to roll down the slope. It would be simple for him to stop himself; he has only to grasp at some roots. But he has no wish to. He will roll to the bottom. Each time his legs come over his head it is as though for an instant the side of the hill is a flat plain and the lights in the windows of the farmhouse below are mysteriously large lights on the distant horizon. Each time his head comes off the ground it is as though he is falling across the sky. The dog, running behind him, begins to bark excitedly and to nose the ground. Each turn is like a door opening and shutting. Plain shut sky shut plain shut sky and the smell of the wet bracken on either side of the door. Bang, shut, bang, shut. The level. The sound of hosing in the dairy.

After the incident in the wood that autumn night he not infrequently climbs up to the near edge of the wood and deliberately rolls head over heels down the bracken slope.

The cook sees him one late afternoon.
You'll break your neck, she says.
My neck won't break.

TAKING A FALL

He saw the branch as though it were created to sweep him from his pony. All consequential reasoning, all the speculation which pertains to being able to choose among possibilities, was swept away in the same moment that it became clear to him that the branch must inevitably sweep him off the pony.

Time is measured not by numerals on a clock face but by the incidence of our apprehended possibilities. Without these—in face of the branch already above the galloping pony's ears, time suffers an extraordinary change. The slowness of it cannot be imagined.

The boy lies on a bed in a farm-labourer's cottage, calm, waiting for the pace of time to revert to normal. When it does, he may moan.

The old man moves about the room. It is like an outhouse with a bed in it. There is a window with very green leaves outside it: on the sill is a candle. The bed on which he is lying is covered with rags and an old horse blanket. It smells of damp foul cloth.

The old man is lighting a fire beneath a blackened kettle. The ceiling of the room is stained brown and in places the plaster has fallen off and the laths are visible. The brown of the ceiling is the colour of tea. The old man moves slowly and with difficulty. The boy believes that he is an old man of whom he has heard his uncle speak. His uncle said that he would die in the Workhouse.

He can feel how swollen his mouth is. With his tongue, cautiously, he feels the holes from which his teeth have been knocked out. (What will come to be known as his leer has been born.) The pain in his chest breathes in and out like the old man blowing into the fire on his knees.

Who are you? he asks the old man.

The old man comes to the bed and sits on it. In face of the arrested time just ending, the boy may be as old as the man.

What the old man says I do not know.

What the boy says in reply I do not know.

To pretend to know would be to schematize.

Meanwhile development is so retarded, progress and consequence so slow that the determination not to cry out is left inviolate. It can endure for hours.

The branch struck him on the chest and face. It may be like this at the instant of being shot. The violence of the impact is so great that the self withdraws from all further contact. This is not the same phenomenon as unconsciousness. He was conscious, but suddenly his own body, its sensations and acquired memories became a vast estate in which he could wander without concern about his means of locomotion. Far away from where he was in his estate he saw a dark mass, composed of stone surfaces and water. He was approaching it fast. He entered it as his back struck the pony's haunches. He lay vertical in a fissure of a cloud-like substance as his feet shot up into the air above the pony's withers. When he hit the ground, curtains of whole fields were drawn back to reveal the blue sky without any land but him beneath it. Then he lost consciousness.

His courage on the bed, when he regains consciousness, derives from his original decision, when he first saw the branch, not to cry out. That was an hour ago and before the old man found him. On the bed he is still deciding. In time as he now experiences it, sustaining his decision is not what demands courage: on the contrary, it is the making of the decision which never ends.

(It is in order to break and destroy the concession of this experience of time which the body invents to protect itself, that torturers alternate torture with comfort.)

Everything you write is a schema. You are the most schematic of writers. It is like a theorem.

Not beyond a certain point.

What point?

Beyond the point where the curtains are drawn back.

Come back to the boy.

Who says that?

The old man does.

What does the boy feel?

Ask the old man.

Look at him, says the old, man, poor bugger. Not a cry out of him.

The last barrier against consequence is the home. This is why the dying want to die at home.

The boy is not dying.

But he is in a home in bed with the bedclothes that smell of damp foul cloth over him.

In the time which his fall and his pain arrested, he found a home.

The old man was there as the boy emerged from his estate.

They met as equals. No rules governed their encounter. Bone to bone.

But when the boy's sense of time began to revert to normal, he became young again.

That was a nasty toss you took, sir. Don't fret yourself. Lie quiet.
Your uncle's coming to take you home in the buggy.
I don't want to move.
You can't stay here can you?
Why not? Whose is it?
Whose what?
Whose bed is this I'm on?
It's mine, sir. I found you on the edge of Hawk's Rough, and I carried you back and laid you on the bed.
Whose home is it?

He will look through the windows of other labourers' cottages and he will climb up to the window of the dairymaid's room. He will try on her aprons. He will strap on one of Tom's leather leggings and it will come to the top of his thigh. To be another!

Don't fret. I'm going to see to the fire. We must keep you warm mustn't we?
What else did you do?
I cleaned the blood off you and laid you down.
Am I badly hurt?
Nothing that won't mend itself.
It hurts when I talk.
Don't fret.
Stay with me.

The sound of the buggy, and his uncle is in the doorway. His uncle makes the old man look almost as small as a dwarf. Jocelyn looks down at the boy and speaks gently to him, smiling. To Jocelyn it is a form of initiation that his ward has undergone. The curtain has gone up on his life.

He confers with the old man and gives him a two shilling piece. The boy sees the money change hands, and the old man continually tapping his forehead to convey gratitude.

His uncle lifts the blanket, lets it fall to the floor, and takes up the boy in his arms. The pain in his chest is such that he screams and loses consciousness.

Jocelyn whispers tenderly to soothe, to propitiate.

You've the making of a real thruster my boy.

Carrying the boy through the door, he hisses quietly, mollifyingly, as a groom does grooming a horse.

A thruster, my boy, a hard-bitten thruster.

All history is contemporary history: not in the ordinary sense of the word, where contemporary history means the history of the comparatively recent past, but in the strict sense: the consciousness of one's own activity as one actually performs it. History is thus the self-knowledge of the living mind. For even when the events which the historian studies are events that happened in the distant past, the condition of their being historically known is that they should vibrate in the historian's mind.

3.

In the Piazza San Michele on the waterfront at Livorno there is a statue of Ferdinand I. At each corner of the pedestal on which the archduke stands, a bronze figure of a naked African slave is chained. For this reason the statue is often referred to as *I Quattro Mori*. There is an inscription on the pedestal, the last part of which reads in Italian as follows:

> '... made in 1617 after the death of Ferdinand. Later (between 1623 and 1626) Pietro Tucca added his admirable slaves, the models for which he chose from the local prison.'

THREE CONVERSATIONS OVER THE YEARS ABOUT HIS FATHER

Why don't I have a Papa?
Your Papa died.
Dead?
Yes.
In the cemetery he's dead?
If you are good, you go to heaven when you die.
Was Papa good?
I'm sure he was.

Always?

We didn't know him. I don't think your uncle or aunt knew him either.

But Maman—

Your mother met him in Italy I think.

What was he doing in Italy?

He had something to do with ships.

Was he English?

I think he was Italian.

What did Maman call him?

Now finish your soup and no more silly questions.

Was he run over by a train?

Who?

Papa when he was dead.

I don't know.

Couldn't Maman stop him?

Finish your soup.

I'm dead too! Ha! Ha! Dead! Dead!

Finish—

O

Why will nobody tell me anything about my father? Whenever I ask about him, you change the subject.

I never saw him. Nor did your uncle. You must ask your mother about him.

You are only pretending not to know. Please who was he?

He was a merchant from Livorno in Italy.

Was he Italian?

Yes, an Italian merchant.

Were they married long before he died?

A very short time.

And did he really die in an accident with a train?

Who told you that?

That's what Cook used to tell me.

I didn't know.

Was he very old when he died?

He was much older than your mother.

Am I like him?

I've told you I never saw him.

But guess.

Perhaps your dark eyes. You certainly don't get them from her.

○

Would you like to go to Italy?

When?

Next week—to Milan.

Is Milan near Livorno?

It's quite a long way.

I should like to visit Father's grave in Livorno.

Who told you he had a grave?

Nobody told me. All dead people have graves.

I meant why did you think it was in Livorno?

Because that's where he lived.

What would you say if your father was alive?

He can't be.

And supposing I told you he was?

You told me he was dead.

It was a terrible mistake. We thought he was dead.

But why didn't you hope he was alive?

It was all a terrible mistake.

You mean he's alive.

Yes.

The train didn't kill him.

Would you like to visit him? The two of us together.

Us? If he's alive, I'd say the question is whether you want to see him.

There's no need for impertinence.

○

The train journey to Paris, two days spent there with friends and then the journey on to Milan comprise the longest period that the boy has spent with his mother since infancy. She is unlike anybody else he knows: yet he has known about her ever since he can remember. She is both strange and familiar. With her he has the sensation of playing a part in a story which concerns a life he might have led. Everything about her suggests an alternative.

She talks a lot to him, but not as one talks to a child. (From the moment she abandoned him to her cousins she has wanted to think of him as grown up, as formed: then pride in him could supersede her guilt. Now that he is eleven she thinks of him proudly as a man: a man to whom she can refer for support and justification: a man who, in many respects, is like a father to her.) She talks to him about Socialism, the importance of Education, the future of women, about art—they will see Leonardo da Vinci's *Last Supper* in Milan—about her friend Bertha Newcombe who is in love with Bernard Shaw, about the different nations of Europe and their characteristics.

Some of what she says he does not fully understand. But all of it seems to pass by like the views seen through the train window: distant, continuous, almost disembodied. It is the same with her voice which is unlike any other he has heard (she still talks incessantly), but which does not seem to belong to her. When he returns to their compartment having walked along the train corridor, the fact that his mother is still there in the same place half surprises him. He had half expected her to disappear. When she falls asleep he presses her arm, presses it hard until he can feel how solid it is. He is mystified by this solidity as he might be by an image in a mirror moving of its own accord.

She has certain characteristics by which he recognizes her instantly in his dreams and thoughts. The smallness of her plump hands, and their surprising lightness of touch; the way she opens her hazel eyes very wide (like the china eyes of a doll); her large bosom and square body (like a silk sack stuffed); the firmness with which she says certain words—RIGHTS, IDEAL, DISGRACE; a scent, hyacinth-like which covers, as lightly as tulle, another (for him) unnamed but older smell. But these characteristics do not create a person in his mind: they remind him of the fact that his mother happens to have these characteristics.

When, through the train window or the carriage window in Paris, a woman for some reason or another attracts his attention—it happens rarely—and he has time to observe her, he plays a game of imagining her as his mother. The game is impossible if the woman is in the carriage and likely to talk to him or to Laura: she must be and must remain a stranger. The woman there with a tiny waist, wearing blue satin, who is shaking with laughter and whose screams first attracted his attention and separated her from the crowd, what would it be like, he wonders, to have her as a mother? Or the fat woman who is carrying too much away from the market and who looks as though she is too fat to climb up into the train: or the woman in the landau with ostrich feathers, wearing narrow trousers beneath her slit skirt? He does not compare these women with the woman beside him. If the game were just one of judging between them, of deciding which mother he would prefer, it would soon pall: furthermore, if his judgement were to go against Laura, he would be assuring his own unhappiness. The imaginary mothers he sees through the window are candidates for filling the absence which Laura represents. The game is always to try to imagine more about having a mother. It is the first time he has played the game. It is Laura's presence which supplies the necessary sense of absence from which to begin.

It is more than eleven years since Laura and Umberto have met, and their son is there in breeches and a cap to remind them both of how long eleven years may be.

On a platform in Milan railway station the son sees his father for the first time: the father sees his son for the first time: the lover sees his ex-mistress as mother to his son, and the mother sees her ex-lover as her child's father. On the platform beneath the distant and extensive glass roof of the station the three of them assemble as a family group: prosperous and to be envied. Mother and father do not kiss, but the mother proffers her son (who is as tall as she) for the embrace of the father. For an hour or so the three of them seem to each other to be huge, improbable, giant apparitions—like faces drawn on kites.

Laura explains to herself how Umberto has changed. He has become like a caricature of a capitalist. Her Fabian friends in London would find it hard to believe that he was the father of her child. He must have taken advantage of you, they would say, taken advantage of your naivety and your good heart. He is heavier and more stupid than before. She sees in his face the obstinacy and stupidity of all the letters he has written to her. His skin has become darker and coarser. He has huge bags under his eyes. She compares him with her son. It is far easier, she has already decided, to talk intelligently and naturally with him than with Umberto. Umberto is like a rich fat old child. He is incoherent: his eyes become tearful: his massive fat hands bang and grasp and he keeps on repeating phrases like All my life! All my life!

Umberto scarcely notices how Laura has become shapeless, how she clenches her small hands when walking, how she has acquired the habit of baring her teeth in an ironic smile when she is impatient. These are all details beside the single transformation he was expecting: she has become the mother of his son who is no longer a child. He has eyes only for the boy.

The hotel is full of rumours according to which Italy is on the brink of Revolution. It is said that shooting has already begun in the industrial suburbs of the city.

To Umberto the red leather furniture, the winter garden plants, the lifts with gilded cages, the dragooned maids in white suddenly seem absurd. His long-cultivated taste for grand hotels ends in disgust. He wishes to take his son home. In such a hotel intimacy (except sexual intimacy in bed) is impossible. The staff carry messages from guest to guest. There is nothing of his own which he can show his son. The grandeur is anonymous and false. It seems to him that his one-time mistress and his son hide from him in their rooms behind innumerable doors: he has the sensation that everyone in the hotel is being forced to wear a disguise. And so, for a few hours, and despite his hatred of Revolution, Umberto listens to the rumours with a kind of anticipation. Because he is conscious, now that he has found his son, that nothing will ever be the same again for him, his fear of violent change is momentarily reduced. He sees the nervousness in the eyes of some of the other hotel guests and he distinguishes between himself and them: they need their disguise whereas he does not. For a few hours he feels an uncertain correspondence between the violence of his emotion, to which he cannot in this hotel give proper expression, and the violence threatened by the crowds already gathered in the northern suburbs.

When he explains the political situation to his one-time mistress, he does so with unaccustomed vehemence. He speaks of the senility of Crispi: the impotence of Rudini 'the gentleman': the genius of Giolitti. There are only two choices, he says, Giolitti or the anarchists! Progress or revolution! We may even need a little revolution to strengthen Giolitti's hand! He raises his own large hand and opens it wide in front of Laura's face. Dimly (because without any emotive associations) she remembers that she used to think of him as a bandit. She feels her own motives for coming to see him generally confirmed by his manner and by the events he is describing. She too has come to demand—not for herself, but for her son—the share which is his right. The word JUSTICE, silently spoken in her mind, is spoken with the characteristic intonation which her son has noticed.

Why hasn't your government a plan for solving the problem of poverty? All over the world people—
The problem of poverty! Umberto interrupts, repeating the words very loudly and laughing. In our country, he says, poverty isn't a problem. It's a life. There is only one way of being rich but there are a thousand ways of being poor.
And look what happens! snaps Laura.

Both parents frequently glance at their son as though appealing for his support. His father looks at him protectively, his mother seeking protection. The boy senses that the three of them have met too late; he is no longer the child who can receive what each of them, independently, wishes to give, and what he might once have welcomed. In the history of his own life he is older than they: about the history of his own life their innocence makes them like two children.

As he watches his parents, he returns again and again to the same question: what was his mother like before she was so shapeless and his father was so fat? How is it that she, who rejects him in every word she utters, every gesture she makes, must once have accepted him? What force then disarmed her? Or could she have yielded of her own accord? He cannot find the answer.

Meanwhile they talk of the alternatives to Revolution.

Towards evening clouds mass above the city. The leaden light makes the cathedral look like a gigantic piece of shrapnel. The canals in the suburbs appear to turn black. The open spaces are airless as though the whole city had been placed in a box.

Milan is noted for the violence of its thunderstorms and during the moments preceding them one can experience this strange sensation of a distorted, inconsistent size-scale. The scale of the buildings and the extent of the city remain overwhelmingly large in relation to one's own size; one feels dwarfed; and yet, simultaneously, one has the sensation that the city—with oneself in it—has been reduced to the size of an exhibit in a glass case in a museum. The experience may be related to dramatic changes in air pressure. This evening the sensation of distortion is particularly strong.

In the hotel more and more electric lights are switched on. The bulbs are a sulphuric yellow. The colonnade of the Scala is visible from the first-floor hotel lounge. The colonnade is lit up; evidently the evening's performance has not been cancelled.

Guests stand at the tall windows looking out. There is the sound of distant shouting. The Piazza is unusually empty. A man wearing a stock runs his hand up and down the velvet curtain at his side; the texture of the material reassures him.

The Head Porter hurries up the stairs and into the lounge with the news just delivered to the Junior Porter at the front entrance. He whispers to an old man in an arm-chair who, having received the news, raises his head and announces in a high voice: *Signore, Signori!* Whereupon the Head Porter delivers the news in the manner of a Master of Ceremonies. The workers of the Pirelli factory have seized a police barracks. A column of insurgents from Pavia is marching upon the city. The anarchist leaders are inciting the workers to attack the centre. They have already set fire—

Another old man shouts out to his two sons standing near by (one of them is in officer's uniform): The cavalry! Don't delay! Martial law and the cavalry! The sons shrug their shoulders.

A few seconds later thunder rattles the tall windows and the force of the rain is such that it sounds like fire. The guests look towards the streaming dark windows. The lights on the colonnade of the Scala have gone out. Laura whispers to Umberto that she wishes to lie down in her room.

The boy stares at the dark life-size portraits on the opposite wall: they represent Piedmontese notables of the Risorgimento. Alone with his son for the first time in his life, Umberto wants to make a ritual gesture. He approaches his son from behind and lays his hands upon his head in the manner of a bishop. The boy remains motionless. He is more aware than he has ever been of the question he cannot formulate when he looks down at the farmhouse before daybreak.

It is now as if the rain is beating upon the glass case in which the city is being exhibited. From a stair-well at the back of the hotel there ascends a woman's long-sustained scream.

A waiter hurries to the heavy wooden door with brass fittings which opens on the corridor leading to the back of the hotel. But the scream (the scream of a new kitchen-maid from the country who fears lightning and thunder because they are a sign of the wrath of God) has already had its effect. It has already reminded many of the guests that they have been awaiting such a scream in such circumstances—with dread or with inexplicable expectation—for years. For them the scream is a signal.

The immediate effect of the storm is to disperse the open-air meetings of workers and demonstrators. It achieves what Turati, the socialist leader, failed to achieve in his appeals for order and calm.

But there are other effects. It is not only the country kitchen-maid whom the storm has frightened. Those responsible for law and order in Milan have been reminded of the ineluctable nature of storms when once they begin. In the flashes of lightning which, although they emanate from the sky, appear to light up the piazza from below, in the rolls of thunder echoing between the far mountains and the near buildings, in the incontestable force of the downpour and in the hysteria of the electrical tension, they have seen the spectre of their working population in revolt. Two workers and one policeman have been killed during the day. After the storm the spectre looms larger than the facts. The forces of order must immediately take the most extreme measures against the least provocation: only thus can the revolutionary storm, of which the natural one that has just passed was only a harmless symbol, be averted. The massacre of the following days is assured.

Dinner in the hotel dining-room is well attended. The guests wear evening dress. Thus the male diners and the waiters, both wearing black and white, are distinguished by their positions and actions rather than by their appearance, and one has the impression that all the men in the large room are attendant upon the women in their multi-coloured dresses. A fountain plays, and around it are arranged lemon trees and oleanders in wooden tubs. On the tables are roses.

Umberto takes a white rose from the chalice on his table, carefully trims its stem, wipes it with his folded handkerchief, stands up and, holding the barely open white rose in front of his vast, untidy face, the colour of yellow clay, bows to Laura, pouting his mouth in the vulgar Italian manner which, describing a kiss, denotes appreciation. Yet Umberto modifies the vulgarity of the gesture: the symbolic kiss is restrained and he holds the rose in front of his mouth—as though the flower were the word which his lips were forming.

Please, dear Laura, accept—

Put it down, she says, furiously embarrassed by his theatricality

64

and by the implication of present courtship: an implication which, in her mind, unpardonably confuses the past with the present.

Umberto gently hands the rose to his son who is seated between the two of them.

You give it to her, he says.

The boy places the rose by his mother's soup spoon.

Suddenly she is reassured. She considers it possible that Umberto has understood what she wishes to establish: namely that all his dealings with her must be made by way of her son. Picking up the rose she slowly twirls it between her fingers, raises it to her eyes, and lays it down again on the table in front of the boy.

Umberto, noticing the sudden change in her attitude and incapable of not exploiting an unexpected success, says: Shall we eat *Pollo alla Cacciatore?* If I am not wrong, dear Laura, you always liked *Pollo alla Cacciatore.*

This is the first time that he has mentioned the past. The boy is immediately alerted. Laura is momentarily touched by his remembering. The remark confirms what she wishes to be confirmed: the fact that, a long time ago, Umberto was in a position to be the father of her child. Unaware of the eloquence of her expression, she half smiles at Umberto. The boy, intercepting the glance, recognizes it. He has seen Beatrice look at Jocelyn with a similar expression. It is a look which confesses a secret common interest deriving from some past experience from which, by its nature rather than by its timing, he is conscious of being inevitably excluded. It is a look which makes him conscious of being the third person.

What does *Pollo* something mean? he asks.
It is a chicken cooked in wine with mushrooms and peas and young vegetables. *Pollo alla Cacciatore.*
But is that what it means?
It means chicken cooked like hunters cook it.

The look and the dish henceforward became associated in his mind. It is the look of the *Pollo alla Cacciatore*.

The Mediterranean breaks along the long coasts of Italy. In places the waves are phosphorescent in the dark. Between the coasts millions are hungry. In the south they riot without hope.

An assault on the town hall, devastation and destruction of the tax registers; then the arrival of police or soldiers, volleys of stones from the crowd, opening of fire by the troops. The crowd retreats, cursing, leaving its dead and wounded on the ground. In a few months in another commune the story repeats itself.

The tax on flour is over 50 per cent: on sugar 300 per cent, on meat and milk 20 per cent. Salt is so highly taxed that many peasants never taste it. Meanwhile it is an offence against the excise for those who live by the coast to draw salt water from the sea. Guards have shot at women coming down to the beaches with buckets. It is safest at night. Phosphorescent drops form for a moment along the rim of the bucket, in whose illegal water she will cook tomorrow's pasta.

I FATTI DI MAGGIO 1898

The boy wakes early, as he intended to do. He slips out of the hotel before either of his parents are astir.

Because the people in the streets are speaking a language which he cannot understand, the significance of most of what he sees is ambiguous. The commonplace and the exceptional are mysteriously confused. Is the gentleman who flings himself into a carriage and shouts at the driver frightened or late? The six girls advancing with linked arms (and their hair tied up in scarves)— do they sweep the other pedestrians off the pavement every morning as they are doing today? A man by the kerb is reading out loud from a newspaper. Is it a tram stop? The men who gather round him begin to shout. Are they shouting in approval or anger? A jeweller has closed his shop and pinned a piece of paper with writing on it to the shutters.

There are so many people that the carriages and trams can pass through only with difficulty. The wheels of the trams screech against the rails. He wonders whether they always screech like that.

A young very short man with a beard is puzzled by the presence of the boy, whose clothes make it clear that he comes from a rich bourgeois family. The entire crowd is made up of workers on strike, assembling to listen to their speakers near the Giardini Pubblici.

What are you doing here, he asks in Italian, this has nothing to do with you!

The boy, almost as tall as the young man, shakes his head and shrugs his shoulders. This increases the suspicions of his questioner.

It won't help you spying on us, he says.
I do not understand, says the boy in English.
So you're not an Italian.

They try to talk but the boy understands nothing. The young man puts his arm round the boy's shoulders. Within a few seconds his whole attitude is reversed. If the boy cannot understand their language, he is immune to the hypocrisy of deception of words and thus can be the pure witness of their actions. The boy's wordlessness now appears to him, in an unclear paradoxical way, to be comparable with the universality of the Revolution in which he believes. He calls to his sister in a nearby group of mill-girls: Come and meet our *pulcino*, he says. *Ecco il nostro pulcino.*

Despite his diminutive shortness, the young man with a beard has a wide flat brown chest. His face is like a ferret's. He works as a maintenance mechanic in a cotton mill. Since 1894 he has twice been arrested and deported under Crispi's law of Public Security (the *decreto-legge*).

Let him stay with you, he says to his sister, he can't speak our Italian.

Out of the six mill-girls to whom the boy has been entrusted, he notices particularly a Roman girl, only two or three years older than himself, whose face is pock-marked and who already has a growth of black hair above her upper lip. He notices too—for she wears a white short-sleeved bodice—that her arms are unnaturally thin, like long brown handles to her hands. Her moustache intrigues and embarrasses him.

To them he is a fascinating enigma. They can talk about him as though he were not there.

He has beautiful eyes.
Look at the leather of his shoes.
Where does he come from?

Yet they can also approach him, touch him, study his reactions. Half child and half man, he appears to them as an ambassador between the romantic dreams of their own childhood and the men from whom in reality they must soon choose. (The eldest of these girls earns less than 10d a day).

Let us call him my *affianzato*, cries the Roman girl, made brazen by the excitement, her acknowledged ugliness and the fact that the boy will never understand.

The crowd in and around the Corso Venezia numbers fifty thousand. Some are organized into columns and contingents from particular factories; other groupings are smaller and less organized. They do not know exactly how many they are; but all of them sense that they represent the majority. This majority can claim what each has felt but cannot say when alone: Look at this head, this body— ill-taught, badly-fed, poorly-dressed, overworked. It deserves the best the world is able to offer.

Near the edge of the Giardini Pubblici, the boy sees the young man with a beard standing in a tree and addressing the crowd. He is giving them directions about where to go.

The crowd see the city around them with different eyes. They have stopped the factories producing, forced the shops to shut, halted the traffic, occupied the streets. It is they who have built the city and they who maintain it. They are discovering their own creativity. In their regular lives they only modify presented circumstances; here, filling the streets and sweeping all before them they oppose their very existence to circumstances. They are rejecting all that they habitually, and despite themselves, accept. Once again they demand together what none can ask alone: Why should I be compelled to sell my life bit by bit so as not to die?

Of the reality of politics most of the crowd are ignorant. Politics are the means by which they are kept suppressed and impoverished. Politics are the means by which they are deceived and disarmed. Politics is the State which oppresses them. In the heart of each there is a desire to challenge the entire political armoury of their oppressors with the single and simple weapon of justice: the justice of their own cause, crying out to the sky above Milan and to the future. Yet justice implies a judge. And there is no judge and no judgement.

The cavalry charge as the first shots are fired. The shots are above the heads of the crowd.

They ride out in lines of five or six. After a line has passed, sections of the crowd appear to re-form—not in order to resist, for resistance at this instant is unthinkable, but because in order to avoid the horses they have pressed themselves into unimaginably tight units which, as soon as the danger has momentarily passed, inevitably enlarge again. The lines of cavalry turn and wheel. Sections of the crowd repeatedly contract and expand like pumping hearts. Screams ascend and dissolve. Shouts persist.

A line of cavalry approaches. The nearest horse rears above a huddled group. The boy has never as yet seen from the ground a horse used as a weapon. Like his uncle he has always been a rider. The under-side of a rearing horse seen from below is awful in a very particular way. The body is large and heavy with four metal-shod hooves on legs whose pounding power is utterly evident. But the physical threat is compounded with something else. The horse too is made of sinews, bones, flesh and blood. It is breathing hard and is frightened. The rider's violence has already distorted its nature. The horse shares your defencelessness as it is about to

69

crush you. It is as though your fear has uncontrollably entered the horse which threatens you.

The eyes of the rider stare fixedly into the middle distance, with only quick furtive glances downwards. His back teeth are clenched so hard that he cannot swallow. His head is like a head strung through its eyes on a line five feet above the faces of the crowd: the line of his orders. His spurred boots kick out blindly at the hands and arms trying to grab them. Repeatedly his spurs jab into the horse's flanks to force it forward.

Hypnotized by the sight of horse and rider, the boy does not move until the Roman girl pulls his arm so abruptly that he almost falls. Then they begin to run. With her free hand she holds up her skirts as she runs. He notices again how unnaturally thin her arms are; but her hand is big and encloses his. She does not hesitate about where to run—towards the trees in the Giardini Pubblici.

They pass a group carrying a wounded man. Others are running. Screams gush in accompaniment to the blood—but not always from the same person. Blood runs down a woman's face, the eyes behind the blood tightly shut. An enormously fat man is half lifting her, his arm round her back. The cleared spaces enable the cavalry to charge more rapidly against those who remain. A middle-aged man alone in the middle of the Corso, fists in the air, curses the soldiers. Cowards! he shouts, *Rinnegati!* He advances towards a line of horsemen drawn up in stationary formation awaiting orders. An officer behind the line orders him to stop. He continues to advance. When he is shot he falls on his face.

Butterflies the colour of grey sandstone, others the colour of honeysuckle. Grass and wild flowers as high as the knee. Petals faded by the sun so that they are almost white, but not clay white like the miniature snails to be found in places on the dusty earth. Delicate wild gladioli the colour of amethysts, transparent and smaller than a finger joint. The red of poppies—the colour in which a child pictures fire. Fading poppies, damp, their fallen heads the colour of wine stains. Shallow outcrops of flat rock smooth and grey like the sides of dolphins. The whole field surrounded by ilex trees. To die in that field, blood flowing into the dry earth. To be shot, to fall across the tram lines, blood making the cobbles slippery. I picture the first death to make a wreath for the second.

She leads him across the gardens to the railyards and the streets near the station of the Piazza della Republica. She never lets go of his hand. She holds it neither amorously nor protectively but impatiently as if to make him run or walk fast, or, when they stop, as if to make him understand more immediately what they are watching. Occasionally she speaks to him in Italian although she knows that he cannot understand what she says. Shock, the strangeness of their situation and perhaps an innate desperation make her develop the fantasy which began as a joke. Soon she is pretending that one day they will get married. This pretence is no more unlikely than the events taking place round them. And so she establishes, intuitively, a balance between the violence of their circumstances and the violence of her imaginative preoccupation, and this balance enables her to become quite calm.

They watch a tram being overturned to make a barricade. As it falls the glass of all its windows is smashed. Having unharnessed the horse, men and women drag a carriage to overturn beside the tram. A line of railwaymen are carrying picks and crowbars from a railway depot. The news has spread that the army has been ordered to clear the city, street by street, and to hunt down every 'insurgent'. Another group of railwaymen are dismantling the track.

Everything is about to be transformed.

Imagine the blade of a giant guillotine as long as the diameter of the city. Imagine the blade descending and cutting a section through everything that is there — walls, railway lines, wagons, workshops, churches, crates of fruit, trees, sky, cobblestones. Such a blade has fallen a few yards in front of the face of everyone who is determined to fight. Each finds himself a few yards from the precipitous edge of an infinitely deep fissure which only he can see. The fissure, like a deep cut into the flesh, is unmistakably itself; there can be no doubting what has happened. But there is no pain at first.

The pain is the thought of one's own death probably being very near. It occurs to the men and women building the barricades that what they are handling, and what they are thinking, are probably being handled and thought by them for the last time. As they build the defences, the pain increases.

A man from the rooftops shouts that there are hundreds of soldiers at the corner of the Via Manin.

Umberto and four of the hotel staff whom he has specially paid and to whom he has offered a further reward of a hundred lire if they find his son, are searching in the streets behind the hotel where there are neither soldiers nor barricades.

At first, says the Roman girl in Italian, we'll live in Rome because I think we'll be happier there.

Whenever she speaks, he looks at her in the same way as he would if he understood her. The meaning of her words seems unimportant to him; what is important is that what he is seeing, he is seeing in her presence.

And you will buy me, she says in Italian, some white stockings and a hat with chiffon tied round it.

At the barricades the pain is over. The transformation is complete. It is completed by a shout from the rooftops that the soldiers are advancing. Suddenly there is nothing to regret. The barricades are between their defenders and the violence done to them throughout their lives. There is nothing to regret because it is the quintessence of their past which is now advancing against them. On their side of the barricades it is already the future.

Every ruling minority needs to numb and, if possible, to kill the time-sense of those whom it exploits by proposing a continuous present. This is the authoritarian secret of all methods of imprisonment. The barricades break that present.

The Roman girl leads him into a doorway a few yards from a barricade. We will wait here a little, she says in Italian, like a wife to an elderly husband on the occasion of a cloudburst.

The soldiers draw nearer. The last doubt that the action may be deferred disappears. Kneeling at one end of the barricade with his back against a basement grille is a white-haired man with an old pistol across his knee. It is loaded; he has one other bullet in his pocket. Younger men and women are still dismantling the road and adding to the pile of cobbles. Others are armed with bars and sticks.

Everyone falls silent. There is a distant noise of hammering from the yards and, nearer, regular as the sound of a clock (its promise of a seemingly endless time lulls him; but the way it fills the time, whose passing it records, oppresses him) the noise of marching feet. *La Rivoluzione o la morte!* shouts the white-haired man into the silence. And then: Sing, damn them, sing! They must hear us singing.

When he first commanded Sing! the Roman girl went forward to the step of the doorway, simply, as to the footlights, and began to sing the '*Canto dei Malfattori*'.

It is hard not to romanticize her voice. At first I thought it frail like her arms which so impressed him. But it is full and coarse. For a moment nobody in the street joins in, the better to appreciate how

73

her voice fills the street and seems instantaneously to soften every surface and edge.

The soldiers fire their first volley into the barricade.

The first volley simplifies, its echo killing every distraction. Nothing remains but what is in hand. A few men throw stones towards the soldiers; they fall short. A shutter bangs and an officer fires with his revolver at the window of the house. On the road between the soldiers and the barricade, absolutely still, are the seven stones that have fallen short.

Behind the barricade women get down on their knees to gather stones along the perimeters of the holes already made and to feed them to the men. A railwayman, still wearing his cap with a red and gold braid round it, shouts: Wait! Wait till we can break their heads in! Wait! And when I say—all of us at once! Wait! He has a bony, quick face and he is smiling.

The soldiers close up. A second volley. For the second time nobody is hurt. Nobody believes it, yet nobody fails to consider that the justice of their cause may be a protection. Now! Twenty men hurl their stones through the air. The soldiers edge back. A woman jeers at them: *Faccie di merda!*

A youth in an apron says of the railwayman: That one is like an officer of the artillery. On the word '*fuoco*' there is the crack of a single shot and the railwayman falls. The shot came from an upper window, not from the street. The bullet is in his face. The bullet belongs, he believes, to the past, preceding his own childhood. The wound in his face, attended by three women, gives birth to his death.

A cubic metre of space; empty it of your conception of that space; what remains is like death.

The soldiers advance again, and are driven off in the same way. But this time they withdraw a hundred yards, and there is a lull whose quiet deceives no one. Behind the barricade it is probably the moment of greatest fear. The enemy have taken the measure of the defenders' defiance and are re-planning the attack accordingly;

the defenders can do nothing but tend their dead comrade and wait, hopelessly out-armed and outnumbered.

In Italian she whispers to him: I promise you if a soldier lays hands on me, I'll drive a knife down between his shoulders. She touches him lightly with her finger where the blade will strike. As if he had understood what she said and were pretending to die, he lets his weight lean against her. I promise, she says. His head falls on to her shoulder. His legs are trembling and he fears that he is about to lose consciousness. With her arm round him she leads him through the passage of the house to a yard where she splashes his face with water from a tap and tells him to drink. The water is sharply cold and as he gulps it, he hears another volley of shots from the street. The sound in his ears and the swallowing of the cold water in his throat become a single sensation. He sees her face, her heavy eyebrows meeting in the middle, her heavy mouth and moustache, a squashed blemished face with slow eyes; he sees her expression; never before has a second person's expression appeared to express what he is feeling.

Che Dio li maledica, she says.

Along the street several riflemen have been posted in the windows of upper rooms from where they can fire, over the barricade, at its defenders. Under their covering fire the soldiers in the street are advancing. Already three defenders have been wounded.

Let me speak of one of the wounded. The bullet has entered just beneath his right collarbone. If he keeps his right arm still, the pain is constant but it does not move: it does not lunge out and devour his very consciousness of what remains unhurt. He hates the pain as he hates the soldiers. The pain is the soldiers in his body. He picks up a stone with his left hand and tries to throw it. In throwing it he inadvertently moves his right shoulder. The stone goes crooked and only hits a wall.

Write anything. Truth or untruth, it is unimportant. Speak but speak with tenderness, for that is all that you can do that may help a little. Build a barricade of words, no matter what they mean. Speak so that he can be aware of your presence. Speak so that he knows that you are there not feeling his pain. Say anything, for his pain is larger than any distinction you can make between truth and untruth. Dress him with the words of your voice as others dress his wounds. Yes. Here and now. It will stop.

There is no judge.

When the soldiers are twenty yards away, two women climb up the iron bars, which are meant to prevent people or animals falling under the tram, onto its side. As they emerge into view as targets at point-blank range, they scream at the soldiers: Shoot us! Why don't you shoot us? Several rifles point at them but nobody fires. They stand upright, straddling the broken tram windows. They continue to scream at the soldiers. *Figli di putana!* And then: *Castrati! Castrati!* The boy in the street stares up at them from behind. The heel of one of them protrudes through a large hole in her stocking. On the ankle of the second, who is without stockings, is a smear of blood. *Castrati! Castrati!* More women are climbing the bars to join the first two.

An officer notices a man on a sixth-floor parapet, further down the street, behind the barricade. The man is gesticulating. The officer orders a section of soldiers to fire at him.

The man on the parapet sees the soldiers bring their rifles to the shoulder and aim at him. If I jump, he thinks, they will kill me before I hit the ground. He jumps.

To the officer the young women swearing and prancing on the tram are sluts whom he will later have arrested. But for some of the soldiers, sons of peasants or workers from other cities, they evoke childhood memories. The women's voices show that their rage is solemn and passionate, precluding all answers. For these soldiers the women on the tram seem to have attained, whatever their actual age, the authority of elders; their rage is inseparable from judgement; before such rage one must ask for pardon.

The soldiers are ordered to advance. This order re-establishes the sense of manhood they were for a moment in danger of losing. Obediently they move forward, rifles at the ready: some to round up the men, others to drag the women off the tram.

Castrati! Cowards!

The words concentrate into a yell. It is not a yell of fear but of total refusal. They are like women yelling on behalf of the stillborn.

I cannot continue this account of the eleven-year-old boy in Milan on 6 May 1898. From this point on everything, I write will either converge upon a final full stop or else disperse so widely that it will become incoherent. Yet there was no such convergence and no incoherence. To stop here, despite all that I leave unsaid, is to admit more of the truth than will be possible if I bring the account to a conclusion. The writer's desire to finish is fatal to the truth. The End unifies. Unity must be established in another way.

Between 6 May, when martial law was declared in Milan, and 9 May one hundred workers were killed and four hundred and fifty wounded. Those four days marked the end of a phase of Italian history. Socialist leaders began to lay more and more stress on parliamentary social democracy and all attempts at direct revolutionary action—or revolutionary defence—were abandoned. Simultaneously the ruling class adopted new tactics towards the workers and the peasantry; crude repression gave way to political manipulation. For the next twenty years in Italy—as in most of the rest of Western Europe—the spectre of revolution was banished from men's minds.

O

In the garden in Livorno the fountain is playing. The fountain, the palm trees, the hibiscus and flowering shrubs have not been allowed to deteriorate since the death of Umberto's wife, three years ago in

1895. He employs two gardeners. He travels specially to Settignano to order rare plants. Each year his memory of his wife approximates more closely to the picture of her preserved by her acquaintances and friends. He no longer disputes that his wife was a person of great spirituality.

Occasionally there is a noise which suggests a marble dropped into water. It is made by a perch, basking on the surface of the water, abruptly plunging. Umberto cannot enjoy the peacefulness of the garden alone. Alone he feels old and nervous. He will agree to anything Laura asks in exchange for being able to have his son in Livorno.

Umberto thinks that his son is not like a modern Italian but like a youth painted during the Renaissance; his face is like a window onto his soul. He finds the gaps in the boy's teeth a little disconcerting when he smiles, but these he will have stopped with gold. He tells Laura of all the advantages which the boy would enjoy if he lived in Livorno. Laura does not say what she thinks. Instead she complains, hints, contradicts herself. The more persuasive Umberto becomes, the less encouraging she is. He pleads with her, he begs her on his knees.

No, No, she cries, holding his arms to make him get to his feet.
He reminds her of times they have spent together.
Ah my little one you were mad, quite quite mad.
Italy, she insists, is not a country for a child.
Come with him, says Umberto becoming more agitated, I'll buy a house. I'll buy you . . .
The father's sentimentality will ensure that the mother has her way.

Whilst his unknown mother and newly-discovered father argue about where he should live and with whom, the son returns again and again to his memory of being led into the yard where the water-tap was. Again the Roman girl throws water on his face. Again he is amazed by her expression. Again something is revealed to him. The revelation is as wordless as the water she threw was colourless.

Where he is (in the garden in Livorno) or where he was (in the Via Manin) is unimportant; what he sees in front of him (his mother's round face and her hair impeccably arranged in a bun) or what he saw (the Roman girl's blemished open mouth) belongs to the particular moment; what he hears (the sound of the fountain playing) or what he heard (screams and curses of women) are simple alternatives; what matters is what her expression in the yard confirmed but what, until this moment, was wordless. What matters is not being dead.

4.

It has begun, the struggle unto death against what is.

The veil of St Veronica: a kerchief with the image of Christ's head wearing the crown of thorns imprinted upon it.

I see another image miraculously printed on cloth. Her body with her head thrown back and her eyes shut. The image is naturalistic, quite unstylized. Dark areas of hair. Her pale skin almost indistinguishable from the colour of the linen sheet on which she lay.

Again and again two pigeons fly into the wood and out of it: the male always in pursuit. As the pair approach the wood with the hen bird in the lead, she checks herself in mid-air by holding herself vertical, with her tail down and her outstretched wings now acting as a brake. Her head is thrown back, her beak points to the sky. She hangs there motionless and yet not falling. The male bird finds himself at her side. She begins to drop, puts her head down and her tail up, dives, and they enter the wood together. A moment later they emerge from the far side of the wood to circle once more and repeat the same flight.

The description so far as it goes is accurate. But my power to select (both the facts and the words describing them) impregnates the text with a notion of choice which encourages the reader to infer a false range and type of choice being open to the two pigeons. Description distorts.

On an afternoon in late May 1902 (a few weeks before the end of the Boer War), Beatrice seduces him. What happens happens like an undescribed natural event.

O

When Laura and her son returned from Milan at the end of May 1898 they found that Beatrice was engaged to be married to Captain Patrick Bierce of the 17th Lancers. The boy was sent to a boarding school. During most school holidays he stayed alone with Jocelyn on the farm. (Beatrice accompanied her husband when he was posted to South Africa.)

The type of school to which he was sent has been frequently described. Its daily routine was spartan: its ideology imperialistic and religious: its social life authoritarian and sadistic. The purpose of the education which the school offered was to produce empire-builders.

Like many other boys he adapted himself to school life. A certain aloofness reinforced what his companions immediately recognized as his foreignness. He was not, however, unduly persecuted. His very indifference was a kind of protection. He was nicknamed Gari-baldi because he claimed that his father was Italian. He spent an unusual amount of his free time playing the piano in the school music rooms. His interest in music was entirely disproportionate to his small talent.

At the age of fourteen his face was no longer that of a child. The change is sometimes thought of as a coarsening process; this misses the point. The change—which may occur any time between four-teen and twenty-four—involves a simultaneous gain and loss in expressiveness. The texture of the skin, the form of the flesh over the bones, become mute; their appearance becomes a covering, whereas in childhood it is a declaration of being. (Compare our response to children and to adults: we give to the existence of children the value we give to the intentions of adults.) However, the openings in the covering—especially the eyes and mouth—

become more expressive, precisely because they now offer indications of what lies hidden behind.

The process of maturing and, later, of ageing involves a gradual but increasing withdrawal of the self from the exterior surface of the body. The skin of the very old is like a garment. The mouth of the man next to the boy—it was Jocelyn—was already inexpressive; he had withdrawn from his mouth: his lips were no more than a flange of the outer covering. This covering offered a certain amount of information: country gentleman, outdoor life, taciturn, disappointed. It was only through his eyes that one could still sometimes glimpse that part of his self still capable of response.

They were walking up a steep winding path with high hedges on either side. It was a late November afternoon (1900), very similar to the one when the men in sack-cloth had shown the boy the dead dray-horses. He had spoken to nobody of this incident. He remembered it vividly without seeking any explanation. It had acquired the isolated absoluteness of a vision. For him his experiencing it was its explanation.

It had been raining hard during the day. Beside the path water was running fast downhill along a stone-bedded ditch, overgrown with grass. They could hear but not see the water. Both carried guns under their arms.

Earlier, the boy had been telling Jocelyn about a dream he had had.

. . . I was down in the Martin and it was very hot, like it was last summer. I was swimming and there were big birds flying very low over the water—not predatory birds. Sometimes a bird's foot touched my hair. Then more and more birds came so that I was forced to swim to the bank and climb out.

Tedder was telling me it's going to be an exceptional year for duck on the estuary, said Jocelyn.

I started looking for my clothes. But somebody had changed them. They weren't the same clothes as before. They were a uniform, a soldier's uniform. It was a perfect fit—I mean it must have been a uniform made for me.

Do you remember what regiment? asked Jocelyn.

I didn't know in my dream what regiment it was.

Were you a cavalry officer?

I didn't know.

Perhaps the Eighth Hussars, said Jocelyn. They had arrived at a gate. Jocelyn put his hand on the barrel of the boy's gun to remind him to break it before climbing over. As he did so he looked at the boy, and was suddenly overwhelmed by how foreign he looked. He looked like an Italian: he looked like the son of his Italian shop-keeper father. His rigid mouth hardly moving, but in a kindly tone, he said: No, not the Eighth Hussars, even when you are dreaming.

I put my hand into the tunic pocket, continued the boy, and inside was—a crab! A large crab and it nipped me. I pulled out my hand and the extraordinary thing was that my hand was the crab! I had an arm, a wrist, and a crab for a hand.

What a preposterous dream! Why do you tell it to me?

I think it means that if I join the army I shall be wounded.

A light wound perhaps.

No, severely.

I saw a sow badger this morning, said Jocelyn, you should have come with me.

I heard you go off. You shouted at Tedder about the mare being under-bitted.

I haven't found the key to that mare's mouth yet, said Jocelyn.

Then they had both fallen silent.

In the narrow steep lane the boy asked: Have you heard from Aunt Beatrice?

Jocelyn appeared not to hear. The boy glanced sideways at him.

The man's eyes were screwed up and his face was thrust forward into the damp, increasingly cold air. He could have been trying to spot something in the light which was beginning to fail. Or he could have been a man leaving his house with the determination never to return, a man thrusting his face forward so that it might the sooner be immersed in the unknown and the indifferent.

Several minutes later he said: She says they're saying in Durban, that the war is as good as over. Lord Roberts is on his way home.

She'll be here soon then.

You forget that she's married, said Jocelyn.

Where will they live?

I've no idea.

Why are all the things still kept in her room?

Because it is still her room.

Will they both come here?

Again Jocelyn appeared not to hear. They emerged from the lane into a spinney. At the end of the lane Jocelyn's dog was awaiting him. A springer spaniel called Silver.

Do you know why you have bad dreams, said Jocelyn, it's because you spend too much time indoors. You don't exercise yourself enough. Too much in the house. It's a woman's life that. Not a man's. You should come out with me more.

I'm sorry if I disappoint you, said the boy. He said it insolently as though it were inconceivable that the man could have any real grounds for disappointment. When I give my first concert you'll be proud of me.

We've only got about twenty minutes more in this light, said Jocelyn, let's clear the wood and cross the quarry field. You work the left and I'll take the right below. Silver, come here Silver!

His voice changed when he spoke to the dog, becoming both firmer and softer. To the boy he spoke more loudly and yet hesitantly.

They separated and began to go forward through the wood. The trees and the slope of the ground made it impossible for them to keep in sight of one another.

Hup! Hup! cried Jocelyn to show how far forward he was.

Hup! Hup! replied the boy to show that they were advancing in level line.

It is a cry which is thought not to alert the birds. It sounds more like a wooden stick striking a hollow wooden vessel (the wood of the vessel water-logged) than a voice speaking.

Nothing stirred in the wood. The tree trunks looked grey. The spaniel was seeking half-heartedly as if it found the damp entirely vegetable odour of the wet leaves disagreeable.

Hup! Hup!

For Jocelyn the cry belonged to a language which was theoretically infinite. Those two repeated wooden monosyllables filled the spinney with the splendour of a tradition as no sentence or speech or music ever could. Through the cry and the response to it, was invoked the understanding of honourable men acting in concert, disinterestedly, to experience certain moments of pure style.

Hup! Hup!

This time Jocelyn's cry was addressed gently and specifically to the boy. He was talking to the boy, including him in the tradition. The boy noticed the difference in the man's cry, but he answered as before.

Hup! Hup!

The tradition envisages men in close but special contact with nature. The men are unspoilt by comfort yet they are free of the necessity of having to exploit nature. They enter into nature rather as a swimmer, who has no need to cross it, enters a river. They play in the current: in it and yet not of it. What prevents them being swept away are time-honoured rules to which they adhere without question. The rules all concern ways of treating or handling specific objects or situations—guns, boots, bags, dogs, trees, deer, etc. Thus the force of nature (either from within or from without) is never allowed to accumulate; the rules always establish calm, as locks do in a river. Such men feel like gods because they have the impression of imposing an aesthetic order upon nature merely by the timing and style of their own formal interventions.

Hup! Hup!

If Silver puts up a woodcock, thought Jocelyn, it will be almost too dark now.

The tradition envisages that at the end of the day tiredness finally forces the men to cease. They return home stiff, hungry, chilled or soaked, caked with mud. At home they offer to women and friends the invisible unmade masterpieces which they have fleetingly constructed in nature; they offer them in the soiled or torn clothes they throw off, in their stiff bodies, in their excited distant eyes, in the names they possess and the names of where they have been with whom.

Hup! Hup!

It was the boy's turn to respond. He did so, as before, flatly—without the conspiratorial intensity of his uncle.

Advancing level with Jocelyn, doing what was expected of him, his presence indicated only by his prescribed responding cry, it occurred to him that he could be any man walking up with his uncle. Under cover he had entered the company of men.

They emerged from the wood and proceeded across the open quarry-field. The cries were no longer necessary for they could see one another. Jocelyn whispered urgently to his dog, checking him so that he should not get too far ahead. His way of talking to the dog was part of the same language.

A hare leapt from covert some twenty-five yards away. Jocelyn fired one barrel. The report and its echo from the quarry face momentarily supplied an axis to the uniform grey dusk, as though the two sounds were magnetic poles to which every particle of the dusk turned and pointed.

The hare ran on, the pulse of its leaps undisturbed. It was running cross-wise, offering the boy a broadside shot.

He saw it running. He saw it as a brown furry smudge. He saw the muscles along its shoulders and down its haunches flex as it zig-zagged. He was unaware of squeezing the trigger, unaware even—for a second's delay—of the recoil: he simply saw the hare in mid-leap going small and falling.

Imagine an invisible net which can fly through the air but remains open-ended like a wind-sock: the net flies towards the hare, the hare leaps into the net whose neck is only wide enough to admit the animal's head and shoulders, so that the hare, entering the net, has to bunch itself up as a rabbit does when scuttling into its burrow. As the hare bunches, the foot of the net is filled with lead. It drops immediately to the ground.

The dog was whimpering. In this light, said Jocelyn placing a hand under the boy's elbow and holding the hare by its hind legs level with their two faces, I couldn't have done that.

O

What does *castrati* mean? he had asked Umberto in Italy.

Castrati? Castrati!

Umberto was surprised but delighted by the question. It was the antithetical question to all that he wanted to tell the boy.

Un castrato cannot be a father.

Umberto began to explain at length and fulsomely. He poured out wine and insisted that his son drink. As he talked Umberto's fingers chopped themselves off, made hooks of themselves, wagged.

The boy had seen Tom castrating lambs: a flick of the knife and then the two testicles sucked out into the mouth and spat upon the ground. But he had not connected the Italian word with the English.

Umberto cited himself as a father, and hit the lower part of his stomach with his flat hand. He leant across the table so that his huge face was close to the boy's. But *il castrato* today, he said, is an insult. It does not mean it properly. It means a weak man, a man who is not capable, a feeble one. Him. *Quest'uomo è castrato*. He could be called that. *Un Castrato*. Umberto was so close to his son's face that he could not resist touching it. *Ecco* my boy my boy, he said.

○

The gun room was small and square with a high ceiling. High on one wall hung a pair of mounted antlers, dusty and grey. An oil lamp was reflected in the black curtainless window. Jocelyn stood at a bench-like table on which his gun lay in three parts. The boy sprawled in a sagging arm-chair in front of the fireplace in which there was no fire.

Why, asked the boy looking towards the black window rather than towards Jocelyn, do you disapprove of Aunt Beatrice's marriage?

It is not a subject we should discuss.

The boy took in the crowded room: boots, mackintoshes, fishing rods, baskets, piles of old copies of *The Sportsman*, two foxes' masks, a pipe-rack, a ladder—and on everything pointing upwards an old hat or cap hung. He remembered the room as he had been aware of it as a child. He had never been allowed in. But he had noticed through a half-open door men in their shirt-sleeves, a fire burning and an unusual smell. After a pause, he re-started the same conversation.

Everything has changed since she went, he said.

Jocelyn was screwing together the brass joins of two lengths of a cleaning rod. The table smelt of gun oil. The smell reminded Jocelyn of his father. It was associated in his mind with the smell of cordite and metal—the smell of sport. It suggested to him the smell of food being prepared for company. This last was associated with returning home with friends after a shoot, but is perhaps inherent in the smell itself. The smell of gun oil, for all its graphite, has something about it of the smell of butter in shortbread or pastry when they are still very hot in an iron oven. It is the antithesis of the smell of lilac. In the chill fireless room, Jocelyn shivered and heard himself saying: There was no stopping her.

Did he sweep her off her feet, then? asked the boy.

He fawned at her feet like a dog.

Is she happy with him?

She couldn't be happy with him, Jocelyn said and then, with the gesture of a romantic 'cello-player, drove the cleaning-rod through the barrel. The action always pleased him. He ran his hand along the bluish polished metal of the underside of the barrels. Again he was speaking before he had decided to do so. She has the highest standards, he was saying, that is how she is made.

He was handsome, said the boy in a tense intended to provoke.
He is a cad, said Jocelyn, his hand beginning to tremble.
Did you have it out with him?
I could not.
A cad you think?
Jocelyn put the barrels down and steadied himself with both hands on the table.
This is not a subject we should pursue, he said.
He was not thinking of the boy's age. He wished to talk to nobody about this subject.

The boy, however, was determined to force Jocelyn to say more: not out of personal animosity but in order to claim his own right— and his ability—to know, to touch on no matter what subject. It seemed to him that nothing familiar now remained in his life: hence his right to pursue every question.

I doubt, said the boy, whether there are any marriages which the families of both parties are really happy about.

There used to be.

One side always makes a sacrifice. Usually the side with the least money.

Surprised by the odd sense and wording of those remarks, Jocelyn turned to look at the boy who was leaning deep back in the armchair, his face in shadow. He could discover no insolence in his expression. When their eyes met, the boy said:

You didn't approve of my mother and father did you?

That was a very different case.

You mean because they were never married?

Who told you that?

A boy at school called Charles Hay.

Jocelyn turned to the window. The whole of the boy's upbringing, he considered, had been compromised by half-measures and his mother's sudden whims.

The boy was still speaking: You can tell by looking at them that they've never been married. They don't treat each other like husband and wife. They don't possess anything in common—except me.

That is no way to speak of your mother and father.

Is lying better?

I find it regrettable that you should come across such stories at school.

They call me Garibaldi because they say my mother might have been his mistress too.

It is terrible.

I laugh.

Laugh?

Do you expect me to defend my mother's honour?

Jocelyn wanted to tell the boy that he had argued many times with Laura that it was necessary to tell him the truth. Yet he felt that anything he said would now be incomprehensible because it belonged to a past which existed only in his own memory.

He turned back to the table and began wiping the stock of his gun.

Why is Captain Bierce a cad? asked the boy in a gentle, almost tender voice.

He's a bullying Irish braggart—a mutton-fisted loud-mouthed
pack-horse captain!
That's no way to talk about your brother-in-law!

Having said this, the boy laughed. And Jocelyn laughed too. They
laughed at the collapse of the formalities which had surrounded
them. In face of this collapse they were for a moment equal. The
boy got up from the chair and went over to the table. The man sat
down and leant back in the arm-chair. He was trembling.

The boy, picking up the stock, noticed that the firing-pins had not
been released. Pressing the front of the stock against the table top,
he squeezed each trigger. The two sharp taps of the pins against
the wood broke the silence. The surface of the table there was
already scarred with thousands of tiny pock marks caused during
the years by this method of releasing firing-pins so that their springs
should not be weakened.

Jocelyn began to speak from the depths of the chair, staring at the
fire grate, and softly as though almost to himself:

He tore her out of her own place. I know what she is like. She is as
fine as china. She's like that figure there with flowers around her
waist. She needs to be protected and free.

The boy could not see the man for he was hidden by the back of
the chair. Above the chair he could see the mantelpiece: on it
were a dusty packet of envelopes, a ball of twine, a leather strap and
a porcelain figure of a shepherdess, about eight inches high.

He tore her out of her own place. She was part of this place. She
knew it. There were no secrets from her. She was the spirit of this
place and this house. She was why I lived here.

The boy stared at the porcelain figure, its pink, almost white glaze
shining in the lamplight.

I begin to be glad I've lived half my life. A fair part of it has been
good. But from now on everything will get worse. Everybody is
becoming ignorant and mutton-fisted and too busy judging everybody else. We're going to have sermons and commerce. I hate this

damned farm now. No one knows how to wait any more, because they haven't anything worth waiting for. I don't know how to wait myself. I used to wait for her.

The man stopped talking.

I'll go and change, he said later, it's cold here.

The boy approached the mantelpiece still staring at the porcelain figure of the shepherdess.

O

How did it happen that on 2 May 1902, Beatrice was in her bedroom, her hair loose, wearing only a nightdress and wrap, in the middle of the afternoon?

The previous day, walking through the walled vegetable garden, she had noticed that several boughs of lilac had come out on the tree in the north-east corner. She wanted to pick some to take into the house. But to get to the tree she had to cross a bed of wet earth and rotting brussel sprout plants. She took off her shoes and stockings and left them on the path. Her feet sank into the mud up to her ankles. When she reached the tree, she discovered she was not tall enough. A little way along the wall was a black, rotten ladder. (During her absence in South Africa the house and farm had deteriorated dramatically.) She tested the first three rungs and they seemed strong enough. She moved the ladder to the lilac tree and climbed up. A wasp, caught between her skirts and the wall, stung her on the instep of her foot. She cried out (a small cry like a child's or a gull's), took little notice, cut the lilac and went barefoot into the house to wash her feet. By evening, her foot was inflamed and during the night she slept badly.

The next morning she decided to stay in bed. She knew that it was not the kind of decision she would ever have made before her marriage, before she left the farm. Jocelyn expected her to run the house and keep an eye on the dairy: he was away at a point-to-point in Leicestershire. A surveyor who was coming that afternoon expected her to prepare papers for him. Everybody would expect her to treat a small, already less swollen wasp bite as though it were nothing. Before her marriage she did what was expected of her. Now she did not.

She gave instructions and took a bath. Still wet, she stood looking at herself in the tall tippable mirror in the bathroom.

She did not pretend that her gaze was that of a man. She drew no sexual conclusions as she stared at herself. She saw her body as a core, left when all its clothes had fallen from it. Around this core she saw the space of the bathroom. Yet between core and room something had changed, which was why all the house and the whole farm seemed changed since her return. She cupped her breasts with her hands and then moved her hands slowly downwards, over her hips, to the front of her thighs. Either the surface of her body or the touch of her hands had changed too.

Before, she lived in her body as though it were a cave, exactly her size. The rock and earth around the cave were the rest of the world. Imagine putting your hand into a glove whose exterior surface is continuous with all other substance.

Now her body was no longer a cave in which she lived. It was solid. And everything around, which was not her, was movable. Now what was given to her stopped at the surfaces of her body.

In nightgown and wrap she returned to bed. She lay back against a bank of pillows and imitated the cackling noise of a turkey. When she noticed the portrait of her father she stopped. Some women might have considered the possibility that they were going mad. She began to move her head from side to side on the bank of pillows, thus tilting her view of the room from side to side. When she felt giddy, she got out of bed and dropped on to her hands and knees: the carpeted floor was level and still. On the level ground in the free space she was conscious of being happy.

At her dressing table with a silver-backed mermaid-embossed hair-brush in her hand she asked herself as she had many times during the previous six months: Why do I feel no deep loss? Her way of answering the question was to search in her mind to make sure that its supposition was correct. Then her answer, which entirely satisfied her, was: Because I don't.

Captain Patrick Bierce was killed on 17 September 1901, in the mountains north of the Great Karoo, Cape Colony. A British encampment was attacked by Boer commandos under General Smuts. The commandos were desperate, lacking both supplies and ammunition. In some close fighting among rocks Captain Bierce had half his head blown away. The Boer who shot him at close range had used an explosive Mauser cartridge (generally used for big game) because he had no other ammunition. Later, after the British had surrendered, the Boer found the mutilated officer whom he had shot dead, and was distressed at having had to use such ammunition. He argued to himself, however, that there was not a great deal of difference between killing a man with an explosive bullet and smashing him with a lyddite shell.

The colonel who broke to Beatrice the news of her husband's death said: We soldiers count as our gains—our losses. Those men we love most to honour are those who die in a great cause.

What afflicted her was the shock which she imagined her husband feeling at his own death. She imagined him dying in mortal disappointment. But the fact that their life together was over impressed her too as a gain rather than as a loss. She could leave Africa. She could leave him. She could leave his brother officers.

I do not know for how long the relationship between Jocelyn and Beatrice had been incestuous.

I do know that Beatrice must have married Captain Bierce in order to simplify her life.

The power which Jocelyn exercised over his sister was essentially the power of the elder brother of childhood prolonged into adult life. He was protective and possessive; he was the moral arbiter in a world he knew better than she. Her virtue must lie in her obedience to him and her indifference to the judgement of others. Yet after adolescence this power of his over her depended upon her collaboration. More than that—this collaboration contributed more to their relationship than any adult ability on his part to be masterful. His domination was the result of her willing it for him. Hence the strangely circular nature of their moods and intimacy . . .

Into this circle stepped Captain Bierce, confident, huge, beaming, straight-speaking—simple and uncomplicated as only a man in uniform can appear to be. He courted her. He knelt before her and said he was her servant—her giant servant. He worshipped, he said, the very ground on which she trod.

He seemed to demand neither connivance nor complicity. Instead he asked her formally for the gift of her hand in marriage. The conventional metaphors became persuasive in their very simplicity. Leading her by the hand, he would show her the world.

She accepted his proposal.

They were married in the parish church of St Catherine's.

They left for Africa.

The land surface of the earth is estimated to extend over about 52,500,000 sq. miles. Of this area the British Empire occupies nearly one quarter, extending over an area of about 12,000,000 sq. miles. By far the greater portion lies within the temperate zones, and is suitable for white settlement. . . . The area of the territory of the Empire is divided almost equally between the southern and northern hemispheres, the great divisions of Australasia and South Africa covering between them in the southern hemisphere 5,308,506 sq. miles while the United Kingdom, Canada and India, including the native states, cover between them in the northern hemisphere

5,271,375 sq. miles. The alternation of the seasons is thus complete, one half of the Empire enjoying summer while one half is in winter.

Within a few weeks of their arrival in Durban, Beatrice began to suffer a delusion: she came to believe that everything was being tilted, that everything around her was taking place on an incline which was gradually becoming more acute. As the angle of incline increased, so everything on it began to slip downwards, nearer to its bottom edge. The inclined plane extended over the whole sub-continent, and the bottom edge gave on to the Indian Ocean.

One early afternoon in February 1899 in Pietermaritzburg she took a rickshaw despite the fact that Captain Bierce had recently been mysteriously insistent that she should not do so. However, she had few illusions left concerning her husband's mysteries.

The Zulu rickshaw-boy wore a head-dress of tattered, dyed ostrich feathers which smelt of burnt hair. His long legs were crudely white-washed. The previous night there had been a thunderstorm and the sky, cleared by the storm, was an unusually harsh blue. The frayed ostrich feathers above her, shaking as the Zulu between the shafts ran, appeared to brush the blue sky as though it were a tangible, painted surface.

They passed a company of marching British soldiers. Under the blue sky, in front of the low, shack-like hastily constructed buildings, along the unmysterious absolutely straight streets, each platoon looked like a box in which twenty or thirty men were helplessly vibrating.

Here, as in Durban, the activities of her countrymen never ceased. Every moment had its duty. The rickshaw passed some officers on horseback who bowed slightly without looking at her. To them she was an officer's wife. She had selected among Captain Bierce's brother officers those whom she would prefer to be killed at Lady-smith if a certain number had to be.

She began to stare at the running whitewashed legs, one, unflexing, continually giving place to the second, flexing. The movement was very different from that of a horse's hind legs as seen from a trap; and the difference disturbed her. Yet her feeling led her to no conclusion. What separated her from the British wives with whom she was obliged to pass most of her time, was her lack of opinions. She had come to hate the sound of talking. She trusted certain feelings in herself precisely because they did not lead to conclusions.

They turned into a narrower but equally straight street which led past the backs of bungalows and some unused sites of land. Trees cast intermittent shade. They came upon a file of African women walking along the grass verge. By their costumes it was clear that they had walked to the city from a Location kraal. (For certain brief occasions women were allowed to come to the city to visit their menfolk employed there.) On their heads they carried immense gourds. The rickshaw slowed down. One of the women shouted something at the Zulu which Beatrice could not understand. Another made a gesture and laughed. None of the women looked at her. Two were old with withered breasts. Another carried a baby.

At the end of the narrow street they joined a busy avenue and reached her destination: the entrance gate to the botanical gardens. She climbed out and asked the rickshaw-boy what was in the gourds the women were carrying. Looking down at her—for she was much shorter—he told her that it was kaffir beer. It was then that everything tilted for the first time. She had to cling to the railings of the botanical gardens. She clung to them, facing them, her head thrust between two bars. The rickshaw-boy stared at her, dumbfounded, until a policeman arrived and started to threaten him.

The second time was in Durban at a dinner party given by the harbour master. She saw the dinner table tilting. She put out her hand to prevent a silver candelabra with candles burning in it from falling over. In making this abrupt movement (which was incomprehensible to those sitting around her) she knocked over a guest's glass of wine.

Later that night, made tender and menacing by drink, Captain Bierce hissed at her affectionately: A clumsy slave, my dove, must be chastised, I have no choice but to tie you up again. Try to slip out,

Beatrice, I must tighten the bindings. Speak to me, Beatrice. Declare your allegiance. . . .

As her delusion became more and more frequent, the physical sensation of everything being tilted gave way to a conviction that it was being tilted. She suddenly knew it instead of feeling it.

She is aware that there is another way of seeing her and all that surrounds her, which can only be defined as the way she can never see. She is being seen in that way now. Her mouth goes dry. Her corsets constrain her more tightly. Everything tilts. She sees everything clearly and normally. She can discern no tilt. But she is convinced, she is utterly certain that everything has been tilted.

Even when the delusion had passed, the idea of the sub-continent being tilted did not strike her as implausible; on the contrary it seemed to correspond with the rest of her daily experience and to make that experience more credible.

Gradually the anguish accompanying the delusion lessened. She consulted nobody. She ceased to be worried by its abnormality. She accepted it. She accepted it as the consequence of living first in Pietermaritzburg, then in Durban, and later in Capetown. She no longer wondered whether she was going mad; instead she awaited her chance to escape.

Beatrice's disturbance was probably partly due to her discovery of what her husband was like out of his uniform. All that he demanded was that she should allow him to tie her up and gently maltreat her. The mere sight of her tied up was usually sufficient to bring him to a sexual climax; she suffered not from his violence but from her own shame and disappointment. The unfamiliar climate of Natal and Cape Colony may have further exacerbated her nervous condition. But there was another factor.

THE GREAT AMAXOSA DELUSION

On 23 December 1847, the British Governor of Cape Colony, Sir Harry Smith, summoned together the chiefs of the Amaxosa tribes on the Eastern Frontier. He told them that their territory—the most fertile in South Africa—was to be annexed and made a crown dependency: British Kaffraria. After a while it became clear that the Gaika tribe and their chief Sandila were determined to offer the most stubborn resistance. Sir Harry Smith re-summoned the chiefs. Sandila refused to come. Whereupon Sir Harry deposed him of his chiefship, and in his place, as chief of the Gaikas, appointed an English magistrate called Mr Brownlee. Convinced that they had now dealt with the matter masterfully, the two Englishmen ordered the arrest of Sandila. On 24 December 1850 the force sent out to arrest him was ambushed and the Gaika tribe rose in revolt. White settlers in the military villages along the frontier were attacked and killed whilst celebrating Christmas. Thus began the Fourth Kaffir War: the penultimate stage in the Amaxosas' long defence of their independence, which had continued for sixty years.

By 1853 the British, with their prodigious military advantages (the war cost the Colonial Office nearly a million pounds), were able to impose a military defeat on the tribes. In 1856 there followed what the British were later to call 'The Great Amaxosa Delusion'. This 'delusion' constituted the ultimate stage of the Amaxosa nation's defence of its independence.

A girl named Nongkwase told her father that when going to draw water from a stream she had met strangers of commanding aspect. The father went to see them. They told him that they were spirits of the dead who had come to help their people drive the white men into the sea. The father reported to Sarili, an Amaxosa chief, who announced that the people must do what the spirits instructed. The spirits instructed the people to kill all their cattle and to destroy every grain of corn they possessed. Their cattle had become thin and their crops poor as a result of the land already stolen from them by the white man. When every head of cattle was killed and every seed of corn destroyed, myriads of fat beautiful cattle would issue from the earth, great fields of heavy ripe corn would instantly appear, trouble and sickness would vanish, everybody would be young and beautiful, and the white man, on that day, would perish utterly.

The people obeyed. Cattle were central to their culture. In the villages heads of cattle were the measuring units of wealth. When a daughter was married, her father, if rich enough, gave her a cow, an ubulungu—'a doer of good': this cow must never be killed and a hair from its tail must always be tied round the neck of each of the daughter's children at birth. Nevertheless the people obeyed. They slaughtered their cattle and their sacred cows and they burnt their grain.

They built large new kraals for the new fat cattle that would come. They prepared skin sacks to hold the milk that was soon to be more plentiful than water. They held themselves in patience and waited their vengeance.

The appointed day of the prophecy arrived. The sun rose and sank with the hopes of hundreds of thousands. By nightfall nothing had changed.

An estimated fifty thousand died of starvation. Many thousands more left their land to search for work in Cape Colony. Those who remained did so as a propertyless labour force. (A little later many were to work as wage slaves in the diamond and gold mines further north.) On the rich, now depopulated, land of the Amaxosa, European farmers settled and prospered.

○

Who is that? asked the boy.
The Grand Duke: Ferdinando Primo. He was the father of Livorno. He founded the city and he came from Firenze, said Umberto.
What is it made of?
I do not understand.
Is it made of stone? asked the boy.
It is made in bronze, a metal *precioso*.
Why are the men chained?
They are slaves. Slaves from Africa.
They look very strong.
They must be strong. They—how you say? Umberto mimed a man rowing.
Rowing a boat?
Yes. Yes. Yes.

Why did they want to make a statue of them?
Ma perché son magnifici. They are beautiful.

◯

Beatrice laid aside the silver-backed, mermaid-embossed hairbrush and going to the window stopped by the vase of lilac.

When the boy came into the room she said : I cannot ever remember any lilac having a scent like this lot. Then she asked him whether he would please find out whether the second cowman was still sick. After he had left the room, she thought : I am more than twice as old as he is.

POEM FOR BEATRICE

Continually mists change my size
Only territories on a map are measured
The sounds I make are made elsewhere
I am enveloped in the astonishing silence of my breasts
I plait my hair into sentences
Never let loose
I walk where I wish
My cuffs admit my wrists alone
Break
Break the astonishing silence of my breasts.

THE BOERS

'Our century is a huge cauldron in which all historical eras are boiling and mingling.'   Octavio Paz

African civilization in South Africa was destroyed by the Boers. The

Boers colonized South Africa for the later benefit of the British. The British intermittently aided them in this colonization but the essential relation between the colonizers and the colonized was created by the Boers. Yet the Boers were themselves fugitives—in both a geographical and a historical sense. They defeated in the name of defeat. When, in the eighteenth century, they began to penetrate into the High Veld, they did so to escape the controls of the Dutch East India Company in Cape Town, and as soon as they did so, they regressed historically. They abandoned fixed farms; they became nomadic herdsmen and hunters.

The Great Trek of 1835 which led the Boers into Natal, the Transvaal and Orange Free State was a retreat from the demands and disciplines in all spheres of social activity—productive, political, moral—of nineteenth-century Europe. Unlike other colonizers it could not occur to the Boers that they were taking 'civilization' into 'the dark continent': they themselves were withdrawing from that 'civilization'.

Their productive means were no more advanced than those of the Bantu whose land they seized, whose crops they burnt and whose herds they stole. Their fire-arms, fast horses and wagons gave them the necessary tactical advantages. But they were incapable of developing what they seized. They were even incapable of exploiting the labour force of impoverished squatters which they created. With all their rights of mastery and property, which they held to be sacred and God-given, they could do nothing. They were impotent; and they were alone among those whom they had uselessly defeated.

In the rest of the world which Europe colonized, enslaved and exploited, native populations were massacred and destroyed (in Australia, in North America): deported elsewhere (from West Africa as slaves): or else they were accommodated within a moral, religious, social system which rationalized and justified the colonizations (catholicism in Latin America, the princely kingdoms and the caste system integrated into the imperial rule of India). In South Africa the Boers were unable to establish such a self-justifying 'moral' hegemony. They could accommodate neither victory nor victims. They could draw up no treaty with those whom they had dispossessed. There was no settlement possible, because they were unable to use what they had taken. There was consequently less hypocrisy or complacency or corruption among the Boers than among other colonizers. But it seemed to them that the existence of every African was an incitement to that great black avenging which they continually feared. And since no settlement was possible, the justification, the explanation of their position had to be continually reaffirmed through individual emotion. Day and night every Boer had to insure that his feeling of mastery was stronger than his fear. All that could relieve the fear was hatred.

Politics, so far as Beatrice was concerned, was one of the careers open to men: no more and no less. (She saw Laura's devotion to politics as proof of her heartlessness.) She was interested in the stories and characters of Greek mythology—but not in history. She knew nothing of the fate of the Amaxosa. When people spoke, as they did continually in Musgrave Road, Durban, or at the Royal Hotel, of the 'treachery of the Boers' and the 'Boer atrocities', she had the impression that everyone was waiting their opportunity to compete, like singers at an audition, in saying the necessary phrases with their own individual gestures and signs of emotion. The competition never ended so long as there was a second person present. Other subjects included The Empire, The Character of the Kaffir, The Qualities of The British Soldier, The Role of the Missionary. She never questioned the assumptions which underlay the phrases. Both assumptions and competition bored her. She acquired the habit of appearing to listen whilst studying the speaker's fingers, or looking out of the window or wondering what she herself would be doing in half an hour. Thus her time and her attention were frequently unoccupied. And this is what led to her disturbance, to the possibility of the sub-continent haunting her.

Precisely because she lacked the protection of ready-made generalizations and judgements, because she allowed her thoughts to wander aimlessly, because she lacked what all administrators and troops oppressing another nation must always maintain—a sense of duty without end, she began to feel, between the interstices of formal social convention, the violence of the hatred, the violence of what would be avenged.

In Pietermaritzburg she saw a loyal Dutchman (loyal to the Queen) beating his kaffir servant. As he beat him he made a noise in his throat like a laugh. His mouth was open and his tongue was between his teeth. His passion was such that he did not wish to stop until he had annihilated the body he was beating: yet however hard he beat it, he could not annihilate it. From this arose the necessity of his cry which resembled a laugh. His expression was like that of a small child deliberately shitting himself. The servant, absolutely silent, hunched himself against the blows.

Sometimes in the way an African ran she saw the defiance of all his race.

She could not explain her feelings to herself. There is an historical equivalent to the psychological process of repression into the unconscious. Certain experiences cannot be formulated because they have occurred too soon. This happens when an inherited world-view is unable to contain or resolve certain emotions or intuitions which have been provoked by a new situation or an extremity of experience unforeseen by that world-view. 'Mysteries' grow up within or around the ideological system. Eventually these mysteries destroy it by providing the basis for a new world-view. Medieval witchcraft, for example, may be seen in this light.

A moment's introspection shows that a large part of our own experience cannot be adequately formulated: it awaits further understanding of the total human situation. In certain respects we are likely to be better understood by those who follow us than by ourselves. Nevertheless their understanding will be expressed in terms which would now be alien to us. They will change our unformulated experience beyond our recognition. As we have changed Beatrice's.

She is aware that there is another way of seeing her and all that surrounds her, which can only be defined as the way she can never see. She is being seen in that way now. Her mouth goes dry. Her corsets constrain her more tightly. Everything tilts. She sees everything clearly and normally. She can discern no tilt. But she is convinced, she is utterly certain that everything has been tilted.

○

She sat down cross-legged on the rug by her bed to examine the wasp bite on her instep. There was still a pink circle, the size of a halfpenny; but her foot was no longer swollen. Her foot lay on her hand as though it were a dog's head, whose gaze was concentrated upon the door. Abruptly unbuttoning her wrap and pulling her nightdress up over her knees, she lifted her foot and, bending her head forward, placed the foot behind her neck. The hair that fell over it felt cool. She tried to straighten her back as far as she could. After a while she lowered her head, lifted her foot down and sat cross-legged, smiling.

I see a horse and trap drawn up by the front door of the farmhouse. In it is a man in black with a bowler hat. He is portly and unaccountably comic. The horse is black and so too is the trap except for its white trimming. I am looking down on the horse and trap and the man who is so comically correct and regular, from the window of Beatrice's room.

On the table between the window and the large four-poster bed is the vase of white lilac. The smell of it is the only element that I can reconstruct with certainty.

She must be thirty-six. Her hair, usually combed up into a chignon, is loose around her shoulders. She wears an embroidered wrap. The embroidered leaves mount to her shoulder. She is standing in bare feet.

The boy enters and informs her that the papers for the man in the trap were the correct ones.

He is fifteen: taller than Beatrice, dark-haired, large-nosed but with delicate hands, scarcely larger than hers. In the relation between his head and shoulders there is something of his father—a kind of lunging assurance.

Beatrice lifts an arm towards him and opens her hand.

Pushing the door shut behind him, he goes towards her and takes her hand.

She, by turning their hands, ensures that they both look out of the window. At the sight of the man in black on the point of leaving they begin to laugh.

When they laugh they swing back the arms of their held hands and this swinging moves them away from the window towards the bed.

They sit on the edge of the bed before they stop laughing.

Slowly they lie back until their heads touch the counterpane. In this movement backwards she slightly anticipates him.

They are aware of a taste of sweetness in their throats. (A sweetness not unlike that to be tasted in a sweet grape). The sweetness itself is not extreme but the experience of tasting it is. It is comparable with the experience of acute pain. But whereas pain closes anticipation of everything except the return of the past before the pain existed, what is now desired has never existed.

From the moment he entered the room it has been as though the sequence of their actions constituted a single act, a single stroke.

Beatrice puts her hand to the back of his head to move him closer towards her.

Beneath her wrap Beatrice's skin is softer than anything he has previously imagined. He has thought of softness as a quality belonging either to something small and concentrated (like a peach) or else to something extensive but thin (like milk). Her softness belongs to a body which has substance and seems very large. Not large relative to him, but large relative to anything else he now perceives. This magnification of her body is partly the result of proximity and focus but also of the sense of touch superseding that of sight. She is no longer contained within any contour, she is continuous surface.

He bends his head to kiss her breast and take the nipple in his mouth. His awareness of what he is doing certifies the death of his childhood. This awareness is inseparable from a sensation and a taste in his mouth. The sensation is of a morsel, alive, unaccountably half-detached from the roundness of the breast—as though it were on a stalk. The taste is so associated with the texture and substance of the morsel and with its temperature, that it will be hard ever to define it in other terms. It is a little similar to the taste of the whitish juice in the stem of a certain kind of grass. He is aware that henceforth both sensation and taste are acquirable on his own initiative. Her breasts propose his independence. He buries his face between them.

Her difference from him acts like a mirror. Whatever he notices or dwells upon in her, increases his consciousness of himself, without his attention shifting from her.

She is the woman whom he used to call Aunt Beatrice. She ran the house and gave orders to the servants. She linked arms with her brother and walked up and down the lawn. She took him when he was a child to church. She asked him questions about what he had learnt in the School Room: questions like What are the chief rivers of Africa?

Occasionally during his childhood she surprised him. Once he saw her squatting in the corner of a field and afterwards he wondered whether she was peeing. In the middle of the night he had woken up to hear her laughing so wildly that he thought she was screaming. One afternoon he came into the kitchen and saw her drawing a cow with a piece of chalk on the tiled floor—a childish drawing like he might have done when younger. On each of these occasions his surprise was the result of his discovering that she was different when she was alone or when she believed that he was not there.

This morning when she had asked him to come to her bedroom, she had presented a different self to him, yet he knew this was no longer a matter of chance discovery but of deliberate intention on her part. Her hair was loose around her shoulders. He had never seen or imagined it like that before. Her face seemed smaller, much smaller than his own. The top of her head looked unexpectedly flat and her hair over the flatness very glossy. The expression of her eyes was serious to the point of gravity. Two small shoes lay on their sides on the carpet. She was barefoot. Her voice too was different, her words much slower.

I cannot remember, she said, any lilac ever having a scent like this lot.

This morning he was not surprised. He accepted the changes. Nevertheless this morning he still thought of her as the mistress of the house in which he had passed his childhood.

She is a mythical figure whom he has always been assembling part by part, quality by quality. Her softness—but not the extent of its area—is more familiar than he can remember. Her heated sweating skin is the source of the warmth he felt in Miss Helen's clothes. Her independence from him is what he recognized in the tree trunk when he kissed it. The whiteness of her body is what has signalled nakedness to him whenever he has glimpsed a white segment through the chance disarray of petticoat or skirt. Her smell is the smell of fields which, in the early morning, smell of fish although many miles from the sea. Her two breasts are what his reason has long since granted her, although their distinctness and degree of independence one from the other astonish him. He has seen drawings on walls asserting how she lacks penis and testicles. (The dark beard-like triangle of hair makes their absence simpler and more natural than he foresaw.) This mythical figure embodies the desirable alternative to all that disgusts or revolts him. It is for her sake that he has ignored his own instinct for self-preservation—as when he walked away, revolted, from the men in sack-cloths and the dead horses. She and he together, mysteriously and naked, are his own virtue rewarded.

Mythical familiar and the woman he once called Aunt Beatrice meet in the same person. The encounter utterly destroys both of them. Neither will ever again exist.

He sees the eyes of an unknown woman looking up at him. She looks at him without her eyes fully focussing upon him as though, like nature, he were to be found everywhere.

He hears the voice of an unknown woman speaking to him: Sweet, sweet, sweetest. Let us go to that place.

He unhesitatingly puts his hand on her hair and opens his fingers to let it spring up between them. What he feels in his hand is inexplicably familiar.

She opens her legs. He pushes his finger towards her. Warm mucus encloses his finger as closely as if it were a ninth skin. When he moves the finger, the surface of the enclosing liquid is stretched — sometimes to breaking point. Where the break occurs he has a sensation of coolness on that side of his finger — before the warm moist skin forms again over the break.

She holds his penis with both hands, as though it were a bottle from which she were about to pour towards herself.

She moves sideways so as to be beneath him.

Her cunt begins at her toes; her breasts are inside it, and her eyes too; it has enfolded her.

It enfolds him.

The ease.

Previously it was unimaginable, like a birth for that which is born.

It is eight o'clock on a December morning. People are already at work or going to work. It is still not fully light and the darkness is foggy. I have just left a laundry, where the violet fluorescent lighting bleaches most stains out until you unwrap the washing and look at it in your own room. Under the fluorescent lighting the girl behind the counter had the white face of a clown with green eye shadow and violet almost white lips. The people I pass in the rue d'Odessa move briskly but rigidly, or hold themselves stiff against the cold. It is hard to imagine that most of them were in bed two hours ago, languid, unrestrained. Their clothes—even those chosen with the greatest personal care or romantic passion—all look as though they are the uniforms of a public service into which everybody has been drafted. Every personal desire, preference or hope has become an inconvenience. I wait at the bus stop. The waving red indicator of the Paris bus, as it turns the corner, is like a brand taken from a fire. At this moment I begin to doubt the value of poems about sex.

Sexuality is by its nature precise: or rather, its aim is precise. Any imprecision registered by any of the five senses tends to check sexual desire. The focus of sexual desire is concentrated and sharp. The breast may be seen as a model of such focus, gathering from an indefinable, soft variable form to the demarcation of the aureola and, within that, to the precise tip of the nipple..

In an indeterminate world in flux sexual desire is reinforced by a longing for precision and certainty: beside her my life is arranged.

In a static hierarchic world sexual desire is reinforced by a longing for an alternative certainty: with her I am free.

All generalizations are opposed to sexuality.

Every feature that makes her desirable asserts its contingency—here, here, here, here, here, here.
That is the only poem to be written about sex—here, here, here, here—now.

Why does writing about sexual experience reveal so strikingly what may be a general limitation of literature in relation to aspects of all experience?

In sex, a quality of 'firstness' is felt as continually re-creatable. There is an element in every occasion of sexual excitement which seizes the imagination as though for the first time.

What is this quality of 'firstness'? How, usually, do first experiences differ from later ones?

Take the example of a seasonal fruit: blackberries. The advantage of this example is that one's first experience each year of eating blackberries has in it an element of artificial firstness which may prompt one's memory of the original, first occasion. The first time, a handful of blackberries represented all blackberries. Later, a handful of blackberries is a handful of ripe/unripe/over-ripe/sweet/acid, etc., etc., blackberries. Discrimination develops with experience. But the development is not only quantitative. The qualitative change is to be found in the relation between the particular and the general. You lose the symbolically complete nature of whatever is in hand. First experience is protected by a sense of enormous power; it wields magic.

The distinction between first and repeated experience is that one represents all: but two, three, four, five, six, seven ad infinitum cannot. First experiences are discoveries of original meaning which the language of later experience lacks the power to express.

The strength of human sexual desire can be explained in terms of natural sexual impulse. But the strength of a desire can be measured by the single-mindedness it produces. Extreme single-mindedness accompanies sexual desire. The single-mindedness takes the form of the conviction that what is desired is the most desirable possible. An erection is the beginning of a process of total idealization.

At a given moment sexual desire becomes inextinguishable. The threat of death itself will be ignored. What is desired is now exclusively desired; it is not possible to desire anything else.

At its briefest, the moment of total desire lasts as long as the moment of orgasm. It lasts longer when passion increases and extends desire. Yet, even at its briefest, the experience should not be treated as only a physical/nervous reflex. The stuff of imagination (memory, language, dreams) is being deployed. Because the other who is palpable and unique between one's arms is—at least for a few instants—exclusively desired, she or he represents, without qualification or discrimination, life itself. The experience $= I + $ life.

But how to write about this? This equation is inexpressible in the third person and in narrative form. The third person and the narrative form are clauses in a contract agreed between writer and reader, on the basis that the two of them can understand the third person more fully than he can understand himself; and this destroys the very terms of the equation.

Applied to the central moment of sex, all written nouns denote their objects in such a way that they reject the meaning of the experience to which they are meant to apply. Words like cunt, quim, motte, trou, bilderbuch, vagina, prick, cock, rod, pego, spatz, penis, bique —and so on, for all the other parts and places of sexual pleasure— remain intractably foreign in all languages, when applied directly to sexual action. It is as though the words around them, and the gathering meaning of the passage in which they occur, put such nouns into italics. They are foreign, not because they are unfamiliar to reader or writer, but precisely because they are their third-person nouns.

The same words written in reported speech—either swearing or describing—acquire a different character and lose their italics, because they then refer to the speaker speaking and not directly to acts of sex. Significantly, sexual verbs (fuck, frig, suck, kiss, etc., etc.) remain less foreign than the nouns. The quality of firstness relates not to the acts performed, but to the relation between subject and object. At the centre of sexual experience, the object—because it is exclusively desired—is transformed and becomes universal. Nothing is left exterior to it, and thus it becomes nameless.

I make two rough drawings:

They perhaps distort less than the nouns. Through these drawings, what I have called the quality of firstness in sexual experience is perhaps a little easier to recall. Why? Being visual, they are closer to physical perception. But I doubt whether this is the explanation. A skilful Roman or Renaissance pornographic painting would be still closer to visual perception and yet, for our purpose, it would be more opaque.

Is it because these rough drawings are schematized and diagrammatic? Again, I doubt it. Medical diagrams are sometimes more schematic—and again more opaque. What makes these drawings a little more transparent than words and sophisticated images is that they carry a minimal cultural load. Let us prove it obversely.

Take the first one. Put the word *big* above it. Already it is changed, and the load increased. It becomes more specifically a message addressed by writer to reader. Put the word *his* in front of *big* and it is further changed.

Take the second one and put the following words above it: *Choose a woman's name and write it here.* Although the number of words has increased, the drawing remains unchanged. The words do not qualify the drawing or use it syntactically. And so the drawing is still relatively open for the spectator's exclusive appropriation. Now carry out the instructions. Write the name of, say, Beatrice. Once again the increase of its cultural load renders the drawing opaque. The name Beatrice refers the drawing to an exterior system of categories. What the drawing now represents has become part of Beatrice, Beatrice is part of an historical European culture. In the end we are left looking at a rough drawing of a sexual part. Whereas sexual experience itself affirms a totality.

Take both drawings and put the word *I* above each one.

I am writing about the lovers on the bed.

Her eyes refocus upon him. Their look is for him something as specific and permanent as a house or a particular door. He will find his way back to it.

It is a look for which the Roman girl's prepared him four years ago. Behind such a look is a total confidence that at that moment to express something—without thought, without words, but simply through one's own uncontrollable eyes—is to be instantaneously understood. To be, at that moment, is to be known. Hence all distinctions between the personal and the impersonal disappear.

Do not let us even by a hair's breadth misinterpret the meaning of this look. The look is simultaneously and in absolutely equal terms appealing and grateful. This does not mean that Beatrice is grateful for what has passed and is appealing for what is to come.

Don't stop, my sweet, don't stop, is what she may have said or will do: but not with this look.

Such an interpretation implies that eventually, if all is well, her look will be transformed into one which is purely grateful. An interpretation particularly dear to the male as provider and master. But false.

The look in Beatrice's eyes being in equal measure appealing and grateful is not the result of these two feelings co-existing. There is only one feeling. She has only one thing to say with her uncontrollable eyes. Nothing exists for her beyond this single feeling. She is grateful for what she appeals for; she appeals for what she is already grateful for.

To follow her look, we enter her state of being. There, desire is its satisfaction, or, perhaps, neither desire nor satisfaction can be said to exist since there is no antinomy between them: every experience becomes the experience of freedom there: freedom there precludes all that is not itself.

The look in her eyes is an expression of freedom which he receives as such, but which we, in order to locate it in our world of third persons, must call a look of simultaneous appeal and gratitude.

A little later she strokes his back and whispers: You see. You see.

The world is not as we have subsided into it. Within us there is the keenness, the sharpness to perform surgery. Within, if we have the courage to wield it, is the cutting edge to sever the whole world as it is, the world that pretends to be part of us, the world to which by compromised and flabby usage we are said to belong. Say now to me. Now to me say to me.

She places her hand so that his testicles may rest upon the palm.

From the long tight bud the longer petals loosen: their tips begin to separate so that at the far end of the flower there is an open mouth. Then, freed, the petals slowly revolve like propellers: in eight hours one may turn between forty-five and ninety degrees. As they revolve they retreat till they are pointing backwards from their small round calyx which is now thrust forward.

Thus a cyclamen opening. And thus too, greatly accelerated, the sensation of his penis becoming erect again and the foreskin again withdrawing from the coronal ridge.

The clocks keep another time.

I was walking through a forest with a woman, smaller than I and blonde. We were happy but not specially preoccupied with one another.

We came to a dead animal's head, half detached from its body. The animal might have been a fox, a donkey, a deer. The head was hollow like a mask or a glove. The sight should have been disturbing, but it was not. On the contrary it encouraged us. The mouth of the animal seemed to be grinning, its eye peaceful. The tattered skin of its neck was like a wide tattered sleeve. This sideways-lurching grinning severed head of an average-sized animal did not signify the death of that animal; it was purely a sign, put there to encourage us to continue.

We came out of the forest on to a large plain. The sky there was dark and purple but the plain was pale gold. The beauty of this plain, shimmering, many degrees lighter than the sky, made me (and I think her too) entirely happy. Quite near us were two rows of wooden buildings, like stables except that each was separate from the rest like very small wooden Russian houses. Around these buildings were men and women dressed in long whitish clothes. They were buying and selling cattle. (The people were not rich buyers and sellers: they were nomadic herdsmen.) We saw a herd of white cows (bison?) charging over the plains and vaguely in our direction. They were kicking up clouds of golden dust against the blackish sky. Suddenly she was frightened. I was not—perhaps because of the sign in the forest. I put my arms around her and pressed her against me. The intense pleasure of doing this became indistinguishable from that which I derived from what was happening around us. Be still, I said to her, if we are absolutely still, they will avoid us. The cattle thundered past, covering us, pressed tightly against one another, with gold dust. Not a single tail touched us.

○

They lie abandoned, side by side. The air from the open window cools their bodies and makes them aware of how damp they are, on the front of their stomachs how wet.

It should go on for ever, she says. It is not a complaint. She grips two fingers of his hand. She knows that the pace of time is reverting to normal. She crossed a threshold beyond which space, distance, time were meaningless. The threshold was warm, damp and quivering: animate to a degree for which the inanimate has no qualitative equivalent—unless it be jurassic mountains: animate to a degree at which it seemed that substance became sound alone.

It should go on for ever.

They lie on their backs. He has a sensation of being extended horizontally. He is conscious of the flatness of the bed, the floor, the earth under the house. Everything that is standing looks incongruous and incomplete to him. He is on the point of laughing. Suddenly he notices the portrait of her father on the wall opposite the bed. It is a provincial clumsy painting so that the image of the man oscillates between being a likeness and a childish stereotype of a ruddy-faced country gentleman at an inn. The face looks as though it has been tinted pink. The eyes are blankly fixed. Looking at this portrait of her father, he waves a hand.

POEM FOR HIM

éblouir to dazzle
like silk
her body is borderless
its centre a mouth of earth

liquid throat
(o nightingales of 19th century verse)
    passage of unprotected being
        cul de sac

to have reached there
    to dazzle the earth
        éblouir

3.

5.

THE BEGINNING AS DREAM

The strange thing about dreams is not so much what happens in them, but what one feels in them. In dreams there are new categories of emotion. In all dreams, even bad ones, there is a sense of imminent resolution such as one scarcely ever experiences when awake. By resolution I mean the answering of all questions. In my dream we were crossing a city. The city might have been London; it was a city, anyway, which was familiar; a city in which everything was interesting, in which everything was both striking and intimate. I was crossing this city in a bus and at the beginning I was on top of the bus (it was a double-decker bus without a roof). At the beginning of the journey in the bus it was dusk or night. I remember the coldness of the air outside, the coldness of the wind which swept over the seats on top of the bus without a roof, and at the same time the affirmative warmth of myself in my clothes. The bus passed through many streets with crowds of people, lights, cinemas, underground railway stations. It was a long journey and we had an appointment at the other end of the city, an appointment which at that moment it seemed important to keep. But after we had been travelling for about an hour, it became clear that although this bus was going in the right direction, it was taking a much longer time than we could possibly have imagined. And so I decided that we would get off the bus at the next stop, in a crowded place where we might be able to find a taxi. We would go the rest of the way by taxi. Deciding this in no way made me regret what we had done; it had nevertheless been a good idea to take the bus. No sooner had I made this decision than the bus left the main thoroughfares and drove, without stopping now, along narrow back streets beneath warehouses, bridges and high brick walls that we couldn't see over. These were the outskirts of the city, still familiar, still intimate, still a pleasure to see. And I had the sense that we were getting near an estuary or perhaps even the sea. By now it was clear that the route the bus was taking was the wrong one; it was more than that even, it was a route that had been abandoned, yes, that is how it felt to me, although I did not formulate it in my dream quite like that. And yet in riding in this bus which was following an abandoned route there was still the same strong sense of rightness. And this was confirmed when the high wall beside the bus suddenly disappeared and there was a view of water below, with ships along the quayside and, nearer than the ships, a pool of vivid green light on the water, across which a white bird, a huge white bird flew. It didn't fly like a swan; it flew, not with its legs tucked up but with its legs hanging down, its neck curved not stretched straight out, its big, heavy wings, rather clumsy, white, tinged with green reflexions from the water beneath it. It was a vision of a bird such as I had never known before. And it was enough to justify, to explain everything else that had happened and was happening or would happen. The bus didn't stop. We sat back in our seats, the cold night air blowing against our faces.

And then the bus, never going very fast, changed into a train, a train which we were responsible for driving. There was nothing very complicated mechanically about this. We were now in the front of the vehicle and it was running along lines, still following or continuing the same route as the bus had taken. I keep on saying 'we' because I wasn't by myself, but I wasn't with any other specific people either, I was in the first person plural. We were now in front of the train which was running a little faster along a single track. Although we were in a deep cutting with high stone walls (or were they brick? they were black brick), although we were in this cutting, I had a sense of being at a very high altitude.

I saw a bend in the line ahead. I wasn't the one who was driving at this moment, but I was looking up at the configuration of the lines of bricks at the top of the cutting wall, high above us, and I could tell by the way that they were converging that round this next bend the cutting would open out and that we would be flooded with light. It was now no longer night. The fact that I could read this in the walls gave me a great sense of satisfaction (although perhaps partly my pleasure came from my anticipation of that opening out and the bright light which was awaiting us round the bend). The train was now going fast. As we turned the bend, there, as I had foreseen, the cutting walls fell away. We were high up, high up, above a whole landscape and a whole bay, a bay of the sea—an idyllic landscape, blue sea, hills, gentle beaches, woods. All laid out below us. But at the same moment as we turned the bend we saw that the lines of the railway descended at an extremely sharp angle, like the lines of a switchback train; and not only this, we saw that they led, several hundred feet below, straight into the sea.

This constituted one of those moments of imminent resolution of which I spoke. The end of the line, like this, leading into the sea, explained the strange nature of all our previous journey and the reason why the route had been abandoned. The view beneath us was of an ineffable beauty, which made even more sense of the whole journey than the white bird had. The white bird in that small circle of light. And now the whole landscape and seascape beneath us. There was no question of stopping the train. For an instant we were balanced at the top of the steep descent, and then we began to descend, fast and dangerously. This had been foreseeable from the very instant that we had turned the corner but had in no way diminished my pleasure. And although there was a grave inevitability about the end we were approaching, it seemed neither tragic nor pathetic. To the rest of us I shouted out: Swim! as we hurtled down. The train disappeared deep under the water. I was not drowned. But some of us (belonging to my first person plural) were.

O

'The progress of today in every field is nothing else but the absurd of yesterday.'
                    Luigi Barzini, *Corriere della Sera* 1910

Today I wish to write about an event which took place in September 1910.

The Aero Club of Milan had offered a prize of £3,000 to the first man to fly over the Alps. Geo Chavez, twenty-four years old, a Peruvian already famous in the aviation world, has been waiting for several days in Brig, beneath the Simplon Pass in Switzerland, for the weather to improve. Several other competitors are also waiting.

Most of the pilots are of the opinion that it is already too late to attempt the flight this year; June or July would be more suitable months. During the last five days they have made trial flights, climbing to over a thousand metres but then returning to the small field called Siberia where canvas hangars have been erected. All of them have complained of the treachery of the air currents which tug at their planes as soon as they approach the entrance to the massif: all except Weymann, the American, who wears a pince-nez and says about everything that you have to get used to it.

A few weeks ago, Chavez broke the world altitude record. Across the Alps there is no need to climb as high as he did then. Yet the mountains appear to constitute an absolute frontier. The buildings of Brig crouch low on the ground before them. The mountains induce the idea that there is nothing beyond them. To believe that Italy and Domodossola are on the far side is an act of faith, supported, it is true, by the traffic on the Simplon road and by history, for it was near here that Hannibal and Napoleon crossed the Alps with their armies, but denied by the five senses within whose pentagon each man is alone.

I quote from the report by Luigi Barzini, a well-known Italian journalist, in the *Corriere della Sera* of 23 September 1910: 'This morning around ten o'clock the news from the Simplon was not at all encouraging. On the north side the weather was calm. But a wind was blowing through the valley at the bottom of which, like white stones after a landslide, were the small snow-covered houses of the village. On the Monscera and in Italy the weather was splendid.

' "I would like very much to go," Chavez told me sadly, "I will never find better weather conditions on the Italian side."

'He kept on telephoning his friend Christiaens who was making meteorological observations on the Kulm.

'All of a sudden Chavez says: "I must go and see. A car." We took a racing car belonging to a young American and sped up the mountain, deafened by the roar of the engine, and hanging on to our very seats so as not to be thrown out at the corners.

'A very strong east wind was blowing against the very highest peaks, at perhaps 3,000 metres, dragging clouds along with it. But lower down the weather was perfect. The trees were still. The smoke of fires lit by tourists in the woods was rising slowly into the sky. It was not too cold, although above 1,300 metres everything was white with snow . . .

'Chavez looked around him, studying the air. A continuous working of his jaw showed that he was grinding his teeth. Nothing else showed that he was preoccupied or anxious. He had not shaved, he had got up quickly in the morning and he had just forgotten this detail of his toilet in the dawn of the victorious day.

'He spoke little. He asked the time. "I must go," he exclaimed. And after a few minutes he added, "If I can't get through, I'll land at the Simplon Hospice, I'll certainly be able to get as far as that."

'Christiaens climbed into the car and exchanged a few words with the aviator—serious words.
' "The wind?" asked Chavez.
' "There's still wind," Christiaens replied.
' "No chance of going through?"
' "No."
' "What's the wind speed?"
' "Fifteen and increasing."
'In the valley of Krummbach the pines were moving and the grass was bent low under the icy wind.
' "It's very strong!" said Chavez, "it's making the pines sway and it takes some wind to do that . . ."

'A car was coming up from the valley. It was Paulhan, who had gone ahead to explore. We stopped and Paulhan told us that towards the Monscera the weather was absolutely calm. The two aviators became engrossed studying the likely air currents.

'The wind was blowing from the Fletschhorn, which was covered in snow.

' "It's not very likely to change," said Paulhan, "and the currents will make whirlpools. If you get caught in one of them—." An eloquent gesture concluded the sentence.

'Chavez and Paulhan climbed a few hundred metres towards the Hubschhorn and then watched from there for a few minutes. The wind seemed less strong. Coming down Chavez was torn by doubts.

' "Wait till tomorrow," said Christiaens.
' "I'm going now," Chavez said suddenly, "let's go quickly to Brig." '

He must dress accordingly. There are no rules save his own. But these he has repeatedly checked with himself, so that what he is doing does not seem to him to be for the first time. Nothing will seem original from now on—except his luck over which he has no control, and his welcome when he lands in Milan. He puts on a tight-fitting suit of thick Chinese paper—the same kind of paper which the great Chinese calligraphers used to write on. The sight of his own legs as he dresses encourages him. He has been a champion runner. Before a race he has many times felt the weakness in his legs which he feels now and which is not a weakness but is a waiting for the beginning. On an impulse he asks one of the mechanics in the hangar to lend him a pencil and he writes on the paper on both legs: *Vive Chavez!* Over the paper suit he puts on water-proof working overalls, specially quilted with cotton, then some sweaters, and on top a leather shooting jacket.

When everything was checked and the cloths wrapped round the pipes against the cold, Chavez prepared to take off. He glanced at the mountains; against the blue sky they looked nearer than they had ever done during the last week. He glanced across at the spectators along the side of the field: he was determined not to come back and land once more in Siberia.

There's a priest over there, he said to one of his mechanics, all we need now is a gravedigger.

He waved to his friends. He is enclosed, made secure, by the familiar deafening roar of the engine, which after a run of sixty yards lifts him into the air.

The spectators see the plane take off and gain height easily and well. The engine sounds regular. They look up at the plane with its elegant curved wings against the sky and in different ways they all think of it as a bird. But when Chavez heads for the entrance to the massif, they lose sight of the plane. It totally disappears from view.

He has crashed! someone shouts.
He has gone into the hillside where the pine-trees are.
He can't have done, he was higher than that.
You can't tell.
Look! Look! There he is.
Where?
About half-way up the forest!
And they find the plane again. But it is no longer like a bird in the sky. Against the greyish pine-trees and then against the grey shale face, it is like a moth, but a moth that can no longer fly and is crawling slowly across the surface of a grey window.

Chavez is fighting the wind that is already blowing him too far to the east, but he is also fighting a sense of unreality. He has never flown like this: the more he gains height, the lower he is: it is the mountain that is gaining height.

When it was clear that this was not another trial flight, the news was telephoned to the cities of Europe. In Milan a white flag was run up on the roof of the Duomo. This was the agreed sign that an aviator had taken off from Brig to cross the Alps with the intention of coming to Milan. As soon as he had crossed the mountains, a red flag would go up. In the piazza round the cathedral a crowd began to collect. Whilst waiting for the red flag to be hoisted, they chatted and often glanced up at the sky. In spirit and formation this crowd was very different from the crowd which had assembled in the piazza in May 1898.

The Hotel Victoria in Brig is full of journalists, flying enthusiasts and friends of the competitors. Among them is the principal protagonist of this book, whom I will now call, for the sake of convenience, G.

He is twenty-three years old and a friend of Charles Weymann, the American pilot with the pince-nez.

A few months previously he flew as Weymann's passenger in one of the first night flights ever made. Weymann had been impressed by his calm and his good navigating sense. Unexpectedly clouds had obscured the moon and the sudden total darkness had compelled them to make a forced landing in unknown hilly country. It was an experience, Weymann was reported by the press as saying, that I would rather not have again. But it would have been a damn sight worse if I'd been alone.

Weymann found it hard to understand why his young friend, who was an enthusiast for flying, didn't want to learn to fly himself. I'm willing to teach you, he said, and they're lining up for that privilege in Pau and New York.

G. was recognizably the same person as the boy of fifteen. Beatrice would have recognized him at once. But his complexion was sallower and his face thinner, which made his nose appear larger than before. When he smiled the gaps of his missing teeth still made him leer.

It would be different, said Weymann in his slow American voice, if you had no money. You need money to fly. But I guess you have plenty.

I have too many other interests.
What are your other interests? What do you do?

He smiled at Weymann ironically, for he knew that Weymann was a man incapable of discovering the truth even when it was placed in front of him. I travel, he said.

The pince-nez magnified the simplicity of the American's blue eyes. Exactly, he said, so you could fly. You have the attitude and the determination, the two things needed.
Weymann counted the two on the fingers of his hand.

I am too impatient. I wouldn't last a month by myself.

You need to be quick, said Weymann. He was small, dapper and wore a bow tie.

My mind would be on other things.

Such as? asked Weymann, his eyes open wide.

The maid who serves us breakfast.

She's sweet, conceded Weymann, his eyes blinking.

She fills my life.

But we've only been here a day.

She's engaged to a clerk who works in the Town Hall and they are going to get married at Christmas.

You're joking, said Weymann, beginning to suspect that he was being teased.

No, said G.

Weymann spoke like a patient schoolmaster: We are making history. We are pioneers, we are the first to open a new chapter. I guess we are a little mad. But how can you compare what we are doing—the early birds like us—with a twenty-four-hour infatuation with a little Swiss waitress whom you haven't even spoken to. How can you put one before the other like that. You're not a schoolboy. You're not being serious. I just can't believe you. He grasped his companion's arm. Tell me what your worry is.

Whether she got my note before lunch.

Weymann burst out laughing. He had decided that since this ugly, intense young man (whom he liked because of what they had experienced together) did not want to talk truthfully about himself, it was better to stop talking. His laugh was a way of withdrawing from the conversation. Poker tonight? he asked.

The next day Weymann said to another friend: He's so damned secretive. I don't know what he is up to. I can't make out whether he's interested in the money or the adventure—or both, like us, I guess.

The news that Chavez has taken off with the determination not to turn back arrives at the Hotel Victoria during lunch. Everybody rushes out on to the terrace to see the plane as it flies down the Rhone valley before turning south towards the massif. They shout and wave.

After a week of false rumours and disappointments everyone was reconciled to the idea that the Alps would not be crossed by an aeroplane this year. Why does it not occur to them that this attempt may end in disappointment too, that Chavez when he approaches the Saltina gorge may find the currents too strong and be forced to turn back? Perhaps because it is the last chance: tomorrow everyone is leaving: and so they seize upon the last hope of an event. Perhaps also because they have seen Chavez, they have watched him for a week and they have read his face. This is not to talk of his fate but of his character.

Chavez sees the crowd on the terrace below but does not wave back to them. He feels superstitious. The next time he waves must be on arrival.

During the last week many peasants have come to Brig in the hope of seeing a flying machine disappear over the mountains. And now the hotel staff, the waiters, the maids, the cook, the dishwashers, the gardener and his wife, appear to be as excited as the guests. There are many elements in such excitement—curiosity, the uncertainty of the outcome, a vicarious sense of achievement because they have all been near to the man they can see in the sky; but what may be deepest is the satisfaction of witnessing, and so of taking part in, what they believe will be an historic occasion. This is a very primitive satisfaction, connecting the time of one's own life with the time of one's ancestors and descendants. The great pole of history is notched across at the same point as the small stick of one's own life.

When G. left the dining-room, he did not go out on to the terrace but ran to the courtyard at the back of the hotel, where there was a large wooden building. Its ground floor was open like a barn, and there was a stone trough and a fountain around which the hotel laundry was washed. Above, on the second storey, were the maids' rooms. She was standing on the outside wooden staircase, gazing up at the sky. He called her by name—Leonie! and held out his hand to indicate that she should come down. Taking her by the arm, he told her to be quick: they would see best from the balcony of his room.

She might then have declined. It was the weakest moment of his strategy. She knew perfectly well that two things were happening at the same time: the plane was flying overhead like a bird, and the man who had pursued her with notes, with jokes, with whispered conversations, with declarations of love and extravagant compliments during five days was now hurrying her up into his room; more than that, she knew that he knew that she had two hours off duty every afternoon. She followed him because the unusualness of both the things which were happening confirmed that the occasion was exceptional. The noise of the engine, the excited shouting and the fact that everybody, with their backs turned towards her, was pointing up at the sky, encouraged her to take advantage of her normal, unexceptional self. He stood at the doorway to let her pass and it was as though under his cover she slipped past this self. On the stairs she began to giggle.

In his room she fell silent. He strode across the floor and flung open the French windows on to the balcony above the crowded terrace. The plane was banking as it turned, and both of them in the room could see the silhouetted head and shoulders of Chavez, smaller than a boot-button.

Leonie was frightened to come near to the window lest somebody on the terrace, looking up, caught sight of her. She stood well back from the window in the middle of the room, without any possibility of pretending any more that they were there to watch the plane heading for the mountains. (She could have fled the room, you say. Yet she was not frivolous. He had proposed nothing to her yet. She knew parts of what he would propose. She was neither frivolous nor naive. But there was the other part, his proposal to her exceptional self, that self which was surrounded by life other than her own as the receding roar of the aircraft engine was surrounded by silent air.)

Within an instant he had shut the windows and had turned round to face her. That he had succeeded, that it was indeed she, Leonie, who was standing there, looking with uncertainty at him, was established once and for all in his mind by the most characteristic facts about her: her large fingers, her broad squashed-looking nose, the coarse stringy wisps of hair escaping from under her maid's cap, her peasant's unpowdered complexion with, to the left of her chin, a pale slight discoloration the size of a small fingernail, her rounded shoulders and bosom, her brown eyes the colour of dark wood. He scarcely noticed the features which had made Weymann call her sweet, for these she had in common with many others.

He put his arms round her. She stood there, her cheek against his chest, waiting. She listened to his words. My heart. My happiness. My brown-eyed lamb. Leonie, Queen of the Alps. (But such words recorded for a third person lose their precision and their outrageous eloquence.) She was passive neither in her listening nor in her apparent submission to his will. She was constructing, precisely and furiously, the meaning of what had happened to her.

A week ago she had never seen him nor even imagined a man like him. He was rich. He was the friend of men who flew aeroplanes. He had flown in an aeroplane himself. He travelled from country to country. He spoke a peculiar German. He had a face like a man in a story. She counted on none of these facts for what they might say in themselves. They were merely items of proof that he was different from anybody else who had spoken to her. Yet, if this had been all, she would have attached no great significance to his being different. Her expectations in life were modest. She knew very well that the world was full of people who were utterly different from the townspeople of Brig or the peasants of the Valais, and that they could have nothing to say or do with her. But he—and this is what so profoundly impressed her—addressed himself to her, Leonie. For a week he had concentrated on nothing else but seeking her out, offering her presents and compliments, talking with her and demonstrating to her her own uniqueness. Like all people who are not set upon deceiving themselves, Leonie was able to distinguish intuitively between sincerity and insincerity. She knew that he was not lying to her, even if she remained ignorant of the truth he was telling her. She could distinguish, too, as most women can, between a man who is begging for favours, or, alternatively, may try to grasp them, and a man who, in face of a particular woman, is compelled to present himself to her as he is. This is some of what she meant when she said to herself: he has come for me.

When Zeus, in order to approach a woman he had fallen in love with, disguised himself as a bull, a satyr, an eagle, a swan, it was not only to gain the advantage of surprise: it was to encounter her (within the terms of those strange myths) as a stranger. The stranger who desires you and convinces you that it is truly you in all your particularity whom he desires, brings a message from all that you might be, to you as you actually are. Impatience to receive that message will be almost as strong as your sense of life itself. The desire to know oneself surpasses curiosity. But he must be a stranger, for the better you, as you actually are, know him, and likewise the better he knows you, the less he can reveal to you of your unknown but possible self. He must be a stranger. But equally he must be mysteriously intimate with you, for otherwise instead of revealing your unknown self, he simply represents all those who are unknowable to you and for whom you are unknowable. The intimate and the stranger. From this contradiction in terms, this dream, is born the great erotic god which every woman in her imagination either feeds or starves to death.

When he answered Weymann's question: what do you do? by saying: I travel, the answer was neither superficial nor evasive. The constant stranger must continually travel.

For a moment longer her arms hung straight at her side. Out of the window she could see the sky above the mountains, September blue, familiar as the colour of a plate. The Blériot engine was still just audible.

The plane fell fifty metres, like a dead plaice dropped. Chavez wanted to turn back. What prevented him was what he had previously said to himself even although, at the time of saying it, it was unimaginable to him that his plane might drop like a dead fish.

Never again will a single story be told as though it were the only one.

Her upbringing and education at home, at school and in church has prepared her for the situation she now finds herself in. She must reject this unknown man who is about to ruin her life. She must save her honour. She must guard herself, her womanhood, for her beloved Eduard who has courted her for two years and with whom she will live in the house near the river where he keeps the bee-

hives, and who will be the father to her children who will go to the
same school in Brig as she went to. She is in danger of mortal sin. She
must resist the evil temptation. In this way Leonie had been prepared. She must think of her own mother and of what she would wish
for her daughter now. She, the daughter of her mother, she, the child
of God, she, the *promise* of her beloved Eduard, she, the bride of
her bridegroom in two months' time, she, the mother of her future
children, she, the elder sister of her younger sisters, she must preserve her honour as daughter, Christian, *promise*, bride, mother,
sister. But she as I? I, Leonie, what should I do to preserve my
honour? *I did not know what to do.* For this she had not been prepared. In her life as it is she cannot kiss this man. But he is not in
her life; he is outside it. *I was alone with him. There was nobody
else.* She will never again, she senses, be in the arms of a man outside her life. *It was like a dream.* What she does with him is not
part of her life — although others will consider it so and its consequences may continue all her lifetime. What she does with him will
be the doing of that part of her which is not in her life. *My weakness
was stronger than I was.*

He slid his hands down her back until they were under her buttocks.
Then slowly and deliberately he lifted her up. Her feet left the
ground. He lowered her, but not so that her feet took her full weight.

She had the sensation that wherever his hands went they lifted her
and took away some of her weight. He was putting his hands between
her and gravity. She looked up into his eyes, which were entirely
concentrated upon her. He was smiling and the gaps in his teeth
looked as dark as his eyes. Although she could still recognize the
sunlight streaming through the window, she could believe that there
was a black curtain behind her back, black like his eyes and the
gaps in his teeth, and that this black curtain was being slowly drawn
around them until finally it would be like a black round tent. She
felt him touching the parts of her which were naturally down-
weighted, heavy, pendant, and each time he touched them he lifted
them up and took away some of their weight. It was then that she
put her arms round him.

His hands, which had counteracted the pull of gravity on all those
parts of her body of whose mass — however slight — she could be
conscious, had a further effect. Within the mass of each of these

parts she felt a force of attraction, drawing it, not yet continually but in broken impulses, towards him and the larger mass of his body. (The sensation was comparable to the obvious one in her breasts but was deeper and more diffused.)

She began to repeat his name.

Any attempt at an exhaustive description of what she was experiencing is bound to be absurd. The experience was central to her life: everything that she had been, surrounded her present experience as land surrounds a lake. Everything that she had been was turned to sand and shelved at the borders of this experience to disappear beneath its waters and become its unseen, mysterious lake bed. To express her experience it would be necessary for us to reconstruct around ourselves her unique language. And this is impossible. Armed with the entire language of literature we are still denied access to her experience. There is only one possible way of, briefly, entering that experience: to make love to her. Then why do I want to describe her experience exhaustively, definitively, when I fully recognize the impossibility of doing so? Because I love her. I love you, Leonie. You are beautiful. You are gentle. You can feel pain and pleasure. You are tiny and I take you in my hand. You are large as the sky and I walk under you. It was he who said this.

He placed her seated on the bed and went to the door. From the bed she held out her arms to him.

No, he said, not like drunken peasants.

The sudden harshness of his words did not hurt or surprise her. She simply waited to see what he would do next.

He told her to undress. She hesitated—not because she was unwilling but because she did not know how she should undress with him watching her. He started taking his own clothes off. She undid the buttons of her cuffs but no more. He stood there on the far side of the room, naked. She had often swept and cleaned this room. He stood there naked. Remembering the past, remembering that she had washed the curtains which he had just pulled across the window, she lowered her head.

Leonie, look up. He sees you. Look at him seeing you. You are being seen as you are. When you were born, before you opened your round crinkled mouth and cried out, you were first seen, not as yourself, but as the alternative to a boy. Their eyes went to your sex—a line drawn on your pink damp tummy—before they looked at your expanding eyes. You were a girl and they called you Leonie. Look, his looking surrounds you. He recognizes you as each mirror you have ever stopped in front of has reflected you. The mirror reflects: he recognizes. He stands naked seeing you. As you bend forward to take off your worn slip with a hole in it under one arm, he sees your two breasts fall forward not quite silently.

Your image covers the entire surface of his body like another skin. All your appearances surround his penis.

You have never seen yourself like this.

Looking at you he recognizes you. His recognition cannot be put out. It burns what it recognizes. And by the light of its burning it recognizes more and more until it is so bright that it recognizes as familiar what it has never seen.

He has never seen you naked and now you are.

Some say of my writing that it is too overburdened with metaphor and simile: that nothing is ever what it is but is always like something else. This is true, but why is it so? Whatever I perceive or imagine amazes me by its particularity. The qualities it has in common with other things—leaves, a trunk, branches, if it is a tree: limbs, eyes, hair, if it is a person—appear to me to be superficial. I am deeply struck by the uniqueness of each event. From this arises my difficulty as a writer—perhaps the magnificent impossibility of my being a writer. How am I to convey such uniqueness? The obvious way is to establish uniqueness through development. To persuade you, for example, of the uniqueness of Leonie's experience by telling you the story of what happened when Eduard discovered that Leonie had been unfaithful to him. In this way the uniqueness of an event can be explained by its causes and effects. But I have little sense of unfolding time. The relations which I perceive between things—and these often include casual and historical relations—tend to form in my mind a complex synchronic pattern. I see fields where others see chapters. And so I am forced to use another method to try to place and define events. A method which searches for co-ordinates extensively in space, rather than consequentially in time. I write in the spirit of a geometrician. One of the ways in which I establish co-ordinates extensively is by likening aspect with aspect, by way of metaphor. I do not wish to become a prisoner of the nominal, believing that things are what I name them. On the bed they were not such prisoners.

On the road across the Kulm pass Chavez sees figures waving to him. Among them are Christiaens and Luigi Barzini. In a few hours the *Corriere della Sera* will carry a report of this moment.

'A profound emotion nails us to the spot. We do not move. We are lifeless, our souls shining in our eyes, and our hearts beating fast. We are spellbound by the great beauty of what we are seeing. A thousand years of life cannot annul this memory.

'After a few seconds we jump back into the car. Christiaens is beside us. Two Swiss police climb in also—and we are away! We look at each other; our eyes are red. The Swiss guards too have tears in their eyes as they mutter germanically: Mein Gott, mein Gott. The plane is now just about to enter the Krummbach valley which two hours ago was rent by wind and lightning. It is above the fields around the hospice. It looks as though he is losing height.

' "He's landing," we yell. "There he is! He's landing!"

'It is clear that the aviator has a moment of doubt. He may be thinking of landing; then he decides that the wind is not as terrible as he feared and he continues . . .'

All pilots at that time took their bearings from what they could see on the ground. And the ground reassured them, for on it they could expect to land and to receive help. When Blériot, the year before, had flown the Channel, a French destroyer had escorted him. Briefly, for about ten minutes, he lost contact with the ship and saw only the sea; he said afterwards that during those long minutes he had felt terrifyingly alone. Chavez' decision now makes him the first man to fly deliberately beyond the sight and reach of other men.

The cold surrounds him like the four walls of a cell; but the cold also enters the cell. One wall presses relentlessly and continually against him. The right side of his face and body are icy. It is the wall of the wind: the wind which he once (twenty minutes ago) so wrongly under-estimated. The wrong no longer appears to him a matter of miscalculation but of transgression. It is the original sin to explain his life, now identical with this flight. The wall opposite that of the wind is made of rock and snow.

On his left he can see Monte Leone. The snow, white in the sunlight, both emphasizes the presence of the mountain and transforms it into a kind of absence.

Not a stain would remain on that white.

He tries to break through the wall of wind. Whenever he turns to the right, the roar of the Gnome engine becomes louder, because the wind blows it back at him, but the plane hangs almost stationary in the air. He has lost height which he must regain if he is to cross the Monscera. Yet he is frightened to climb. The wind above him is stronger than the wind blowing at him and it blows up there from all directions at once. It is bad when the plane drops, but it is even worse when it is lifted up by the wind. Then his own legs, his own feet in their boots above the engine move in a sickening way: the linen on the top surface of the wings blisters irregularly as though the wind had already torn holes on its underside.

Below the shoulders of Monte Leone and much nearer to him, the lower mountains rise like the broken eroded galleries of a semicircular amphitheatre in which he is alone in the centre.

He remembers Paulhan's last words of advice: Keep high! Keep high! The words have become absurd.

His immediate difficulty will be to clear the far ridge of the amphitheatre after he has flown across the arena. The wind is edging him further and further into the semi-circle, towards the blind galleries. If he can clear the ridge where it breaks (west of the Glatthorn), there will be worse difficulties to face. He is too far east and he believes he has to climb three or four hundred metres to cross the Monscera. The wind, holding him down, and forcing him to the east, is cornering him and the corner where it will smash him to pieces will be in the gorge of the Gondo.

He must have considered whether he should turn into the wind and circle the arena to gain height. Yet, I believe, the idea of turning round, even momentarily, filled him with horror. If he once circled this theatre of blind gulleys and ridges, he would never break out of the circle but would die in it when his engine stopped. He would rather fight in a corner.

He can no longer distinguish between rock and silence. The surfaces of his body are by now completely numb from the cold. The most that his consciousness can oppose to the rocks which surround him is air and the noise of the engine at his feet. He flies on towards the Glatthorn like an arrow towards its target.

He is beside a rock face which is like the loose hide of a gigantic mule stretched across the frame of the letter A and, apparently, blown inwards, between the legs of the letter, by the same wind which is blowing against him and his plane. On the mule-hide of this rock Chavez sees the shadow of his wings, sometimes lurching away, sometimes rushing towards him as the shadow crosses folds. Looking down he sees rock rising up at him. Ahead he can see higher peaks still. Reverberating and echoing against the rock beside and below him, the noise of his engine falls and rises like his shadow, and his shadow seems to clatter with the noise of his engine and of falling stones.

Here there could have been no question of conscious decisions.
Here I cannot calculate as I write.

Chavez has the impression that he is about to enter the jaws of an animal whose passages and gullet and stomach and arse are made of solid rock, an animal whose digestion is geological. An animal that can kill before it is alive, and eat when it is dead.

Here it is not a matter of courage or the lack of it; here men divide themselves into those who still want to live and those who do not. Which they are may be revealed in the way they scream. Some ascend with their screams; some die with them. Chavez climbed, indifferent to the risk of stalling, indifferent to everything, except to the necessity of escaping from the jaws of the animal: upwards.

He was in the Gondo.

O

At Domodossola, in communication with Brig by telephone, everyone waits. The factories have stopped work. The workers are watching the sky. The old forego their siesta. The young are making their way to the field where Chavez will land, refuel and then take off for Milan. On every balcony and in every window which has a view of the Ossola valley, green, peaceful but climbing up to pine forests and then to rocks, people stand, eyes half-shut, staring into the sky above the Alps. There is no wind.

It is a tragedy! We ought to be able to see him by now.
Perhaps he has turned back.
But he crossed the Simplon.
How do you know?
Roberto told us.
And Roberto?
Signor Lucchini, the clerk of the Mayor, came into the Garibaldi twenty minutes ago and said that he had passed the hospice.
Praise be to God.
Since this morning I knew it was going to be a tragedy. I dreamt about him last night.
That's because you are in love with him.
To clap my eyes on him just once!
And we'll all call out his name—Geo! Geo!

Thousands in Domodossola pick out the plane, minute against the pine forest. It is lower than they expected. With shouts the watchers try to quieten each other, so as to be able to hear the engine. It is too far away. Slowly the movement of the aeroplane becomes clear. It is coming down towards Domodossola.

Duray, racing-car driver and friend of Chavez, unrolls two lengths of white calico on the grass of the landing-field to make a cross, visible from the air; a crowd of boys compete to help him peg the cloth to the ground.

The plane is flying and losing height so regularly, so serenely, that all of those watching feel personally elated.

He is the first man to fly the Alps; he has done what was previously thought impossible. It is a momentous event that we are witnessing, yet, look! it is simpler than we imagined, he is flying straighter than a bird and effortlessly, and that is how he has flown over the Alps; achieving greatness is perhaps less hard than we have been led to believe. This sequence of feelings (formulated in many different ways) leads to a conclusion of sudden elation. Why can we not all achieve what we wish?

The Mayor, being driven in a car to the landing field and wearing his ceremonial robes in order to welcome the great aviator, announces to his companions on the back seat that the town will name a street after Chavez to commemorate his victory over the mountains.

An express train for Milan left Domodossola station at 14.18 hours. A young man in the train spots the Blériot monoplane through the carriage window and pulls the alarm signal. The train comes to a sudden halt. The young man jumps down on to the track and runs along the length of the train shouting to the other passengers to watch and pointing with his arm at the plane which is now only a little higher than the tree, and in which Chavez is clearly visible. When he reaches the locomotive, the young man stops and waves with both arms at the sky, hoping that Chavez will see him and wave back; he will then have been the first to salute the hero. But Chavez does not wave back. A fact about which the young man and his friends who were flying enthusiasts were to speculate for many years.

Leonie's head is thrown back like a singer's singing. Her eyes too have rolled back so that he sees only the whites of them, not the irises. Her mouth is open and her throat swollen. She makes a noise in her throat which is a word said very slowly but he does not decipher it.

Some cry, some lie motionless, some thump with their fists, some lie curled up, some push their tongues between their lips, some clench their brows and set their mouths in determination, some wave their hands and others open them until they are like starfish: no two are the same until they leave behaviour behind, until they come with him to that moment when everything is simultaneous and every one of them is there together.

He experiences every orgasm as though it were simultaneous with every other. All that has occurred or will occur between each, all the events, actions, causes and consequences which have and will separate in time woman from woman, surround this timeless moment as a circumference surrounds the circle it defines. All are there together. All despite all their differences are there together. He joins them.

Sexual desire, however it is provoked or produced circumstantially, and whatever its objective terms and duration may be, is subjectively fixed to two points in time: our beginning and our end. When analysed, sexual desire has components which are violently nostalgic and lead us as far back as the experience of birth itself: other components are the result of an ineradicable appetite for the unknown, the furthest away, the ultimate of life—which can finally only be found in its negation—death. At the moment of orgasm these two points in time, our beginning and our end, may seem to fuse into one. When this happens everything that lies between them, that is to say our whole life, becomes instantaneous. It is thus that I explain the protagonist of my book to myself.

He lay on his back beside Leonie, holding her hand, his eyes shut.

She no longer saw secret promises in his face. She knew what he promised and the secret involved the two of them. With her hand he wasn't holding, she touched his face. She followed with the tips of two fingers the contours of an eyebrow and then down the side of his nose, past the corner of his mouth, which twitched when she passed it, to his chin. By touching his face in this way she could make her feeling of familiarity more natural and destroy a little of its mystery. She could localize the feeling of familiarity in what she felt in her fingertips. And thus she was less overwhelmed by it. She wanted to cup her hand over his nose. She raised her hand to her own nose to smell it. She placed it on his forehead instead. She would have played like this, with isolated words occurring to her with a sense of odd illumination in her head (as though she knew that there was light, white like snow, behind all that she saw or pictured and that this light gave everything a white outline until the instant she saw it), she would have continued like this until he spoke or moved. But a man shouting on the staircase interrupted her. A moment later a woman shouted on the terrace just under the window. Several more shouts followed.

Had Leonie belonged to a different social class, she might have reacted differently. Her immediate response might well have been to question the right of others in a hotel to raise their voices and disturb her. As it was, a raised voice was a warning signal; she had learnt since childhood that when you heard somebody raising their voice, you either disappeared or prepared yourself to be unjustly abused. She feared that the people were shouting because they were looking for her.

She pulled her hand away from his. He opened his eyes.

They are looking for me, she whispered, they are coming to look for me. Nobody will come in here, he said, and closed his eyes again. There was a knock at the door.

What is it? he asked.
A man's voice on the other side of the door: Chavez has crashed.
Where?
When he came down to land at Domodossola.
You mean he made the crossing and then crashed?
At the very last moment, yes, a couple of metres above the landing

field, he didn't level out, he just dived into the ground at about a hundred kilometres an hour.

Is he dead?

No. He has broken both his legs, but they said on the telephone he isn't badly hurt otherwise. He's been taken to hospital.

All right. Thank you for telling me.

Are you coming down?

I'll see you later. He turned to Leonie. You see, he said, they weren't looking for you. And he began to laugh.

How can you laugh, she asked, when your friend must be suffering so much.

I'm laughing at us.

At me because I was frightened?

No, at the two of us here whilst he was crossing the Alps.

He may die.

And one day I'll die and you too, with your beautiful brown eyes and your white teeth. There is never any time to lose.

Don't you have any feelings for him at all?

I had no time.

I don't understand what you say.

No chance ever comes twice.

They just told you he crashed.

Then I will try to console his fiancée.

Who are you? She said this fiercely but in a whisper as though she were frightened that he might answer in a voice loud enough for the whole hotel to hear. She believed that he might be the Devil. Abruptly she turned her back on him and buried her face in the pillow. Why me? she asked.

You are like you are, that's why.

Why me out of all the others? There are so many.

You as well as many others.

Am I—she raised her head to look at him and then changed her mind about what to say: I must go, she said, they'll be looking for me. Let me go.

Yes, he said.

Don't you really care about your friend who is hurt?

You talk about him but you don't mean him.

I don't understand what you say.

When you ask about him, you are thinking of yourself.

No—when I saw him flying off—

—but by then I had already come to find you.

144

He placed his hand on her shoulder. Her whole body turned towards him and she lay on her back looking up at him. She could see in his face what had happened to them both after he had come to find her; his face was different; but it was not the face of the Devil.

She knew that he could not take her with him when he left. It was not worth her asking. It was not even worth asking whether he would be leaving tomorrow or the day after. That much she could discover from the hall porter. She might ask whether he would return to Brig. But she already knew the answer. Chavez had crossed the Alps. No aviator would try from here again. He would not come back. Everything she had ever noticed in the world stood between his life and hers.

Will I see you tomorrow?
Yes, I will find you.

She recognized that he was lying. The total unexpectedness of what had happened did not mean that it was likely to happen again. A more sophisticated and privileged woman would have found it hard to accept that the encounter was unrepeatable, and so would probably have needed the lie and have failed to recognize it as such. For Leonie it was not hard to accept. The choices open to her had always been limited; she thought of most of the conditions of living as unchangeable; and so the idea of the extraordinary was central to her life. She was superstitious.

She shivered. He pulled up the sheet to cover her. As he did so, he saw her body stretched almost straight, save that one hip was slightly raised. There are women—often they are wide-hipped and plump—whose bodies become unforeseeably beautiful when recumbent. Their natural formation, like a landscape's, seems to be horizontal. And just as landscapes are for ever continuous, the horizon receding as the eye of the traveller advances, so, to the sense of touch, these bodies seem borderless and infinitely extended, quite regardless of their actual size. His hand set out. The large dark triangle of hair on her pale skin announced unequivocally the mystery which it hid.

She would have liked to have said before washing, whilst they were still extraordinary, lying on the bed, that if he asked her to go away with him, she would go. It would have been a way of telling him how she felt: all he had supposed about her had been right: he had known more about her than anybody else had: so now he must know—because she did not believe that she would see him again—that she loved him, loved him like her own child. Yet if she spoke of going away with him, he would lie and misunderstand what she said. She must find another way to tell him. She feared that if she did not tell him, Eduard might kill himself or her. She believed that her telling him would protect them all later.

And so it happened that the young peasant bride who, an hour and a half earlier, had been shy to undress in front of him, suddenly threw off the sheet and kneeling on the bed seized hold of his head, pressed his face against her stomach, and, with her own head thrown back, so that she saw blue light in the pear-shaped blobs of glass hanging from the candelabra in the centre of the ceiling, repeatedly called out his name, whilst tears ran down her face.

○

Later, in the evening, G. saw Weymann. Weymann, normally so imperturbable, was distinctly nervous. During the afternoon, after the news of Chavez' crash, Weymann took off in his plane and tried to climb towards the Simplon; the prize for reaching Milan still remained to be won. But the wind proved too strong and he turned back to land again in the field with the canvas hangars.

What time did you take off?
At 3.43, about two hours after Geo.
Was the wind much stronger?
Not appreciably on the ground. But when I climbed to about a thousand metres, just after the Napoleon bridge, there I hit it full force. It's always been there, about the same spot. Suddenly it comes at you, and it knocks you sideways, like the slipstream of an express train. It couldn't have been much less when he went through. But I don't believe in taking unreasonable risks, and he did.
He succeeded though. So didn't the risks seem less? He'd proved the risks weren't that great.

He's proving it in hospital I'm afraid.

But he crossed!

You don't think like that when you hit that wind. You can feel it straining every strut and joint of the kite.

Supposing he crossed and landed safely but then had engine trouble on the ground, would you have turned back then? Supposing he proved it without mishap, would you have turned back?

Yes, I study my plane and the weather conditions, nothing else. You have to stay very sober in the air, my friend. You have to be quite sure of what you can or you can't do. And if you're in doubt, don't do it. Geo wanted to be a hero. And that's fatal in the air.

He has shown that something was possible which people thought impossible. Isn't that an achievement?

I pay my respects to his courage, but it's a dangerous example.

That's why there's a prize offered. If there wasn't any danger—

No. No. I don't mean the natural hazards of flying. I mean the danger of encouraging foolhardiness and the taking of unnecessary risks. In the end flying's like everything else, the secret of success is a healthy respect for what you're up against. If you want to get on, you don't pee into the wind. I'm not a coward, but I'm not an idiot either.

You're saying he is an idiot.

He's a hero. But I'll lay you whatever odds you want that at this moment he's cursing himself for an idiot. They say it's not at all sure that he'll ever have the proper use of his legs again.

You feel bad about turning back.

Come with me. I'm driving to Domodossolo tomorrow to go and see him. I've borrowed a Fiat. Or are you still waiting for a reply to your letters to that maid? What's her name?

She's called Leonie.

The same as the mountain over there? Leone.

It's spelt differently.

I wouldn't trust either of them! joked Weymann.

I'll come to Domodossola.

6.

This morning as I was shaving I thought of a friend of mine who lives in Madrid and whom I haven't seen for fifteen years. Looking at my own image in the mirror I asked myself whether, after so long, we would recognize each other immediately if we met by accident in the street. I pictured to myself our meeting in Madrid and I began to imagine his feelings. He is a friend to whom I am deeply attached, but I hear from him only once or twice a year and he does not occupy a constant place in my thoughts. After I had shaved, I went down to my letterbox and there found a ten-page letter from him.

Such 'coincidences' are not uncommon and everyone is more or less familiar with them. They offer us an insight into how approximate and arbitrary is our normal reading of time. Calendars and clocks are our inadequate inventions. The structure of our minds is such that the true nature of time usually escapes us. Yet we know there is a mystery. Like a never-seen object in the dark, we can feel our way over some of its surfaces. But we have not identified it.

The way my imagination forces me to write this story is determined by its intimations about those aspects of time which I have touched but never identified. I am writing this book in the same dark.

A SITUATION OF WOMEN

Up to then the social presence of a woman was different in kind from that of a man. A man's presence was dependent upon the promise of power which he embodied. If the promise was large and credible, his presence was striking. If it was small or incredible, he was found to have little presence. There were men, even many men, who were devoid of presence altogether. The promised power may have been moral, physical, temperamental, economic, social, sexual —but its object was always exterior to the man. A man's presence suggested what he was capable of doing to you or for you.

By contrast, a woman's presence expressed her own attitude to herself, and defined what could and could not be done to her. No woman lacked presence altogether. Her presence was manifest in her gestures, voice, opinions, expressions, clothes, chosen surroundings, taste—indeed there was nothing she could do which did not contribute to her presence.

To be born woman was to be born within an allotted and confined space, into the keeping of man. A woman's presence developed as the precipitate of her ingenuity in living under such tutelage within such a limited cell. She furnished her cell, as it were, with her presence; not primarily in order to make it more agreeable to herself, but in the hope of persuading others to enter it.

A woman's presence was the result of herself being split into two, and of her energy being inturned. A woman was always accompanied—except when quite alone—by her own image of herself. Whilst she was walking across a room or whilst she was weeping at the death of her father, she could not avoid envisaging herself walking or weeping. From earliest childhood she had been taught and persuaded to survey herself continually. And so she came to consider the surveyor and the surveyed within her as the two constituent yet always distinct elements of her identity as a woman.

A woman had to survey everything she was and everything she did because how she appeared to others, and ultimately how she appeared to men, was of crucial importance for her self-realization. Her own sense of being *in herself* was supplanted by a sense of being appreciated *as herself* by another. Only when she was the content of another's experience did her own life and experience seem meaningful to her. In order to live she had to install herself in another's life.

Men surveyed women before treating them. Consequently how a woman appeared to a man might determine how she would be treated. To acquire some control over this process, women had to contain it, and so they interiorized it. That part of a woman's self which was the surveyor treated the part which was the surveyed, so as to demonstrate to others how her whole self should be treated. And this exemplary treatment of herself by herself constituted her presence. Every one of her actions, whatever its direct purpose, was also simultaneously an indication of how she should be treated.

If a woman threw a glass on the floor, this was an example of how she treated her own emotion of anger and so of how she would wish it to be treated by others. If a man had done the same, his action would only have been an expression of his anger. If a woman made good bread, this was an example of how she treated the cook in herself and accordingly of how she as a cook-woman should be treated by others. Only a man could make good bread for its own sake.

This subjunctive world of the woman, this realm of her presence, guaranteed that no action undertaken within it could ever possess full integrity; in each action there was an ambiguity which corresponded to an ambiguity in the self, divided between surveyor and surveyed. The so-called duplicity of woman was the result of the monolithic dominance of man.

A woman's presence offered an example to others of how she would like to be treated—of how she would wish others to follow her in the way, or along the way, she treated herself. She could never cease offering this example, for it was the function of her presence. When, however, social convention or the logic of events demanded that she behave in a manner which contradicted the example she wished to give, she was said to be coquettish. Social convention insists that she should appear to reject something just said to her by a man. She turns away in apparent anger, but at the same time she fingers her necklace and repeatedly lets it drop as tenderly as her own glance upon her breast.

When she is alone in her room and sure of being alone, a woman may look at herself in a mirror and put out her tongue. This makes her laugh and, on other occasions, cry.

It was with a woman's presence that men fell in love. That part of a man which was submissive was mesmerized by the attention which she bestowed upon herself, and he dreamt of her bestowing the same attention upon himself. He imagined his own body, within her realm, being substituted for hers. This was a theme which occurred constantly in romantic poems about unrequited love. That part of a man which was masterful dreamt of possessing, not her body—this he called lust—but the variable mystery of her presence.

The presence of a woman in love could be very eloquent. The way she glanced or ran or spoke or turned to greet her lover might contain the quintessential quality of poetry. This would be obvious not only to the man she loved, but to any disinterested spectator. Why? Because the surveyor and the surveyed within herself were momentarily unified, and this unusual unity produced in her an absolute single-mindedness. The surveyor no longer surveyed. Her attitude to herself became as abandoned as she hoped her lover's attitude to her would be. Her example was at last one of abandoning example. Only at such moments might a woman feel whole.

The state of being in love was usually short-lived—except in unhappy cases of unrequited love. Far shorter lived than the nineteenth-century romantic emphasis on the condition would lead us to believe. Sexual passion may have varied little throughout recorded history. But the account one renders to oneself about being in love is always informed and modified by the specific culture and social relations of the time.

For the nineteenth-century European middle classes the state of being in love was characterized by a sense of excessive uncertainty in an otherwise certain world. It was a state exempt from the promise of Progress. Its characteristic uncertainty was the result of considering the beloved as though he or she were free. Nothing that was an expression of the beloved's wishes could be taken for granted. No single decision of the beloved could guarantee the next. Each gesture had to be read for its fresh meaning. Every arrangement became questionable until it had taken place. Doubt produced its own form of erotic stimulation: the lover became the object of the beloved's choice in full liberty. Or so it seemed to the couple in love. In reality, the bestowing of such liberty upon the other, the assumption that the other was so free, was part of the general process of idealizing and making the beloved seem unique.

Each lover believed that he or she was the willing object of the other's unlimited freedom and, simultaneously, that his or her own freedom, so circumscribed until now, was at last and finally assured within the terms of the other's adoration. Thus each became convinced that to marry was to free oneself. Yet as soon as a woman became convinced of this (which might be long before her formal engagement) she was no longer single-minded, no longer whole. She had to survey herself now as the future betrothed, the future wife, the future mother of X's children.

For a woman the state of being in love was a hallucinatory interregnum between two owners, her bridegroom taking the place of her father, or later, perhaps, a lover taking the place of her husband.

The surveyor-in-herself quickly became identified with the new owner. She would begin to watch herself as if she were him. What would Maurice say, she would ask, if his wife (that is me) did this? Look at me, she would address the mirror, see what Maurice's wife is like. The surveyor-in-herself became the new owner's agent. (A relationship which might well include as much deceit or chicanery as can be found between any proprietor and agent.)

The surveyed-within-herself became the creature of proprietor and agent, of whom both must be proud. She, the surveyed, became their social puppet and their sexual object. The surveyor made the puppet talk at dinner like a good wife. And when it seemed to her fit, she lay the surveyed down on a bed for her proprietor to enjoy. One might suppose that when a woman conceived and gave birth, surveyor and surveyed were temporarily reunited. Perhaps sometimes this happened. But childbirth was so surrounded with superstition and horror that most women submitted to it, screaming, confused, or unconscious, as to a punishment for their intrinsic duplicity. When they emerged from their ordeal and held the child in their arms they found they were the agents of the loving mother of their husband's child.

I hope the preceding few pages will throw some light on the story

I am about to tell and in particular on G.'s insistence upon Camille being 'solitary' (i.e., unsurveyed by her own agency).

O

KARL MARX HAS BEEN RELEGATED
TO THE ATTIC

Giolitti in 1911

Since his father's death in 1908, this is the first time G. has returned to Italy. Lawyers in Livorno settled the problems of his inheritance; he owns three factories, two cargo vessels and fifteen houses near the centre of the city.

The evening haze over Lake Maggiore gives everything the look of a backdrop to a theatre set. The islands seem painted. On the hill rising up behind Stresa are the large villas of the rich. Most of them were built in the nineteenth century. Around their windows and doors are painted vine leaves and oranges and birds. At one of the largest villas with an imitation Renaissance watch-tower, Weymann and G. have been invited to dine.

Why did he crash?

Although there were hundreds of witnesses, accounts of what actually happened vary considerably, as do the explanations. Around the dinner table several theories are suggested.

Chavez was in complete control and was about to make a perfect landing. But unhappily, as a result of the strain of the flight and the buffeting of the wind, one of his wings folded a few seconds before his wheels touched the ground. This immediately forced the nose of the plane down and it dived, engine first, into the earth.

This theory is proposed and defended with authority by Monsieur Maurice Hennequin who, since he is an engineer working for Peugeot, was indeed the semi-official Peugeot representative at the competition, has to be listened to with respect. He has a habit of holding his listeners' attention by suddenly stopping in the middle of a sentence to take in a mouthful of food. He gesticulates rigidly with his large hands, as if they were wooden doors opening and shutting to let his words out and to prevent anybody else's ever entering into the home of his argument.

It would not have been a perfect landing. Chavez misjudged his speed. He was trying to land at about ninety kilometres an hour instead of sixty. What, however, caused the crash was not one but both wings folding, folding up like the wings of a butterfly when it alights.

This is the opinion of the Italian host, a director of the Pirelli rubber firm in Milan who has made generous donations to the Aero Club and believes, like Lord Northcliffe, that aviation has a great military and commercial future. His voice is habitually modulated to express the sweetness of reason itself. The position of his villa, its painted ceilings, the idea of dining beneath Chinese lanterns on the open platform of the imitation watch tower, the live flamingoes in the garden below, the new factory opened, all testify, he feels, to the reasonableness of his views. He believes in encouraging trade unions and offering incentives to his workers. How often has he quoted to his less successful and more belligerent business colleagues the words of the great Giolitti as Prime Minister:

'The upward movement of the popular classes is accelerating day by day, and it is an invincible movement, because it is common to all civilized countries and is based upon the principle of the equality of all men. Let no one delude himself that he can prevent the popular classes from conquering their share of political and economic influence. It depends chiefly on us, on the attitude of the constitutional parties in their relations with the popular classes, whether the emergence of these shall be a new conservative force, a new element of prosperity and greatness, or whether instead it shall be a whirlwind that will be the ruin of our country's fortunes.'

Only as a last resort would the host think in terms similar to those of his uncle: The cavalry! Don't delay! Martial law and the cavalry! And then he would not shout such words in a Milan hotel; he would quietly pick up a telephone.

His wife asks whether it would not have been safer to land in the lake.

As the result of the cold experienced during the crossing, the pilot's hands became so numb and frozen that he could no longer handle his controls properly.

This is the suggestion of the Contessa R., who is a great patron of the Milanese opera.

The Contessa raises her hand, its fingers supplely converging towards an apex. It is a dancer's miming gesture for a flower about to open: it is also the gesture of a child trying to pick something out of a jar. Suddenly, on the word 'frozen', she shoots out fingers and thumb and holds them stiffly outstretched while she passes her other hand over the supposedly frozen one, indicating by tentative touches how icy its surface must be.

What intelligence! a man whispers to the young lady beside him, what intelligence behind those grey hairs! By Christmas, the young woman replies, she will have recovered from the loss of Gino, and her hair will be as black as five years ago.

Why does nobody consult Monsieur Chavez himself? The speaker is a woman of about thirty. Her voice is slightly rasping, as if it had once been ruined by a fit of inordinate demonic laughter. Are not most of the controls worked by the feet?

Could you please tell me her name?
Madame Hennequin. Surely you were introduced?
Her first name, I mean.
I do not know her maiden name.
Her *prénom*.

Ah. I am so sorry. Camille.
Geo remembers nothing after the Gondo gorges.
Poor Geo!

The hostess, wearing a golden bracelet made in the form of an ancient Etruscan one, extends her arm in beckoning invitation to Weymann. Monsieur Weymann, she says (Weymann is a friend of Maurice Hennequin—hence the invitation), you are the flyer and our guest of honour, tell us your opinion.

Weymann smiles but replies tersely in English: You can't trust a plane like that. Do you know what its wings are made of? Cotton and wood.

Chavez was suffering from a kind of euphoria. He believed that he had succeeded in his venture and the worst was behind him; at the last moment he became reckless.

This is the theory of Harry Schuwey, a Belgian industrialist.

A woman who was just previously smiling at Camille Hennequin and sharing some joke with her says: I don't find that very convincing, Harry. Her manner of address indicates that she is probably his mistress.

And she?
Mathilde. Mathilde Le Diraison.

My dear Mathilde, replies the Belgian, that is because you have no imagination at all. A young man of twenty-four who has just flown over the Alps for the first time in history believes that he is immortal, the world seems to lie at his feet (the Belgian gives a little laugh), believe me, moments of success are the most dangerous.

But he *is* immortal, says Madame Hennequin, schoolchildren will learn his name in the history books.

If she were not so well dressed one might mistake her for a schoolteacher. Her features and her figure possess a kind of angularity which suggests a distinct if circumscribed independence of mind.

That will depend, says her husband, on what he does in his further exploits. (In Monsieur Hennequin's choice of the word 'exploits' there is an unconscious condescension, the result of jealousy.) His is a great achievement, I would be the last to deny it, but in the coming years there will be many more even more spectacular ones. Am I not right? He addresses himself to his host whose agreement is certain.

In ten years somebody will fly the Atlantic, says the host.
The first man to fly round the world! says the host's wife wearily.
Will somebody fly to the moon one day? asks Madame Hennequin.
Monsieur Hennequin smiles indulgently at his exotic wife and says with pride: She is an extremist, a dreamer, is Camille.

I am scarcely less interested in her than G. I will describe her to you as I now see her. She is thin. Her bones look as though they are too big for her skin; an effect not unlike that of a child wearing clothes she has outgrown. Her movements are very fastidious, as though they too are too small for her and she must take care not to outdo them. Her face glows, and her eyes are both soft and very translucent, like absolutely clear water in which fur is reflected.

She notices G. gazing at her. Most men when they stare at an unknown woman who attracts them, have already begun in their imagination the process of seducing and undressing her; they already see her in certain positions with certain expressions on her face; they are already beginning to dream about her. And so, when she intercepts their look, one of two things happens: either they continue to stare at her shamelessly because her real existence does not disturb their dream: or else she will read a flicker of shame in their eyes expressed as a momentary hesitation to which she will be obliged to respond either encouragingly or discouragingly.

He stares at her without shame or insolence. In his imagination he has not laid a finger upon her. His purpose is to present himself as he is. Everything else can follow. It is as though he imagines himself naked before her. And she is aware of this. She recognizes that the man looking at her is utterly confident that he has no need to hide anything, no need of any deception or covering. How is she to respond to such imprudence? This time the choice is not between encouragement or discouragement. If she lowers her eyes or looks away, it will be tantamount to admitting that she has appreciated his temerity: to turn away will be to admit that she has seen him as he is. (She will guard for herself, she will preserve the memory of his magnificent imprudence.) The more modest response is to hold his gaze, to stare blatantly back at him in the pretence that she has noticed nothing. This is what she does. Yet the longer they look at each other, the more conscious she is of him addressing himself unreservedly and exclusively to her. Although surrounded by observers, and although he is several metres away and she does not yet know his name, the mere act of their looking at each other has been transformed into their first secret encounter.

What were those extraordinary lines of Mallarmé you quoted to me this morning? Monsieur Hennequin asks his wife.
A woman dancer, she recites slowly and distinctly, is not a woman who dances for she is in no way a woman and she does not dance.
The Belgian gently rolls the wine in his glass.
It is beautiful, says the Contessa, and it is true. A great artist is more than a man or a woman, a great artist is a god.
In my opinion Mallarmé was trying to destroy language, says Monsieur Hennequin, he wanted to deny words the meaning they have, and I suppose it was a long-drawn out act of revenge.
Revenge? I don't follow, says the host, looking at the palm trees silhouetted against the lake and in the back of his mind playing with the idea of installing an electrical generator so that the house and gardens may be lit with electric light.
A revenge against his public, the public who didn't appreciate him as he wanted to be appreciated.
It is beautiful, repeats the Contessa, a dancer is not a dancer, a singer is not a singer. How true it is. Sometimes I myself wonder who I am.
I have one or two acquaintances in Brussels, says the Belgian, who wouldn't agree with you there. They have, if I may so put it, they have first-hand experience of a number of women dancers. Only Mathilde laughs and the Belgian bows his head to her in pretended gratitude. (He wields power. He sits with his big arse on everything that might give him cause to doubt anything he does or says.)
You don't accept, Maurice, the genius of your Mallarmé? asks the host. In this house above this garden he likes to encourage talk about poetry.
Mallarmé may or may not have been a genius. I am not in a position to judge. But he was an obscurantist, and I believe in clarity. As an

engineer it's almost a professional article of faith. Confused machines just aren't possible.

Mallarmé was a genius, he was immortal, said Madame Hennequin, far ahead of his time.

If we could all live a thousand years, says G., we would each, at least once during that period, be considered a genius. Not because of our great age, but because one of our gifts or aptitudes, however slight in itself, would coincide with what people at that particular moment took to be the mark of genius.

You don't believe in genius! says the Contessa, shocked.

No, I think it's an invention.

Several guests have left the table to look over the parapet at the moonlit gardens below. He sees a statue, white, sinuous and indistinct at its edges. Yet the way it is placed makes it part of the geometry of the garden with its straight paths, stone steps and polygonal fountains. The lights on the islands across the lake flicker, but otherwise everything is as still as the past.

Such an historical silence cannot last.

G. turns round to address Monsieur Hennequin: I know little about Mallarmé: I do not read poetry, but is the thought of Mallarmé's which Madame was so good as to quote to us really so confused? Some experiences are indescribable but they are nonetheless real. Can you, for example, Monsieur Hennequin, describe the tone and quality of your wife's voice? But I am sure that you would recognize it anywhere, as I would too, Madame Hennequin.

Madame Hennequin watches her husband to see how he will respond to the strange young man who has singled her out.

We talk of the mysterious tragedy of Chavez' crash, says G., hundreds of people witnessed it, yet nobody can describe what he saw. Why? Because it was too unexpected. The unexpected is often indescribable.

He looks at Camille. He will call her, he decides, Camomille.

Mallarmé, G. continues, is saying that when a woman dances she can become transformed. Words which applied to her before, will no longer apply. It may even be necessary to call her by a different name.

Monsieur Hennequin places himself between the young man and his wife. Monsieur Hennequin is slim for his age but he has large heavy thighs. Women are women, he says, putting his hands up to bar entry, whether they are dancing, dressing, entertaining our guests, looking after our children or making us happy. And let us be grateful for that.

Our beautiful ladies, says the host, must be beginning to feel the cold night air rising from the lake. Let us go indoors.

They talk of attraction and magnetism; these notions suggest a force acting between two given bodies; what is left out of account is how utterly the bodies appear to change in themselves; they are no longer the given bodies. The fact of being given has changed them.

It is not that you see her so differently; it is that she frames a different world. The shape of her nose doesn't change much. In outline she is the same. But within her unchanged contours everything you perceive is different. She is like an island whose coastline still corresponds to what was shown on the map, but on which, and surrounded by which, you now live. The sound of the sea on all her beaches—unless you accept the dictatorship of your intelligence—ultimately that is the only thing you can oppose to death.

For bruises sand is cool and like silk to the touch. For wounds it is inflaming and harsh, each particle contributing its degree of pain.

But by abstract metaphor I distance myself from my unique perception of her.

The tip of each of her fingers, with its bitten nail, is as expressive as an eye looking at me. I follow from the tip of each finger past the two knuckles to where it joins her hand. Her hand looks curiously thin and ineffective. As an object her hand looks as though it has been discarded. I can imagine or foresee it being different. It might caress me. It might hammer against my back. It might present itself as a five-teated udder to my mouth for me to suck each finger. None of this, however, is of any importance. My attention happened to fall upon her hand. It might just as well have been another part of her. Her elbow. Sharp with her bone pressing against her skin and making it white and bloodless. What can I foresee her elbow doing? Nothing of significance. Yet I perceive it in the same way as her hand. I receive from it the same promise and in the same way it fulfils its promise. I isolate parts in order to follow my eyes, instant by instant, faithfully. But my eyes move, reading her, at incredible speed. The fresh evidence of each part, of each new sight of her, contributes to my perception of her as a whole, and makes this whole continually move and pulsate like a heart, like my own heart.

What is her promise? Of her love in the future? But that is not yet fulfilled. If I made love with her it would be to complete, to put an end to, something that had already happened to us. When you describe something, when you name it, you separate it from yourself. Or to some degree. To fuck is like naming what has happened in the only language adequate to expressing it. (Only when nothing has happened is it possible to separate sex from love.) All acts of physical love are anticipatory and retrospective. Hence their unique significance.

My eyes touch her almost but not quite in the same way as my hands might. If I touched her, her skin, the surface of her body, a contradictory sensation would accompany my sense of touch. I would have the feeling that what I was touching also enclosed me: that this exterior surface (which is her skin with its variegated pores, its degrees of softness and heat and its different smells) that this exterior surface was at the same time, according to another mode of experience, an interior surface. I do not speak symbolically: I am referring to sensation itself. Touching her from the outside would make me aware of being inside.

I look at her fingers as though I were on the point of inhabiting each one, as though I might become the content of its form. I and her phalanxes. Absurd. Yet what is the absurd? Only a moment of incongruity between two different systems of thinking. I am speaking of her fingers, the flesh and bones of another person, and I am speaking too of my imagination. Yet my imagination is not separable from my own body; nor is hers.

The light which, falling upon her, discloses her, is like the light that falls upon and discloses cities and oceans. The facts of her physical being are the events of the world, the space in which she moves is the space of the universe, not because I am unmindful of everything except her, but because I am prepared to risk all that is not her for the sake of all that she is.

The way she plants her feet, the exact length of her back, the tone of her rasping voice (which he said he would recognize anywhere) —each of these and every other quality I see in her, appears as significant as a miracle. There is no end to what she can offer: it is infinite. And I am not deluding myself. I desire her single-mindedly. The value of everything about her, the significance of her smallest movement, the power of what differentiates her from every other woman—this may be determined for both of us by what I am prepared to risk for her. And that is the world. And so she will acquire the value of the world: she will contain, so far as she and I are concerned, all that is outside her, myself included. She will enclose me. Yet I will be free, for I will have chosen to be there, as I never chose to be here in the world and the life which I am ready to abandon for her.

Je t'aime, Camomille, comment je t'aime. That is what he must say.

The guests entered the large room where the furnishings were dark and heavy and the lamps cast bright distinct circles of light—like those lit arenas on conference tables in which it was traditional to depict statesmen signing treaties. The arrangement of the room suggested its principal use as a place where Milanese politicians and businessmen came to work out their plans undisturbed: it offered comfort but not distraction: it was a male room, like a minister's private reception room in a parliament building. There was nothing in it (except now the women's bare arms) which was equivalent to the flamingoes in the garden. As the guests entered this sober but comfortable room through the large double door beneath a portrait painting of Giolitti, he noticed Madame Hennequin talking with her friend Mathilde Le Diraison and there was something in the relationship between the two women which intrigued him. They had an air of scarcely disguised conspiracy, such as sometimes sisters preserve between them even after they have become adults and their parents are dead.

In a corridor Madame Hennequin had passed a huge mirror in the shape of the sun and in this mirror she had found herself trying to see the mantle over her shoulders and the fringe over her forehead as he might see them. Through his eyes she found herself pleasing.

Now in the room she compared him with her husband. They were unequally matched. Monsieur Hennequin was stronger and had greater authority. He was like a father; with her two children at home she often referred to her husband as Papa; he was a man who understood the world. His discretion about his mistress—even this—was an example of how well he understood it. Whereas the other, who spoke French badly, did not read poetry but could explain Mallarmé: Mallarmé whose poetry she loved so much because it was inexplicable: the other was imprudent and careless. But since they were so unequally matched she could allow herself to smile at him. Circumspectly, in her own rather distant manner and always in reference to her husband who could at any moment rescue her from the consequences of her own childishness, she was willing, for the duration of the evening, to flirt with this friend of the American aviator: to pretend that a relation existed where in fact there was none.

She asked him what kind of man Chavez was. He replied that he had only met him once or twice, but that Chavez was a nervous man and perhaps also a desperate one. He addressed his reply, however, as much to Monsieur Hennequin as to Madame Hennequin. It was as if he were aware of the comparison she had made and the conclusions she had reached. Having alerted her to his interest, he was now content for them both to concentrate on her husband, the owner.

On a low table near which they sat was a large glass statue of a swan, rose-coloured, and mounted on a silver turntable which revolved. It was neither art nor toy, but an ornament denoting wealth. Madame Hennequin, looking directly at him, put her hand on the swan's neck and murmured the famous line of Mallarmé:

> *Un cygne d'autrefois se souvient que c'est lui*
> *Magnifique mais qui sans espoir se délivre ...*

The harsh rose-coloured glass made the skin of her thin hand seem milkily translucent.

No more? asked Monsieur Hennequin encouragingly. He was aware that the American aviator's friend had roused his wife's interest and he hated Mallarmé, but he wanted to demonstrate his tolerance in such matters.

It goes on like this, said Madame Hennequin, but don't try to understand it, just listen to the sound of what I'm saying.

She recited the whole four-line stanza and the following one, allowing her voice to transform the nostalgia of the poem into a kind of longing. The poem is about opportunities missed, but, by the very act of saying it out loud, she seized an opportunity. By reciting some lines from it she took the opportunity of letting the sound of the words express all that she felt to be independent to herself, all that was outside the reckoning but not the protection of her husband. She was like a tree, she considered, that grew in the soil of her husband's garden but the leaves of which moved independently in the wind.

Whilst she spoke Monsieur Hennequin leaned back in his chair and smiled at the ceiling, painted with garlands. It was her spirituality, he congratulated himself, which made her such a good mother, although it also explained her reticence, her excessive modesty towards him. His heavy thighs and stomach pressed against his clothes and creased them. She lacked heat, he concluded, but on the other hand she would always be innocent.

G. refrained from glancing at her.

You have a poet's voice, said the host, and then repeated the last two words in Italian to make them sound more appropriately poetic.

The Contessa quickly started her own conversation with those around her.

G. leant forward and pushed the glass swan quite forcefully so that its silver turntable began to revolve. It ceased to look like a swan and resembled a tall-necked, many-sided carafe of rosé wine.

The swan is drunk, said a young man.

G. turned towards Monsieur Hennequin and said: There is something I have often noticed which I do not fully understand and which I believe, Monsieur, you may be able to inform me about.

I will do my best.
Perhaps you do not often have the opportunity of visiting fairs?
You mean trade fairs?
Fairs in the street where there are shooting stalls and moving pictures and performing fleas and roundabouts and switchbacks . . .
I have seen them from a distance, yes.
I am an habitué of such fairs. They fascinate me.
Why do they fascinate you? interrupted Madame Hennequin.
They are full of games for adults and there are very few places where you can watch adults playing.
Simple-minded adults, said Monsieur Hennequin, those who patronize these fairs are of very low calibre.
You are entirely right, Monsieur Hennequin. You must surely have visited one once to understand them so well? Now, to come to my question. Do you think that flying round repeatedly in a circle, as happens on a certain kind of roundabout, do you think this might have a temporary effect—for purely physiological reasons—on the brain?
It can induce a sense of giddiness . . .
I mean more. Could character be temporarily changed by it?
Please explain, said Monsieur Hennequin, what you have in mind.
At these fairs there is a special kind of roundabout, a combination of a roundabout and a series of swings. The seats are suspended on chains and when they turn—
A centrifugal force comes into play, said Monsieur Hennequin, and

165

they are thrown outwards. I have seen the kind of which you are speaking. We call them *les petites chaises*.

Good. Now you can control—up to a point—how you swing outwards and in what direction. It's all a question of how far you lean back, how high you push your feet up, how you swing with your shoulders and how you pull with your arms on the chains either side. It's not very different from what every girl learns on an ordinary swing.

I know, said Madame Hennequin.

The game which most of the riders play as soon as the roundabout starts to turn, is to try to swing themselves near enough to whoever is behind or in front of them so as to join hands with them and then to swing together, as a pair, holding on to each other's chains. It's quite difficult to do this, often only their fingertips touch—

The seats are spaced in such a way, interrupted Monsieur Hennequin, to ensure that they never come into contact. Otherwise it could be dangerous.

Exactly. But everyone who rides on this kind of roundabout is transformed. As soon as it begins to turn and they begin to gain height as they swing out, their faces and expressions are changed. They leave the earth behind them, they throw back their heads and their feet go up towards the sky. I doubt whether they even hear the music which is playing. Each tries to take hold of the arm trailing in front of him, they cry out in delight as they gather speed, and the faster they go, the freer they play, as they rise and fall, separate and converge. The pairs who succeed in holding on to one another fly straighter and higher than the rest. I have watched this many times and nobody escapes the transformation. The shy become bold. The awkward become graceful. Then when it stops most of them revert to their old selves. As soon as their feet touch the ground, their expressions again become suspicious or closed or resigned. And when they walk away from the roundabout, it is almost impossible to believe that they are the same beings, men and women, who a moment ago were so free and abandoned in the air.

Madame Hennequin set the swan turning as he had done earlier.

Now what I want to ask you, Monsieur Hennequin, is whether you think this transformation might arise from the effect on the nervous

166

system of gravity being modified by a centrifugal force? Is that possible?

It is more likely the result of the very low mental capacity of the class of people who go to such places. For the most part they are little better than children.

You don't think it would have the same effect on us?

I doubt it very much.

Hasn't it always been man's dream to fly? Is that so childish? asked Madame Hennequin.

I fear, my dear, your imagination takes too much for granted, said Monsieur Hennequin. A fairground stunt like this has got nothing to do with flying. You should ask Monsieur Weymann.

The conversation changed. Somebody remarked on the painting of Giolitti. The host laughed and said the painter must have been a political opponent. Do you know what Giolitti's enemies call him? They call him a Bologna sausage, because, they say, he is half ass and half pig!

I understood you admired him, said the Belgian.

In Bologna pig may be a pet name, said Mathilde Le Diraison.

Yes, I do admire him, said the host. He is the creator of modern Italy. He has often been here, in this room, and it was he himself who said that about his own portrait, and he added that the painter was from Bologna! And this is exactly how he is a great man. He knows how unimportant personal opinions are. What matters is organization. Organization and persuasion.

The conversation turned to politics and then to Germany and the news of the continuing riots in Berlin. Monsieur Hennequin feared that a revolution breaking out in one country in Europe might quickly spread to the others. Monsieur Hennequin was always oscillating between supreme confidence and sudden fear.

His host shook his head reassuringly. There will be no revolution in Europe, the danger is past, and the reason is simple. The leaders of the working masses do not want power. They only want improvements. They have learnt the techniques of bargaining. They have to pretend to ask for more than they want to receive what they do want. From time to time they bring out the word Socialism. This word is the equivalent of temporarily breaking off negotiations, but always with the intention of re-starting them. If we educate people properly, if we use the benefits of modern science, if we curb the power of monarchy and rely upon parliamentary government, there is no reason at all why the present social order should ever change violently.

The host came over, stood behind Monsieur Hennequin and put his hand on his shoulder. You are sceptical, he continued, come, let me show you a recent photograph of Turati and the Socialist Deputies in Rome. It is a curious picture. And very reassuring.

Monsieur Hennequin got up. Madame Hennequin began to say something but was interrupted—

You are beautiful. You have eyes which say everything. And you have the voice of a corn-crake.
She laughs. A corn-crake! Is that a compliment?
I love you. How I love you. I must see you tomorrow.

In the year 1910, which in this respect was in no way exceptional, over half a million Italians emigrated abroad in order to find work and avoid starvation.

THE NATURE OF LIKENESS

In writing about Camille I cannot get close enough to her.

Who is drawing me
between pencil and paper?

One day I shall judge the likeness
but she who judges
will not be the woman who now
so expectantly poses.

I am what I am.

What I am like is how you see me.

O

Domodossola, like Brig, was crowded with journalists and flying
enthusiasts. It is a small town of narrow cobbled streets. Its roofs
are covered with clumsy irregular tiles of blackish-red stone, similar
in colour to the rocks of the Gondo. When seen from the air the
overhanging eaves hide the small streets and the whole town looks
like a scattered pile of blackish-red slivers of shale, the deposit of a
landslide.

In the Piazza Mercato the Mayor had ordered a large blackboard to
be put up. On it, with white chalk in copperplate script, was written
the latest medical bulletin concerning Chavez.

Being Sunday morning, there was a market and the square and streets
were crowded. During the night the weather had changed and it
was hard to believe that they had dined, twenty kilometres away,
on the open platform of the tower above Lake Maggiore. He was
slowly making his way towards the hospital. When he saw Camille
walking in front he was not surprised.

She was wearing a *trotteur* of pale lilac grey. Its cut and its colour
made her look more enterprising than she had in g dress.
Her walk was light and decided. On her head she wore a low-
crowned hat with white flowers, tilted forwards. Her brown hair was
swept up at the back into a chignon. He guessed that her trim

elegance early in the morning in this provincial town meant that she had slept little or badly.

The temperature of hair to the touch varies considerably from person to person, regardless of the surrounding temperature. There are heads of hair which always tend to be cool; others which seem to generate their own heat in the coldest conditions. In the cold air, whilst she remained quite oblivious of his presence a few metres behind her, he could foresee that Camille's hair would be unusually warm.

She stopped to look into a shop window of gloves and furs. Abruptly he took her arm from behind. She wheeled round with a little cry and with her fists clenched in anger. When she saw that it was he and not a stranger, she could not prevent the relief from showing on her face. She continued to frown, but a smile wavered along her mouth.

He asked after her husband and said that he wanted to propose to him that if the weather were not worse this afternoon, they, with Monsieur Schuwey and Madame Le Diraison, might accompany him on a motor trip to Santa Maria Maggiore.

During the night she had asked herself many times about his absurd declaration of love. Why had she not turned her back on him? Why had she not protested? She told herself it was because she was too surprised. Yet she might have been forewarned. She had after all consciously encouraged his evident interest in her. But what she could never have foreseen, what still confused her, was the way in which, suddenly, and clearly by an act of will, he was addressing her in the room as though they were alone, as though he had dropped from the sky, or come up from the earth, exactly beside her, without having to interrupt or cross the territory of those who surrounded her. She did not protest because there seemed to be nobody to protest to; nobody could have seen him. Had she made a scene, it would have been about something which had already ceased to exist. At one moment during the night she woke up convinced he was standing by the window. For the same reason she could not cry out.

She was telling him how she had lost a pair of gloves on the train coming from Paris. He asked if he might accompany her into the shop. She hesitated. He assured her there was no other shop in the town and he would be glad to interpret for her.

This morning she saw yesterday's incident differently. What had happened (mysteriously) had happened; but it was without consequence thanks to the order and routine of her normal life. She was in Domodossola with her husband. In four or five days she would return to Paris and her children. This man (with whom she was in a glove shop explaining that she wanted long white gloves) had taken advantage of one moment at a dinner party such as could not occur again. The incident had been finished before it began.

The woman who served them in the shop spoke at length about the heroism of Chavez. Geo Chavez, he translated to Camille, was a victor over the mountains, a conqueror, to whose present pains the woman behind the counter would gladly minister all night and to the least of whose wishes she would be proud to be a slave. She spoke as a mother although to her great regret she never had a son. One of her daughters worked in Milan, a second helped her with the shop.

The gloves which Camille wished to try on were of the thinnest white leather and tight-fitting. The woman, who was proud to live in the town which would nurse Chavez back to health, brought one of the gloves to her mouth and breathed into it before handing it across the counter to Camille. If it was still difficult to put on, she explained, she would sprinkle some talc.

When memory connects one experience with another, the nature of the connection may vary considerably. There are connections by contrast, connections by similitude, connections by way of sensuous metaphor, connections of logical sequence, etc., etc. The relation between the two experiences may sometimes be one of mutual comment. In this case the connection is multiform and complex. Yet the comment, although extremely precise, cannot be verbalized any more than a chord in music can be. The experience of watching the Italian shopkeeper breathing into a glove summoned up and commented upon his memory of the mysterious warmth he once found in the clothes of Miss Helen, his last governess. Likewise his memory commented upon his present experience. The comments, however, remain unwritable.

The Italian woman blew into the second glove before passing it
to Camille. Filled with her breath, the glove took on the form of a
hand which suddenly and deeply frightened Camille. It was a languid
boneless hand, a hand without will, a hand floating in the air like a
dead fish with its white stomach uppermost. It was a hand she did
not want. It was a hand that could not clench itself. It was a hand
which in caressing would in no way be a hand and would not
caress; it would lead away. At that moment she knew what he was
offering her. He was offering her the possibility of being what she
pretended to be. He was proposing that she turn Mallarmé's
words into lived mornings and afternoons. But she immediately
put her knowledge out of her mind by dismissing the self which
recognized it, as unserious. All she had to do to remain safe, she
told herself, was to be wary of being unrealistic.

The gloves fitted her perfectly. The leather across her tiny bony
knuckles was so tight that it shone as if it were wet.
Take one hand in the other, he told her.
She did so.
You see, he said, you take your left hand in your right.
Is it strange? she asked.
No, he said, but it means you are confident, you are the mistress of
your own fate.
She laughed, reassured that he recognized this. I am quite content,
she said.
You can be content and a slave. Contentment has little to do with it.
Why do you say content?
She thought it best not to answer. I am easily startled though, she
said, like I was in the street just now.
Startled! You turned upon me with the fury of a virago defending
her honour, and when you recognized it was me you extended me
an utterly confident welcome.
Camille pulled off the gloves angrily, lay them on the counter and
turned towards the door. He asked the shopkeeper how much they
were.
I don't want them, said Camille.
He paid for them. The shopkeeper folded them in mauve tissue
paper. Camille stood facing the door. From behind he took both of
her elbows in his hands.
(What can I foresee her elbow doing? Nothing of significance. Yet
I perceive it in the same way as her hand. I receive from it the same

promise and in the same way it fulfils its promise. Her elbows are in his hands.)

Trust me, he said. Nobody else knows why you take your left hand in your right. It doesn't compromise you.

I don't want the gloves, she said.

They won't compromise you either, he said, it is certain that you would have bought them. And I offer them to you only as a modest homage to your elegance, Madame Hennequin, this morning.

The formality with which he spoke confused her. It was impossible to decide whether its falseness was deliberate or the result of his far from perfect grasp of the language. Either way it emphasized how by showing her anger she had been indiscreet.

It is too early for us to disagree, he said, and he held out the gloves to her and bowed.

She took them.

Je t'aime, Camille, he said, opening the shop door.

O

The hospital is near the centre of the town. A square yellow building, it looks like a classical early-nineteenth-century villa in its own garden. The main door is flanked by camellia trees. In the doorway is a table with a book open upon it. The book is for passers-by or visitors who do not wish to disturb the flyer, to write messages or tributes in. For some, however, it seems a sinister omen, for in certain parts of the Mediterranean a book is placed by the front door when there has been a death in the house; and in this book neighbours and acquaintances sign their names as an expression of condolence.

Weymann is waiting for him at the top of the stairs.

He says he remembers nothing after the Gondo, Weymann whispers.

How does he seem?

Very shaken and erratic.

What do the doctors really think?

His injuries are not serious. He has no concussion. There's nothing to prevent him making a complete recovery.

Except?

I didn't say except.

But except?

He's too nervous, says Weymann.

They enter the room in which there are already half a dozen men, including Christiaens and Chavez' close friend Duray. On the wall opposite the bed are pinned telegrams from all over the world: enough to cover the entire wall.

To the wounded man the wall might have represented a vast transparent window on to the world's view of his achievement; but it does not, it remains a wall with confused meaningless rectangles of paper pinned to it, some of which stir slightly when the door is opened. His temperature is only slightly above normal. His brain is lucid. Time and again his imagination approaches the irreversibility of the events since he announced 'I'm going now'. Their irreversibility confronts him like a rock face which moves with him as he turns his head or shifts his gaze. However high he climbs, however daringly he breaks through the wall of the wind westwards, it is still there, in front of his eyes and above his swollen lips. He repeatedly makes the approach but the geology of the events never changes. Meanwhile these silent endlessly recurring private approaches make everything else said or seen in his room seem as far away as the words he cannot read on the telegrams.

They found him under the débris of his plane with his face pressed against the earth. He did not lose consciousness.

G. takes Chavez' hand and offers his congratulations. He is unaccustomed to finding a man mysterious; mystery, for him, is the prerogative of women. About men he asks only questions to which the number of answers is limited, as one asks what time it is—according to a clock or a watch. He looks into Chavez' dark eyes, whose expression is suspicious, at his swollen lips which, even when unbruised, were absurdly full and curved, at the backs of his hands, and he sees the whole appearance of the small young man, forced to lie unexpectedly there in a bed in a hospital in a garden in Domodossola, as an outer covering no less arbitrary or opaque than the misshapen cylinders of plaster round his legs. A hand on a woman's breast conjures up the same mystery. Beneath the tangible extends the enormity of what is intangible and invisible. A doctor can take the plaster off his legs. But a surgeon making an incision in his flesh and opening up the organs within would not disclose the mystery. The mystery lies in the vastness of the system by which Chavez, so long as he is alive, constitutes the world in which he is living (which includes your hand shaking his) as his own unique experience.

This morning I went into a glove shop and the woman who served me spoke of you as though you were a saint, a saint with the courage of a hero.

I know, interrupted Chavez, they think of me like that. Perhaps they are right or perhaps they are not. Anyway the question will never be settled because, meanwhile, I'm dying.

O

The weather improved. He suggested that Monsieur Hennequin should drive the motor car. In the late afternoon they were driving through a pine forest which overlooked the lake. Madame Hennequin wanted to stop so that they could walk a little in the forest.

The light enters the forest almost horizontally. Each entry between the trees into the depths of the forest acquires in this light an exaggerated stereoscopic quality. The trees which are against the light look entirely black. The tree trunks which are sunlit are a greyish honey colour. The same light falls upon the taffeta and silk of the two women's dresses which are pearly and luminous. As the women walk, their feet in their buttoned boots tread lightly but deeply into a carpet of pine needles, rotted cones, moss and the leaves of flowers. Every surface is more than usually vivid, but in the forest everything loses something of its substantiality.

To Camille he has been no more than formally polite, so as to emphasize to her the depth and seriousness of the conspiracy which now links them. He has concentrated his attention upon Monsieur Hennequin and Harry Schuwey. He is encouraging the latter to talk about the resources of the Congo. He appears to listen with interest; every so often he asks a supplementary question or makes an encouraging sign of agreement. Yet despite the impression he gives, he is scarcely listening to what is being said. In a mixed language, where words are only one of the expressive means—a language not essentially different from that in which he questioned himself as a child but now possessing a wider range of references —he addresses, silently, the two men whom he is walking between.

How did you choose them? You chose them for exactly the same reasons as you would have chosen any other woman. Men in your position must have the best. The best is not an absolute, though. Men in your position must have the best for men in your position. If you choose a woman without considering this you may jeopardize your position and the putting of your position in jeopardy may cause you—and therefore her—unhappiness. Cut the cloth according to the purse, and choose the wearer of the cloth according to its cut. But apart from being men with positions you are men with penises.

On their left, the ground rises steeply so that the roots of the distant trees are level with the top branches of the near ones. Beween the higher distant trees there are rocks, jagged in shape but covered in green moss. On their right, when there is a sufficiently straight avenue to look down, they can see the surface of the lake shimmering like mica below.

And your penises are much given to idealizing. Your penises want the best possible—and to hell with your positions. How can you satisfy both?

A forest is not incontrovertible like a mountain. It is tolerant, like the sea, of everything which occurs within it.

You cannot. But you can protect yourselves or you can try to protect yourselves against the worst consequences of an open rift. And this you have done from the moment you attained the age of responsibility, with the help of your colleagues, your friends, your church, your professors, your novelists, your dressmakers, your comedians, your lawyers, your forces of order, your public men and of course your women.

Monsieur Hennequin wonders whether what his friend is saying might be of interest to Peugeot. Everything that motor cars will need should be of interest to Peugeot. He would like to visit the Congo himself. He has been to Algeria but in his opinion that is scarcely Africa. Africa begins with the jungle. He picks up a stick

from the path and with it he lightly taps the trunks of the trees which
are within his reach as they pass them.

You had to find a third value, a third interest that your social
ambition, which, unlike pure ambition, must always wear the dress
of conformity, and the idealism of your penises could acknowledge
as arbiter. And this third value was property. The third interest was
an interest in owning. Not a remote merely financial interest, but a
passionate one which stirs you physically, which becomes a sense
as acute as the sense of touch. Indeed you have seen to it that your
children are taught to touch nothing that is not theirs, not a flower
nor an animal nor the hand of a stranger. To touch is to claim as
property. To fuck is to possess. And you take possession either by
paying rent or by buying outright.

The women were walking behind the men. Harry Schuwey is
explaining that whereas ivory is a luxury material today, rubber
with the development of the motor industry is becoming an essential
one and that therefore the future of the Congo lies in rubber. The
forest is very still except for the party advancing along the path.
Occasionally, high up among the topmost branches, a bird sings a
few notes and then stops.

Has nobody told you about your houses? I discovered it a long time
ago. You are walking leisurely—in any city in Europe—through a
well-off residential quarter down a street of your own houses or
apartments.

The trees are spruce firs or larches. Lichen grows more readily
on the former. Many dead branches are festooned with matted pale
green hair, like dried seaweed. On other branches lines and clusters
of lichen algae are fixed like tarnished white silver press-studs.

Their window-frames and shutters have been freshly painted but
their colour barely differentiates them from the façades around them,
which absorb the sunlight but give off a slight granular scintillation
like starched linen table-napkins. You look up at the curtained
windows in which the curtains are so still that they might be carved
out of stone, at the wrought iron-work of balconies imitating plants,
at ornamental flourishes referring to other cities and other times,
you pass polished wooden double doors with brass bells and plates,

the silence of the street consists of the barely perceptible noise of a distant crowd, a crowd made up of so many people so far away that their individual exertions, their individual inhaling and exhaling combine in a sound of continuous unpunctuated breathing, gentle as a breeze, this silence which is not entirely a silence, receives and contains the noise of a front door being shut by a maid, or the yapping of a dog among upholstered furniture and heavy carpets, as a canteen with its green baize lining receives the knives and forks deposited in it. Everything is peaceful and well-appointed. And then suddenly you realize with a shock that each residence, although still, is without a stitch of clothing, is absolutely naked! And what makes it worse is their stance. They are shamelessly displaying themselves to every passer-by!

As the party strolls on, the spaces they see between trunks and branches change in shape and colour. Colour and shape can conspire to suggest the presence, there, between two trees, of a deer.

Look! whispers Mathilde.

The process is the obverse of that of natural camouflage whereby animals merge with their surroundings; her knowledge that deer live in the forest has led Mathilde to create an animal out of the surroundings.

He has deduced from the way Mathilde smiles at him that Camille has confided in her. In her attitude there is an openness, an undisguised curiosity such as women can only afford to show to a new lover or suitor of an intimate friend.

I really thought it was a deer, says Mathilde.

The path leads to a clearing, a meadow of tall grass in which every blade is rendered separate and distinct by the horizontal light and which is full of the stillness and peace of early autumn wherein it seems that all development has been suspended, all consequences indefinitely delayed. Monsieur Hennequin, ignoring the present arguments of Harry Schuwey, stoops to pick some meadow saffron which he presents to his wife. The moment reminded him of the year in which he had courted her.

You chose this woman as you made her your own. At any moment the degree of conviction in your choice depended on your estimate of how exclusively she belonged to you. In the end she belonged to you entirely, and then you were able to say: I have chosen her.

Camille takes the flowers in her gloved hand. And Mathilde pins them to her friend's blouse.

It is necessary to believe that what you choose for yourself is good. But a part of yourself—the part that was cunning, listened to other men and had known since childhood that life benefits those who benefit themselves—this part remained sceptical. By marrying her, you would lose the opportunity of marrying another. By possessing her you would limit your possible powers of possession. True, you could still choose your mistress. But in the end the same would apply to your choice of her. And so the sceptical part of yourself asked: is she desirable enough to convince me consistently of my own good sense in making her mine? Is her desirability such that it can console me for finding her, rather than any other, desirable?

Camille laughs at a joke of Mathilde's. Monsieur Hennequin walks through the high grass like a man walking into water. Harry Schuwey is explaining why the official annexation of the Congo which occurred two years ago will benefit trade.

Had the answer been No, you would have dropped her as though she had ceased to exist.

I have never seen such large butterflies, shouts Monsieur Hennequin and running a little distance tries to catch one in his cap.

In order to console you for the loss of all or nearly all the other women in the world, she had to become an ideal. She collaborated with you in the choice of the qualities to be idealized. You chose Camille's innocence, delicacy, maternal feeling, spirituality. She emphasized these for you. She suppressed the aspects of herself which contradicted them. She became your myth. The only myth which was entirely your own.

Schuwey is arguing that the colonial methods of King Leopold and his private Congo Free State were effective enough twenty years ago and that it was hypocritical of the other European powers to condemn the use of forced labour and harsh repressive measures when they themselves had once used similar methods—less effectively. Nevertheless, Schuwey says, it is perfectly true that kings make bad businessmen because they always put revenue before investment.

You—you have idealized different qualities in Mathilde. She is different in temperament and she is not your wife but your mistress. She has, you say, the most beautiful neck in the world. She is lazy, you believe, as only a pleasure-loving woman can be. She is, you pride yourself, devilishly attractive to men. To idealize the last quality is uniquely satisfying—so long as a second proposition, about which you feel less confident, pertains: and she does not deceive me.

When you consider leaving Camille, when you find that Mathilde, is, after all, too extravagant and erratic, it will not be because you are dissatisfied with what they are but because they will no longer be able to compensate you for what they are not!

I hate you. You have power not because of your wealth but because most men obey you. Everything they learn makes them envy you and envy leads to obedience. They want to be like you. So they live by the same laws, and in the end they choose obedience as their own good.

Your power in yourself is paltry. Your eyes peer out like dead men propped up at their windows to make the crowds in the street below believe they are being watched. Ears, which are the most innocent, the most receptive feature of the face, become either side of your head useless vestigial appendages from a former age, like the useless nipples on your chests. Where do you live? At your fingertips? In your heart? At the bottom of your dreams? Across your shoulders?

You live in the ill-lit, airless space between your last skin and your clothes. You live in your own perambulating mezzanine. Your passions are like rashes.

I hear the lark, says Camille, but I can't see it.

You cannot threaten me. Your existence reconciles me to the idea of my own death.

I do not want to live indefinitely in a world which you dominate;

life in such a world should be short. Life would choose death rather than your company. And even death is reluctant to take you. You will live long.

Monsieur Hennequin approaches the group standing in the corner of the meadow. He holds his clasped hands out in front of him. Apparently he has caught a butterfly.

Let it go, says Camille, you are worse than a small boy.

You wouldn't have said that to Linnaeus, replies Monsieur Hennequin.

Who was he? asks Schuwey.

Monsieur Hennequin throws his hands up into the air above his head and opens them. There is no butterfly. He roars with laughter.

When you laugh, you laugh crazily (panting in momentary relief) at the person you might have been, and of whom the joke briefly reminded you.

As soon as one of you disappears, there is another to take his place, and the number of places is increasing. There will be shortages of everything in the world before there is a shortage of you!

After the meadow, the path leads to a point which commands a wide view of the plain and the first southern slopes of the Alps. When they stop talking, the silence, the expanse of the lake, the snow on a single Alpine peak, the late extension of the autumn afternoon, combine to make an amalgam which is like a lens for the imagination of even the habitually unimaginative: the lens enables them to glimpse the space surrounding their own lives.

Why should I fear you? It is you who speak of the future and believe in it. You use the future to console yourself for the youth you never had. I do not. I shall be beyond the far reaches of your ridiculous and monstrous continuity, as Geo Chavez has gone. I shall be dead, so why should I fear?

I fear the idea now: the idea of your immortality: the idea of the eternity you impose upon the living before they are dead.

On the return walk to the car he again affably accompanies the men. The forest is darker and cooler. The smell of pine is stronger. In the dusk of the trees the unity of the trees is more pronounced. A single twig of a larch has small bossy protuberances running on alternative sides along its length. When the twig was smaller, each of these was a needle. When the twig becomes a branch, each of these will be a twig. And branches grow from the trunk in the same way. The forest is the result of the same stitch being endlessly repeated.

As he helps Camille into the back of the motor car, he passes her a note. She will read it later. In it is written: My corn-crake, my little one, my most desired, I have something to tell you and you alone. Meet me tomorrow afternoon. I shall wait for you in a car outside Stresa Station tomorrow afternoon.

Monsieur Hennequin discovered the note the same evening. Camille had put it between the pages of Mallarmé's *Poésies* which at that time she always kept by her side. The oil lamp on the writing table started to smoke; she called her husband from the adjoining room and asked him to adjust it. (In their Paris house they already had electricity.) By accident Monsieur Hennequin knocked the book off the table. The note fluttered separately to the ground. He stopped to pick up both paper and book. The folded piece of paper intrigued him: he wondered whether Camille had begun to write her own poetry. He unfolded it. The note was signed. He put it back in the book, kissed Camille on the top of her head and left the room as though nothing had happened.

Camille, unsuspecting, instructed her maid to prepare a bath. She had decided that she would ignore the note. But she could not cease asking herself and trying to answer the question: what is it in me that makes him so heedless and so insistent?

After a quarter of an hour Monsieur Hennequin had assessed the full magnitude of the wrong done to him, and he entered his wife's room without knocking and as though he had just at that instant discovered her infidelity. The door banged against the wall. Camille had unpinned her hair and was in a dressing gown. Monsieur Hennequin did not raise his voice. He spoke harshly between his teeth.

Camille, you must be mad. Can you explain yourself?

She looked up at him, surprised.

Open that book, you know already what is in it. There is a note—a note of assignation addressed to you. From whom is it?

You have no right to spy on me. It is humiliating for both of us.

From whom is it?

Since you have read it and it is signed, you obviously know.

From whom is it?

You tell me—and you can tell me, too, how many other notes I have received from the same gentleman. You are being very stupid, Maurice.

From whom is it?

He stood upright in front of her, his fists clenched, his head slightly inclined so that he could see the place on her head where he had kissed her before leaving the room to decide what it was necessary for him to do. She, in her chair, either had to lean back as though cowering away from him, or else stare at his watch-chain, a few inches from her face. She stared at the gold chain.

I have nothing to be ashamed of, she said. I did not intend to reply to his note, which I found very foolish, and I have done nothing whatsoever to encourage him. You must really believe me.

From whom is it?

Can you say nothing else, Maurice? Why don't you ask me what has happened. Me. Before jumping to your own conclusions.

From whom is it?

My God, what is the matter with you?

I want to hear you speak his name.

Then I am afraid I shall not give you that satisfaction.

Exactly. Because you know as well as I do that your voice will betray you. You will not be able to keep your feelings—if they can be called feelings—you won't be able to keep your feelings out of your voice. Say his name now.

I refuse. You are being absurd.

You refuse. Of course you refuse, I have seen the two of you together. I was blind. Blinded by my own trust in you. But now I can see. From the first moment you met him, you ogled him, you put yourself at his side, eyeing him, murmuring—

You have gone out of your mind. You have no right to say these things to me. I have done nothing.

Done nothing! In two days you haven't had the time to do anything

—as you so delicately put it. But you have wanted to, and like—like a prostitute you have interested him.

She tried to push him away with her hands. Then she lowered her head and began to cry.

We shall leave for Paris tomorrow afternoon, he said. You can tell Yvonne to pack. He strode to the door and turned to face her again. The shamelessness of it is what I find so disgusting, he said, the vulgarity! In two days under my very eyes in a small town where we are all of us of necessity on each other's doorsteps!

Doorsteps! she said, angry whilst crying.

I shall warn him tomorrow morning, he said, if I catch sight of him again with you, I shall shoot him—and have every court in France on my side. I shall shoot him down like—

Would it not be more honourable to challenge him to a duel?

I daresay you see yourself as a great courtesan. But you have neither the tact nor the charm for that. And you happen to be living in the twentieth century.

I beg you not to speak to him.

Him!

Where her gown crossed over he could see her white, rising breasts. Let us go back to Paris, she said, if that will really satisfy you, but do not speak to him.

Evidently, my dear Camille, you are frightened of what I will learn from him.

Very well.

He took the key out of the door and left the room. He took the key because otherwise she might lock him out. She had done so on several occasions after disputes; and later tonight—he was aware of it now—it was possible that he might decide to fuck her like a prostitute.

○

Camille slept fitfully. At six she got up. Her husband was not in his room and had apparently not slept in his bed. She opened the shutters. The sky was blue without a cloud in it. The pace of the day had not yet established its rhythm; time, like the street with only a few people in it, seemed elongated. The length of the day and the depth of the blue sky constituted a stage whose dimensions suddenly made her shiver. From the window she could see the railway station.

She waited impatiently for the time when she could decently send Yvonne with a message to Mathilde, asking the latter to join her as quickly as possible because she needed her help.

Whilst waiting she ordered coffee.

From the window she saw a cat cross the courtyard with that undeviating fleetness which characterizes cats when they have direct access to what they want. The cat had heard the noise of the coffee grinder being turned by the peasant girl in the kitchen, who sat on a stool and held the grinder between her knees. For the cat the noise signified cream. When the maid finished grinding the coffee, she would go to the wooden larder in the wall and take down a large jug of cream. She would pour the cream from this jug into small silver jugs, and if the cat rubbed itself against her leg, she would also pour some into a chipped blue and white plate and place it by the door to the yard for the cat to drink.

She looked several times through her wardrobe to decide what to wear today. They would be catching the train to Paris. She was being taken home to her children, herself like a child who had misbehaved. She had a dark travelling suit in linen lined with patterned satin, which would be highly suitable. She decided, however, to wear her *trotteur* of pale lilac grey. She was being taken home under protest.

It was not for her advice that she needed Mathilde but for her assistance. Mathilde was a person, Camille considered, with different standards from her own and with far more luxurious tastes. Mathilde understood contracts and because she understood them, she was able to keep them. When she married Monsieur Le Diraison, aged sixty-four, she undertook to make the rest of his life agreeable in exchange for the inheritance she would receive at his death. And for five years she had spoilt the old sick man like a child. She, Camille, would be incapable of carrying out such a bargain; she believed that life should be finer than that. She believed in a justice whose essence was spiritual, not material. She liked the parable of

185

the labourers in the vineyard of whom the last to be hired, who worked for only one hour, were nevertheless paid the same amount as those who had borne the burden and heat of the whole day.

She needed Mathilde's assistance precisely because she wanted to redress an injustice. If her husband had spoken to him as he had threatened to do (and his absence seemed to confirm that this might be the case) she wanted to go out into the town this morning, accompanied by Mathilde, in the hope that they might meet him. She never wished to see him again, but she wanted to give him her assurance that however unsuitable, imprudent and mistaken his pursuit of her had been, she had never for one moment considered it base.

She foresaw that Mathilde would dismiss this plan as quixotic and childish. But she knew that Mathilde would do what she asked: partly out of friendship, even more out of her fear of boredom.

What are we waiting for in this horrid little provincial town? Mathilde had said yesterday morning, I believe we are waiting, my dear, for the hero to die.

O

As the local train drew into Domodossola station, Monsieur Hennequin opened the carriage door, ready to jump down on the platform. He was not impatient and he knew he had time to kill, but the more briskly he acted, the more certain he was of the correctness of his decision. A number of workers got out of the same train, but instead of making for the exit they crossed the lines towards the shunting yards. There were no cabs waiting outside the station and he could only see one other person at the far end of the Corso.

He passed his hand over his side pocket to satisfy himself once again that the automatic pistol, to obtain which he had made the tedious night journey, was solidly there. Its solidity, like the briskness of his actions, acted as a confirmation; it was like hearing an acquaintance say of him: Maurice acted calmly and firmly.

Passing the hotel, he looked up at his own bedroom window and remembered Camille's taunt about fighting a duel. It was the traditional time of day for duels and for executions. He told himself that after a night without sleep, in the early morning, before the day for most people had begun, you might have an unusual sense of your own destiny.

He walked into the old centre of the town where there is an irregularly shaped piazza and the pavement in front of the shops is arcaded. The blackboard on which was written last night's medical bulletin concerning Chavez had been placed under the arcades in case it rained during the night. The writing was smudged at one corner. *The instability and irregularity of the patient's cardiac functions give rise to continuing anxiety . . .*

The shop windows under the arcades had large wooden shutters folded across them. They were painted green, but because they had been painted on different occasions, each had its own distinctive shade. Above the shutters were the shop signs. Several family names occurred more than once over different shops. When the shops were open, it was obvious from what was displayed in their windows that they were little more than poorly stocked stalls in a remote provincial town. But with their shutters up they looked different. It was possible to imagine that they were shops full of rare articles. Monsieur Hennequin walked several times round the arcade.

He would have liked Camille to witness the forthcoming encounter. She would see the young man shown up for what he was—a cynical philanderer with the mentality of a petty criminal. And she would also learn how far he, her husband, was prepared to go in order to protect her.

He no longer blamed Camille. Last night he had glimpsed in her the tart who, according to Monsieur Hennequin, is found in every woman but who only makes herself evident if the woman is denied the controls which her nature requires. He had ignored the warning contained in her infatuation with Mallarmé's poetry: this poetry had stimulated and irritated her taste for the limitless, the boundless. But finally, he convinced himself she was not to blame: she was innocent. Her weakness was the weakness of her sex.

In protecting her from this weakness, in putting a stop to the leering young man's felonies, he was acting on behalf of all husbands for the sake of all wives. Women who were far more cunning than Camille, far more capable of pursuing their own interests, suffered from the same weakness: the weakness of succumbing to their own false first impressions. Women, able to twist men round their little fingers as soon as they knew them, could be rendered as impressionable as an eleven-year-old before a stranger whom they did not yet know. Women could calculate, they could make elaborate strategic and tactical plans, they could be patient and persistent, they could be merciless and generous—but their first impressions were invariably faulty. They could not see what was in front of them. This was why philanderers, so long as they were dealing with women, had need of so little diguise or distinction.

Monsieur Hennequin came to believe that what he intended to do was a duty placed upon him as a consequence of the weakness and inferiority of others. He was in no way aware of having to defend his own interests, or of having to try to escape from the solitude being imposed upon him. He left the arcade and the shuttered shops.

Monsieur Hennequin stood in the doorway of the bedroom. I don't imagine you are surprised to see me, he said and shut the door behind him. We men are not the fools you take us for, he continued, and we know exactly how to deal with your type.

The bedroom was a modest one with a wooden plank floor. On the bed, instead of blankets, there was a large eiderdown in a white coverlet. The pillows were stuffed, not with feathers, but with grain. It was the hotel where the drivers of the Simplon mail coach used to stay. G. was still in bed but had raised himself up on one elbow.

As soon as he had shut the door behind him, Monsieur Hennequin pointed the pistol at the man in bed. Either you stop or I will kill you.
The man in bed stared at the pistol. (Is it the mere sight of gun metal which reminds him so strongly of the smell in the gun room of his childhood?) He heard Monsieur Hennequin's voice continue as though in the room next door.

If I see you in my wife's company again, here or anywhere else, I swear that I will shoot you on the spot.

Monsieur Hennequin was perfectly well aware of which way the gun in his hand was pointing—it was not his life that was in jeopardy. Further, he had reckoned since his first discovery of the note that it supplied him with evidence which would assure his receiving a purely nominal sentence even if he killed the man lying in the bed. Very little in his own life was menaced and he was now putting a stop to what might later have become a serious danger. Yet the invocation, the use of the threat of death may sometimes have a wider effect than the intended one. When once death is invoked, the choice of who must die may seem oddly arbitrary. In any case Monsieur Hennequin began to tremble.

He was not frightened, but he sensed that at this moment he was justifying his whole life. It was as if he was now prepared to choose death for himself rather than compromise or deny the meaning of his life. The important thing was the choice of death; whether for himself or another—always with the gun in his hand pointing at the man in the bed in front of him—seemed unimportant. It no longer mattered whether or not Camille witnessed the scene. To threaten or take the life of an avowed enemy was to enhance his own. He was discovering with excitement a new power.

If I have the slightest reason to suspect that you have seen her, I will shoot you like a dog whilst you sleep.

G. began to laugh. The pretences had been dropped and the truth which was revealed was absurdly familiar. The truth was Monsieur Hennequin, visibly trembling, the words coming out of his mouth with strange cries of pleasure, a pistol in his hand.

If I see you approaching the wife of any colleague or acquaintance of mine I shall shoot you as you leave the gathering.

Often he had been asked: why do you laugh, love?

After days of intrigue and hope and calculations, after doubts and heart-searchings, after boldness and timidity and further boldness, what truth is disclosed? His trousers flung across a chair, her wrap put aside or the coverlet of the bed pulled back, two rough triangles of darkish hair are disclosed and within them the parts whose exact forms first-year medical students are taught to recognize as typical of the entire human species. There is no mistaking any of it, and in this total lack of ambiguity there is a truly comic banality. The longer the mask has been worn, the longer the familiar has been hidden, the more comic the revelation becomes, for the more the pair of them are meant to be astounded at what they have always known.

You tried to take advantage of the innocence of my wife—as I'm sure you have taken advantage of God knows how many other unfortunate women. But this time, thank God, it is not too late.

When Beatrice fell back on the bed laughing, she was no longer laughing at the absurd man in black in the trap, but at what she knew would now become obvious on her bed, beneath the portrait of her father, according to a freedom apparently granted by a wasp sting.

Keep quiet. Stop laughing. Or you will get a bullet in your chest now.

He continued to laugh because at last he was face to face with the unexceptional. It was partly a laugh of relief, as though, against all reason, he had feared that the other might, in this, be exceptional. And partly he laughed at the great first joke of the commonplace becoming inexorable, like a penis becoming erect.

Monsieur Hennequin considered that his laughter was like that of a madman alone in his cell. And this idea that the leering man in the bed might be mad disturbed and discouraged him, for he believed that, although the mad must be forcibly restrained and in certain cases exterminated, madness itself was nevertheless self-defeating, and so his avowed enemy appeared to represent a less substantial menace than the one he had resolved, without hesitation or compromise, to put a stop to.

You are mad, he said. But mad or not you will have no second warning.

Monsieur Hennequin walked backwards out of the door, prolonging to the last possible moment the excitement (which the mad laughter had done so much to diminish) of pointing the gun at the man who had tried to seduce his wife.

O

Madame Hennequin and Mathilde Le Diraison are riding in a dilapidated carriage with a hood with holes in it and a driver with a straw hat, along the Via al Calvario, towards the church of San Quirico, which lies to the south, ten minutes from the centre of Domodossola.

They met G. in the Piazza Mercato. He greeted them quickly and, looking at Camille, said: Your husband with a pistol in his hand has just threatened to shoot me if I speak to you again. I must speak to you again. I will wait for you both at the church of San Quirico. We cannot talk here. Come as soon as you can. Then, without allowing them time to reply, he stepped back into the arcade and was gone.

Your friend is nothing if not dramatic, remarks Mathilde.
Do you think it is true?
That Maurice threatened him, yes.
He didn't have a gun.
Every man has some friend who has a pistol.
Do you think Maurice is capable of killing him?
For you, my dear, men will do anything! Mathilde laughs.
Please be serious.
Do you feel serious?

When Camille heard that her husband had threatened him with a gun, she was reminded of her wedding day. Her anger at the injustice of her husband's action, her shame on her husband's behalf, her resentment at the fact that her husband had ignored her protestations and appeals, made her acutely aware that she was his wife, or, more accurately, that she had become his wife according to her own choice. Up to this moment being Madame Hennequin had seemed to be part of her natural life; her marriage was part of the same continuity which led from her childhood through young womanhood to the present. There had been misunderstandings and disagreements between her and her husband, but never before had she felt that the course of her life was out of her control, that what was happening was unnatural to her. She remembered how, at their wedding, Maurice and she had knelt, isolated, alone, in front of the entire congregation, but side by side so that she could feel his warmth, in order to receive communion. He had knelt shyly and with what she then believed to be true humility. Now she imagined him getting to his feet with a pistol in his hand and a look of blank unfeeling on his face.

Suddenly amazement overcame her anger with a thought which restored to her a little of her natural identity, which suggested that she was not entirely helpless and which confirmed her sense of being blindly wronged by her husband. This thought was: Under the threat of being shot, he still wants to speak to me because he can see me as I am.

No, I do not feel serious, says Camille.
You should persuade them to fight a duel for you.
That is what I told Maurice. He said it wasn't modern.
I don't see what being modern or not has to do with it. Men don't change in that respect.
Do you think we do? asks Camille.
You are changing. You are transformed. You are a different person from what you were two days ago. If you could see yourself now—
What would I see?
A woman with two men in love with her!
Mathilde, please promise me one thing—do not, on any account, leave me alone with him.
Not if you both insist?
I am serious now. I cannot see him unless you promise me this.
Fortunately Harry is not jealous. Well, he is jealous, but not to the point of shooting or threatening. Afterwards he may make a scene in private with me, but I can put a stop to that quite quickly.
It would be as much as his life is worth, says Camille, please promise me.
I think Harry is the type of man who might under certain conditions shoot himself, but he would never shoot anybody else. What do you think *he* would do—Mathilde nods in the direction they are going —if he had reason to be jealous?

Jealous of me? asks Camille.

Yes, says Mathilde smiling.

When she thought: Under the threat of being shot, he still wants to speak to me, her vision of his appearance altered. The alteration was also retrospective. What she had noticed but not remembered came to light. Hundreds of details assembled to form the whole man before her. He attracted everything she had seen him do. Her impressions rushed towards him, attached themselves to him, as though magnetized, and, covering him, became his characteristics. His head addressed her. She saw into it. The head was larger than average. It lunged forward when he spoke. Thick curls fell over the back of his neck. The tops of his ears entered other thickets. His hands with which he gesticulated were smaller than average. The veins on them were rather pronounced. The missing teeth, when his mouth was open, made it seem wider than it was. The gaze of his eyes was insistent. His feet, like his hands, were small. His walk was light and fastidious and in contrast to the heavy thrust of his head and shoulders. She found each physical characteristic eloquent of an aspect of his nature, as a mother may find the characteristics of her infant before it can talk or sit up.

I think he would kill me and then himself, says Camille, laughing. Where does he live? It would be fortunate if it were Paris.

I don't know. He says he is half English and half Italian.

That might explain a lot, remarks Mathilde.

Please promise me, says Camille.

Has he told you how he lost his teeth?

Mathilde, listen to me, this could be a matter of life and death.

He has an expression that I've only seen on one other man.

Who? asks Camille.

He was a friend of my husband's, an Armenian who fell in love with me.

Exasperation wells up with tears in Camille's eyes. Mathilde lowers her voice and whispers: Camille, you can trust me. But you are naive about such situations. The danger is Maurice, and there you can depend on me.

Camille rests her head back against the dusty leather upholstery and lays her gloved white hand on Mathilde's arm.

How hot it is today! says Mathilde. There are days when grand passion is just not possible. The weather is a woman's best friend!

We shall be there too soon. I don't want to have to wait for him. Mathilde, ask him to drive more slowly.

Camille touches the fringe of her hair and stares at her own hand. It looks to her extremely small and delicate, likewise her wrists and forearms. She wants to appear as fresh and as intricate as white lace (she remembers a painting she once saw of a girl on a swing in a garden in Montpellier whose petticoats were bordered with white lace). She wants to appear like that in this green, overgrown, remote landscape for a few minutes before her enforced return to Paris where there are more clothes than trees and the streets are like rooms.

The carriage stops by the church. The same Fiat car in which they made the trip to Santa Maria Maggiore is parked in the shade of a plane tree. There is nobody to be seen. They ask the driver to wait. He nods, gets down and lies on the grass by the side of the road. One of the brass lamps on the Fiat is dazzling in the sun. Camille lowers her head and, pointing her parasol towards the ground, opens it; Mathilde points hers at the sky to open it. They walk together round the church.

He is on the north side sitting on a stone bench. He kisses Camille's hand and then immediately takes Mathilde's arm and saying: You are her friend, she confesses to you and so I need not explain what has happened to us. He leads her away towards a path bordered by gravestones. Camille makes as though to follow them. He turns. No, he says, please wait. Sit where I was sitting.

It is very quiet. The doors of the church are locked. There is nobody on the road. It is hard to believe that they have driven no further than the outskirts of the town. To Camille the silence sounds abnormal. She believes that on ordinary mornings carts pass along the road, children play near by, the priest prays in his church, peasants work in the fields. In the silence she can hear the beating of her own heart and his voice, but she cannot distinguish his words.

He is telling Mathilde that he and she will surely meet again and that he will always be in her debt, if she agrees to his plan. He loves Camille: he has never been alone with her: he can no longer write to her: all he asks is that Mathilde take the carriage and wait by the Rosmini College—the driver will know it—where he and Camille will join her by motor car in half an hour. He needs that little time to explain his feelings to the woman with whom he has fallen so desperately in love. He speaks lightly, as though he has no need to convince Mathilde, or as though he knows it is hopeless to try to convince her.

Whilst appealing to Mathilde, he is careful to remain in sight of Camille, to speak conspiratorially in Mathilde's ear, to make Mathilde laugh once or twice, to continue holding her arm and to give their collusion every appearance of intimacy.

The lightness with which he speaks intrigues Mathilde. It does not force her to decide whether he is telling the truth or not. If what he said was too credible, she would be obliged, as Camille's friend, to find it incredible. If what he said was obviously untrue, she would be obliged to tell him so. As it is, the question of the truth of what he is saying does not arise, because in the way he speaks he assumes that she already knows the truth. Which she doesn't. And the fact that she doesn't arouses a very acute curiosity in her. If she cannot discover the truth directly, then Camille must discover it and tell her. The truth, she feels, will not be terrible for, if it were, he would not assume so easily and naturally that she already knows it. She trusts him immediately because he gives her no reason to. It is Maurice that Mathilde does not trust. And in order to convince herself that she is not being reckless on her friend's behalf, she imagines how it would be possible for her to ask Harry, who is in a position to put considerable professional pressure on Maurice, to persuade Maurice to be more reasonable. She says she will take the carriage to the college if Camille agrees.

Camille watches them walking up and down behind the gravestones which, old and eroded, are the shape of half-eaten biscuits. The anomaly of the situation makes Camille angry and impatient. Why, she asks, must she, after all the risks she has taken, sit here whilst Mathilde jokes with him over there? She decides that she must speak to him by herself.

A few minutes later the driver gets up from the grass, rubbing his knees. Mathilde steps into the carriage and waves to Camille. Don't be long, she cries, I can't work miracles. As the carriage, which is crookedly suspended over its back axle, departs down the deserted road, Camille thinks: Mathilde believes that in Paris I may become the mistress of this man with whom I have just agreed to be left alone.

There is a look which can come into the eyes of a woman (and into the eyes of a man, but very rarely) which is without pride or apology, which makes no demand, which promises no adventure. As an expression, signalled by the eyes, it can be intercepted by another; but it is not addressed, in the usual sense of the word, to another: it takes no account of the receiver. It is not a look which can enter into the eyes of a child for children are too ignorant of themselves: nor into the eyes of most men for they are too wary: nor into the eyes of animals because they are unaware of the passing of time. By way of such a look romantic poets thought they saw a path leading straight to a woman's soul. But this is to treat it as though it were transparent, whereas in fact it is the least transparent thing in the world. It is a look which declares itself to be itself; it is like no other look. If it is comparable with anything, it is comparable with the colour of a flower. It is like heliotrope declaring itself blue. In company such looks are quickly extinguished for they encourage neither discourse nor exchange. They constitute social absence.

His desire, his only aim, was to be alone with a woman. No more than that. But they had to be deliberately, not fortuitously, alone. It was insufficient for them to be left alone in a room because they happened to be the last to leave. It had to be a matter of choice. They had to meet in order to be alone. What then followed was a consequence of being alone, not the achievement of any previous plan.

In the company of others women always appeared to him as more or less out of focus. Not because he was unable to concentrate upon them but because they were continuously changing in their own regard as they adapted themselves to the coercions and expectations of the others around them.

He was alone with Camille, walking back to the north side of the church which was in the shade. He took her arm. He could feel with his fingers that it was warmer on the inside than on the outside. He was overcome by a sense of extraordinary inevitability. The feeling did not surprise him. He knew that it would arrive, but he could not summon it at will. He felt the absoluteness of the impossibility of Camille being, in any detail, in the slightest trace, different from what she was; he felt she was envisaged by everything which preceded her in time and everything which was separate from her in space; the place always reserved for her in the world was nothing less than her exact body, her exact nature; her eyes in tender contrast to her mouth, her small breasts, her thin rakelike hands with their bitten fingernails, her way of walking with unusually stiff legs, the unusual warmth of her hair, the hoarseness of her voice, her favourite lines from Mallarmé, the regularity of her smallness, the paleness of—with this concentration of meaning which he experienced as a sense of inevitability, came the onset of sexual desire.

I want to tell you, she said—

Your voice, he interrupted, is also like a cicada, not only a corncrake. Do you know the legend about cicadas? They say they are the souls of poets who cannot keep quiet because, when they were alive, they never wrote the poems they wanted to.

I want to tell you, she repeated, that I love my husband dearly. He is the centre of my life and I am the mother of his children. I consider he was wrong to threaten you, and I want you to know that I gave him no grounds, absolutely no grounds, for believing that he needed to threaten you. He discovered the foolish note you wrote to me—

Foolish? We have met, we are alone, we are talking to each other—and that is all I asked of you. Why was it foolish?

It was foolish to use the words you did, it was foolish to write a note at all.

What foolish words?

Camille stared at an impenetrable cypress tree. Everywhere there was still the same abnormal silence. I do not remember, she said in a hoarse whisper. And saying this she remembered a line by Mallarmé:

> ... *vous mentez, ô fleur nue*
> *De mes lèvres.*

I called you my most desired one, my corn-crake.
That was foolish.
But you are.
The inscriptions on the tombstones were mostly illegible. The letters which were formed with curved lines (like U or G) appeared to be more quickly effaced than those composed of straight lines (N or T).
Then you must go. Please go.
The heat of the morning made anything which was out of reach or sight seem unusually distant.
It was not wrong of your husband to threaten me, he said, he has every reason to be jealous.
He has no reason! I am his wife and I love him. And I cannot he held responsible for your feelings. You are mistaken, that is all—mistaken in me. You are not base. I believe in the nobility of your feelings. And this is what I wanted to tell you, I did not encourage my husband to protect me from you for I don't need any protection. I have known you for two days. Do you really suppose that a woman's affections can be gained in such a short time? In two weeks or two months perhaps. But in two days! You are mistaken. I think you believe life is like that swing you described. It isn't. Talking here we are already running a risk for nothing. There is nothing to be gained. Please take me back to join my friend in the carriage. My husband and I are leaving for Paris this afternoon.

Camille spoke with difficulty. It was no longer easy for her to say these things. Yet she said them with sincerity. She saw renunciation as the only proper way of putting an end to the present situation and of undoing the injustice and indignity of her husband's threats. What she was renouncing was still of little importance. But she believed in destiny. Nothing in her life had led her to believe that she was entirely the mistress of her own fate. She did not think of the future as unmysterious, as entirely foreseeable in the light of decisions made today. She wanted to be able to look back at this moment of genuine renunciation because she considered it a neces-

sary one. But she did not feel compelled to answer for the consequences, expected or unexpected, that might follow from that
moment. They might be beyond her control and she recognized
this with modesty, with hope and with misgivings.

Then I will find you in Paris! he said.
He will shoot you.
Not if you don't betray me.
Betray!
It was foolish to keep the note. In Paris you must be wiser.
In Paris I will refuse to see you.
If there was nothing conspiring against us, he said, we would never
find out what we are each capable of.
You do not know, you cannot know, what I am capable of. Nobody
will ever know. Please take me back.
I think I have dreamt of you all my life without knowing that you
existed. I can even guess what you are going to say now. You are
going to say: you are mistaken.
You are mistaken! she repeated, unable to stop herself, and unable
to repress a laugh.
It was you, Camomille.

By the car he explained to her what she must do with the controls
in the driving seat whilst he cranked the engine. She was pleased to
do what he instructed her to do, for it offered her an opportunity of
showing him that she was capable, that her renunciation was in
no way a disguise for incapacity.

At the end of the bonnet she could see his powerful head and
shoulders lunging from side to side as he turned the crankshaft.
His arms were thin. His forehead was shiny with sweat. After several
unsuccessful turns, the engine started. The whole motor car began
shaking and her gloved hands on the steering wheel shook in time
with the engine. He shouted something which she could not hear.
She had the impression that if she climbed down from the car she
would have to make a small jump from the trembling car into the
absolute stillness of the dust on the road and the walls of the church.
She jumped. On the other side of the car he offered her his hand as
she climbed up into the passenger seat. When she was seated, he
lifted up her arm so that it trailed over the door, then he kissed it
between glove and sleeve. She stared at his bowed head. She saw

her other hand lay itself upon his hair. He gave no sign of having felt her touch.

We will go back by the small road through the Viezzo valley, he said, it is only three or four kilometres longer.

SI TU VEUX NOUS NOUS AIMERONS AVEC
TES LEVRES SANS LE DIRE
                                    Mallarmé

To morality there are no mysteries. That is why there are no moral facts, only moral judgements. Moral judgements require continuity and predictability. A new, profoundly surprising fact cannot be accommodated by morality. It can be ignored or suppressed; but when once its existence has been recognized, its inexplicability makes it impervious to any immediate moral judgement.

She knows that the man driving her away in his car is indifferent to the chaos he is creating in her ordered life. Because of this indifference she wants to see him as an enemy. He is indifferent to the way she has defended him against her husband. He is indifferent to the effort by which she has renounced him. He is indifferent to the happiness with which she has been satisfied. Every reason which she can find to call him an enemy of her interests she welcomes, and with every reason which she finds she becomes more critically conscious of her own life.

The open motor car creates its own cool breeze. It seems to Camille that there is a correspondence between the cool air blowing against her face and neck and arms and the silvery colour of the underside of the leaves continually shifting on the branches of the trees they pass. Between the trees are green slopes of grass. The landscape is in every detail the setting for the conspiracy of their being alone together.

She contrasts his indifference with the love of her husband, her children, her own family. She hears them addressing her by name.

There is no distinction between the name they call her and what they expect from her. Camille is her life.

Camomille, he says. A classmate used to make the same joke at school. There is only the difference of a syllable.

What is it that you love in me? she asks.

Your dreams, your elbows, the doubts at the four corners of your confidence, the unusual warmth of your hair, everything that you want but are frightened of, the smallness of—

I am frightened of nothing in myself and you know nothing about me.

Nothing? I know all that I have written about you.

Who is speaking?

You don't care what happens to me, she insists.

Then why do you ask me?

Because I am curious to see myself through your eyes. I wonder what has misled you.

Nothing has misled me. My whole life has led me to you.

You are as mad as he.

Who?

Maurice and you are both mad.

But not you and I.

He will shoot you in Paris.

He stops the motor car after a bridge, at a point at which a path appears to lead down to a stream.

I will be in Paris in eight days, he says.

She jumps from the running-board of the car into the stillness of the grass and dust. She lands on her stiff legs and, turning round towards him, scowls. Then she runs a few steps towards the wild acacia trees away from the road. All that she has learned of deportment, all that has become the second nature of her movement as a woman, deserts her. She moves like an awkward child, or like an adult overcome by grief.

And if, she cries out, in her hoarse voice, if I say this—she flings out both arms either side of her—this is Paris a week from now! If I do!

She runs on, stumbling a little, between the trees.

He begins to run after her. She hears him and turns round towards him. Near by is a wooden trellis construction over which a thick abandoned vine is growing.

Stay where you are, she cries out, and lunges out of sight behind the trellis towards some trees.

Out of his sight, she stops running. Unhurriedly and pausing from time to time to look around her, she begins to undress. Above the trees, above the near wooded hills which are like fists covered with green fur, she can see improbable peaks with snow upon them. She looks down to negotiate the hooks of her corset.

It is not myself I will give you. Not the self of mine. Or, if I were you, and believe me I can at this moment imagine it as easily as I can turn the palm of my hand upwards or downwards—or if I were you, the self of you. If you want to number me part by part I shall be as any other, for nobody has found the judge of parts, nobody has found the nipple to judge the breast, the brow to measure the light in the eye, the ear to decide the note of the way, the only way, in which I might walk towards you now between the trees. Part by part I am a woman undressing in a clearing like a room by a stream, hidden from you and waiting, who a few minutes ago renounced you, who will return to my children in Paris tonight, who cannot imagine myself other than the loving wife of my husband, who has never before been what I am now. But I am not the sum of my parts. See me as wholly as your own dear life demands that you see yourself. I have as many hairs on the back of my neck as you may have ways of touching me. It is not myself I give you, it is the meeting of the two of us that I offer you. What you offer me is the opportunity for me to offer this. I offer it. I offer it.

She speaks out loud to him: I am waiting here.
The incongruity of her tone of voice does not surprise him. (It is as though she is calling out a little impatiently through an open dressing-room door.) The words employed at such a moment are bound to be incongruous.

She is sitting in the grass. Her hair falls over her shoulders. Her chemise is loose. Her grey skirt and jacket lie folded on the grass with some other garments.

Because Camille has chosen a setting which reminds her of some

Renaissance painting of fauns and nymphs, we are liable to picture her as having the body of a goddess as painted by Titian. This is far from the case. Her arms are thin, her neck knotted and taut, the insides of her thighs have so little flesh upon them that were she standing with her feet together her thighs would scarcely touch each other.

She awaits him as he expected. And yet he is surprised. This combination of surprise and of expectations being precisely fulfilled is unique to moments of sexual passion and is another factor which places them outside the normal course of time. At some moment prior to birth we may, at a level as yet unknown to us, have perceived the whole of our life like that. Before he touches her he knows what touching her will reveal to him. When he touches her he will fully appreciate how alone she has become. Undressing was the act of shedding the interests of those who make up the interests of her life. With her clothes she discarded the men he hates. Her unclothed body is the proof of her solitariness. And it is her solitariness—her solitariness alone—that he recognizes and desires. He has led her from her conjugal bedroom, from the overfurnished apartment, from the street in which the curtained windows are so still that they might be carved out of stone, from the overread pages of Mallarmé, from the clothes which she orders from her costumier and her husband pays for, from the mirrors which are falsely impartial to husband and wife, further and further away from where she belongs until she is herself alone. From that solitude of hers and from his they can now set out. *Andiamo.*

As he stares at her with eyes more intensely fixed than any she has ever imagined, she sees herself as a dryad, alert in a way that is more animal than human, quick, sensitive, fleet-footed, soft-tongued, shameless. She sees him and the dryad together as a couple, and the sight of them fills her with tenderness. The dryad undoes his shirt. She anticipates the dryad offering herself on all fours, face to the ground, and he mounting her like a goat. She crawls on all fours until she is facing his head and then kisses his eyes from above.

Camomille.

The feeling of tenderness wells over and makes it impossible for Camille to imagine anything viewed from a distance; the idea of the dryad is momentarily obliterated. Gradually such moments become longer and longer until the dryad disappears into the smell of the crushed grass and the surrounding silence, never to return, and Camille becomes entirely concentrated in the act of following with her tongue the underseam of the penis of the man over whose thigh her head is hanging.

He is there under her, above her, beside her. He has no claims on her; he has made none. He is there like the trellis with the vine overgrowing it. He is there like a wall against which she could repeatedly bang her head. He is there, outside herself, like everything else in the world which has not claimed a second residence in her consciousness. She has not said to herself that she loves him. He has convinced her of only one thing. Unlike any other man she has ever encountered, he has convinced her that his desire for her —her alone—is absolute, that it is her existence which has created this desire. Formerly she has been aware of men wanting to choose her to satisfy desires already rooted in them, her and not another, because among the women available she has approximated the closest to what they need. Whereas he appears to have no needs. He has convinced her that the penis twitching in the air above her face is the size and colour and warmth that it is entirely because of what he has recognized in her. When he enters her, when this throbbing, cyclamen-headed, silken, apoplectic fifth limb of his reaches as near to her centre as her pelvis will allow, he, in it, will be returning, she believes, to the origin of his desire. The taste of his foreskin and of a single tear of transparent first sperm which has broken over the cyclamen head making its surface even softer to the touch than before, is the taste of herself made flesh in another.

This can never stop, she whispers, slowly and calmly. My love, my love.

They were fucking in the grass. Both half believed that they were no longer lying down but standing up and walking as they fucked; towards the end they began to run through tall wet grass. He had the further illusion that others were running towards him.

All are there. How can I ever open those words to let their original and still potential meaning out? All are there in their own time and at the same time. It is a matter of supreme indifference to me whether the sweet throat is mine or yours. And here, now, here let the word supreme attain its supremacy. It is of no consequence whose is whose. All parts are one. All are there together. All despite all their differences are there together. He joins them. There is no more need. There, desire is its satisfaction, or, perhaps, neither desire nor satisfaction can be said to exist since there is no antinomy between them: every experience becomes the experience of freedom there: freedom there precludes all that is not itself.

He and Camille lay alone, dishevelled, side by side on the slope by the vine. A peasant passing by on the far bank of the stream spotted them although they were lying quite still. He saw a white arm like a statue's and a stockinged foot. The peasant was curious and crouched down to observe what would happen next.

Whom were we walking?
I was a knee which wanted the thigh on the other leg.
The sounds of my most tender words were in your arse.
Your heels were my thumbs.
My buttocks were your palms.
I was hiding in one corner of your mouth. You looked for me there with your tongue. There was nothing to be found.
With your throat swollen, my feet in the pit of my stomach, your legs hollow, my head tugging at your body, I was your penis.
You were the light which falling on the dark petals of your vagina became rose.

The blood-vessel was lifted up in the lock of your flowers.

○

Normally a shooting incident in Domodossola would only have been reported in the local Italian press, but since the town was full of journalists from all over Europe, who were awaiting the death or recovery of Chavez, the story was printed in many different papers. According to their time-honoured tradition when dealing with incidents affecting respectable members of the bourgeoisie, the Swiss newspapers tactfully withheld the full names of those involved.

'The small town of Domodossola was yesterday the scene of a dramatic *crime passionnel*. Monsieur H—, a French businessman with interests in the motor car industry, found himself in the town in connection with the recent triumphal crossing of the Alps by the aviator Geo Chavez. At 3.30pm in the crowded Piazza Mercato, Monsieur H— fired three times with an automatic pistol at Monsieur G, a young Englishman who is likewise said to be a flying enthusiast. The latter had just come out of a fruit shop and was walking in one of the picturesque arcades which border the square. The life of the victim, who was wounded in the shoulder, is not in danger. He was taken immediately to the hospital where the aviator hero is also being treated.

'After the incident Monsieur H— offered no resistance to the police and declared that his only mistake had been to fire from too far away. He claimed that he had already warned the Englishman that he would shoot him if he did not desist from embarrassing and pursuing his wife, Madame H—. "It is an affair," he said, "of elementary honour and I am certain that when the facts have been established, I will be assured of the sympathy of all decent society." The Englishman, although he evidently speaks fluent Italian, declined to answer questions.'

○

On the wall of the old hospital at Domodossola—a new larger hospital has since been built near by—there is a plaque with an inscription which pays tribute to Chavez' heroism and indicates the room on the first floor where he died on 27 September 1910.

All accounts of his last hours suggest that Chavez remained haunted by his flight. He could not understand what still separated him from the life continuing around him: the life which, with all the ardour of his determined youth, he wanted to re-enter. His achievement, in so far as he could separate it from the disaster which had befallen him, only increased the mocking appeal of this life.
'I'm going now. Let's go quickly to Brig.' Vive Chavez! He remembered writing that on his own legs. What had he done wrong? Whether the fault, the transgression, had been technical or moral was by now hopelessly confused in his mind. He tried to recall what he had screamed when he had entered the Gondo. He could not. And he feared that he would not be able to until he had come out of the Gondo. He was still in it.

There is no plaque on the hospital wall to indicate the room, only three windows away, where G. was taken from the operating theatre after a bullet had been removed from his wound. A middle-aged nurse with the complexion of a Neapolitan was washing his face and neck.

For the first time since the shooting, it was comparatively quiet. From his bed he could see the hospital garden. The absolutely still leaves of a willow tree were sharply distinct in the horizontal evening light. It occurred to him how brief moments of drama are; how swiftly order can be re-established. He was reminded of his father's garden in Livorno and the pool with the perch in it. And he remembered the exhilaration with which, in that garden, he had discovered that what mattters is not being dead. He let out his breath in a hiss.

I'm sorry. Did I hurt you?

No, no. I thought of something. He paused a moment. Then, in a lighter voice, he said: Now, you tell me, you are an experienced woman, I can see that, and you are not over-fastidious. Now, would you say I was like the devil?

Shhhhhh! Don't think about such things.

You haven't answered me.

She glanced at the young man's face, leering, and his dark eyes looking at her and she thought of the story of how an outraged husband had tried to shoot him dead and she said: You don't look like a devil to me.

(Later when she told the story she pretended that she replied like that because it is the duty of a nurse to keep a patient calm.)

That is what he called me. But imagine trying to shoot the devil! Do you know the only way to get rid of the devil? Offer him what he asks. Would you do that?

In drying his face with a towel she tried to stop him talking by clapping her hand over his mouth.

Now, would you offer him what he asked? he insisted. It's the only way—even if it's your soul he wants!

It is wrong to blaspheme even in jest. You shouldn't talk like that.

Bo! he cried.

(She confessed later that she had been so surprised that she couldn't help laughing.)

The face of his fiancée who had come from Paris and was sitting by his bed was the length of the Gondo away from Chavez. If he stretched out his arm to touch her, he had the impression that his arm was the sleeve of the Gondo, from which his fingertips, moving round her mouth, could just emerge but not the remainder of his body.

His agony of mind was the result of an axiomatic truth, in which he had believed all his life, having been inexplicably overturned. In face of his courage and his survival without serious wounds, God, nature and the world of men should have found themselves in accord. Why were they not? He had proved his right to succeed and he had been forced to forego it. The wind he so wrongly under-estimated, the mountains, the treacherous icy air, the earth which entered his mouth and now his own blood, his very own body refused to accord him his achievement. Why?

During the night he repeatedly muttered: *Je suis catholique, je suis catholique.*

G. woke up and found himself re-hearing word for word what Camille had said in the motor car on the way back from Domodossola.

I will write to you. Where shall I write to you?

No, do not write. As soon as I arrive in Paris I will give you a sign.

You will be amazed to see what I am capable of. I will astonish you. I shall be cunning. I shall be as cunning as an *avocat.* I will disguise myself. Can you imagine me as a baker? I will come to you disguised as a baker. Or as an old woman. (She laughed a little.) You will be horrified—and then I will take my disguise off and you will see your corn-crake. If Maurice wants to kill me, he can. I am not afraid. But it is you he will try to kill. It is you who must wear a disguise. What would suit you? You might be a Spaniard. A Spanish priest! It must be something unlike you, so that I can hardly believe —but now I would know you, however you were disguised, I would recognize you anywhere, and Maurice would recognize you because of the light in my eyes when I saw you. Supposing you knew afterwards you must die? And I too knew that you must die? I wouldn't try to stop you now. Now I wouldn't. Before, I would have done. I would have tried to save you. I would have refused you. Perhaps I would have been afraid myself. I know now. I would welcome you. That is what you would want. And you would want me then under threat of death more than you have wanted any woman. And afterwards I would die with you—happy.

Next day, Chavez' last words, whose meaning cannot be interpreted, were: *Non, non, je ne meurs pas . . . meurs pas.*

○

Weymann came into the room with a pained expression on his

face. He greeted G. coolly and then went and stood by the window, through which he kept looking out as though something surprising were happening on the lawn below.

The funeral is tomorrow, Weymann said.

I hear everything from the corridor. The walls aren't very thick here. He died at three o'clock yesterday afternoon.

The whole town is in mourning, said Weymann.

If Hennequin had been a better shot, we could have had a double funeral!

That is a remark in very poor taste.

It would have been my funeral, not yours. Why are you so solemn?

Because it is a solemn occasion and your—your—he struggled for the right word and looked out on the invisible events taking place on the lawn below—your philanderings are most inappropriate. The whole town is in mourning. The factories have stopped work.

It will be like an opera by Verdi. The Italians love deaths. Not Death but deaths. Have you noticed?

They feel the tragedy of the occasion.

You said he was an idiot.

That was before I knew he was dying.

Does it make any difference? He asked this in a gentler voice, and Weymann, somewhat mollified, left the window and approached the bed.

He has passed over into the sky, said Weymann in the voice of the priest whom he often resembled, a bit of the sky which the rest of us, who are still alive, call the paradise of lost flyers.

I shall be out of here by tonight and then I will be able to pay my respects too. Have the Hennequins left?

I must tell you that the whole affair in which you were involved has been a considerable embarrassment to all of us. Scenes like the one you provoked give the flying community a bad name. It makes us out to be adventurers—

But aren't you?

You know exactly what I mean.

Tell me, have they gone back to Paris?

Madame Hennequin was in a state of collapse, if it gives you any satisfaction to know that.

And Monsieur?

He had to be constrained from coming to find you in hospital. The second time he wouldn't miss, he said.

You should have let him come. I should have liked to have seen him again.

Suddenly Weymann was angry. His thin face became red and his eyes protruded as he stared at the figure in the bed: Yes, I think we should have let him come. What are you doing? What are you playing at? Let me tell you something. This town is full of men. Tomorrow it will be fuller—men coming from all over the world to pay their homage to the magnificent contribution, the historic courage of Geo. Do you know there are peasants who have walked from the mountain villages into town today to line up and pay their last tributes to the man they loved. You should look at their faces. You might learn a little modesty. You might see what it means to be offered hope for your children after a lifetime of toil and sacrifice. You might understand what achievement is. And amongst these men, these men who fill the town like pilgrims and lend it their own dignity, there is a little—there is a little runt!

He banged the door and was gone.

O

The crowd made the town look like a village. Figures in black pressed against the walls of the narrow streets. In an open doorway several children were barred and held back by women with straight rigid arms, lest they run out into the street as the procession passed and by this single act diminish the long-lasting gravity of the moment. From first-floor windows and from the balconies above hung improvised flags of black crêpe and tricolours with black upon them. It was sunny, The streets through which the cortège would not pass were deserted. All shops and offices were shut. The bells in the campanile tolled very slowly. The last note of each peal seeped almost completely away before the next refilled the silence. The sound was such that even in the arcade from where you could see neither sky nor mountains you were reminded of solitude. In the precincts of the Piazza Mercato there was an unusually strong smell of horses and leather, for carriages and carts had brought mourners from all over the countryside and many had been left there, unattended, while the mourners followed the coffin on foot.

The stationmaster, wearing a gold-braided cap and a long coat, glanced once more at his own reflection in the glass doors of the waiting-room. It was not a question of vanity at this moment but of vocation; in the same spirit an actor may glance in a mirror before going on stage. Within the waiting-room journalists from all over Europe jostled to book their telephone lines to their capitals.

Assembled outside the hospital the town band began to play a funeral march. The cortège moved off, shuffling at first. In front of the four horses of the hearse, girls in white veils strewed tuberoses on the cobbles and dust. Boys darted back and forth between the main street-corners and the head of the procession to keep the girls supplied with baskets of flowers. The Mayor had announced that the cost of the funeral would be met by the municipality. When they were standing upright, one girl might timidly smile at another; but when they were strewing the flowers on the road, bending forward as if trying to cast a net in a fast-flowing stream, they did so with grave, concentrated expressions, one with her teeth biting her lower lip.

Close behind the hearse walked the hero's grandmother, brother, fiancée and family friends. The fiancée held her head high with the air of a wife following a cart which is taking her husband, a heretic, to his execution; she defied the occasion; she defied the forces which had killed him. Geo's brother, a rich young banker, walked with his head down, looking at the flowers on the road, many as yet untrampled. The grandmother walked with a stick, jabbing the ground. Sometimes her stick skewered a flower.

Behind the family came the diplomats, the senators, Chavez' fellow pilots, the Mayor, the journalists, the representatives of aircraft-engine firms, the local rich. And after a discrete gap there was the straggling procession of thousands, most of whom had seen Chavez when he first appeared, triumphant, on their side of the mountain, when he was coming down to land in the field where Duray had pegged out the white cross in calico. At this sight of a victory being apparently so easily gained, in face of the impossible being so quickly transformed into the possible, they had felt elated. In the newspapers they had read, or had heard others read, sentences like: The great utopia of yesterday has become reality. And so some had asked themselves: Why should we too not achieve what we wish? Those who were in the habit of answering such speculative questions had given their usual answers. The rich must be overthrown. Private property must be destroyed. Others had maintained that Italy must be united, must be given Trieste, must have more colonies; only then would all Italians fulfil their destiny. To those who asked, all the answers seemed theoretical. But the question had remained.

Now with the unexpected death of Chavez, the question was closed. It was as they had always been taught. Achievements are never easy. There is a price to pay for daring. The true heroes are dead ones. When what is desired is immoderate, it lies beyond death. The choice is between accepting life as it is and dying a hero's death.

Outside the Duomo the speeches began. The crowd listened in a mood of acknowledgement and acceptance. The young, faced with the familiar choice, chose once again in their imagination heroic death. Their elders looked back on their lives, gently, tenderly, as they might look at their own children, trying to find in them proof that a certain kind of cunning and a certain kind of modesty offer the best means for tricking and coaxing the best out of life: life which, when all is said and done, is better than being dead, although the naive courage of the dead hero touches them profoundly because they too were naive like him, and they know full well that the lessons which rid them of their naivety were not ideal, were not what they once wished. The young among the crowd celebrated the heroism of early death; their elders recalled the price of survival.

The Peruvian Ambassador: I am proud to be your compatriot, O Chavez, and I have come to place on your coffin your own country's homage. We leave to your dear ones the sad duty of tears: strong nations must neither complain nor weep: they can only exalt and glorify their sons who, like you, Chavez, sacrifice their life for the bright light of an ideal . . .

There was a commotion in the front ranks of the crowd drawn up in a semi-circle round the hearse and the steps of the Duomo. A dozen men pushed their way forward and mounted the steps. They were dressed like Alpine guides and each pair of them carried an object like a stretcher. On these stretchers were arranged massed patterns of wild flowers—edelweiss, arnica, forget-me-nots and red rhododendrons. They placed the stretchers on either side of the church door. As they came down, one of the men shouted out: Above four thousand metres we'll see you in the air! Then he slapped his own cheek several times.

The Peruvian Ambassador: From your earliest childhood you were a master of energy, and for us your death is a glorious lesson. You were strong, you were great; above the eternal snows, amid the sublime peaks, you flew upon your fragile machine, a token of the audacity and genius of man.

The Mayor announced that a piazza would be named after the dead aviator.

Inside the Duomo there was a short service for Chavez' family and the distinguished foreign visitors. They remained standing, staring straight ahead of them into the half-light from which gold objects emerged without glitter. They felt the cold air rising from the stones. It is here, not in the streets strewn with flowers outside, that the devout try to relinquish the blind will to live.

The canon: Chavez, the bold and audacious youth who had the fabulous vision of the Alps conquered and fleeing under his glance; the proud, courageous youth whom we saw soaring through the air above us, crossing our valleys more swiftly than an eagle: Chavez, who made us tremble with enthusiasm in anticipation of the imminent triumph—Chavez is no more.

Among the congregation in the cathedral, G. stood near Monsieur Schuwey and Mathilde Le Diraison. His thoughts drifted towards the Hennequins in Paris. Camille was waiting to become his mistress. He doubted whether Monsieur Hennequin would shoot again; he had failed to prevent his wife from cuckolding him and he had failed to avenge himself: after the first time the number of subsequent times made little difference. Taking note of Camille's determination in the matter, he would concede his wife's right to a lover provided he suffered no inconvenience and provided she realized that his tolerance was conditional upon her curbing her more extravagant tastes, and upon her never questioning his own arrangements. Camille, in an access of gratitude, would find it in herself to love both husband and lover—in different ways. She would submit to Monsieur Hennequin's occasional conjugal demands with the reservation in her own mind that she could only truly belong to her lover. She would lend herself to her husband for her lover's sake.

A mass of candles had been lit for Chavez. The flames created their own air currents so that when a group of them flickered and leaned in one direction, this disturbed another group, making them blow inwards together as if in panic to confer, and then this agitation provoked other flames to burn a little higher, which caused yet others to flatten themselves and circle, unsteadily, round their wicks as if searching for air.

For her husband's sake she would demand from her lover discretion, punctuality and a certain financial arrangement. She would no longer read Mallarmé for it might remind her too vividly of her approach to that moment when, for the first and only time, she made herself alone, as he was alone. Perhaps one day she would become enthusiastic about another, more sober poet. Time would pass. Everybody would be accommodated. Through boredom or on a sentimental impulse, Camille would give herself, without her accustomed reserve, to Monsieur Hennequin and afterwards she would feel that it was to her husband that she really belonged. But no sooner would she feel this than she would rush to her lover begging him to re-take her and insisting that she wanted to belong to him and to nobody else. Once convinced that she had become her lover's, she would await an opportunity—which might take months during which time she would occupy herself with the lives of her children and friends—an opportunity to test her attachment by once more offering herself to her husband. And so she would traffic to and fro, each oscillation marked by apparently inexplicable excitability. At first she would await re-possession by her lover far more impatiently than by Monsieur Hennequin. But gradually, so that she might feel, as she would on peaceful days, that she belonged to them both and to her almost grown-up children more than to either, she would commend to her lover more wit and less passion. Ten years later, if she were fortunate, she might acquire a second lover and the first would be cast, with certain minor variations, in the role of the original husband. If she were less fortunate, she would arrange occasional meetings between Monsieur Hennequin, who by then would have a place on the managing board of Peugeot, and her lover, so that by talk and reminiscence she might belong to them both. In old age she would catch sight of herself in a mirror, unawares, solitary, unowned, but then she would think of death: death before whom you have no choice but to make yourself alone.

The canon: He ascended to heaven and he came down having achieved the most dramatic victory yet on the long road of civilization's conquest. A pioneer, he has advanced the progress of man. Imagine the future that his glorious achievement has opened to us — nation will no longer be separated from nation, the advantages of civilization will reach the furthest corners of the earth . . .

Mathilde Le Diraison noticed him standing a few pews away. His arm was in a black sling. She had spoken briefly with Camille before her departure for Paris. Together they had decided that he was a Don Juan, that already in his life there must have been hundreds of women. But it makes no difference, Camille had˙ cried, it makes no difference to know that.

Mathilde Le Diraison asked herself two questions. What was his secret, why had Camille succumbed so quickly? The second question concerned herself. What would it mean if, after loving hundreds of women, he made no attempt to approach her? The two questions were intertwined like the strands of the red silk rope which hung across the end of the pew and which she continually flicked with her fingers so that it kept swinging.

She had a face which might be considered stupid. It was the face of a person, slow to go beyond the immediate, who had no particular wish or talent for abandoning herself to flights of fantasy or of deep emotion. At any moment her face declared: WHAT IS HAPPENING IS HAPPENING TO ME, TO ME, TO ME.

The swinging red silk rope caught G.'s eye. He made his plans quickly. He would go to Paris, visit the Hennequins, make a point of ignoring Camille, reassure the husband and would quickly begin an obvious, public affair with Mathilde Le Diraison. In this way he would avenge himself on Hennequin by making the whole shooting incident appear ridiculous, a question of a doubtful flirtation on the part of his wife which, unfortunately for Hennequin, she was incapable of sustaining; and he would disabuse Camille of her fond illusion that passion can be regulated and that a lover can be something different from a second husband. He would see to it that the affair was as brief as possible and afterwards he would disappear from their circle. He regretted that between Monsieur Schuwey and Mathilde Le Diraison there was scarcely more than a purely contractual relationship. But he supposed that even Schuwey must have some pride invested in the woman he paid to be with him. He would discover where.

. . . He has fallen, but he has fallen as a hero who has accomplished a great feat, which everyone thought impossible and mad. Honour and glory to him!

As they came out of the Duomo, the mourners screwed up their eyes against the sunlight and bowed their heads. They had the air of having partaken of some secret which they could not share; the more so because, for those who had remained outside, the solemnity of the occasion was lessening. Boys handed more baskets of tuberoses to the girls in white. Some of the girls were laughing. The band struck up another funeral march and the procession slowly moved off towards the station.

A schoolmaster explained that the guide from Formazza who had slapped his own cheek had meant that the spirit of Chavez would live in the mountain air so that, high up, climbers would feel his spirit on their cheeks like you can feel the wind or the heat of the sun.

The train waited silently. It was the second time a train on this line had been specially stopped for Chavez. The pall-bearers who carried the coffin from the hearse to the train were all aviators, among them Paulhan. The station master saluted as they passed. The journalists were already telephoning. The girls in white veils lined the platform. Suddenly the locomotive gave a shrill prolonged whistle.

He thought again of Camille. Not Camille as she would be when he saw her in Paris but Camille as she had been when she challenged him to come to Paris under threat of death, a threat in which he could no longer believe but in which at that moment, before her husband had failed to kill him at point-blank range, he could still believe. She had offered this challenge like an invitation. And in issuing this invitation she had spoken, as no woman had spoken to him before, with the unconfoundable authority, the distance, the astonishing familiarity of a sibyl. Had she been right not only about him but also about her husband, he would have immediately accepted.

The whistle, arranged by the station master and the engine driver as a salute to the hero at the beginning of his last journey, was unlike any of the other sounds which had been heard that morning. It had no resonance, no echo, no meaning. It was a squeal without a soul, like the squeal of a saw. Long after everyone expected it to stop, it continued. It drove out every thought except the anticipatory one that surely it must stop now. Now! Now!

Chavez' grandmother banged her stick up and down on the platform, but it was impossible to know whether she did this in anger at such an inappropriate initiative being taken by an engine driver, or in the agitation of unbounded grief.

4.

7.

Nuša considered that G. was unlike most other men. She was apparently alone and yet he did not approach her as though she were a prostitute. He said he was Italian but he was polite to her. (He must be, she decided, an Italian from far away.) He was very well dressed yet he suggested that they should sit down on a stone seat together. He said the seat was over two thousand years old. He did not try to touch her except when he took her hand to help her up the steps to the seat. (She was prepared to shout as soon as they sat down but there was no need.) I come here every day at this time, he said, why do you come here? She was about to say she had come with her brother when it suddenly occurred to her that he might be a police agent. I come here, he continued, because I hate Christian tombs. This remark mystified her. Then he spoke normally about the weather and Trieste and the war.

After a while he asked her where she came from. The question seemed harmless and she told him she was born in the Karst. In that case, he said, please say something to me in Slovene. She said in Slovene: It is sunny today. He asked her to say something longer. She said: Most Italians despise our language. She said this loudly, with a certain defiance in her voice. She wondered whether he could understand, but he continued to smile. Say something more, he asked, tell me a story or whatever comes into your mind. She asked him if he could understand what she said. He smiled directly at her. I promise you, he said, not a word; your secrets are safe. She could think of nothing to say. He waited and then he looked at her with raised eyebrows to express surprise at her silence. She said in Slovene: You see the cat over there in the grass?

She stopped and put a hand to the shoulder of her blouse. She had large arms and hands. When either walking or sitting, the way she held her shoulders and neck gave the impression that her whole body was leaning very slightly backwards. In another life this would have given her a somewhat imperious air.

It is not a place I like, she said. I would not come here by myself. She stopped, alarmed that she had inadvertently betrayed the fact that she had come here with her brother. Then she remembered that she was talking in Slovene. If I found one of these broken stones in one of my uncle's fields, I would say it was disgusting and throw it away. I have heard people say they are worth a lot of money. But if they are worth a lot of money, why do they leave them here lying in the grass? If they were precious, they would have taken them to Vienna. Over there by the arch there are several plum trees, she continued, people say if the war goes on the city will starve; they will take everything to Vienna.

You speak beautifully, he told her. It is our language, she said, but she had to say it in Italian. He asked her where she worked. In a factory. What do you make? It is a jute mill, she replied. Have you worked there long? Three months. It smells of fish which is bad. Why fish? It is the oil used on the jute to make it soft and mixed with the water.

As they talked, different suspicions occurred to her. Again, that he was a police agent for the Austrians. That he was mad—this garden made her think of madness. That he intended to offer her a job as a servant in his house. (She would never accept this.) That he was a 'friend' from abroad who was waiting to make contact with her brother.

Her brother, Bojan, was somewhere else in the overgrown garden of the Museo Lapidario. Since his return he had come here every Sunday, and sometimes she accompanied him. He came to meet his friends because the museum garden was usually deserted and on Sundays there was no entrance fee. They called it Hölderlin's garden, and Bojan explained to Nuša that Hölderlin was a German poet who loved Greece and wrote an epic about a Greek patriot, a great hero, who took part in a rising against the Turks, like the Serbs had done, but that Hölderlin lived too long and had gone mad. A broken stone foot, always on its side in the grass, and a child's white body without arms, propped against a wall, made the German poet's madness more credible to Nuša.

At a time when national independence has become or is becoming a conscious issue, one may find in an undeveloped and colonized society, within one family and even within one generation, extraordinary differences of knowledge and sophistication; yet such differences do not necessarily constitute a barrier. The one who has received a higher education at the hands of the imperial power (for there is no other education available) is aware of how consistently his own people's history and culture have been denied, and he values in his own family the vestiges of the traditions which have been suppressed; at the same time the other members of the family may see in him a leader against their foreign oppressors whom until now they have only been able to fear and hate dumbly. Educated and ignorant share the same ideals. The difference between them becomes a proof of the injustice they have suffered together and of the rightness of those ideals. Ideas become inseparable from aspirations.

Nuša was taught to read by her brother, who was two years older, when she was twelve. At that time she lived in the village where her father was a peasant.

The Karst is composed of high, hard limestone ridges and much of the land is uncultivable. It is a mineral landscape, offered up to the sky without much covering. The rock is porous and there are many caves. She remembered her brother drawing a map which showed all the caves he knew. He gave each one the name of one of his friends : Kajetan, Edvard, Rudi, Tomaz. The chasms, gulleys and loose rocks of the Karst make you think of the remains of a city constructed without geometry or man. On the coast where the ridges of limestone descend to the sea, there is the modern city of Trieste, most of it built in the 1840s to realize the dream of Baron Bruck, the Minister of Finance in Vienna, who needed a large southern port for his proposed German-speaking 'Empire of Seventy Millions'. Between outcrops and steep slopes of scrub, there are small hidden valleys and hollows, painstakingly cultivated as fields and vineyards.

Nuša's father had three cows and he sold fruit and flowers to the markets in Trieste. Through the help of a local schoolmaster, Bojan obtained a place in the Realgymnasium in the city. When Nuša was sixteen her mother died. The father was disconsolate and Nuša was unable to take her mother's place; she was moody and her father accused her of being too talkative. (Her brother had encouraged her to talk even when nothing practical depended upon it, but in this, unlike her reading, nobody else in the village encouraged her.) The following year, 1913, her father died. She went to work in Trieste as a maid for an Italian family.

After 1920 when Trieste was Italian and the Fascists had forbidden the Slovene language to be used in any public situation, an Italian doctor was asked: But how can the peasants explain their symptoms to you if they don't know Italian? The doctor replied: A cow doesn't have to explain its symptoms to a veterinary surgeon.

Nuša's spoken Italian improved but she left the family and found a job in a warehouse. Bojan went to the School of Commerce in Ljubljana where he earned his living as a waiter by day and studied at night. When he received his diploma he went to work in Vienna for a firm which imported non-ferrous metals. Ever since attending the School of Commerce in Ljubljana he had been a member of a small, clandestine group of students and secondary-school pupils associated with the Young Bosnians.

Two months earlier, in March 1915, he had returned to work in the Trieste branch of the firm.

The sight of his sister sitting on a kind of throne beside an unknown, conspicuously well-dressed man, shocked Bojan. He had not expected anybody else to be there. He had pictured his sister walking slowly by herself among the fruit trees. In addition, this man was morally unprepossessing. He might be an Austrian (Bojan was too far away to hear what kind of Italian he spoke). He was obviously rich. He had a cunning, disenchanted face. Seated together on the carved stone seat raised up on a dais, overhung by a fig tree, the two of them looked like characters in an illustrated story of some cheap Viennese magazine. Their difference of class, compounded

with the fact that they were man and woman, precluded any innocent interpretation. The degree to which the man's clothes were
spotless and elegant was an index of his inner corruption; just as
his sister's skirt and blouse and the scarf tied round her head
were signs, despite her own will, of her easy availability. Bojan
tried to argue that Nuša might have a good reason for talking with
such a man; yet the way the man regarded her was too eloquent to
be ignored. The fact that his sister could provoke such looks made
him angry. He asked himself how she had lived during the years he
was away. She was too large, he thought: she filled her clothes too
obviously, it was a form of immodesty. Why was she so large? Why
did she continue to grow large long after most girls stop? He could
not avoid the suspicion that it was a question of will. In accordance
with a precept of the Young Bosnians, Bojan had vowed to abstain
from sexual relations and he knew how important it was to develop
the will. She did not wish sufficiently strongly to preserve her innocence. Her innocence as a girl, when he taught her to read, had
become fixed in his mind as an ideal. Caught between his anger
and an onrush of tenderness released by the memory of his sister's
soul, which could not have entirely changed, he ran forward into
the detestable, cheap, soulless illustration. He ran lightly on his
feet, like a messenger who may have a long distance before him. On
reaching the steps he did not mount them, but came to a halt,
stood like a soldier and addressed the man in formal Italian: You
must forgive us, sir, but I and my sister are already late. Then in
Slovene he said: Nuša, please come immediately.

She rose and followed her brother.

The Young Bosnians named themselves after *La Giovane Italia*,
formed by Mazzini in 1831 to fight for an independent republican
Italy. The aim of the Young Bosnians was to liberate the Southern
Slavs (in what is now Yugoslavia) from the domination of the
Hapsburgs. Groups were strongest in Bosnia and Herzogovina — par-
ticularly after these two provinces were annexed by Austro-
Hungary in 1908; but they also existed in Dalmatia, Croatia, and
Slovenia. They were terrorists and their principal political weapon
was assassination.

The assassination of a foreign tyrant or his representative served two purposes. It reaffirmed the natural law of justice. It demonstrated that even crimes committed in the name of order and progress would not go forever unavenged: crimes of coercion, exploitation, oppression, false testimony, intimidation, administrative indifference. But above all, the crime of denying a people their identity. The crime of compelling a people to judge themselves by the criteria of their oppressors and so to find themselves inferior, helpless, and wanting. The justice of natural law demanded that the innumerable victims of these crimes in the past be redeemed. The act of political assassination might also rouse the living and make them realize that the power of the Empire was not absolute, that death, for once serving justice and not indifferent to it, could question that power. If the example of the assassin was followed by the mass of his people, they would rise up against their foreign oppressors and throw them out. To do this was no more impossible than killing a tyrant in public in the street.

'There is no duty more sacred in the world,' wrote Mazzini, 'than that of the conspirator who sets out to avenge humanity and to become an apostle of natural law.'

On 2 June 1914 Francis Ferdinand, heir to the Hapsburg throne, was shot dead with his wife, as they drove through Sarajevo in an open limousine, by Gavrilo Princip, a Young Bosnian of nineteen.

Six other Young Bosnians were in the crowd waiting to assassinate the archduke. For different reasons five of them failed to act. But the sixth, Nedeljko Cabrinovič, threw a bomb. It exploded behind the royal car wounding several people in the crowd but leaving the heir presumptive unhurt. Cabrinovič tried to kill himself on the spot by taking poison and jumping into the river. The dose of poison was too weak. Hauled out of the river, he was asked who he was. I am a Serbian hero, he replied.

Earlier the same morning Cabrinovič went to a photographer's shop and had his portrait taken with a school friend. He ordered six prints of the photograph. They would be ready in an hour. He asked his friend to send the photographs later the same day to addresses which he gave him. At the trial—where there were twenty-five accused—the Judge was perplexed by this story of the photographs.

I thought posterity, explained Cabrinovič, should have a photo of me taken on that day.

One of the photographs was sent to a certain Vuzin Runič in Trieste. Cabrinovič had worked in Trieste in a printer's shop until October 1913. He had left Trieste saying: You'll hear of me again. Wait and see what happens when certain people with red stripes down their trousers and helmets with feathers on their heads come to Sarajevo!

Shortly after his return to Trieste, Bojan took this photograph out of his wallet and asked Nuša if she knew who it was of. She shook her head. Then he told her his name. And now, Bojan said, he is dying, dying in chains of cold and damp and starvation. The conditions where he is are so bad that even the gaolers fall ill there. His chains weigh ten kilograms. At night there's ice on the floor of the cell. Gavrilo is there too. But the prisoners are in solitary confinement day and night. Nedeljko was willing to die. We are all willing to die. Why did they not execute him? Because our imperial and royal majesty prefers his prisoners to die slowly in agony.

Nuša saw a photograph of two young men in dark suits and stiff white collars. They wore the same kind of clothes as her brother. Nedeljko was on the left. He had black hair, dark eyebrows and a moustache. His friend beside him had placed his hand on his shoulder.

When the photograph was taken, said Bojan, he didn't expect to live for more than three hours. Everything was badly arranged—including the poison.

Sometimes Nuša was disturbed by what her brother said; he spoke too quickly of too many things.

The expression on Cabrinovič's face is grave but calm. It is his friend that looks determined; for Cabrinovič there is nothing more to decide (or so he believes at the moment the photograph is being taken, the moment which he intends to represent his whole life). He has chosen his destiny. And if, in the next hour, he should hesitate, his portrait will be there, already developed, printed in black and white, forbidding him to relent.

I despise the dust of which I am composed: anyone can pursue and put an end to this dust. But I defy anybody to snatch from me what I have given myself, an independent life in the sky of the centuries.

Nuša thought the photograph was like a photograph on the headstone of a grave. She had never seen any of these in the village cemetery. But in the Cimitero di S. Anna in Trieste there were many. The only difference was that being out in all weathers they were more faded. Looking at the photograph she knew that whatever her brother or his friends asked her to do, she would do, because they were heroes, and because, flowing through her large body, mixed with her blood, there was something unchanging, which each of them loved, not in her but in itself, and which each of them was prepared to die for.

Princip and his accomplices wished by an irrevocable act to draw attention to an incontestable reality: the wretchedness of the Southern Slavs under Hapsburg rule. Their act, however, was interpreted in terms of the phantasmagoric unrealities of Great Power diplomacy. Austria maintained, without evidence, that the Serbian government was involved in the plot. Russia, Germany, France, Britain took up their respective positions. The words their ministers dictated and the orders they issued referred to a view of war and of national interests which no longer had any basis in reality. Not one of them foresaw the simplest facts about the war they were about to launch. Moltke, the German commander-in-chief, who was perhaps the least deceived, said that nothing could be foreseen.

Have you ever heard an artillery barrage? asked Bojan.
I have stayed here.
You think your eardrums are going to break.
Bojan, what?
When you hear an artillery barrage you think: it's enough to wake up the damned in hell. But you're wrong. The noise of the artillery is the noise of the nations snoring in their sleep. And a few poets and revolutionaries suffer from insomnia. What is happening to the world, Nuša, has never happened before.
What will you do? asked Nuša anxiously.
I will leave soon. Even non-ferrous metals won't save me from the draft much longer. I will go to Paris.
Paris!

Vladimir Gacinovič is there and I want to see him. We must correct our mistakes. We must be ready for when the war ends.

They will arrest you in France.

All I need is an Italian passport. Hundreds of Italians are crossing the frontier illegally all the time, to avoid the army. I will go with them. But if, unlike them, I have an Italian passport, I can go further.

The Museo Lapidario is near the castle on the hill of St Giusto which overlooks the whole bay of Trieste. From the top of the hill several narrow streets descend towards the southeast. Nuša is walking with long strides, letting the soles of her feet bang against the cobbles and leaning back against the gradient. Her skirt billows like a heavy flag. Her large arms swing a little across her body. When I reach the Corso, she says to herself, I will walk like somebody from the city.

She believes that Bojan is far-seeing: he can see all that she cannot. He and his friends acclaim today the good which the rest of the world will only acclaim tomorrow; they condemn the evils to which everybody today turns a blind eye and which in the future will incur the wrath of all. She believes, too, that Bojan is incapable of being unjust. He is willing to die for justice.

She passes a trattoria from which the smell of fried batter is wafted and the noise of people laughing. She stops to look through the open door. At the far end of the eating room a group of Italians are seated round a large table on which many plates, half-empty carafes of wine, a bundled napkin, broken rolls of white bread are strewn in the oddly suspended disorder which may descend upon a table when lunch continues into the late afternoon and nobody wants to leave. If I went in there, Nuša thinks, and started to sing, they would fall silent and afterwards they might give me money because they have eaten well and it is Sunday; but it would have to be an Italian song. She dares herself to try. Before she has resolved to do so, one of the Italians turns round and beckons her to come in from the doorway. She hurries on.

She wonders whether their ability to judge and their love of justice comes from the many books Bojan and his friends read or whether it is their ability to judge which enables them to find and choose the books. She admires their patience. She has seen them pass hours with books in front of their faces. They take no notice of anything else in the room. You have to move round them as though they are trees which have grown up through the floorboards. And then suddenly one of them comes to the end of his patience. He might have been struck by lightning. He throws the book on the table, leaps to his feet and shouts something like: We must act now. Already too much time has gone by! Sometimes the others stand up, equally excited, questioning each other with their eyes. Then, without a word, they put on their coats and caps and go out. Once she looked at a book left on the table. It was written in German which she could not read.

The street turns and becomes on one side like a bridge from which one can look down on the buildings of the city centre, around the Exchange. Most of them are the sepia colour of the wood of cigar boxes. Every window and doorway has its Corinthian pilasters, architrave and pediment. The German-speaking Empire of Seventy Millions was meant to preserve the heritage of Classical Greece. Its authority was carved and moulded upon the façades of its port.

Nuša begins to sing in her head one of her favourite songs she would not have sung to the party in the trattoria. It is a song about a young man who crosses range after range of mountains but who continually promises that he will come back to his mother in the village. Irresistibly the tune prompts her throat and opens her mouth and in a moment Nuša is singing out loud. Her walk changes. She ambles. One hand she clenches and the other she opens. With the open hand she combs the air and with the closed one she slowly beats upon it. She imagines, as always during this song, a stream flowing between rocks. The clearness of the water with its silver edges which undulate in the mountain light like lines of millions of silver pins round the hems of skirts is what she sometimes thinks of, faced with the jute, saturated in its oily slush. She passes an old couple proceeding very slowly down the hill. The wife holds the husband's arm and on his other side he keeps within touching distance of the wall. There is a connection between the way they walk and the little they eat. As a child in the village Nuša never saw such old people. There, the old were either housebound or robust; either they awaited visits or else they were sturdy and could make visits themselves. The old woman, on hearing Nuša singing, says in Slovene: Good, my little one! It's Sunday, isn't it?

Nuša recalls Bojan's reproaches. As soon as they left the museum garden, he began to scold her. He said she was losing her self-respect. He said it was despicable to let oneself become a victim. He told her men like the Italian wanted to make her into a prostitute. What do they call us? he asked. They call us *Sc'iavi!* don't they? And they laugh like thunder at their joke! (*Schiavi* in Italian means Slavs; *sc'iavi* means slaves.) By agreeing to sit down with such a man, he said, you show you are willing to become a slave. Do you remember the summer when I came home, he said, and we read Preseren together and you declared you would like to live like he wrote? Your soul, he said, can't have changed, but then you lived in a village; now you live in this city—this city without a soul, this city with a German mind and an Italian stomach—and here you must question everything you do if you want to live in the way we once aspired to, which is the only way worthy of modern men and of women who are the equals of men. To be found laughing with an Italian who has accosted you in a public garden is a long way from Preseren, he added.

Later, when he was calmer and they were sitting a little apart from his friends on the grass near the castle, he asked Nuša whether she had ever thought of getting married. She shook her head. He seemed pleased by her answer. From where they were sitting they could see the three hills on the slopes of which Trieste is built. The three hills are bracketed together by the sea. There was a very gentle breeze. The leaves of a tree were slightly agitated so that their shadows on the ground shifted quickly, like coins falling or rolling, yet the breeze was not rough enough to sway the branches. Nuša noticed none of this but she felt a very slight breath of wind on one side of her face because it was hot where she had blushed at her brother's anger. The time will soon come, Bojan said, when we will break out from this anachronism (she did not know the word), we will be free—and then will be the time to marry and have children, the free sons and daughters of our own country. To have children now, Bojan said, is to breed soldiers and slaves for those who tyrannize the world.

The Corso is almost deserted. All the large streets have a neglected air. Since the outbreak of war the trade of the city has disastrously declined. There is considerable unemployment. The port handles only a fraction of the shipping it was built for. Nuša stops before a dress displayed in a shop window. Her hair, still invisible beneath her scarf, is fair, the colour of dark honey. She can see the colour of her hair as though it were on a white cloth in front of her. The dress is in *crêpe de chine*.

When the right time according to Bojan has come to marry and have children, will she and her friends each have a dress like this? As soon as she imagines asking Bojan the question, she becomes ashamed of it because she knows he would consider it frivolous. She frowns. She can see a dim reflexion of herself in the shop window. She has strong shoulders and large hips. The lower part of her face is soft and large like her bosom. But her forehead is wide and hard. She is standing solidly on her feet. She cannot see her eyes, but she does not appear to herself to be frivolous. Bojan's reproaches about her conduct in the garden now strike her as undeserved. He had no idea, she says looking hard at her reflexion, what I had in mind. And at this moment a new idea enters her mind. She sees how, out of the very incident which led Bojan to reproach her, she can prove herself to him.

Leaving the Corso, she makes her way through many side streets to the Via dell'Industria where she lives. If only, if only, she prays as she walks, it is true that the Italian stranger goes to Hölderlin's garden every day at noon.

O

When G. left the museum garden he walked in the opposite direction from Nuša; he made his way north-west and she south-east.

Those were the significant geographical co-ordinates of the city. Trieste was considered the last station of modern Europe; southeast lay the Balkans, the Near East and Asia leading imperceptibly, according to West Europeans, from one to the other, from ignorance to cruelty, from barbarism to famine. It was the last city—or the first, depending on which way you were travelling or fleeing—where the virtues of European protocol, honour and production could almost be taken for granted. On this one point both the Austrians and

Italians of Trieste were agreed. And the crucial differentiation was visible within the city itself. The north-western end of the city and waterfront was comparable with the modern port of Venice. The eastern end was populated by hordes of Slavs and small colonies of Mohammedans, Turks, Persians, Arabs, of whom the male children, it was believed, all carried knives. Even the trees and the grass and the earth by the sides of the roads looked different—and indeed were different because of the dust caused by the bad state of repairs of the roads in the east, the many unstabled horses there, the broken fences, the dumps, and the immigrant families from Galicia and Serbia and Macedonia who, during every summer until 1914, whilst waiting for a ship to the United States or South America, slept out like tramps on the grass under the trees.

G. had been living intermittently in Trieste for several months.

His face was considerably aged. The process of maturing and, later, of ageing, involves a gradual but increasing withdrawal of oneself from the exterior surface of the body. People took him to be nearer forty than thirty. His eyes were dark and keen as before. (Eyes of agate, a woman in Warsaw had written about him.) But the lines of his face and the corners of his mouth were over-worn. An interest easily awakened in his eyes was registered by the rest of his face as an effort which called upon some reserve of energy. He was fatter than five years previously, and more evidently his father's son. Whether, however, this increased resemblance to his father was a natural or a deliberate development it is hard to say, for he was in Trieste under the pretence of being a rich Italian candied-fruit merchant from Livorno, who wished to investigate the possibilities of setting up a plant for canning the fruit grown in Carniola. He was there pretending to be his father's legitimate son.

In August 1914 he was in London. At first he welcomed the news of the outbreak of war. In Britain it was clear from the very first day that tens of thousands of men wanted to enlist immediately, leave the country and go and fight in France. They were convinced that the war would be over by Christmas. Their principal worry was that it should not end—naturally, so far as they were concerned, with an Allied victory—before they had fought in it. Such a situation offered a prospect of a multitude of women being left behind without fiancés or husbands or brothers, and a prospect, within a few weeks, of thousands of widows. Some of these women he would choose. The men were going to war like Captain Patrick Bierce had done, and he would find further Beatrices.

To describe the nature of his memories of Beatrice would require a book with its own uniquely established vocabulary. (It would be the book of *his* dreams, not mine or yours.) He never made the slightest effort after he had left the farm to see Beatrice again. When he arrived in England in July 1914 after an absence of five years, it did not occur to him to inquire how or where Beatrice was living. Yet his memories of her were inerasable. He did not individually compare other women with her, but, because she was the first, she was equal in his memory to the sum of all the others. As the sum of the others increased in his life, so did her value, or, more precisely, the value of his sexual encounter with her, increase in his memory.

Very soon his attitude to the war began to change. He had never made a distinction in his mind between women who had given themselves to him and women who had not. Every woman had in common with all others her possible susceptibility to his propositions. In London at this time he met women whose behaviour was so unlike any he had previously met that he began to doubt whether they had anything in common with other women. These women were not the property of other men; they belonged to, they were the creatures of, an idea. He had met fanatical women before, but their fanaticism always involved a faith or an idea which was like a heart in the body of their own lives; they lived by it, and it, however rigid or absolute, pulsed with their own blood. The fanaticism could be embraced with them. The women in London were possessed by something outside themselves. They were possessed by the idea of hatred. They knew nothing of the passion of hatred. And what they hated was entirely unknown to them.

G. had often observed the certitude of the bereaved widow who is convinced that she can love only the memory of her husband. Unlike a wife, a widow is likely to despise the time still left her. A wife of a certain age may find herself trapped within the press of time:

234

behind her, her life till now with the man she married: in front of her, coming closer every day and soon to form a monolithic block in which she will be encased, her life, from now until she dies, with the man she married. Trapped like this, she considers infidelity in the hope of proving that her husband's gradual accumulation of each hour, day, year, decade of her life is not inexorable.

A widow, by contrast, embraces the inexorable. She recognizes her husband's absence as final. She returns to the past. She pretends that time is repetitive. If she thinks of the future at all, she thinks of it as eventless. Her refusal to consider any possibility of remarrying, her insistence on having ceased to be, in a sexual sense, a woman, are not so much an expression of a permanent and absurd fidelity as of her conviction that no important event can ever occur again in her life. She believes that her life will always be full with the event of her husband's absence: an event which can be endlessly reproduced so long as she lives with her memories in the past. She tries to make her own life timeless. She considers the passing of time a trivial affair. Her husband has entered eternity. (This is an accurate formulation even if she is without religious belief.)

If a man puts his arms around her, she is convinced that this does not constitute an event. She believes that her compliance is of no more significance than the placing of her head, as a child, on the lap of her father. She is convinced that within the emptiness of her life, an emptiness which she accepts as proof of the depth of her loss, the man's caresses and her responses are utterly without significance. And this is actually a proof of her grief.

The wife so values the time still left her that she is desperate to fill it with new experience.

The widow so despises the time still left her that she is certain that no true experience can enter it.

Both are deceived.

In London G. met widows whose certitude was of a different order.

MRS. CHRISTINA FENTON

I lost my husband in France six weeks ago. He was serving under General Sir Hubert Gough and the General wrote to me telling me of the circumstances of his death. He was killed by a German machine-gun while leading his men—

May I offer you my condolences.

On the day war was declared he was already impatient to embark. In the last letter I received from him he wrote that he hated to see the Boche so close to Paris. Nothing would have stopped him. He never hesitated.

Hesitation is always dangerous.

Men look to us women to see what we admire.

And what do you—not the others—*you* admire?

There is no difference between us. We admire those who are willing to die for their king and country. I admire my husband, there is no reason why I should not say so. He died as I would wish a man I loved to die. I never thought he would be killed, I never thought this (she picks up a corner of her black silk shawl and drops it again) would happen to me. But no more did I ever think we would live in a time as inspiring as the time we are living now.

Do you dream of Joan of Arc?

It is not our place to lead. Our duty is to set an example. You are not entirely British, are you?

An example of what?

I trust you have no German blood. But you haven't, I can see. If I had to guess, I would guess you had a Persian ancestor, a long way back, on one side of the family.

The Persians have the swiftest cavalry troops in the world.
You do have Persian blood. And if you are not in the army, you must be in the Royal Flying Corps.
How did you guess?
You can fly an aeroplane.
Yes, I can fly.
I knew it. You have the face of a flyer. Have you seen the Boche from the air?
They look like kangaroos.
Why do you say that?
To surprise you.
I hate them. By next spring we must take Berlin.
It is the colour of their uniforms which makes them look like kangaroos.
Would you come and meet the Patriotic Penelopes? No, you cannot refuse, it is your solemn duty, and when you are killed in the air, we shall hold a memorial service for you. I shall send a car for you tomorrow evening and you will see the example we are setting.
What are you?
We call ourselves the Patriotic Penelopes because we are widows whose husbands have made the supreme sacrifice or sisters whose brothers have done the same. Nobody else has the right to join us. (She looks up at him with her light grey eyes and a light expression on her face as though she were talking about gardens.) We are going to start another circle for mothers who have lost their sons. We decided at the beginning not to admit mothers into the same circle as our own because of the difference in age. We—the Penelopes—are all young women, or fairly young. We don't for one moment believe that it means less for a mother to lose her son but we feel the loss is of a different kind. We shall invite the mothers to join us on many occasions but we shall remain separate circles. For public events our being young widows is important because it brings home the truth to people more tellingly. It began when two or three wives who lost their husbands in France met and began talking. This was just before my husband was killed. One of them was the wife of Colonel C.A. Jones, you may have seen his photograph and an account of his heroic action in *The Sphere*. He was awarded the Victoria Cross for his outstanding bravery. We found

we had the courage to bear the first shock more easily if we were not alone too much and if we could talk to other women who were suffering in the same way. Members of the family—we came to notice later—often make matters worse by too much personal sentimentality. When one learns that somebody very dear to one has been killed over there, one must remember why he himself was willing to face death, why he went out to meet the enemy with a clear conscience and such high hopes. He knew we were fighting for a better world. (Her delivery becomes slightly oratorical.) He knew we had to defend little Belgium against the inhuman brutality of the Germans. In Belgium they are cutting off the breasts of women and the hands of little children. He knew we were fighting for freedom and the Empire and for a world safe for children and womenfolk to live in, a world where the meek are not frightened of the strong. If one remembers this, it is as clear as day what one's duty is. We must do everything in our power to continue the fight which he began, continue it until what he gave his life for has been won. We are making great advances. We are twenty now and we plan to start similar circles in every city throughout the land. Of course we no longer just talk amongst ourselves; we call that Common Condolence. Now we have moved on to Patriotic Action. We go out and those of us who are able to speak well speak on public platforms. We encourage recruitment, we urge women to take up munitions works, we talk to nurses. We go to army training camps—we go to them in pairs, not in a group—to express our gratitude to the volunteers. It is a very profound experience, that. One looks down at them sitting there, row after row in front of one; they are fully-grown men but they listen as attentively as children. They will be going any day to France, many of them will not come back, and as one talks one knows that for some of them one's words, simple words of gratitude and determination from two young officers' widows who have lost their very dearest ones in the war, one knows that these words will come back to them when they find themselves exhausted or wounded on the battlefield. We English are often too shy to say what we feel. But who knows of the passions which rage within? And somebody has to tell those lads that what they are going to do is fine and noble. You should hear the way they cheer.

Do you all know what Penelope was weaving?
It was a tapestry of some sort, wasn't it?
Not exactly.

We chose her name because she was the one who was left behind and she kept faith. (She looks down at her own hands lying in her lap.) We see it as part of our task to keep ourselves informed about developments on every front so that we have all possible arguments and facts at our fingertips for our war work and for this reason we invite speakers to come and address us. You simply must come. You will, won't you?

Let us meet in the afternoon first.

At what time? We have not had an officer from the Royal Flying Corps yet. We know almost nothing about the war in the air. You must come in uniform. (She pauses.) What was Penelope weaving? Where will you be at three?

At home.

A winding sheet.

I don't understand. Can I expect you?

He became impatient to leave London, as he eventually always became impatient to leave whatever city he was in. What, however, was unprecedented was that his impatience now included a slight but persistent anxiety. It was not so much a question of his wishing to be somewhere else; he wished to leave because London made him uneasy. There was a further new element in his predicament. The number of places in Europe to which he could go was strictly limited because of the war.

Was his uneasiness partly the result of a premonition of the vast historical changes under way—changes which would transform social and private life and death in Europe to such a degree that he must become unrecognizable to himself? I do not know. He showed no interest in history or politics. From certain things I have already written it would seem that the future filled him with foreboding, but not in a personal sense:

'As soon as one of you disappears there is another to take his place and the number of places is increasing. There will be shortages of everything in the world before there is a shortage of you. Why should I fear you? It is you who speak of the future and believe in it. I do not.'

In early December G. left London for Trieste. The idea of his going into declared enemy territory came about in the following way. Of his contemporaries at school he had remained in contact with only one: an Anthony Wilmot-Smith who worked at the Foreign Office. They had met at various flying events during the past five years because Wilmot-Smith was also a flying enthusiast. G. happened to complain to him about the way he found himself trapped in England. Such an unpatriotic attitude at such a time might have shocked Wilmot-Smith; in the circumstances it did not, for he had always thought of G., ever since their schooldays when he was nick-named Garibaldi, as being more than half foreign.

A few days after their conversation he telephoned G. and asked him how well he spoke Italian. Like an Italian, G. told him. They arranged to meet the same evening. Wilmot-Smith explained that since he worked for the Italian desk in the Foreign Office, he was in a position to make an offer, on a personal basis, to his old friend. He could arrange for G. to be given an Italian passport with the surname of G.'s father. With this passport he could leave the country immediately and travel where he wished. In exchange, he would ask G. to visit Trieste and there meet some fellow Italians who might have some messages for him to take out. He assured G. several times that he would be running no appreciable risk, or anyway a far smaller one than going for a flip in a Blériot. To Wilmot-Smith's surprise and consternation G. acepted the proposition without demanding a single further explanation.

Later Wilmot-Smith tried to point out to G. that the small task he had agreed to undertake would be of great service to the interests of both Italy and Great Britain. The Italians in Trieste, he began to explain, were increasingly restive under the Austro-Hungarian yoke and had to submit to ever more repressive measures; meanwhile His Majesty's government were trying to seek an accord with the Italian government whereby the Italian right to all Italian-speaking parts of the Adriatic coast would be recognized and admitted as an allied war aim. Beginning with these developments, Wilmot-Smith hoped to come reasonably and reassuringly to the aim of British tactics in Trieste. (The British wished to encourage the Italian nationalists there to demonstrate and so provoke savage Austrian reprisals. These reprisals would then strengthen enormously the popular appeal of the war party in Italy). G. cut short Wilmot-Smith's explanation and told him he only needed to know whom he had to meet where. I do not believe, he added, in the Great Causes.

After the Austrian frontier, the train went through a number of deep cuttings and tunnels until it emerged at a point where he could see the whole bay of Trieste before him. He could not think of himself as being in enemy territory. It was winter. The city looked frozen and desolate. The train was ill-heated. The sea was empty of ships. But, as he looked out of the train window down at the streets of buildings arranged sometimes neatly and in other parts haphazardly round the semicircle of the sea, he had a sense of controlled excitement or tension which in itself or by association was pleasurable. It was comparable to what he felt when he was about to enter a house from which he knew the husband or the male owner was absent. This absence, which he has foreseen, fits in with his own presence like a handle to a blade. Inside the house all the furniture and properties which are visible, the curtains and cupboards, the objects on every table, the doors, the carpets, the family beds, the books, the lamps, the portraits have all taken up their positions (without having to be moved a centimetre) to line, like a crowd, the way along which he is about to walk towards the woman who is expecting him.

From the museum garden, on the day he first met Nuša, G. walked slowly towards the Exchange in the Piazza della Borsa. At a corner he stopped to see whether he was being followed. With the streets so empty it must be hard, he thought, to trail somebody and remain unnoticed. He passed the end of the street in which an Austrian banker called Wolfgang von Hartmann lived with his Hungarian wife. Von Hartmann was one of the men with whom he was discussing the fruit-canning project. He retraced his steps and walked down the street, past the house. Behind its windows and its heavy swathes of brocaded curtains, the objects were in place, already lining the route of his arrival of which the exact day and hour had yet to be arranged. To picture Marika, the wife of von Hartmann, he had only to recall her extraordinary mouth and nose.

In a café just off the Piazza Ponterosso, two men were impatiently awaiting G.

He always makes us wait, grumbled Raffaele, the younger of the two men.

Let us watch him when he comes in, said the other, a man in his late fifties who was known as Dr Donato.

When he entered the café the two men were hidden behind the half-closed door of the back room.

He has come! Dr Donato whispered.

We should ask him straight away to explain himself, said Raffaele.

You are too impatient, my ardent young friend, said Dr Donato. The door had a glass window and the elder man was holding up a corner of the curtain so that he could peer through. I have often had occasion to notice in my work, he continued, how much you can learn about a man if you watch him closely without his realizing it. There is a moral language of gestures. The informer sips his coffee in a different way from other people, a distinctly different way. This is not superstition, there are good reasons for it. For example, the idea may cross his mind that his coffee is poisoned, because his mind is accustomed to intrigue. The idea then becomes evident in the way he picks up the cup.

Her nose broke with all conventions. It was so asymmetrical and irregular that it seemed to be almost shapeless. If a cast had been made of it and it had been removed from the context of her face, it would have looked like a delicate piece of a root. Its protuberances and dents, although very slight in themselves, were like the irregularities one finds on those parts of a plant which grow downwards into the earth towards water, rather than upwards towards light. The whole centre of her face suggested a reversed orientation. The outer edges of her lips were already part of the inside of her mouth. Her nostrils were already her throat. When she was seated, she was already running.

Look! He has chosen a table by the window. Now he is trying to peer down the street. He is moving the curtain aside. But he pretends it is because of the sunlight in his eyes. He is sly. There is no doubt about it, he is as sly as a fox biding his time. Look! He is beckoning to the waitress. A little furtive movement of the head—and she goes because she is inquisitive and can't resist secrets. You—take you—you would never call a waitress with a gesture like that. Dr Donato let the curtain fall and placed his hand on the younger man's arm. Everything you do, he explained, has a certain grandeur and confidence. And why, we may ask. Because you want everything to be seen.

Raffaele looked suspiciously at his companion with the thin face and white pointed beard.

Because you have nothing to hide, Dr Donato reassured him.

Dr Donato was by profession a lawyer. His intelligence was evident in his eyes and in his voice which was a little high in tone but very distinct. He took great pleasure in all explanations. He prided himself on being an atheist and a republican. What satisfied him more than anything else was to be able to explain the passion of others. Excess fascinated him because to explain it, in either positive or negative terms, was to demonstrate the full reach of Reason. He had been a member of the Secret Committee of the Italian Irredentist Party in Trieste for twenty years. Many credited him with the famous plot of the tricolour in the Piazza Grande.

On 20 September 1903, exactly as the clock in the Piazza Grande struck noon, a large Italian tricolour unfurled itself and flew from the mast on the tower of the city hall. Police ran into the building and up the stairs to take it down. The door to the tower was locked and barred. Italians ran into the square from all sides to gaze up at the flag against the blue sky. Many thought: when the city is at last Italian, a flag will fly like that every day. 20 September had been chosen because it was the anniversary of the day Rome was declared the capital of Italy. The flag was visible even to ships at anchor in the bay.

When asked about his contribution to this affair, Dr Donato would shrug his thin shoulders and say, as if speaking in a code and wanting to emphasize the fact: We Italians are the most musical race in Europe, and our second most outstanding gift is our ingenuity.

Once more Dr Donato lifted up the corner of the curtain. He has seen something, he said.

What has he seen?

Somebody.

Can you see them? asked Raffaele.

No, but something has reassured him. He looks pleased. Who it was or exactly what sign passed between the two of them, we cannot yet know for we are not yet certain of his motivations. Is he really as interested as he pretends in canning fruit? Who exactly is he? When we have established that —

Raffaele interrupted the older man without trying to disguise the impatience he could no longer contain. Let us confront him with the facts, he said. He led the way across the café floor to the table by the window. A big man, Raffaele had the air of having been anointed since infancy with praises and love. (A semblance which may well signify the opposite.) As he walked across the café, he attracted considerable attention. The clientèle was entirely Italian and Raffaele was well known for the patriotic fervour of his articles in *Il Piccolo* and the way he cunningly evaded the Austrian censorship. He walked across the café as if he were leading, not one thin man with a white beard, but a whole company of his compatriots.

When all three men were seated, their heads close together over the centre of the table, Raffaele asked G. whether he had brought any news from Rome. He spoke quietly, so as not to be overheard, but his jaw was thrust forward and he was scowling.

No, I did not go there.

And the present for Mother?

It should have arrived by now.

You entrusted it to somebody else!

Yes.

To whom?

In an exaggeratedly conspiratorial whisper G. said: If you are working for Mother, the fewer names you know the better. That should be one of the first rules of a clandestine party.

Two weeks ago you told us you were going! shouted Raffaele, pushing his chair back and making people at the nearby tables look up.

I changed my mind.

Men who change their minds are traitors!

When Raffaele was moved he had to make a noise. The first thing he was willing to abandon was secrecy. He considered numbers more important. His own duty, as he saw it, was to rally thousands of Triestine Italians to the cause by setting them an example. The example of a man who would not be intimidated.

Wait until you hear from Mother, replied G., again whispering, then you'll know whether she received our present safely.

You are a traitor and a coward! And either way you are bloodless. At this hour when the whole future of our family is in the balance, you have nothing better to do than dither here discussing how to put fruit into tins — Raffaele lowered his voice at this point in order to underline the fact that he, unlike G., was prepared to use words that indeed required whispering — WITH THE ENEMY! Or do you talk about something else with them? Our Mother, for example!

Dr Donato intervened. *Caro* — he addressed Raffaele — do not let us start accusing each other. He is with us, not against us; he has already helped us on several occasions. He planned to make a journey and he found he was unable to do so and he sent a cousin — shall we say a cousin? — instead. Do not let us jump to conclusions, for my own part I am persuaded — he turned towards G. placing his hands palms down on the table — I am persuaded that we can and must count upon you. Like us you are a dreamer and like us you wish to make the dream reality. The only question, which will eventually answer itself, is whether or not we share the same dream. His voice trailed away and he made his breath whistle softly between his teeth as if he were pretending to fall asleep. Behind his pince-nez his eyelids almost covered his eyes.

You are wrong, said G., I am not a dreamer.

All men dream.

Some less than others.

The dream of our country made great and powerful again is a dream shared by forty millions, said Raffaele. He held a single finger up in the air. This was an Irredentist gesture signifying a United Italy.

G. silently addressed Dr Donato: Twelve young women sitting on the floor at your feet, benefiting from your stories after Trieste has become Italian, you select one and when you take hold of her breasts she cries out lovingly: Papa! Papa! That is your dream.

Have you any daughters, Dr Donato?

Unfortunately not, why do you ask?

A confusion about names, that is all.

Raffaele gripped the table with his hands. It was time, he believed, for plain speaking; Donato should warn G. that if they found any further reason for suspecting him, his life would be in danger. Raffaele distrusted subtlety because he associated it with the intrigues and subterfuges which had bedevilled Italian political life for half a century. Intrigue for him meant the corridor and the lobby; and to these he opposed the battlefield and an overseas empire where Italy would rediscover herself and again impress Roman virtue upon the world. He advocated a return to the austere patriotic purity of a Garibaldi. He saw Donato as a latter-day, obsolete and over-crafty Cavour. He respected his astuteness but he believed that this time, unlike the first, Cavour's influence should be second to the General's. Once, in the Ginnastica Triestina, he had taken a sword down from the wall and cut the air with it round the older man's head and shoulders. Donato also liked to imagine that he had a lot in common with Cavour. And so, as the sword whirred through the air, he calmed himself by recalling how patient Cavour had sometimes to be in face of Garibaldi's childishness.

I want to warn you, said Raffaele, that we are not satisfied with your explanations. You undertook to go to Mother and you failed to do so. What kept you here?

An affair of the heart.

Why did you not inform us?

You know the lady in question, said G.

Raffaele leant back in his chair to suggest the wealth of the possibilities he was considering. May I ask who? He made the question sound as casual as a glove held in the hand.

You may ask them all! said G., laughing.

Raffaele resented the fact that Dr Donato also laughed.

Would you consider helping us in another way? asked Dr Donato. As an Italian from Italy, come here for important commercial negotiations, you are probably in a position to approach certain influential Austrians. Among them there may be one or two who enjoy the confidence of the Governor or the Bishop. Last week a young man—whose Christian name is Marco—was arrested whilst trying to cross the frontier. Would you be prepared to try to use whatever influence you have to persuade your Austrian acquaintances that this young man should be treated as leniently as possible? Best of all we would like to obtain his release.

At a time like this? When the two nations are almost at war?

Wait, wait. The case is an exceptional one. The young man in question is seriously ill with TB; his father, who lives in Venice, is dying;

he is exempt on medical grounds from military service; he has no political record, none whatsoever. He tried to cross the frontier to visit his father on his deathbed and he was arrested.

It sounds unlikely.

That is why his case is exceptional. I have all the evidence here— the lawyer discreetly shook his black dispatch case. A campaign for clemency on humanitarian grounds is quite realistic. Polite society everywhere and especially polite Austrian society, likes nothing better than a temporary good cause. Women are particularly attracted. A little campaign can be mounted, nothing public of course, a purely social campaign which means dropping the right words into the right ear at the right moment at the dinner table.

I don't believe in the credentials you brought us, interrupted Raffaele, and it must be clear to you that at a time like this we cannot afford to make mistakes. Either you prove to us that you are trustworthy, and do so quickly, or—slowly he drove one fist into the palm of his other hand. We have our eyes, he added.

Can you find a better cause? asked Dr Donato as though Raffaele had not spoken. You have a young man suffering from TB, accused justly in a legal sense, but too harshly in a wider sentimental sense, of having tried, out of filial piety, to visit his father on his deathbed. It is enough to bring tears to the eyes of a police inspector. And what is more, the idea of a pardon might well please His Highness the Governor. His Highness, at a time like this, would probably welcome the chance to make a theatrical but insignificant conces- sion to Italian sentiment. Several other men were arrested the same night. Some of them were going to Mother. The courts can make an example of them. But clemency in Marco's case would be an intelligent tactic from the Austrian point of view.

Tactic! said Raffaele.

Why are you so anxious to save him? asked G.

Donato put his hands to his chest in the gesture which announces: And now I shall bare my soul to you, and said: I am a lawyer. I do all I can for my clients. You, you are not obliged to do anything.

But if Marco did receive a light sentence or was pardoned, we would be exceedingly grateful. That is all. I will give you the little dossier I have prepared on this case.

The three men left the café together. Dr Donato took G.'s arm. Our friend Raffaele, he said, drank too much Tokai last night. You can count on me. I shall be extremely grateful if you can help me in the Marco affair. He lowered his voice. You may deny it, but you are a dreamer too.

At the first corner they separated.

Why did you laugh at his jokes? demanded Raffaele. And why did you confide in him about Marco?

Caro, you should have more confidence in me than that. He has no idea who Marco is. True, it is unlikely he can do anything for Marco, but we must try everything. If he is working for the Austrians and they do not know who Marco is, which is quite possible, they may release Marco so that our friend from Livorno can offer us a little present which, they calculate, will increase our confidence in him and hence his usefulness to them. We were not born yesterday, were we? If he obtains Marco's release I will take it as tantamount to proof that he is working for them. So we shall have achieved two things: Marco's release, which is more urgent than anything else, and a clear warning about our friend from Livorno. If, on the other hand, the Austrians know who Marco is—and in that case there is no hope for Marco—then the fact that he tries to arrange for Marco's release will convince the Austrians that he is really working for us, and if they suspect that, I don't think we shall see him many more times in Trieste. There is a chance, a small chance, that he is going to render us, without realizing it, a last service. What can we lose? He put a hand up to his eyes to shade them from the sun.

G. lay on his bed. Across the windows hung white lace curtains. The leaves of the plants embroidered on the curtains were slightly whiter and less transparent than their background. Through the curtains the house on the other side of the street was visible, its curved classical orders and its stucco thrown into relief by the bright evening sunlight. The stone was the sepia colour of cigar boxes. A woman who had apparently just washed her hair and wrapped a blue towel round her head like a turban appeared in a window of the house opposite wearing a loosely-tied teagown. She watched the people in the street below; it was the hour of the *caminada,* when young men from families who consider themselves respectable walk in groups along a route laid down by tradition, to follow and watch the groups of strolling girls from similar families.

At the end of the street a wide canal led into the sea by the main quayside where the liners used to anchor near the Piazza Grande. Before the war scarcely a day passed without a ship, at least as large as the City Hall, closing the fourth side of the square. The canal was a venture which had never been completed. Its entrance was wide and handsome. But two hundred metres from the quayside it stopped. It began as a canal and ended as a dock. The woman who had washed her hair yawned for a full half-minute. She was probably the wife, G. thought, of one of the shopkeepers below. She was quite unaware of being observed. To her, his room behind its lace curtains looked as dark as night. She made as though to go back to her room, hesitated, leant once more on the windowsill and yawned again. A ship blew its hooter, a sound like a seal's bark indefinitely prolonged. The embroidered leaves on the lace curtains were acanthus leaves.

According to gossip, Marika, Wolfgang von Hartmann's wife, had had not long ago an Italian lover who was forced to leave the city. He was a musical conductor and he provoked a public scandal by arranging a concert at which the first syllable of the title of each work, as printed in the programme, spelt out an anti-Austrian slogan. Most of the audience were Italians and they soon spotted the message, gave the conductor an ovation, and at the end started shouting VERDI! VERDI! which meant, in the Irredentist code, Vittorio Emmanuele Re d'Italia. As a result, the conductor lost his post at the Conservatoire and left the city.

Lying on his bed, G. smiled as he foresaw himself pleading the case of Marco to von Hartmann in the presence of his wife.

8.

Each day fresh rumours circulated in the city about Italy's impending declaration of war against Austria. It seemed scarcely possible for Italy to maintain her neutrality any longer—not because of any international incidents which had occurred, nor because of any official declaration by the Italian government, but because of the public campaign in favour of war which was being mounted in all the large Italian cities. It appeared that the will of the people was for war.

The Irredentists in Trieste prepared for the hour of glory. Many young Italians who had often talked of crossing the frontier illegally to join the Italian army but had put off actually packing their bags and setting out in the direction of Gorizia, realized that they must go now or never at all. Early in the evening they made their last *caminada;* the least prepossessing among them could now approach the girl who had never deigned to acknowledge his existence and force tears to her eyes by saying knowingly and gravely: If you do not see me on the Molo tomorrow, do not forget me. The prepossessing, having hinted at their departure in a similar way, advanced like standard-bearers with the tricolour above them, whilst whole clusters of girls followed them with their eyes and squeezed each other's hands so as not to cry out or throw themselves on their knees. The older Irredentists went about the drab city on light feet for they foresaw a radiant Trieste and their life-long struggle achieved before the year was out.

Other Italians among workers and clerks and small shopkeepers listened to the rumours and scanned the newspapers with misgivings. They had much to fear: the reaction of the Austrians in the event of war: fighting in the city: the eventual economic collapse of Trieste under Italian rule. (None of them for one moment imagined that the Austrians would defeat the Italian army.) Yet the very language in which the fears of these Italians had to be expressed made these fears seem shameful. They felt that their mother tongue, as they spoke her, chastised them.

On the Thursday they read in the newspapers about the event which everybody had been awaiting, the unveiling of a statue to commemorate the departure from Genoa of Garibaldi and his Thousand. It was said that the King might attend the ceremony. At the last moment he sent a telegram apologizing for his absence but blessing the occasion.

The principal speaker at Genoa was Gabriele d'Annunzio, self-elected poet of Italian nationalism. He looked like an old hungry fox—but a fox mounted on an invisible horse, a fox so charismatic that he could ride to hounds and lead the hunt. He believed that the aviator was the ideal modern hero. (He had contemplated writing a poem for Chavez.) The crowd applauded him with limitless enthusiasm. His scraggy face seemed to be a proof of the profundity of what he was saying:

'Blessed are those who have much, for they will be able to give much; blessed are those who despise all sterile love, for they will come as virgins to this their first and last love; blessed are those who spoke out yesterday against this event (i.e., the proposed war: the reference may have been censored), for they will accept in silence the law of necessity and will wish to be not the last but the first; blessed are the young, happy and thirsty for glory, for they will be satiated; blessed are the merciful, for they will have pure blood to wipe away and radiant pain to soothe; blessed are those who will return victorious for they will see the new face of Rome. . . .'

It looked as if the will of the Italian people was propelling Italy towards war. But the truth was somewhat different. On 26 April the King and Prime Minister had signed a secret treaty committing Italy to enter the war on the side of the Entente within one month. At that time Parliament was conveniently adjourned, but it would need to be recalled for the actual declaration of war, and it was known that a large majority would be opposed to intervention, as also were most of the peasants, the left wing of the socialist party, many trade-unions and the Vatican. Within one month the nation, and especially the cities, had to be roused in such a way that all opposition, parliamentary or otherwise, would crumble. This was the task allotted by the King and his two chief ministers, who were the only three men in the secret, to interventionist politicians and agitators like D'Annunzio.

At the same time as Britain and France and Russia were negotiating the terms of the secret treaty with Italy, Germany and Austria were making counter-offers in order to persuade Italy to maintain her neutrality. One of the principal differences between the two sets of offers made to the King and his ministers involved the future of Trieste. The Central Powers proposed that Trieste should become a Free City; the Entente proposed that it should become Italian.

Towards the end of the week there was a rumour that Prince Bülow, the Kaiser's negotiator, had suddenly left Rome for Germany with all his staff. Italians who had passports began to leave Trieste sooner than intended. Austrians who had been in Italy hurriedly returned. In this atmosphere of increasing suspense, G. pursued his own interests. It did not occur to him to leave the city. Wolfgang von Hartmann and his wife were away in Vienna and were not returning until the weekend. With every day that passed the proposal to enlist Austrian sympathy on behalf of the young man arrested on the frontier became more blatantly absurd. G. had no intention of speaking of the matter to anybody until the return of von Hartmann and his wife; then, for his own reasons, he would be prepared to plead that absurd and impossible case.

O

Sunday, 9 May, appears to have been a sunny day all over Europe. Wolfgang von Hartmann made a habit of rising early and, since he did not believe in exceptions, he also got up early on Sundays. By seven o'clock he was dressed.

Four thousand men had already been killed along a line of two and a half miles in the Western Front. At 5am the British artillery had begun a bombardment of the German lines. At 5.20 a strong breeze blew across the southern edge of the battlefield dispersing momentarily the clouds of smoke and dust. The German breastwork could be seen with alarming clarity to be almost intact. Ten minutes later the first wave of three infantry divisions clambered over the parapet and began to advance in line into no-man's-land. The diary of the opposing German regiment describes the attack as follows: There could never before in war have been a more perfect target than this solid wall of khaki men, British and Indian side by side. There was only one possible order to give—Fire until the barrels burst! The German machine guns fired. Some of the attacking soldiers tried to stumble back into their trenches, but they were prevented from doing so by the second and third waves of the attack already climbing out.

Wolfgang von Hartmann's wife slept in the same room. She had tried unsuccessfully on several occasions to suggest that, given the onerousness of his work and public duties, it would be better if they had separate rooms. You would always be welcome, she added with a smile that was too eager to be happy. No, he replied, if that is what I had in mind I would not have married you and you could have been my mistress.

A handful of men advanced, no longer aware of who they were; if their mothers had called them by name they would not have answered. A little before the German lines they saw a ditch where they hoped to take cover. When they reached it, they discovered it was full of barbed wire. Some, in their desperation, threw themselves on the wire. The others, one by one, were shot and fell. A second attack, to be preceded by a forty-five-minute bombardment, had been ordered for 7am. This time the gunners were instructed to concentrate their fire on the wire in front of the German breastwork. Those British and Indian soldiers still alive in no-man's-land, who had crawled to find shelter in craters or in small holes which they had frantically scraped out with their own bayonets, were now being killed by the shells of their own supporting artillery.

Von Hartmann paused to watch Marika sleeping. She no longer slept with her hair loose. He was proud of being able to see the expression of his wife's face in repose for what it was. She looked greedy. Yet her greed was not gross, it was a lean greed. And this was what pleased him, for it demonstrated, since she had stayed with him for eight years, how much he was capable of supplying. (She was the daughter of an impoverished Magyar landowner and had married Wolfgang when she was twenty-seven.) A more easily satisfied woman would by now have taken his wealth and power for granted. This had been the case with his first wife. She had trusted him as she unthinkingly trusted the sun to rise each morning. Marika could not afford such complacence, for her next demand might prove inordinate and be refused. Bending over her, Wolfgang pressed his thumb against her teeth which opened a little in her sleep so that mouth and hand were like those of a child who bites on his thumb so as not to cry out.

On an adjacent sector of the front a number of survivors from the Irish Rifles were making their way back under heavy German fire to their own lines. In the British trenches, in which men were milling round like slow dancers, with dead or bleeding partners in their arms, a rumour sprang up that the Germans were making a counter-attack disguised in British uniforms. Men began firing on the returning survivors of the Irish Rifles.

At the railway station in Rome several hundred young men were waiting to meet the train from Turin. They kept peering along the lines which, outside the station, shone like silver forks in the early-morning sun. In the train was Giolitti. He had resigned as prime minister the year before and he was coming to Rome because he believed that the government had not yet reached a decision about entering the war (he knew nothing of the Secret Treaty) and he was determined to use his influence to support the neutralist party. Four years earlier he had championed and organized the colonial war against Libya: but today he feared that in a European war the gains for his country would not justify the cost. The young men had read of his intention to come to Rome in yesterday's morning papers. As the train drew in, they were whistling and shouting: Down with Giolitti! Down with compromise! Long live war! They were trying to climb on to the train before it stopped. The man who had ruled Italy for twelve years was tempted to address them from the train door. They were not having him. Long live Italian Trieste! Down with Austria! War! War! The old man was quickly dissuaded from trying to speak. It was only an hour ago that he had woken up. He wanted a second cup of coffee. An aide suggested he should get out of the train on the far side and so slip away, avoiding the demonstration. He refused. He was unable to take his eyes off the young shouting men. They do not realize, he was saying, that it is not Libya, not Libya.

Each time during the day that Wolfgang von Hartmann finished considering a subject, his thoughts returned to his wife. He asked whether the latest Austrian victory in Galicia on the Russian front was significant. He concluded that it was not. He did not think of his wife as he had left her in bed. He thought of her as she would appear that evening in front of G. He asked whether the initiative undertaken by His Imperial and Royal Majesty's ambassador to persuade the Pope to declare that, in the event of war with Italy, the Holy See would remove itself to Spain, would have the faintest chance of success. He decided that it had not. He had noticed Marika's interest in G. the very first time that G. had come to the house three months ago. Since then G. had been a fairly regular visitor and his wife had not disguised her feelings. He wondered what repercussions were likely to arise from the sinking of the *Lusitania*, four days ago. He feared the Germans had made a mistake. The Germans understood U-boats and nothing else. He had no patience with the hypocritical cries of horror emanating from the Entente; the ship had been carrying munitions and the British had been repeatedly warned that if they persisted in using passenger liners to transport war cargoes, the responsibility for the outcome would be theirs. Nevertheless the sinking had established a bad precedent. It extended the area of war, and by the same token it seriously reduced the area in which common interests of law, insurance, re-insurance and finance could continue, even as between belligerents, to be assumed. According to various enquiries he had made, G., unlike the musical conductor of last year, was a man who could be depended upon to leave Trieste quickly and definitely.

At midday Nuša went to Hölderlin's garden in the hope of finding G. Nobody was there.

Von Hartmann considered that most people wasted energy trying to find absolute answers to transitory questions. Every question, he argued, should be examined in relation to its own time span. One of his favourite examples was that of death. For how long, he asked, do we actually experience death?

Packed together in the assembly trenches, listening for their officer to blow on his whistle which, like the sound of a demented parrot, scarcely audible in the din of bursting shells, was meant to be the signal to go over the top, battalions of men were waiting whilst the German shells exploded around them. When they heard the rush of a shell coming directly at them, they could do nothing but stay standing where they were and close their eyes. There was no space to fling themselves to the ground. Many were packed so tight that they were unable to raise their arms to shield their faces. The wounded could not collapse. Pieces of shrapnel cut through one body to enter a second or a third. It was under these conditions in the forming-up places that between 1.15 and 2pm a further two thousand men were being wounded or killed.

Von Hartmann argued that his wife's adventures and extravagances should be appraised in their special relation to her lifetime with him. The licences he had granted her had to be so graduated that she did not exhaust the possibilities of his compliance until she was too old to find another man. This stratagem was aimed at something more subtle than the preservation of his marriage. He had no doubt that if Marika left him, he would not lack a presentable wife for long. He had no reason to fear solitude in his old age. (He glanced in the mirror above the fireplace. He was rich, a little stout but not bald.) What he wanted to establish and maintain was administrative control of his wife's appetites. He no more believed in absolute insatiability than he believed in infinity. His wife's appetites had to be encouraged and yet never fully met. In this way her apparent insatiability could be preserved and at the same time be subject to his control. The conjugal scene that afforded him most pleasure was the play-acting whereby she tried to deceive him about the money she had lost gambling or a rendezvous she had arranged with an admirer. She was a very poor actress. At any moment of his choosing he had only to look at her gravely, with scepticism, for her to abandon her protests of innocence and to entreat him silently, passionately, with her eyes to allow her to continue. If he consented—his consent communicated by the smallest change of facial expression (they never exchanged a single word on these subjects)—she continued: continued with the performance and the adventure it was meant to hide. If he refused with a frozen expression, she left the room, swearing the vengeance she would never take. The entreaty in Marika's eyes at the moment of one of her broken performances was what made Wolfgang believe that he loved her. On the one hand, it was something very simple: a look of entreaty such as he had often imagined as a child in an animal's eyes: on the other hand, it was the perennial fruit of a complex and unique marriage which he had arranged in detail but which would not have been possible with any other woman except Marika.

At 4pm along the entire attack frontage new lines of men were staggering across no-man's-land, following the pipes of their band. The sound of the mad pipes was a continuation, far beyond music or reason, of the shrill parrot-cry of the officers' whistles. As they were falling, they appeared to fall in heaps rather than lines. This was because, in their last minutes, they were trying to crawl towards each other. The effect was of a crop, cut down, forming itself into stooks.

Marika's infidelities did not disturb Wolfgang von Hartmann because the sexual act (the act which constituted infidelity) was, like the experience of death, so absurdly short-lived. There was of course the obvious difference that death is only experienced once. But if his wife's amorous adventures were considered in gross, it was he, not she, who consented or refused. Her lovers entreated her: she entreated him. Wolfgang viewed Marika's gambling in the same way as he viewed her love affairs. She thought her gambling was wild: he ensured that it never exceeded economic prudence. Every time she drew from her account, he was informed. (This was the least of his privileges as a director of the Kreditanstalt Bank.) In both fields, the amorous and the financial, his control was based on the same principle. His wife must receive continual increments, but the rate of increase, the initial payment and the likely terminal payment were calculated to guarantee that, while always encouraging her to expect more and more, her demands remained easily within his resources, these resources thus appearing to be almost inexhaustible.

Since dawn in the battle of Auvers Ridge, more than eleven thousand men and nearly five hundred officers had lost their lives. Very few were killed instantly and outright. The majority died in an agony which, however great its terror and annihilating pain, offered a relief from the burden of hopelessness induced by the orders they had obediently carried out until the moment they fell.

In the drawing-room after dinner Wolfgang von Hartmann received G. as he received all visitors, politely. It was a large room with a white tiled stove in the form of a Greek temple at one end. On the walls were paintings and heavy mirrors. Before the mirrors were candelabra. Each candle burned in a glass, the size of a leeching glass but with a toothed rim. These glasses which reflected the light of the flames around them and glittered like fish-scales, prevented the flames from flickering as they had flickered in the cathedral at Domodossola. Although the large room was dark in places, the mirror and glasses gave the impression of thousands of candles having been lit.

Marika made her entry five minutes after G.'s arrival. She walked like an animal. I find it hard to describe her walk because the resemblance was not to one animal but several. She resembled a composite animal like a unicorn, but at the same time there was nothing mythical about her. She was no apparition among flowers on a tapestry. Her legs were large-boned and very long. Sometimes I have the impression that they began at her shoulders and that, like the four legs of a horse, they were triple-jointed. As she walked she held her head very still; her neck was thick and muscular; she held her head like a stag; above her red-deer hair you might see invisible antlers. And yet she moved unsteadily, she swayed from side to side, her foothold never appeared quite sure enough for her height and bulk—and in this she resembled a camel.

It is a great compliment, she said, that you come to see us on the very day after our return.

I understand your journey back was very long and tiring.

There is nothing here. Nothing in this godforsaken city. There is you, but how often will we see you?

I have delayed my departure.

We do not see you nearly enough.

If you delay it too long, we may have to intern you, said von Hartmann without smiling but without any overt menace. Let us hope it will not happen.

The casualness of the threat reminded G. of Dr Donato saying: The only question is whether or not we share the same dream.

You say intern like a word you have used all your life, said Marika.

Internieren, we say in German. Like *Internat,* you should know what that means. He looked at G. You, who went to England for your education. *Internat* means boarding school. So if we had to intern you, you would not find life so unfamiliar.

You will not guess what they called me at my *Internat.* I was called Garibaldi.

It is strange how the English made a legend of that man. Somebody told me that when Garibaldi visited London he drew larger crowds than their queen. Is it because, at heart, the English love the idea of the pioneer, sleeping alone under the stars beside his fire, is it because they hate the order of their own terrible cities? They are the opposite of us. Everything that is of value in the empire of the Hapsburgs comes from the order and reason established in our cities —and look at our cities! Vienna, Prague, Budapest! What can we offer you to drink?

I would visit you every day in prison! vowed Marika. She was still standing, swaying a little on her legs, and when she said this she made a movement as though opening a cell door and entering. She was not consciously acting. Theatre bored her. If she 'pretended' to be visiting G. in prison, it was because she made very little distinction between the idea of an action and the action itself; the words which expressed the idea tended to translate themselves straight away into messages to her limbs.

Our cities are like islands in an ocean of barbarism.

I will help you escape, said Marika, the simplest way will be for you to walk out in my clothes.

That would be unwise, said von Hartmann, even I would find it difficult to save you from the consequences of that.

He would strip me by force, of course!

You could always call a guard for help.

You forget who my father was!

You mean your birth makes you incapable of treason.

Yes, that is what I do mean! And I mean that I admire Garibaldi! And I mean that he was a superb horseman! And I am a patriot!

She was not angry. Each sentence made her smile more. At the end she laughed, stroked her husband's arm and sat down.

I fear, said von Hartmann to G., that your countrymen may be stupid enough to declare war on us.

I am not a political man.

If you were, you would not tell my husband, murmured Marika.

I have come nevertheless to plead a case and, with your permission, I would like to plead it before you both.

G. had no doubt that his host would categorically reject his advocacy and that his wife would embrace it. The case of Marco would supply, for a short while, a subject by means of which the woman he desired could openly establish her common interest with him and the necessity of intrigue against her husband could become apparent.

The Austrian banker wanted to give the impression of listening patiently and attentively. He lay back in his chair, occasionally lowering his eyes and turning his head. His eyes were small and very quick, incapable of real attention towards anything except the swift thoughts in the brain behind them.

G. was pleading a case in which he did not believe, but von Hartmann was a man to whom no appeal, however desperate or deeply felt it might be, was possible. By the same token he was immune to most threats. Appeals and threats, when once they have been made, work their way into the consciousness of the person to whom they have been addressed, by a process not unlike that by which a rumour spreads among a crowd. The appeal or the threat is whispered and passed on, but each time it is repeated the whisperer gives it his own stress. In the end one rumour may give birth to several rumours but they will all share the same kind of alarm or hope. Yet who is the crowd? Who goes on circulating and whispering the appeals and threats in the mind until the decision has been taken? The crowd is an assembly of all the other possible selves, commenting on the self in power, whom they believe to be a usurper. They were born from visions in the past; they have failed to establish their own power, but they have not been dispersed, they still inhabit the personality.

Von Hartmann was a man who had eliminated all his possible selves. All that remained from his past were obsolete versions of the same self. He was like a man engraved on a postage stamp.

He would of course have responded to crude physical threats at a reflex level. If his life were threatened he might break down and whimper like a child: more probably he would remain curiously impassive. The silence which emanates from death only continues the silence of such a man's subjective life. Von Hartmann was a man who could be removed, but not challenged. On account of this it might be claimed that he was the ideal administrator.

As Marika listened, the young man who had been arrested at the frontier became inextricably mixed with Garibaldi and with G. in the internment prison from which she would help him to escape. She decided immediately that the young man must be released. More than that, she decided that she would ask the governor herself. Marika's decisions were immediate because she had no interest in justifications. If the needle of her will indicated the magnetic north, all she had to do was to set out; it was incomprehensible to her why anybody should want to adjust the compass to the needle and take other readings. Yet she was a woman who reflected. The difference between her and most others was that her reflexions were exclusively concerned with the past and were in the form of stories and legends. In some she herself played a part, in others, which interested her no less, she did not appear at all. A legend, a story, for Marika was what remained when the necessities which determined it had ebbed away; afterwards the story lay there like a boat cast high up on the beach by an exceptional tide, or like a ring no longer worn but kept in a jewel box. Sometimes what remained was an absence, as in the case of a woman friend who lost an arm in a riding accident. She was galloping away from her lover whom she discovered by chance in a wood making love to somebody else. Before the arm was amputated, when the ring was still worn, when the boat was sailing, life was too fateful to allow for reflexion.

Marika, how I love you! Your smile is more complete than any last judgement. When you take off your clothes you are pure will. We make each other bodiless. All the rest are talkers or sensualists. Marika! When will G. say this?

As soon as he came to the end of his speech, Marika exclaimed: There is only one thing to do, have him released.

Her husband nodded his head. Contrary to convention, he often nodded when about to refuse something. Your eloquence, you see, has won her heart, but I am afraid that under the present conditions it would be quite impossible to intervene in any way on your young friend's behalf. Impossible and dangerous. Let us assume that he is as innocent as you say. In himself he may not be dangerous. But what would be the effect on the city of showing leniency at a moment like this? Many more would be encouraged to try to cross the frontier. The numbers would double. And what would this lead to? Our soldiers on the frontier have orders to shoot at anybody who does not stop or answer their challenge. By relaxing the law in the special case of your friend one might well be responsible for the death of several other young men. And the affair would not stop there. The political and diplomatic repercussions of such frontier incidents might well prove disastrous. It would probably mean war. My wife does not understand politics. In politics nothing is ever merely itself. There is your young Italian whose father is dying, he is arrested crossing the frontier illegally and he stands to be given what may seem a harsh prison sentence, yet to show undue clemency in this one exceptional case could well cause a war in which tens of thousands of sons and fathers would die.

A telephone rang in a distant room. The banker rose to his feet, walked over to his wife and covered her hand, which was resting on the arm of the chair, with his own.

That is why he cannot be set free as you would like, he explained.

She did not look troubled. She no more made arguments than she listened to them. She was like an animal or a person who, having run along a path, turns a corner and finds that it leads to the bank of a wide, fast-flowing river; anger or impatience would be futile. Her expression was calm, stationary. She was looking up and down the river to decide which way to turn before running on. She knew that she lived under licence and she knew that it was too late for her to live otherwise. It was not something she reasoned about, but she sensed it as one can sense the size of a plain or the proximity of the sea without being able to see them. Without a Wolfgang she would become like a gipsy, and she despised gipsies. Furthermore she sensed that the chronicles of the world, the stories that would remain, were passing into the keeping of men like her husband.

A servant came to the door and announced that the telephone call was from Vienna. Von Hartmann excused himself and left the room.

I would like to dance, said Marika, standing up and swaying in slow gliding circles across the inlaid parquet floor towards where G. was sitting. Who are you really? she asked him. You are not he who you say you are. (She spoke an awkward and incorrect Italian.) Who are you really?

Don Juan.

I have met men who thought they were Don Juans, none of them was.

The name is much usurped.

Why do you claim it then?

Did I?

You are right. It was I who asked you, and I believe you.

She moved away and continued in a flatter voice: When shall we make the trip to Verona which you proposed to us?

I love you.

The uncannily still flames of the candles emphasized how tightly the skin of her face was drawn over the pronounced bones of her skull.

If we were at home we would ride into the forest, now, while he is out of the room we would go.

Turn your face towards me.

He places his hand on her nose and mouth so that they are covered. Inside the warmth of his hand he feels her nose like a gentle tonsil. Her eyes are laughing. Then, with his hand a little damp from her breath, he smooths the skin across her hard cheekbones towards her rather red, deeply convoluted ear.

I am not the same, she whispered.

Von Hartmann paused at the door, contemplated the two figures by the fireplace and walked pensively into the room. It occurred to neither G. nor Marika to wonder how long he had stood there.

It seems, he announced, that Rome has decided upon war. It is only a matter of time. He put his hand on G.'s shoulder. So after all you will have to choose between us and the *Internat*.

I have time, said G. You don't have to be a political man to hear war coming, like an avalanche. I haven't heard it here yet.

If there is going to be war, said Marika, we must make our journey to Verona before it is too late. Let us go tomorrow.

Sometimes you astonish me like a child, said von Hartmann to his wife. Verona is nothing but a name for you. Why do you want to go there?

I want to travel.

There are no horses there. There is a theatre.

I hate this city. She began walking towards the far end of the room where the white tiled temple was installed and the walls were lined with books up to the ceiling. Nobody is interested in anything here except insurance. If we are going to be at war before the week is out, we should go immediately.

It is inconceivable that we should leave at a moment like this. Her husband sat down, smiled at G. and continued: It seems as if war is certain, but it will not be for two weeks at least.

Is that what you heard on the telephone? shouted Marika, for she was now at the other end of the room, twenty metres away.

No, that is what I deduce from what I heard.

She climbed a library ladder which stood by the bookshelves and, mounting the topmost step, her hair almost touching the ceiling, her face in darkness and the light falling on the folds of the skirt of her dress which, seen from that angle, appeared to have no waist but to be skirt to the shoulders, she declared: Let us bet on it! I am prepared to bet one thousand crowns that we shall be at war in one week.

Impossible, said von Hartmann.

Very well, she cried again, one thousand crowns. No, there is a better wager. If I win, the young Italian is released. I go to the governor myself and ask him. If I lose, if we are not at war by next Sunday, I will pay you one thousand crowns.

I can only conclude this young Italian must be your lover! said von Hartmann.

She turned her back, as though to look at the books on the top shelf, and said bitterly in German: In the end like all Germans you are *ordinär*.

Von Hartmann replied in dulcet Italian. There is no need to be angry, I have the greatest respect for your feelings. Since he was leaving the country, I doubt very much whether he would have returned. Since he was leaving, your interest in him is both generous and disinterested.

What happened next, happened so quickly that none of the three people in the room would later be able to recount more than a single impression. Their three impressions would, however, confirm one another. Marika jumped from the ladder. Neither she nor either of the two men ever considered the possibility of her having fallen. Undoubtedly she leaped. Perhaps she had intended to land with her feet on the seat of a large leather arm-chair near by and below. In any case the chair was knocked over and she lay on the floor. Yet despite the speed with which it all happened and the impossibility of recording the exact sequence of events afterwards, the moment when she was in mid-air seemed at the time interminable.

Tomorrow morning G. will meet Dr Donato and Raffaele (he has never met either of them singly) in the café off the Piazza Ponterosso. They will ask him about Marco. If he tells them that Marco may be released within the week, they will suspect he is an Austrian agent. If he tells them he has failed to do anything for Marco, they may try to force him to leave Trieste. He will tell them there is a reasonable chance of Marco being released by the twentieth. They will say that that is too late, by then the two countries may be at war. They will insist that G. tries to have something done sooner. He will tell them they are absurdly unrealistic. He will ask them how they expect an Italian businessman to intervene in a question of Austro-Hungarian law. Raffaele, resentful of being told that he is unrealistic, will be on the point of shouting out that they already know G. is an Austrian agent and if he were not, how could he get Marco released even by the twentieth? But Dr Donato will interrupt Raffaele. He only allows Raffaele to blunder when it doesn't matter. He will suggest a walk along the sea front. They will stroll beside the aborted canal until they reach the Molo. All the time Dr Donato will be talking. He will talk about Voltaire. By the waterfront on the fourth side of the Piazza Grande they will see a goods train slowly coming towards them along the quay. Let us watch the train, Dr Donato will say. The wheels of the engine will be taller than the three men who stare up at it. After the locomotive will come the trucks, black, with wheels which appear to be loose after the solemnity of the locomotive's. In the brief spaces between the trucks above the rusty heavy couplings, the three men will glimpse the sea. Dr Donato, having stopped talking, will suddenly take hold of G.'s arm with both hands at the same time. Raffaele will fling an arm round G.'s back and together they will force him forward until his face is a few inches from the blackened boards of the slow-passing truck. G. will try to hurl himself backwards. Dr Donato will kick G.'s heels towards the lines. The right heel and the left. After a brief, interminable moment they will let him break free. You almost tripped, Raffaele will say, you want to be careful in a city like Trieste, there are a lot of accidents here. You see, the lawyer will say, we have very little time.

Let us say Marika was ascending, not falling. Let us say that the floor and everything else in the room was also ascending, but that there was a very slight difference in the speed of ascent, the floor mounting a little quicker than she. That is how it seemed. She leaped upwards. She never seemed to move downwards. Rather, she seemed to hang in the air like a white and damson fuchsia. Her dress lifted a little to disclose white stockings and knees. Her mouth opened but there was no sound. Perhaps the moment was too brief for sound to register. Nevertheless the silence was one of the things which made the moment seem interminable. Suspended there like a fuchsia, she was still herself. She was the woman who had been lying in bed that morning when Wolfgang gazed down at her. She was the woman in every particularity of her physical being whom G. desired. Her very substantiality, there in mid-air, was more far-reaching than any idea. Then she lay in a heap on the floor.

Neither man moved immediately. She made a sound which might have been a laugh. Her husband ran towards her more quickly than he intended. The sight of physical violence always disturbed him. By the time he reached her, she had begun to get to her feet and brush down her dress.

What did you do? he asked. If he had asked: Why did you do it? she might have taken advantage of him.

I misjudged the distance. I am not hurt. Do you accept my bet?

Some brandy, said von Hartmann.

G. noticed that as soon as she took a step she had to disguise a limp.

Your wife has hurt her foot, please allow me to carry her. Before von Hartmann had time to reply, G., leering outrageously, had picked her up. Frau von Hartmann made no protest but laid her cheek against the chest of the man who was her imminent lover.

The trio proceeded down the length of the room.

When the brandy had been served, von Hartmann began to speak softly but distinctly, looking most of the time at his wife who had been laid on the sofa with her legs up.

I will not say that you look like a couple, the two of you, but you look well together side by side. I hope you will not misunderstand my reason for saying that.

He lay back in his arm-chair, holding the large glass in his two hands like a chalice.

Do you remember *Anna Karenina?* I have never been able to believe that Karenin was the successful statesman Tolstoy wanted us to believe he was. The contrast between his well-managed public life and his ill-managed private life was quite unnecessary. Karenin lacked the consistent clarity of mind which a proper administrator needs to have. He probably married the wrong woman, but having married her, he certainly treated her in the wrong way. Why did he not face the truth about her infidelity before it was too late? Because he took it far too seriously. If she was unfaithful it meant the end of the world, and so time after time he postponed the day of reckoning. And what did he do when he could no longer avoid the truth—do you remember, Marika? Anna tells him on their way back from the races.

He held the glass so that the brandy was level with his eyes. His gaze was focussed on the horizon within the glass.

You remember? Karenin went away to think about it and he came to the conclusion that they must both go on living as before. The end of the world when it comes is softer than a whisper. Nobody must see it or hear it. But both of them suffered it silently day and night. Karenin made a tragedy. He made it. There was no need for a tragedy, there probably never is. Anna had to leave him although she knew it would be her undoing. If she had stayed, in the end she would have become as deranged as Karenin. Now, I'm not Karenin, that is what I want you to understand.

He put the glass down on a table, and dabbed once at his lips with a folded handkerchief with his monogram embroidered upon it.

I apply the same realism to my private life as to my public life. It has been obvious to me for some time that you would like to seduce my wife, and it has been equally obvious that she would like to become your mistress. Doubtless this is what, under normal circumstances, might have happened without a word from me. But the circumstances are not normal. Time is running out for all of us. This is why I am raising the matter. I want to tell you that you can count, both of you, on my co-operation.

He paused, looked from one to the other and nodded.

On 20 May, that, to be precise, is four days after the term of your wager runs out, a wager incidentally, Marika, which I absolutely refuse to accept, on Thursday 20 May there is the charity ball at the Stadttheater. It is for the Red Cross, a cause which we would all find worth supporting. You and I (he raised his glass to his wife) will be attending it, always provided that your foot has mended by then. And I hope that our Red Cross will benefit now from the sale of two extra tickets. They cost two hundred and fifty crowns each. Please come (he raised his glass to G.) to the ball and bring, for the sake of propriety, a suitable companion with you. At the ball you will be free to dance with my wife as many dances as she sees fit to grant you. At the end of the evening I am leaving to catch the night train to Vienna. I return here on the Saturday. I repeat that you can count, during those twenty-four hours, on my tact. (Again G. was reminded of Dr Donato who said: I am persuaded that we can and must count upon you.) As for the *Internat,* which may be crossing your mind, I do not think it's going to arise. If I was going to place a bet on the date of the outbreak of hostilities, which I have absolutely no intention of doing, it would not be before the twenty-fifth of this month. I think I am likely to be right. You will therefore have plenty of time to return to Livorno before there is any risk of internment.

Von Hartmann had never before made such a suggestion. But Marika was not surprised. A new legend had begun: she was married to a man who publicly proposed that she should take a lover. She did not fail to notice that he assumed that the story would be a short one because war would break out and she would be separated from her lover. But her husband was a German at heart and was always convinced that everything ended as it began. The end was by no means certain. Before war broke out she might go to Verona with her lover; she might not return to her husband before the war was over. They might all be dead within a week. She would accept to die with the man who put his hand over her mouth an hour ago. She would not die happily with her husband. It would be like dying sitting down.

Marika did not doubt that, if he was Don Juan, he would desert her. She wished only to begin.

Wolfgang was smiling, watching them both. His smile made Marika feel grateful and triumphant. She was grateful for his compliance. She was triumphant because, according to her, nobody knew how it would end. She swung her legs down on to the floor. She needed to disguise the fact that her ankle had swollen. She began to dance slowly down the room towards where she had fallen. You see, my foot is better already, she cried out laughing, we shall go to the ball.

G. took an envelope out of his pocket. I thank you, he said, for your invitation. I shall come to the ball as you suggest. Here are the details of the case I was telling you about. I think you should reconsider the affair. Now that war is certain, the risks in releasing him have become insignificant.

A few minutes later G. got up to leave. How shall we wait till Thursday? asked Marika, and, with the freedom which she believed had just been granted her, proffered a cheek for G. to kiss while Wolfgang stood at her side.

G. took her hand, raised it formally to his lips, bowed and said: Until we meet at the Stadttheater.

It is only now that I understand an incident in G.'s childhood and a prophecy which were mysterious to me when I wrote them:

You'd better watch him if he says so, he says to the boy. The man goes to the head of the first horse, bends over and strikes it. The boy can't see what he strikes with. Perhaps it is the bottle. He does the same to the second head. Not one inch of the horses' flesh such as the boy can see in the lamplight so much as quivers from either blow. The man stands upright, nothing in his hand. So I killed them, you saw I killed them, didn't you? The boy knows he must lie: Yes I saw you. The man approaches him, evidently pleased and pats him on the shoulder. There is blood on his hand which reeks of paraffin. So you saw, he says. Yes I saw, says the boy, you killed two horses. He is aware that it is he who is now talking to the man as to a child. You killed them very well, he hears himself saying.

No terror can match the disgust he feels for the man in front of him. It is a disgust to the point of nausea. In a moment the smell of paraffin will force him to vomit.

Can I go?

Don't ever forget what you saw me do.

Away. The lamp invisible. The smell of paraffin present but now imaginary. He feels his way between the trees.

His fear is overcome, both his fear for himself and (for it is different) his fear of the unknown: not overcome by an appeal to will-power or the summoning up of courage—how often can such direct appeals of a purely formal morality ever work?—but overcome by another, stronger revulsion. It is beyond me to create a name for this revulsion: the ones I think up all simplify. It has nothing to do with the slaughtering of horses or with the sight of blood. It is a revulsion not uncommonly felt by children and men, but one that quickly disappears never to recur if systematically ignored. With him it was always to remain stronger than his fears, for he never ignored it.

When G. descended the balustraded staircase of the von Hartmann house into the massive vaulted entrance hall, from which doors led off to the servants' quarters, he had the impression that permeating the stone-cold darkness was the smell of paraffin. A fact which could doubtless be explained by a lamp having been spilt.

9.

The following morning, after he had met Raffaele and Dr Donato in the café, after the threat of the goods train, G. walked to the garden of the Museo Lapidario and sat there in the sun beneath the plum trees.

Why did he not leave Trieste? He could still have returned to Livorno or London. He could have straightaway taken a ship to New York. After the sinking of the *Lusitania* many bookings were cancelled. Was it a question of sheer obstinacy? He was not an obstinate man; obstinacy is defensive and is deployed round a fixed citadel. There was very little about him that was fixed. Had he then become suicidal? Five years ago he had welcomed the threat of death—Camille was right when she felt that he might have loved her repeatedly if only her husband's threat to shoot them both had been ever-present and credible. But to challenge death is not the same thing as to seek it. I do not believe that G. was any more suicidal than Chavez. Like Chavez, he may have been careless. What then was keeping him in Trieste? The charity ball at the Stadttheater. Not until that Thursday night could he take his revenge on von Hartmann. Beyond this he was incapable of seeing. The degree to which we can postulate or see beyond this is the degree to which we cannot be him. But there is something to be added. Because what G. intended to do at the Stadttheater was the contrary of all he had done since the end of his childhood when he first kissed Beatrice's breast and took her nipple in his mouth, he must have been conscious of the fatality of this intention. Doubtless he was aware of the fateful days Trieste was living through. But he could only be aware of them as an accompaniment to his own—hence they could not directly affect him.

Nuša saw him as soon as she came through the door into the garden. This time she had to pay to go in. She still had the ticket in her hand. The ticket would also have entitled her to look at the more complete classical sculptures arranged in the gallery. She had eyes, however, only for the man she could now see sitting on a broken stone in the tall grass under the plum trees.

Yesterday she had been on the point of giving up hope of ever finding him again. But she consoled herself with the thought: perhaps he comes every day except Sundays. Yet, she argued, this couldn't be true because it was on a Sunday, last Sunday, that she had first met him here. On the other hand, she had never seen him here before on other Sundays when she came with her brother. When he said: I come here every midday, either he was lying or else he meant every day except Sundays. If he wasn't lying, the Sunday she met him was an exception to the exception. She did not reason in these paradoxical phrases but her reasoning led her to a startling, unexpected plan. Tomorrow, Monday, she would not go to the factory, she would go sick, and then she would be able to come and see whether he came to Hölderlin's garden on weekdays. She foresaw she would have to buy a ticket to go in and she thought she might risk losing her job. But all last week she was listening to people talking about war with Italy and she saw that her brother must either go soon or not at all.

She walked towards G. He had his back to her. Had he been watching her, she might have been intimidated. This way she approached him as though he were a load on the ground that she must somehow move.

He is surprised to see a woman advancing towards him with such determination. He supposes that she is the custodian's wife coming to tell him it is forbidden to sit under the trees. When she comes closer he recognizes her and stands up.

The Slovene, he greets her, who told me her secrets!

So you do come here at midday.

I often come here, yes.

But not on Sundays.

I didn't come yesterday, did you?

I came to look for you.

If I remember correctly, your brother interrupted us the last time. Or a gentleman who said he was your brother.

I have something to ask you.

The clumsy way in which she says this—she says it with such bluntness that it is like a command—inspires G. with the idea he needs. Ask me.

You said you were an Italian from Italy.

G. nods, offering her the seat on the stone.

I will sit in the grass, she says. If you come from a foreign country, you have come with a passport. Can you give it to me? She speaks the last sentence very lightly despite the fact that for a week she has feared that she would never have the opportunity to say it.

You have never seen a passport? They are nothing much to look at. They always have a photograph inside.

With an amused smile he takes his false Italian passport from his pocket and hands it to her. She fingers the pages, stops at the photograph. His face looks almost as white as his collar and he is wearing a black suit and a tie. She is reminded of the photograph of Cabrinovič taken on the morning of the archduke's assassination. The face is different but the small rectangle of grey and black and white paper is very similar and like the pictures in the cemetery, except that being out in all weathers they are more faded.

I don't want to look at it, I want to have it.

If you keep it, we will have to stay together here for the rest of our lives. Without a passport I cannot leave.

I need it very quickly.

A butterfly alights in the grass near her hand. Its flight, its stillness, wings upright and congruent, and then again its tremulous movement belong to a time scale so remote from Nuša's and G.'s that if it was applied to them, they would seem like two statues.

What for?

I cannot tell you.

Why ask me?

You are the only Italian I know to speak to.

Trieste is full of Italians.

Not Italians with passports.

I will give it to you on one condition. Let me take you to a ball at the Stadttheater.

Bojan was right, she mutters in Slovene, and she glowers sullenly at the trunk of the nearest fruit tree. It is like a return to her village in the years of poverty. She stares at the implacability of the world. Bojan said that he would want to make her a prostitute, and that was what the Italian meant by a ball at the Stadttheater.

I ask you for your passport, she repeats stubbornly, still staring at the tree trunk, what do you ask?

At the end of the ball when they play the last waltz, you shall have my passport. There is nothing to fear. I am asking nothing else. I give you my word.

You mean a ball at the Stadttheater?

What else should I mean?

I wouldn't be allowed in.

We will buy everything you need. Your dress, a wrap, a bag, slippers, gloves, pearls, everything. You will be my guest.

You do not know what you are asking. She looks puzzled but no longer sullen. I would be thrown out. They will say you have brought a woman-of-the-street to their ball.

Perhaps neither of us know what we are asking, says G., but I will do what you ask if you will do the same.

When is the ball?

On Thursday next week.

It will be too late. Give me the passport now.

One butterfly follows another making loops in the air near her wide feet in their laced boots. The air smells of fresh still green grass. In the depth of the green are purple and white flowers. The fact that she believed he wanted to make her a prostitute and that she was mistaken in this, now emboldens her. She places a hand on his arm and looks up at him with encouraging eyes. Give it to me now, she says.

If I gave it to you now, you would not come to the ball. You are not a fool.

I cannot come anyway. I have to work.

And today?

I told you, I came to ask you.

I will pay your wages.

Give me the passport now and take somebody else. Why does it have to be me? You will find lots of fine women there.

From what I hear I don't believe there will be any war with Italy before Thursday next week.

I cannot dance your dances.

To hell with their dances!

Then why do you want me to go?

He knows that if he flatters her she will again become suspicious. On the steps of the Stadttheater, he says, on Friday morning you can give me your *carnet de bal* and I will give you this. He taps his pocket.

All right, she answers softly but gruffly, I will come.

The deserted garden with its unpruned trees, its walls overgrown with creeper, its stone fragments invisible in the long grass, its dragonflies and cats, has never seemed madder to her than now. She is about to leave it, but what she has just said in it will affect everything else in her life outside it.

G. lightly kisses the back of her hand. Meet me here tomorrow at eleven in the morning and by then I will have found a dressmaker.

She wonders if he is a ghost: it would be no more improbable than what she has agreed to do. The most real thing she can think of is the possibility during the next few days of being able to steal the passport.

Do you know what we call this place? she asks.

I like it, he says, *il giardino del Museo Lapidario*.

I, having written this, cannot forget the garden.

○

Wolfgang informed his wife that, out of sheer curiosity, he had made enquiries about the young man Marco who was in prison. The whole story, he told her, as recounted by G., was a fabrication. The young man carried forged papers. There was no dying father in Venice. 'Marco' was trying to reach Italy in order to speak as a representative from Trieste at the rallies being organized everywhere by the Italian war party. There was already a file on his activities at the Ministry in Vienna. He belonged to the extremist wing of the Irredentists and had the reputation of being an effective orator. Marika asked her husband whether he thought it likely that G. had known the truth. Wolfgang expressed no opinion but made it clear that he was still quite willing to stand by his agreement. The mystery doubled Marika's impatience. First she would yield to the man who was Don Juan and afterwards she would discover what he wanted her to do.

O

G. discovered which was the best dressmaker in the city. The modiste was an old woman from Paris. He discussed with her what kind of dress Nuša should have. He said it should make her look like a queen, an empress. The modiste pointed out that Nuša was young and that to make her so regal would be to age her unnecessarily. He insisted that whatever she wore she would look young, but she must also look commanding. She must look like Sheba, he said.

Nuša submitted to the first visit for measuring like a conscript. She stood there dumb, sullen, apparently locked in the thoughts of her own life which was far away. If other village women had been undergoing the same ordeal, she would doubtless have smiled at them and whispered some truculent comment. She was not cowed but she was entirely alone in a foreigner's world. When she caught sight of herself in one of the mirrors, she saw herself there in that *salon de couture* through the eyes of her mother or some of the girls at the factory and she blushed, her face and neck going a blotchy crimson, not because she was ashamed but because she could hear the story they would tell about her. She had imagined herself being married, being a mother, dying one day. But in none of the situations she had foreseen for herself was she ever as alone and central as she must be in the story they would tell about her. She knew she was justified. What she was doing or allowing to be done was not only just, it was for the sake of greater justice. But to be such a solitary and principal character was like being a criminal. She could speak to nobody about what was happening to her. It was the loneliness of her conspiracy which made her feel like a criminal. Without the slightest pretension she tried to think of Princip and Cabrinovič in their jail in Bohemia, whilst an Italian with a tape-measure called out the measurements of her back to another woman who wrote them down in a book bound in velvet.

G. arranged to see her briefly each day. They met first in the museum garden. Afterwards they went to some shop, which G. had already selected, to buy another item of her toilet. Each day Nuša carried home to her room in the street near the arsenal another parcel. As soon as she had shut the door of the room she undid the parcel and hid the contents at the bottom of the cupboard which served her as larder and wardrobe. She had already decided that after the ball she would sell everything she had acquired. And so, when on the second day she found a number of bank notes stuffed into a dancing shoe, she was not outraged. It did not appear to her as money given her by a man, but simply as part of the sum she hoped to realize when this extraordinary week was over and she must go back to the factory or find other work. She found no opportunity to steal his passport.

Most of those who served them in the shops—the jewellers, the glovemakers, the shoemakers, the haberdasher—were so astounded to see an Italian gentleman accompanied by a Slovene village girl (she was like a carthorse, they said afterwards) that they explained everything by this unusual phenomenon. But one or two may have remained more puzzled. What was the relationship between this couple? They were polite to one another but absolutely formal. They never spoke except when the outside situation demanded it. They looked at each other without rancour but equally without affection. Neither pretended to the other. There was not a trace of the theatricality that goes with prostitution. She was not a tart. Yet neither was she his wife or mistress: there was no intimacy beween them. Then why, with such care and extravagance, was he buying her these presents? Why did she give no sign of gratitude? Or, alternatively, why did she show no disappointment? At times she looked nonplussed. But most of the while she did what was required patiently and with a certain slow natural grace. Two solutions occurred to the puzzled shopkeepers. Either she was simple-minded and the Italian was in some mysterious way taking advantage of her; or else he, the Italian, was mad and she was a servant humouring him.

○

Nuša both hoped and dreaded that she would soon see her brother. She wanted to know what his latest plans were and she thought she might find a way of hinting that she could procure him a passport. At the same time she feared he might have heard that she was not going to the factory and would insist on her telling him what she was doing.

Bojan came to her room late on the Friday afternoon of the first week. Her fears proved unnecessary. He was so distracted by the political situation and the imminence of war that he asked her nothing about herself and assumed she was still working as before.

You must get used to eating less, he said to her abruptly, if you are a little thinner it won't matter.

I never eat so much in the summer, she said.

The Empire will be defeated, that is certain, it cannot survive. When it topples and breaks up, all the cities will be very short of food and supplies.

When are you going to France?

I haven't got everything I need yet. We have to make a whole organization in exile.

Will it be before next week?

I cannot tell you, but I will come to say goodbye before I go, I promise.

If you wait one week I will be able to help you. It will make it safer for you.

What do you mean?

Wait and see.

He sighed and looked out of the small window down the hill on to the docks where a cargo ship was being unloaded. The men looked as small as tin-tacks and the horses with their draycarts on the quay looked no larger than beetles.

She wanted to tell him more, not about her plan, but about her good will. Do you remember on the Sunday before last scolding me in the garden—

When I found you with that unsavoury Casanova? Yes, I remember. And, you see, that is what we fear, now more than ever, the Italians will take over the city and we shall exchange one tyranny for another. And the second tyranny will be worse than the first because between the two there will have been the lost chance of freedom. The Italians will be worse, worse even than the Austrians.

What you spoke to me about then showed me something, she said.

He continued to stare out of the window. The apparent size of the men unloading the ship intensified his pessimism. If you think, he said, of the Italy Mazzini dreamed of, if you think of Garibaldi, and you look at what Italy has become—

In Paris you will see your friend. She knew no other way to reassure him.

Yes, I will see Gacinovič. My life is like a swan flying through the fog towards a light that is very distant but irresistible. Gacinovič wrote that.

Nuša put her arm round her brother's back and her chin on his shoulder. Their two heads close together in the small window, they looked down towards the ship whose hatches were open. Slowly, once, he rubbed his cheek against hers. It was a gesture of tenderness such as normally he would never have allowed himself, but he was overcome by an awareness of how closely their childhood had bound them together. Each of them sensed that the image of the distant light in the fog had profoundly affected the other. To neither was the light a precise symbol or hope. It was not something they could discuss together. But to measure how far away it was, both would begin measuring from the time when he first taught her to read.

○

The final fitting for the dress was on the Tuesday of the second week. In three days Nuša would be paid her wage; she was still earning the passport. She gazed at the extraordinary dress she was wearing in front of the hinged mirrors.

The skirt was made of black silk. Embroidered upon it, in the Indian style, were eight or nine red peonies, a few silver-green rose-leaves and three or four mysterious sprigs with blue fruit hanging from them like sloes. Each rose-leaf was almost the size of one of her hands. The corsage was of muslin, its colour scarcely different from that of her skin. The sleeves were short and wide, bordered with pearls. She stared at her own shoulders and bosom, rounded and solid through the mist of the muslin, and she thought: if this is the dress he has chosen for me, I will be safe at the ball, in this he will not dare to touch me. And then she thought: on Friday morning I will go to where Bojan lodges still wearing this dress and I will wake him up and give him my wage, I will give him the passport which will allow him to go. And then again she thought: it will attract too much attention like that, I must take the dress off before I go to see Bojan.

She did her best not to think about going back to work at the factory after Bojan had gone. When she was working on the softening machine she had to dampen the streaks of jute by pouring an emulsion of whale oil and water on them. Each time the top rollers of the machine pitched down on to the sodden streaks to mangle them against the fixed bottom rollers, her face was splattered with the emulsion. Some of the girls wore a tarpaulin. She had tried, but she found it too constricting. When she was carrying the streaks in her arms from the softening machine to the barrows, they made her blouse wet. At first she thought she would always smell of whale oil. If she could find other work she would never go back to the jute factory.

The modiste was adjusting the very high red silk belt. Inadvertently the old woman's knuckles prodded the young woman's breasts. Nuša felt the huge embroidered flowers with the palms of her hands. The skirt was tight over her hips. Sometimes when she was feeding the streaks on to the delivery cloth of the softening machine the rollers tugged at the streak she was still holding and the sharp tresses caught on her nails or between her fingers. Her present employer had bought a cream like milk for her hands and every day he asked her to hold them out to him and he gravely examined them to see whether they were softer.

The modiste shifted her attention from the belt to the side seams of the skirt. A fraction taken in here, she said to one of her assistants who wore a pincushion on her wrist like a thistle. Nuša could feel hands moving lightly down the outsides of her thighs. Someone else was altering the fastenings at her back. These light touches of fingers she could not see—for she knew she should not move even her head—had a slightly hypnotizing effect.

When she was sick as a child she imagined a swan who came and settled on her stomach as though on the surface of the water. She used to feel a webbed foot trailing along the outside of each thigh. From its position there, bending its long neck forward with its head down—as a swan does when searching under the water—it fed her gently and lovingly from its beak. Surprisingly the taste of the food the swan gave her from its beak was neither fishy nor stale. It in no way resembled the smell of jute. The swan gave her small cakes which were scarcely larger than cherries and tasted of them.

The modiste stood back to appraise her work. *Ça présente drôle-ment bien*, she said in her hoarse voice to herself. Two women knelt on the floor to arrange the train.

Walk a few steps, my dear, said the modiste.

Nuša walked very slowly, as though in the dark, towards the mirrors. One of the women on the floor asked her to pick up the train as she would do if she were dancing. Nuša had no idea how this was done. G., who on other comparable occasions had been there to guide her if she looked lost, was in the ante-room waiting for her to emerge in the almost finished dress. Close to the mirror, she was once again amazed by the fullness of her own radiance through the salmon mist of the muslin. Once again she felt a pang of disappointment that her brother would not see her in this dress when she went to wake him on Friday morning. Then she said: You must show me how I do that.

O

From ten o'clock onwards on the evening of 20 April 1915, the social élite of Trieste drew up in their carriages and motor cars before the steps of the Stadttheater where footmen in uniforms of blue and gold waited to help the parties and couples out. No one expected it to be a ball like the ones before the war. People remarked that it was not the same thing to drive along the Molo to a ball without the liners lit up in the bay. There was not a single ship to be seen in the darkness. Nevertheless the ball was unusually well-attended, perhaps because the idea had occurred to everybody that it would probably be the last one for a good many years.

Among the guests Austrians and Italians were fairly evenly mixed. In most public situations in Trieste Austrians were outnumbered, but this was a special occasion since it was the charity ball for the Austro-Hungarian Red Cross. To put in an appearance at this ball was to demonstrate one's loyalty to the forces of His Imperial and Royal Majesty and to assume as one's own the determination with which these forces had overcome their defeats—hence, incidentally, the urgent need for medical supplies. There were middle-aged and elderly Austrians there who considered it their patriotic duty to dance the mazurkas.

The Italians, mostly from well-established trading and shipping families, were less idealistic but no less anxious for the Empire to survive and to have themselves counted amongst its loyal and influential supporters. The Irredentists in Trieste drew their strength from the professional classes and the intelligentsia. The Italian business and trading community was quite shrewd enough to foresee that without Vienna, Trieste would no longer make commercial sense as a port. If they overlooked this truth they had only to ask themselves why their Venetian competitors were so pleased to finance the Irredentists. The Italians at the ball were nervous. When they went to a window to take a breath of air they half expected to see artillery fire across the gulf.

Wolfgang von Hartmann and his wife came in a carriage. Marika was wearing a dress of lilac and pale green. Her deer-coloured hair was drawn very tightly back. She was breathing through her mouth which was slightly open. The whole day and especially the early part of the evening had seemed endless. She had played patience, she had taken a bath, she had had the hairdresser arrange her hair twice. When she walked through the drawing-room she remembered saying: If we were at home we would go now while he is out of the room. On the parquet floor she traced the path into the forest. She sighed. Waiting ten days had aged her, she would never have waited when she was younger. As the carriage drew up in the small piazza outside the theatre steps, Wolfgang took his wife's hand and told her she looked disarmingly beautiful. She bowed her head without saying a word. The top of her head looked phosphorescent, as if wet from the sea. Remember, he said, I am no Karenin, I. I wish you a very happy time. When her hair was smooth he was convinced of the ultimate control he had over her.

Their carriage drove away. On the steps they heard somebody say in German that although he did not doubt the future importance of the motor car in trade and war, he found it an unsuitable vehicle in which to come to a ball. Marika craned her neck up at the sky. The milky way was just visible. A waltz was being played in the first ballroom.

Whilst they met acquaintances, shook hands, smiled, received compliments, Marika was searching amongst the groups and couples to see if G. had yet arrived. One of the directors of the Trieste branch of the Südbahn railway, an elderly but energetic man with one eye that was always half shut, asked her if he might have the pleasure of the first mazurka. She picked up and dropped her *carnet de bal* into her bag as though to indicate that she need not open it to know that the first mazurka was promised. But abruptly, before she snapped her bag shut, she changed her mind. She would be dancing the first mazurka with the Herr Direktor when G. arrived. He thanked her. She opened her fan and behind it glanced at the wide red-carpeted stairway which mounted to the second ballroom.

During the next few hours most of the guests wanted to forget what the next days or months might bring. Yet what they had to say to each other inevitably and disagreeably reminded them of the following day in their provincial war-threatened city. Their release depended upon the music. The music sounded both familiar and timeless to them. As soon as it started up after each pause, they were reassured and, once reassured, they had the impression of dancing in the same world as they had danced in since their first ball.

Yet to a solitary listener on one of the deserted jetties who had nothing but his ears and memory to go by, the distant music might have sounded different. It was neither timeless nor entirely familiar.

The orchestra, in blue and red uniforms, belonged to an Austrian regiment which had served on the Eastern front and recently been transferred to Trieste in anticipation of war with Italy. The players no longer believed, as they had before, in the time of the waltzes. They were playing them—not to fill the present moment—but to remind themselves bitterly of the past. All Viennese dance music was nostalgic. But this was no nostalgia for a vague past which could always be conjured up and induced to return. This was bitter simple regret for seven brief irrevocable months during which they had seen too much that they would like to forget. Without realizing it, without thinking of it, they played in order to exaggerate, like parodists.

G. entered with Nuša as a dance ended. They stood side by side, surveying the couples who were leaving the floor. She was the same height as he. And she was like no other woman there. This was instantly apparent to all who set eyes on her.

Taking Nuša's arm, G. led her towards von Hartmann and his wife. A silence fell upon that part of the room and several guests ostentatiously turned their backs as the couple passed. He presented Herr von Hartmann and Frau von Hartmann to Nuša, which was the contrary of all that etiquette demanded. Then, in a stentorian voice, he thanked the Austrian banker for inviting them to the ball and, as the music started up again, swept his partner away. Von Hartmann stared at them dancing, his face fixed in an absolutely expressionless mask. His voice when he spoke was calm and flat. The only thing which indicated his rage was his choice of epithet; he wanted to find an expression which came from the same depths as the woman whom G. had had the effrontery to bring to their ball. To come with a plate-licker! he said. His wife smiled. She knew who G. was, and his insolence filled her with enthusiasm.

Nuša's dress was like an iris, tight before it fully opens, when its colour is still folded in upon itself, but an iris upside down, with the tips of its petals on the floor. It was not, however, her dress which differentiated her from the other women there. Her dress merely compelled those who were staring to compare her with themselves. If she had come in her everyday clothes, they would have considered any such comparison ludicrous. Within minutes of their arrival everybody was recounting or discussing the scandal.

An Italian has brought a Slovene to the ball. A Slav girl from the villages, dressed outrageously in pearls and muslin and Indian silk. When she dances the waltz, she dances like a drunken bear, clutching her partner close to her and thumping with her feet.

A young officer in a blue uniform gravely informed a white-haired gentleman that he was willing to challenge the interloper who had had the temerity to insult His Imperial Majesty's Red Cross. The white-haired Viennese was a general who had fought at Solferino. If he spoke German, my boy, you would be justified. But they tell me he has nothing but Italian. And in that case I must forbid you.

A waltz is a circle in which ribbons of sentiment rise and fall. The music unties the bows—and ties them again.

In most circumstances the high society of Trieste would have been far too adept at inflicting snubs for anybody in Nuša's present position to remain self-possessed. Her heart was beating faster than usual and her fingers felt constricted in their gloves. But this was caused by excitement and her anticipation of the success of her plan rather than by confusion or embarrassment. At the ball she enjoyed several unusual advantages. She and G. could pass among the guests without ever becoming engaged in their conversation. They swooped from group to group like birds among heads of cattle. There was the music. It was stronger than the people; they danced to it. And the music was not strange to her. True, she could not dance the mazurka, but she could dance the waltz and the polka, and when she danced with G., she felt secure. She would not trust him until he had paid her. But in the improbable and exposed position she was in, she found familiar things to reassure her. Like the music, he was one of them. The question of why he had brought her there did not occupy her greatly because she knew why she herself was there. She was there to get a passport. She had watched G. warily for ten days and she was confident that, whatever his motives, he would not leave her unprotected. There were also the robes, the jewelry, the flowers, the ribbons. The people were dressed to look their best and this, she felt, limited what they could do. What she was wearing was also a protection. The hostile glances flung at her changed their expression slightly when they took in her turban or her train; for a moment their hostility was checked in its stride. Before it had recovered itself, she could turn her back.

Once they were the first to take the floor. As G. had expected, no other couple was willing to join them. They danced alone. But to a certain young lady the idea of forgoing a dance on which she had placed precise hopes was too much. Why should she stand there whilst her partner goggled at that idiot of a Slav? She raised her hand and placed it decisively on the shoulder of the man she hoped to marry. Obediently, he took her by the waist. Other couples followed.

A waltz is a circle in which ribbons of sentiment rise and fall. The music unties the bows and ties them again.

Very little that happened in the ballroom escaped G.'s notice. The revulsion he had first felt in face of von Hartmann had by now extended to every guest, man and woman, at the ball. He wanted to express this revulsion by insulting and defying them. But he knew them well enough to know that to insult or threaten them openly, to shout or shoot at them, would only have amused and confirmed them. They were all addicts of the theatre. His defiance had to be persistent, devious, and cumulative. Having determined to take this course ten days ago, and having now set out, he was entirely preoccupied, like an aviator in mid-flight, with his immediate situation. He could no longer recall his own motives or think beyond the outcome of the night. Each moment was a moment of tension and triumph. When he spoke to Nuša, he spoke gently and formally—as to his own defiance.

Von Hartmann left the ballroom. It was too late, he reflected, to order his wife to refuse G., for she would disobey him as soon as he left; worse still, she was too primitive, too unintelligent to discern the calculated insult in G.'s behaviour. The insult, which was a public one, amounted to declaring: after a plate-licker, your wife.

A mazurka is simultaneously a race and the music which celebrates the winning couple. For so long as the music continues each couple is the winning one.

Marika, dancing with a young officer, imagines how she will dance with G. as soon as her husband has left; when they wag their heads at the banker's wife dancing with the Italian who came with the Slav, she will show the petty administrators and Jews and insurance clerks of this godforsaken city what disdain is!

Wolfgang has taken the Chief of Police to a window on the grand staircase and is retelling the story about Marco. He should be taken in for questioning immediately, he adds, referring to G.

The Chief of Police, a man of Wolfgang's age and a friend of many years, shakes his head. No, he says, no, that is very unlikely. A man working clandestinely does not draw attention to himself like this.

His cunning is that he relies upon you thinking like that.

He is a little mad, you know. The Chief of Police likes to think of himself, despite his dress uniform which is as ornate as a general's, as being essentially a civilian scientist. Some form of monomania, he continues, he has one idea in his head which is devouring him. Have you noticed the way his face is set? That is typical. And his leer when he smiles? It isn't a smile at somebody or something, he smiles because for the millionth time he has hit upon his idea again.

If he is capable of dancing a polka he is not mad. You should talk to him. He should be questioned forthwith.

You expect me to have him arrested in the middle of the ball?

When he leaves.

No, no, I haven't spent my life studying criminal psychology for nothing. If he became violent he could be a murderer, but a man like him is not a conspirator.

What if the one idea that devours him is the overthrow of the Empire?

I am not so easily frightened. You have only to look at him. That is not his form of madness.

Madness! We play with words. Sometimes I have the impression that we shall leave nothing behind us except word-games. How can you call a man like him mad? The mad are uncontrollable and have to be locked in cells. In fact the mad are relatively harmless. He is not mad. He may be cunning and full of malice, but mad he is not. What you call madness is what you consider to be undesirable but still allow to continue. Madness is what you do not bother to control. I deny your madness and I denounce what you call madness! It is not madness to bring a woman like her here, it is a premeditated insult. He has nothing but contempt for us and this contempt arises from his conviction that he and his friends can destroy us.

Contempt is not a crime. And anyway, I repeat it, to bring a woman like her to a ball is not an insult, for, as you say, insults are calculated, they are rational, it is a form of madness.

You should have him questioned before it is too late.

My dear friend, I have known you for too many years. You do not believe what you are saying yourself. Have your financial negotiations with him been so difficult? You have all my sympathy, to deal in business with a madman like him must be very hard. The Chief of Police laughs. But do not let us make operettas!

I have to leave now. I'm going to Vienna tonight.

You may be right, I will bear in mind what you say, but you haven't convinced me. I have become much harder to convince lately, it may be to do with my becoming a little deaf. In any case do not worry, everything will still be the same when you return.

A waltz is a circle in which ribbons of sentiment rise and fall. The music unties the bows and ties them again.

As the ball continued, the Italians tended to favour the ballroom on the second floor where the theatre's own orchestra, who were civilians, were playing. In both rooms the scandal of the Slav in pearls was still a topic of conversation. The Italians were indignant because it was a compatriot of theirs who had so demeaned himself. Some said only a man from Livorno could behave like that. Others said they had heard his money came from candied fruit which meant he was little better than a shopkeeper. To the Austrians, after the first shock had worn off, the affair was a reminder of how long it would take them to civilize these parts; it might be a task without end; their weariness, which was an indication of how long they had already been engaged in the task, was part of their cultural destiny; meanwhile, until dawn, they could dance to their own music. In the first ballroom everything was now said in German.

After Wolfgang's departure, Marika declined to dance, certain that

G. would now find her. He did not. She passed from one group to another, conversing as she went. So far as she could see, he was no longer in the ballroom. She walked with her swaying walk, her invisible antlers held very still, up the grand staircase. He was not to be seen there. She entered what was now the Italian ballroom. An acquaintance whom she had passed on the stairs whispered to her husband: Frau von Hartmann can never have enough, can she? He was not there either. She concluded he must be sending the Slav woman home in a carriage. She came down the staircase as though already dancing.

A mazurka is simultaneously a race and the music which celebrates the winning couple. For so long as the music continues each couple is the winning one.

The music stopped for supper, it was past midnight. In one of the large foyers long tables were laid with flowers, cut glass and bottles of champagne. The guests arrived, Austrians and Italians now forced to mix again, animated, laughing, making gestures which were a little exaggerated as if with the passing of midnight, everything had become larger and simpler. Young men, specially invited to the ball for this purpose, helped to serve from the buffet. They were not servants but future partners. As they presented a lady with a plate, they would ask after her daughter. Champagne bottles steamed. There were many toasts. Around the centre of one table there was a clearing in the crowd. In that clearing, opposite each other, sat G. and Nuša. Marika watched G. raise his glass to the woman opposite him. They drank. The talk became louder and soon there were trills of laughter.

A few were still drinking when the orchestra struck up. Once again the Italian and his partner with her high breasts beneath muslin and pearls were the first to take the floor. Once again the Italian and his partner with her neck which was neither fat nor thin but like another leg were the first to take the floor. Once again the Italian and his partner whose narrow eyes were indecipherable were the first to take the floor. Once again no other couple joined them. But this time those who stared did so with insolence rather than anger. There were a few guffaws of laughter. Somebody shouted: Go back to the circus!

Immediately G. drew Nuša towards him to whisper a reassurance in her ear. The way they then danced, cheek to cheek, appeared more outlandish than ever; nobody except peasants danced like that.

The waltz is a circle in which ribbons of sentiment rise and fall. The music unties the bows—and ties them again.

It did not astound Marika that she saw him naked as he danced. What astounded her was that she saw his penis. She had never before seen a man on his feet with his penis erect. It changed the whole body of a man. His body no longer stood solidly with its two feet on the ground. It rode on a stick which, despite his body's weight, stayed steadily and consistently in the air, changing orientation only as the woman before him moved. On this stick he rode towards her, his legs and feet dangling either side. His arms were raised the better to keep his balance as he rode. In bed, seen from above or from the side, a penis looks like an object or a vegetable or a fish. His, during the waltz, was indefinable. It was red. It was thrust forward in the direction of its own progress. Its head shifted a little from side to side, as a horse's head when galloping. Often it was so acutely foreshortened that its body became invisible. All she saw was a darkness with a glowing ember at the entrance to it. She could smell the sulphur, she told herself, and it was making her feel giddy.

The General, who as a young man had fought at Solferino, considered the behaviour of the guffawing onlookers most unseemly—they must be drunk. He put an end to the situation by seizing his niece and leading her on to the floor himself.

Marika sat bolt upright in the carriage which drove her home. She had the impression black blinds were drawn over its windows. The story can have only one end, she thought. The music was still audible by the front door of the house.

On the way back to the Stadttheater she sat bolt upright in the carriage, but this time she could see out of the windows. The harbour was very still. A few carriages were leaving the theatre.

During the next thirty years the story was recounted many times. After the occupation of Trieste by the Yugoslav partisans in 1945, when briefly, for the first time, the city was in the hands of Slav patriots, the story lost its allure and began to sound somewhat discreditable. But the versions varied on one point. All agreed that the Hungarian wife of an Austrian banker, a woman with red hair, drew out a whip from under her wrap and began to flog a Slovene woman, whose appearance at the ball had already caused much consternation, down the stairs and out of the building; where the versions differed was on whether she also tried to flog the man who accompanied the Slovene.

Fine horsewoman though she was, Marika was not able to control with absolute precision the lash of her whip and since G. was beside Nuša she may also have struck him. But he bore no marks upon him whereas Nuša had three red weals, one across her neck and two across her back and shoulders.

When Nuša ran down the stairs towards the entrance with Marika in pursuit, G. closed with her to seize hold of the whip. The two figures struggled and Marika fell. Several men advanced upon G. Brandishing the whip in their faces, he broke free and ran down the stairs to join Nuša who by this time was in the street.

With her skirt and train held high up above her knees she was running fast. She had lost or flung off her turban. G. caught up with her. Behind them they could hear shouts and screams. A few of the younger men in evening dress gave chase.

G. took hold of Nuša's hand in case she fell, and they ran together out of the small piazza, away from the sea towards the Exchange. Nuša knew where she wanted to make for—the narrow dark streets by the end of the canal. As they ran hand in hand, panting, without saying a word because they needed all their breath, G. remembered the Roman girl in Milan who had pulled him from under the rearing horse and run with him to the Giardini Pubblici. And you will buy me, she said in Italian, some white stockings and a hat with chiffon tied round it. Yet it was scarcely like a memory. The two moments were continuous; he was still running the same run and in the course of it the Roman girl had grown into the woman, all of whose clothes he had bought, now running fast but heavily beside him.

They took the first street out of the large piazza on the far side of the Exchange. Nuša was beginning to flag. Her hand was wet in his. Her face was red and contorted with effort and pain. They saw a patrol of Austrian police coming down the narrow street towards them. Their pursuers, running more slowly, had turned the corner by the Exchange. He pushed Nuša into a doorway and tried to hide her but they had already been noticed.

At police headquarters they were separated. Left alone, G. remembered Nuša's face as it was just before she was led away. And again he found it impossible to make a distinct separation between her face and the face of the Roman girl in the courtyard in Milan when she splashed water on him and told him to drink. Their features were entirely different. It was in their expression that the mysterious continuity resided. To break this continuity so as to make room for all his adult life between the first and the second face, he had to forget their smeared foreheads, their mouths and intense, silent eyes and remember only the meaning of their expression for him. What mattered the first time was what her expression confirmed and what until that moment had been wordless: what mattered then was not being dead. Now, the second time, what mattered was what her expression confirmed and what until now had been wordless: why not be dead?

10.

Nuša was released by the police the following afternoon. Most of the questions put to her were about G. When she said she knew nothing about him, they asked her why he took her to the ball. She shrugged her shoulders. Are you his mistress? She stopped herself answering No. Please ask him, she said. Did he speak to you about his other Italian friends here? He is not like an Italian, she replied.

They treated her as a half-wit, and this seemed to be justified when they told her she could go. Have you old brown paper, she asked, which you do not want? One guard winked at another. I must be covered, she said, pointing to the muslin top of her dress bordered with pearls. They found her a piece of sacking.

When she got to the quarter near the arsenal, she stopped at the corner of each street to see whether there was anyone she knew; in mid-afternoon the streets were mostly empty. She hurried along close to the walls of the buildings with the sacking over her shoulders. In her room she undressed and sitting on the edge of her bed she bathed her shoulders and her feet from a basin of cool water. She was trembling. If he was released, she asked herself, would he still bring her the passport?

O

The cross-questioning to which G. was subjected was close and repetitive. The reports sent to the Chief of Police suggested that his original impression of G. at the ball had been the correct one. After briefly interrogating the prisoner himself, he was satisfied. G. was released on Sunday morning on condition he left the country within thirty-six hours.

THE STONE GUEST

I went to a friend's house to look at the photographs he had brought back from North Africa. When I came in I said hello to his eldest son, aged ten. A little while later I was concentrating on the photographs and had completely forgotten about the son.

Suddenly I felt a tap on my arm, a rather urgent tap. I turned round quickly and there, the size of a child, was an old man, bald, large-nosed with spectacles. He stood there holding out a piece of paper to me. (Let there be no mystery: the ten-year-old son had put on a mask. But for the duration of perhaps half a second I did not realize this. I started. When the boy saw me start, he burst out laughing and I realized the truth.)

I was surprised and shocked by the old man's presence. How had he arrived so suddenly and silently? Who was he? And from where? Why was it me he had chosen to approach? There was no satisfactory answer to any of these questions, and it was precisely the lack of any answer which startled and frightened me. This was an inexplicable event. Therefore it suggested that anything was possible. I was no longer protected by causality. Probably this was why his size—the most improbable thing about him—did not surprise me. I accepted his size as part of the chaos his very presence proposed.

I do not retrospectively exaggerate either the complexity or the density of the content of that half-second; when profoundly provoked, one's memory and imagination reproduce one's whole life in an instant.

No sooner had he frightened me, no sooner had he pulled away causality from under my feet, than I recognized him. I do not mean I recognized him as the ten-year-old son of my friend. I recognized the bald old man. This recognition of him as a familiar in no way diminished my fear. But a change had taken place. The fear was familiar too now. I had known both man and fear since my earliest childhood. I had the sensation of not being able to remember his name. A small socially conditioned part of me had a reflex of embarrassment. For this part it was no longer a question of how and why he had found me, but a question of what I could say to him.

Where had I first met him? Here it is impossible to avoid paradox. But a single glance back to the depths of your childhood will remind you how common paradox was. I recognized him as a figure in the infinite company of the unknowable. I had not once, long ago, summoned him up in the light of my knowledge; it was he who had once sought me out in the darkness of my ignorance.

There was nothing objectively menacing about him now. But he was threatening because he had figured in a contract to which I had agreed. I had forgotten the circumstances which led to this contract. Hence the initial mysteriousness of his presence. Yet I was able to recognize—without being able to remember—one of its principal clauses; hence his familiarity. The old man, the size of a boy, bald, large-nosed and with absurd round spectacles, had come to claim what that clause promised him.

○

It was a morning of early summer, one of those mornings on which, if one has nothing to do, the evening seems a lifetime away. The sea merged into the sky above Trieste, the same blue hiding them both.

It was fine too in Northern France and Flanders. But those who lay on their backs, dying or wounded, did not stare up at the blue sky with a sense of lucid affirmation as Tolstoy describes Prince Andrey doing on the battlefield of Austerlitz. The finer the day, the greater the confusion death caused on the Western front. Death had been robbed of all significance there; consequently it was easier to accept it as one more condition, like the mud or the cold, in a world fundamentally inhospitable to man, than in a climate and season so full of promise. It's a fucking fine day to croak.

G. walked to his apartment and before changing his clothes lay down on his back. The acanthus leaves on the lace curtains reminded him of how twenty days ago he had foreseen seducing Marika. He clenched his jaw. Not because of what he remembered, but because for two days he had done little else but remember. His memories did not in themselves cause him regret. Mostly he had achieved what he wished, and he would wish the same again. What weighed heavily upon him was the suddenly awakened faculty of memory itself. Or, rather, the prodigious capacity of this faculty. It was the sheer number of memories, their mass, which oppressed him.

He found it impossible to separate one memory from another, just as he had found it impossible to separate Nuša's face from the Roman girl's. It was as if his mind had been turned into a hall of mirrors in which, although all the reflexions moved together, each represented something different. The effect was the opposite of what memory normally does. For example, instead of bringing his childhood closer, the sheer mass of his memories since childhood made his childhood seem absurdly far away. Memories of Beatrice, such as he did not know he possessed, filled his mind, one after the other, each extremely clear, but each inseparable from memories of other women, so that it seemed to him that he must have last seen Beatrice a century ago. Yet I am not conveying the truth accurately enough. The stream of involuntary, precise but concatenating memories which filled his mind appeared to elongate his past life. This I have indeed suggested. But it was equally true that, because nothing remembered could be isolated and set independently within its own time, his remembered life also appeared excessively hurried and brief. Memory alternately stretched and compressed his life until, under this form of torture, time became meaningless.

Last night I heard a friend had killed himself in London. By putting together the three letters of his name, JIM, I do not, even to an infinitesimal degree, begin to reassemble what is now scattered. Nor can I judge his act by invoking the word tragic. It is sufficient for me to receive—receive, not merely register—the news of his death.

G. must leave the city within thirty-six hours. But where must he go? The only place open to him was Italy. From there he could go elsewhere. Perhaps he pictured himself returning to Livorno and living in his father's house. Doubtless he thought of other possibilities. But each of them was a return of one kind or another and he had no wish to return. Thus he began to forget about the *where*. The question became different: how much further could he go? How far could he still put between himself and his past? It was no longer time in itself that would take him further, for time had become meaningless. It was his realization of this which made him decide to walk to Nuša's room and give her his passport. By this act he would go further.

In the Piazza Ponterosso there was a stall with a woman selling fruit. The woman, like Nuša, was from the Karst; he could tell by her features. He bought some cherries. On his way eastwards towards the docks, he began eating them, spitting the stones out on to the street as he went.

Just as in the red of cherries there is always a hint of the brown into which they will disintegrate and soften when they rot, a cherry, as soon as it is ripe enough to eat, tastes of its own fermentation.

He passed groups of men talking sombrely in different languages about the imminence of war. The further he went, the more ragged were the clothes of the men he passed, the more closed their faces.

Because of the smallness of a cherry and the lightness of its flesh and its skin—which is scarcely more substantial than the capillary surface of a liquid—you find the cherry stone incongruous. You may know better but you expect a cherry to be a gob. The eating of a cherry in no way prepares you for its stone. The stone feels like a precipitate of your own mouth, mysteriously created through the act of eating a cherry. You spit out the result of your own eating.

Twice he stopped and turned round because he had the impression of being followed. He sat down on a wall near some shops and watched the women queuing for vegetables and bread. In this part of the city everything was in short supply.

Before you bite the cherry in your mouth, its softness and resilience are identical with the softness and resilience of a lip.

If he was to defy time, he could not hurry.

The house was one in a row of small houses whose front doors opened straight onto the street. He knocked and a woman with two children came to the door. She eyed him suspiciously. He asked for Nuša. The woman said what did he want. She spoke a very halting Italian. He offered the children some cherries but the mother hustled them away before they could take any. Her room is at the top of the house, she said, I shall send my husband up in ten minutes.

Nuša opened the door at the top of the staircase. Her hair was loose around her shoulders. You! she said, and, with a glance down the stairs, she beckoned him in and shut the door quickly behind her.

You have brought the passport!

The room was small with a slanting ceiling. On one side her bed and a cupboard, on the other side a bare table and a chair; between them the dormer window with a view of the docks below. He poured the cherries out of the bag on to the table.

They released me this morning, he said. He took the passport out of his pocket and handed it to her. It seems to her that they have come through their ordeal and reached their destination. She clasps his hand in both of hers. He puts his arm round her. Far from resisting, she leans towards him. Her sense of achievement is so great that for a moment she assumes they have shared the same aim. She leans against him. If he were the weaker, she would have held him up. It is as though they have outrun their pursuers, both of them together, and are now exhausted, limp with exhaustion, but safe.

It is the first time they have been alone together indoors.

Your hair is softer when it hangs down, he says picking up some tresses and letting them fall from his hand.

It hides that! she steps back and throwing her hair forward over her face she shows him the purple weal across the back of her neck.

Slowly he puts his hand on it and she stays quite still as though being examined by a doctor. Between the hairs her scalp is very white. Her hair smells of blankets.

You should put some raw steak on it, he says.

She straightens up, her cheeks flushed because the blood has run to her head, but the pink in them is uneven, visibly distributed in blood vessels as intricate and livid as those at the root of the tongue.

Raw steak! she says, I would eat it, not put it there.

Are the other places worse?

I can't see them properly.

Let me see them.

He is the only person she can show them to and they are part of how she earned the passport. She turns her back and slips one shoulder out of her blouse and chemise.

Across her large full white shoulders run two raised weals, but the skin is not broken. The pores of her unhurt skin emit a kind of light which is indistinguishable from the smell of her skin. He touches her shoulder with the tips of his fingers.

The first night I couldn't sleep, they were like burns.

Through the small open window comes a noise of distant perturbation; a strange confused noise which suggests human voices but is too regular to be speech and too discordant to be music. Two or three sounds are being continually repeated. To G. one of them resembles the Hup! Hup! Hup! of his childhood. Nuša and he glance at one another and then go to the window. Down below on the quay they see people running towards a circle of crowded figures who are waving their arms. Somebody in the crowd is carrying a black and yellow Austrian flag.

Who are they? G. asks.

I do not know.

Her face is impassive but her breast is heaving. They look like our people, she says, the ones who work in the docks.

She steps away and adjusts her clothes, doing up the small buttons with her large hands. I must go, she says, with the passport now.

G. wants to place himself, to intervene between all the forms of her physical being, her heaving breast, her thick hair that smells of blankets, her white scalp, her large hands, her cheeks, the pores of her skin—to intervene between her body as she stands there by the window looking down again at the quayside and her consciousness of herself. He wants to take the place of what she is looking at. He wants to present her to herself as a gift and for the offering to be boundlessly free of virtue. He wants to carry the gift on his own body to satisfy his own need. We have no time, Nuša, he says.

When he spoke her name it was with despair.

For the first time the question of what he would do without a passport occurred to Nuša. She tied a scarf round her hair. We must go. They bundled down the dark stairs.

When G. said: We have no time, Nuša, he might have been referring to Nuša's impatience to deliver the passport, to the crowd coming together on the quay, to the landlady's husband coming upstairs, to the thirty-six hours within which he was meant to leave Trieste, but none of these contingencies presented difficulties which were insuperable and in the past he would have ingeniously found a hundred ways to get round them. The statement meant something more.

For two days he had been oppressed by the abundance of his memories. He had come to the point of feeling condemned to live even the present in the past tense. What had not yet happened was merely a section of his past not yet revealed. When they released him from the police station, he had the impression of walking back, regardless of the direction he chose, towards the past, towards the life he had lived before von Hartmann had offered him Marika and he plotted to take Nuša to the Stadttheater. Whatever he chose was like re-entering a choice he had made before, a choice of which the consequences had already taken place. The opportunities before him were illusory. Time refused to face him. His desire for Nuša was indistinguishable from his despair. Aieeeee!

(Passion must hurl itself against time. Lovers fuck time together so that it opens, advances, withdraws upon itself and bends backwards. Time which their hearts pump. Time whose vagina is moist with timelessness. Time which spends itself when it ejaculates generations.) We have no time, Nuša, he said.

Imagine a character in a legend becoming conscious as he was when alive. The legend is made and cannot be altered. Its unchangeability proffers a kind of immortality. But he, alive and conscious within the legend which is being told, which has already been repeated many times, will feel buried alive. What he will lack is not air but time.

Thus G. descended the staircase with Nuša.

People had come to the doors of their houses and were talking in loud voices together. A young man ran up the street and then down again. G. could not understand a word being said, everything was in Slovene. Several men followed the youth running downhill towards the sea. Nuša asked something. Then she whispered: the Italians have declared war now, today we are at war with them.

G. gripped her arm. It is too late, she said, speaking the words close to his face, if only you had given it to me before.

He did not try to keep her and she ran down the hill. A little way down she stopped to speak to a man. G. saw her pointing up at him. Then she ran on, holding up her skirt with one hand, her boots banging against the cobbles.

To Nuša's surprise Bojan asked only once how she had obtained the passport. She said she found it. He thought that with the passport there was still a hope that he might be able to leave; there would probably be a last train to Italy tomorrow or the day after.

Bojan indeed reached France and lived several months in Marseille where he aroused the suspicions of the French police. In a Marseille police circular during the winter of 1915 his place of birth was given as Livorno, his name as G.'s, his age and occupation as his own. There is a reference number to a file which probably contained a photograph and further details. No specific criminal activity is mentioned—as is the case with other names on the circular. He is simply listed as Suspect.

The British Foreign Office made no attempt to trace the man whom they had supplied with false papers; he was assumed to be missing, probably dead. Years later when working in Yugoslavia against the dictatorship of King Alexander, Bojan still sometimes used G.'s false name (the name G. would genuinely have had if he had been brought up by his father Umberto) as an alias.

G. walked downhill towards the docks. As he passed the man to whom Nuša had stopped to talk, the man smiled and without any attempt to conceal what he was doing, started to follow G. They soon met a crowd of several hundred coming up the hill towards them. In the rear the ranks of the crowd were fairly well organized and a group was carrying a large Austrian standard. But the vanguard, most of whom were men, was very different and advanced like a wave continually breaking and reforming, murmuring and roaring. Everything about them appeared to be diverse—their clothes, their ages, faces, headgear, physique, language. They had come originally from many different places: Slovene and Istrian villages, Serbia, Galicia, Greece, a few from Turkey and Russia, one or two from Africa. All that they had in common was their poverty and their destination.

Once more G. was aware of the absurdity of the question: where should he go? Once again, in place of an answer, he could only think: further. He began to walk with the crowd in their direction.

It was very unlike the crowd he had seen in London on the day war was declared there.

The crowd in London was a static crowd which did not know where to go. It demanded nothing. It bellowed and roared with blank staring eyes because it was impatient to have what it wanted.

But it did not know what it wanted. It was a crowd waiting to be let in and waiting to be despatched. It stood outside Downing Street and Westminster Abbey and the Houses of Parliament impatient to be issued with its own future. It sacrificed itself supremely, without knowing it, in the act of cheering. Its cheers were to become gushes of its own blood hurled up into the air and falling down again over its own staring eyeballs, leaving millions of bloodshot veins in them, down its own jugular choking its exits, down over its stomach interminably bayonetted to where each wound with its unquenchable thirst drank it up, only letting, inadvertently, a few drops of blood dribble from the lip of the wound into the pubic hair. There were many women in the crowd, they pushed with their hands against the smalls of the backs of the men, they pushed them out, they aborted them in blood in the Strand and in Trafalgar Square where they lay, the men-embryos, without hairs or feathers on them, all bones and fleshlings. Yet when it dispersed, the London crowd on the first day of war, it did so calmly; all the men and women went home still calling each other by their usual names, unaware of what they had begun, but buoyant with a sense of unusual pride.

The crowd in Trieste on the day war with Italy was declared, was neither buoyant nor proud nor calm. It proceeded in fits and starts like a drunk sure of his destination but undecided about the exact route there.

Sometimes men ran ahead waving. One had a bell which he rang like a town crier, but he wore no uniform and the bell was black and rusty—perhaps a ship's bell found in the mud of the harbour. Faces appeared in windows. It is war! the men in the street shouted. Come and see what we are going to do! Some groups started to sing but nothing was sustained for very long.

G. walked a little behind the vanguard in the middle of the stream of the crowd. Although he had taken off his jacket and was walking in his shirt-sleeves, his clothes made him conspicuous. The man to whom Nuša had spoken in the street was still walking a few steps behind and each time somebody accosted G. he intervened, speaking in Slovene which G. could not understand; each time the interrogator seemed to be appeased and asked nothing more. G. began to feel that he could leave all decisions to the man walking behind him.

As the crowd made its way north-westwards towards the Exchange and the Italian part of the city, its character began to change. The contrast between its raggedness and the ordered streets down which it was proceeding became more and more acute. By the arsenal it had looked like a crowd of underpaid or unemployed workers; in these streets now it looked like an army of beggars.

A man near G. threw a stone (which he must have been carrying in his hand since they set out) at the shop front of a grocer's. The glass broke. Men started breaking the rest of the glass with their hands, bound round with their overalls or shirts for protection. When they could reach the cheeses and sausages, they threw them back into the crowd. A patrol of Austrian police passed near by, pointedly ignoring the incident. The shopkeeper, terrified, began to hand out his own flasks of wine to the nearest fists thrust out in his direction. It is a good wine, he kept on repeating, as if he were still selling it.

Pressure from the back of the crowd forced them onwards past the grocer's shop. The incident made them all aware, however, of their temporary immunity from the law. When they saw a number of well-dressed people they shouted menacingly: Down with Italy! and sometimes also: The Thieving Rich! The streets became empty. And this again changed the crowd's character. In their own part of the city they had been a spectacle drawing people towards them. Here they put everything into abeyance. It could not occur to them, as it had occurred to the crowds in Milan in 1898, to take over the city. They had no wish to establish their own control or order. They wished to establish only the empty deserted spaces of the streets and piazzas in which anything might happen without order.

The man behind G. tapped him on the back and passed him an open flask of wine to drink from. G. drank, spilling a little on his shirt. Although the progress of the crowd was haphazard and erratic, he had the feeling of being borne along by it ceremonially, almost like a body in a coffin. He looked up at the buildings they were passing between. Caryatid after caryatid dumbly and uncomplainingly bore the weight of pediments intended to prove the culture of those who lived behind their doors and windows.

Sexual acts, like dreams, have no surface appearances; they are experienced inside out; their content is uppermost and what is normally visible becomes an invisible core.

In a room up there Louise had been lying on her back. His arms around her knees, he put his tongue into her vagina. He could recall the taste only of the wine he had just drunk. Slowly a quiver passed from one of her thighs to the other like a wave. It turned, flowed back again, returned. A grain of sand was shifted first one way and then the other way by the alternating movement. From the grain of sand and the warmth between her legs was born a dog's ear. A pointed one. The fur on the outside of the ear was softer and smoother than her own skin. The inside of the ear was transparent pink. From the ear was born a jug of milk. Beneath the surface of the milk, invisible beneath its whiteness, were the trees of a wood, winter trees without leaves. The jug poured the milk over her lap. Upon some parts the milk remained in white pools; from others it ran down; drops of milk hung like white berries in her hair. He could see the branches of the winter trees in the traces made by the milk. The man with the bell started ringing it again. Look at their houses! Further! Further! The words rose to G.'s throat involuntarily but calmly. They were as surprising to him as they were incomprehensible to those around him. Further! Further! He walked with his head right back staring at the blue sky.

The crowd turned into the Piazza San Giovanni and quickly filled it. In the centre was a statue of a gigantic man sitting comfortably in a chair shaded by trees. On the plinth was written VERDI. These letters spelt the name of the man who wrote *Rigoletto*; but in Trieste they also meant Vittorio Emmanuele Re d'Italia. Two men had climbed on to the lap of the statue and were striking the head with iron bars. You could see the shock of each blow jarring their upper arms and shoulders. Women went from door to door round the piazza trying to gain entrance to the buildings. All were locked or bolted. Occasionally a face, half hidden behind a shutter, looked down in alarm at the piazza below filled with *i teppisti*. Some youths climbed into the trees. There was the sudden sound of glass being smashed. It worked like a pre-arranged signal. Everybody near the edges of the piazza began to hurl whatever they could find at the nearest unshuttered windows.

Behind the windows was the property of those who benefited from the existence of Trieste. Those who were beating Verdi's stone head and smashing the windows between the caryatids hated the existence of the city, and they were out to avenge their enforced presence there. They were out to avenge as covertly, as slyly as possible, without further risk to themselves, a small portion of what they had suffered since poverty had forced them or their fathers to leave their villages and settle on the outskirts of the foreign city. The administration of the city was Austrian but its essence was Italian, hence the names of its streets and piazzas, hence the language in which its merciless commerce was conducted. Few of the crowd had any political theory, but all of them knew one thing of which the professors and students of the gymnasium were largely ignorant: they knew that what had happened to them in their villages was part of the same thing as what had happened to them when they arrived in Trieste and had happened every day of their lives since. The unity was historic. Theories may embrace and define this unity. But to each of them it was defined by the unity of his own life's suffering.

Break his head!

Knock his ears off!

Rip the shutters off!

Has nobody told you about your houses? I discovered it a long time ago. You are walking leisurely—in any city in Europe—through a well-off residential quarter down a street of your houses or apartments. Their window frames and shutters have been freshly painted but their colour barely differentiates them from the façades around them, which absorb the sunlight but give off a slight granular scintillation like starched linen table-napkins. You look up at the curtained windows in which the curtains are so still that they might be carved out of stone, at the wrought iron-work of the balconies imitating plants, at the ornamental flourishes referring to other cities and other times, you pass polished wooden double doors with brass bells and plates, the silence of the street consists of the barely perceptible noise of a distant crowd, a crowd made up of so many people so far away that their individual exertions, their individual inhaling and exhaling combine in a sound of continuous unpunctuated breathing ... and then suddenly you realize with a shock that each residence, although still, is without a stitch of clothing, is absolutely naked!

Set fire to the place!

There were rumours that another crowd had already set fire to the building of the Liga Nazionale. It may have been an Austrian agent who first proposed the newspaper office of *Il Piccolo*. A hundred or so men, G. among them, hurried there from the Piazza San Giovanni.

A few Italian printers and journalists including Raffaele had arrived at the *Piccolo's* office for the evening's work. Shouts in the street brought them to the windows. They saw a body of men, some waving sticks and others carrying cans under their arms, running across the piazza towards the main entrance of their building. The scourge of the docks! said Raffaele and in doing so coined the phrase he would later invariably use when describing the rioters. Close the shutters and blinds, he ordered. Then he picked up a telephone and asked for police headquarters. It is very urgent, he said.

By standing close to a blind he could see through the slits the first men reach the building. There were blows and the sound of smashing glass. They were breaking the lamp that hung outside the entrance. He could hear others running up the stone steps to the printing shop. Suddenly he laid the telephone down and pressed his nose against the window pane to be sure of what he could see. He saw G. with a small gang round him point at the windows of the second storey and make explosive gestures with his hands. Raffaele's initial astonishment gave way to a strange satisfaction. In a threatening and unpredictable situation he had found a certitude and this certitude confirmed his own acumen. He could hear them breaking up the furniture on the ground floor.

G. was not only an Austrian agent, Raffaele asserted, he was one of the men employed by the Austrians to mobilize the Slavs. It was now obvious why the Austrians had tolerated his extraordinary behaviour at the Red Cross ball. Everything which had been mysterious about him became instantly clear. With this certitude of interpretation came an equally satisfying certitude of decision. There was no need to consult anybody. He told those who were watching him telephone that they must abandon the building. Make sure everybody leaves, he said. Take this—he took a revolver from the drawer of the desk and handed it to the man facing him. No one else is going to defend us, he added with satisfaction.

He was going to put an end to G. The telephone was still silent. He rattled the earpiece holder violently up and down and asked for another number. I need all of you immediately at the Galleria di Montuzza, he said, I will meet you there. After this call he asked again for police headquarters. He wanted to speak to Major Loneck. He demanded immediate protection for the *Piccolo* newspaper building which was in the hands of *i teppisti* who were about to burn it down. Major Loneck evidently temporized. I am not excited or hysterical, yelled Rafaele, it is a question of civil order.

The incendiaries in the print shop worked quickly and systematically. One of them had found a cupboard full of rags dirty with grease and ink. They placed these rags at the end of the room near the largest press. A man doused them with paraffin from a can. Others were breaking up tables and chairs and laying the wood across the rags. G. emptied some drawers of paper and scattered these too on the pyre. Light it! he urged, for the small of the paraffin was choking him. The man to whom Nuša had spoken in the street was standing guard by the doorway. An old man with shining eyes screwed up a torch of paper, lit it and threw it on the rags.

For a moment they all waited to see whether the fire would catch. Almost immediately there were flames as high as a man. It was about to burn the presses which printed the language of the city, the language of law, insult and demand, the language of the overseer. There was the breathing noise of fire with intermittent very light cracks like those which accompany footsteps in dry undergrowth. The man waiting by the door smiled approvingly at the fire they had made. At first the fire reminded them of their villages; it was still a small fire. Later the same night, after three more attempts to set fire to the building, when it was truly ablaze, they would watch fascinated by the dimensions of their achievement; the more uncontrollable the fire then became, the more they would think of themselves as its master. G. stood somewhat nearer the flames than the others, he felt their warmth on his body.

Quick! cried the man in the doorway, the firemen are here. As the incendiaries ran out, the firemen accompanied by soldiers ran in. There was a scuffle but both parties continued on their way and there were no arrests. A cordon of soldiers was placed round the building and the fire was soon extinguished.

Raffaele was remonstrating with Major Loneck on the other side of the piazza by the corner of the Via Nuova. The Austrian police officer argued that he had other buildings in the city to protect and that as soon as the crowd dispersed he would have to withdraw his guard. If your soldiers go they will try again, insisted Raffaele, the safety of the population is your responsibility.

They should have thought of that yesterday in Rome! said the Major, speaking German.

On another corner G. was speaking to several of the men who had started the fire in the print shop. You see, he was explaining, they are using the hydrant from the building next door. You must put that out of order next time.

Raffaele left Major Loneck and went over to a circle of figures standing in the entrance to the Galleria di Montuzza, the tunnel which runs under the hill on which the cathedral and the castle and the Museo Lapidario are built. He pointed out G. (who appeared to have lost his jacket and was easy to identify in his white shirt) and issued his orders.

A false calm descended upon the piazza and the streets leading out of it. There were many people about, but they were not the people normally to be found in these streets. The firemen went away. The crowd broke up into small loitering groups waiting to see whether the platoon of soldiers would remain or march off. The inhabitants of the area were nowhere to be seen.

G. strolled back towards the Piazza San Giovanni. Ahead of him was a woman whom he thought he had seen before. She was dressed somewhat like Nuša but she was smaller. He stopped in his tracks. Further, he said out loud, further still!

The man in the white shirt whom they were following had a distinc-

tive way of walking: he hunched his shoulders and his head so that
he had the lunging gait of a bull. Suddenly he stopped and said
something out loud to himself. It was not difficult for them to
believe that he was a traitor.

G. walked on. The woman's air of vague familiarity increased his
interest in her. Between the two of them he saw his past self hurrying forward to draw level with her. He would recognize her face, he
would speak to her. He saw her interest being aroused by his past
self. Yet he did not quicken his pace to discover who she was. Whatever it was that separated him from his past self was very slight,
amounting to no more than a whim, to no more perhaps than the
heat he imagined he could still feel on his body from the fire in
the print shop.

If G. had struggled with the four men when they came up to him,
their fight might take several pages to describe. He did not struggle.

If, on the other hand, he submitted to them without any resistance
at all, several pages might be needed to describe his acceptance of
death. He did not submit without resistance.

What happened can be quickly told and the rest can be conveyed
at last by my silence.

They forced him to walk out of the piazza past the church of San
Antonio. On the way he caught a glimpse of the face of the woman
who had seemed familiar: it was from this woman that he had
bought this morning the cherries in the Piazza Ponterosso. Two of
the men held his arms forcing them against his sides like the arms
of a foetus not yet detached from the body. The third man walked
in front and the fourth behind. They went along by the canal down
to the mole. There they turned right towards the railyards. The
waterfront was deserted. From time to time G. tried to release his
arms. He could not. They took him to the water's edge.

Until that moment I do not think he foresaw the exact circumstances of his own death. Certain doubts or hopes must have
remained. Perhaps death when it arrives is always a mounting surprise which surprises itself to the point at which all reference—and
therefore all self-distinction—disappears.

They struck him on the back of his head. He fainted. The taste of milk is the cloud of unknowing. They supported him, moved forward a few inches and then dropped him feet first into the salt water.

The sun is low in the sky and the sea is calm. Like a mirror as they say. Only it is not like a mirror. The waves which are scarcely waves, for they come and go in many different directions and their rising and falling is barely perceptible, are made up of innumerable tiny surfaces at variegating angles to one another—of these surfaces those which reflect the sunlight straight into one's eyes, sparkle with a white light during the instant before their angle, relative to oneself and the sun, shifts and they merge again into the blackish blue of the rest of the sea. Each time the light lasts for no longer than a spark stays bright when shot out from a fire. But as the sea recedes towards the sun, the number of sparkling surfaces multiplies until the sea indeed looks somewhat like a silver mirror. But unlike a mirror it is not still. Its granular surface is in continual agitation. The further away the ricochetting grains, of which the mass become silver and the visibly distinct minority a dark leaden colour, the greater is their apparent speed. Uninterruptedly receding towards the sun, the transmission of its reflexions becoming ever faster, the sea neither requires nor recognizes any limit. The horizon is the straight bottom edge of a curtain arbitrarily and suddenly lowered upon a performance.

Geneva . Paris . Bonnieux

1965–1971

ABOUT THE AUTHOR

John Berger, born in London in 1926, is well known as an art critic, novelist, and film scriptwriter. His many books, innovative in form and far-reaching in their historical and political insight, include *About Looking, Ways of Seeing, Art and Revolution, The Success and Failure of Picasso,* and *Pig Earth.* His films with Alain Tanner include *La Salamandre* and *Jonah Who Will Be 25 in the Year 2000.*

He now lives and works in a small French peasant community with his family. This milieu is the setting of *Into Their Labours,* a three-part project which evokes, in both fiction and essay form, the intricate movement from peasant society to metropolis. The first part, *Pig Earth,* is available from Pantheon Books.